Praise for
Once We Were

"If Hitler and Stalin recognized the Greeks' courage, it's about time the world did, too."

—*Kirkus Reviews*

"*Once We Were Here* is a modern epic, surging with the lifeblood of Greece and her proud history. Beautiful, tragic, and achingly lovely, this story of heroism, survival, and homeland captured my heart."

—Victoria Aveyard, #1 bestselling author of the Red Queen series

"This stirring debut by Christopher Cosmos examines the enduring costs of love and war, and the way family stories—even buried ones—set the course for generations to come. Cosmos is deeply committed not only to his characters and their harrowing experiences, but also to sharing, with insight and empathy, Greece's powerful and often heartbreaking history."

—Paula McLain, author of *The Paris Wife* and *Love and Ruin*

"Winston Churchill said that Greeks don't fight like heroes, but heroes fight like Greeks, and this story proves it; a stunning literary debut about legacy and history, war and peace, fate and destiny, the power of family and stories, and how young love can still shine and endure, even in the face of the greatest evils, and long after we're gone."

— Steven Pressfield, bestselling author of *Gates of Fire* and *The Legend of Bagger Vance*

"Christopher Cosmos gives the reader a front-row seat to six pivotal months in the history of Greece, and the world. Full of both heroics and disasters, *Once We Were Here* shines a vivid light on the human costs of war, and how we inherit family legacies of love, sacrifice, and secrets."

— Caitlin Horrocks, author of *The Vexations*

"As Cosmos highlights throughout the book, the Greek army's bravery was heralded throughout the war by the Allies and Axis alike, and were likened to the Greek mythological heroes in the way they fought and resisted. I could see where Costa and Alexi stand in for those mythological heroes, modern day Greeks, marching off to war as if they were Jason or Odysseus. Romance, long journeys, war, death, tragedy and heroes? Honestly, we might just have a modern day Greek myth on our hands here!"

—Kat Cavano, Katcavano.com

"Fittingly for a story about wartime love and loss, there are also echoes of Ernest Hemingway."

—*Michigan Alumnus Magazine*

"The beauty and history of Greece, World War II, and love are the backbone of this breathtaking and far-reaching novel. Highly recommend."

—ShouldIReaditOrNot.com

"*Once We Were Here* is a gut-wrenching story with cinematic quality. Christopher Cosmos vividly portrays the human side of war, from the untrained Resistance fighters to the villagers and survivors. He reminds us why Greeks are so fiercely proud of their country and defend their legacy."

—Maria A. Karamitsos, "The Windy City Greek"

ONCE WE WERE HERE

ONCE
WE
WERE
HERE

A Novel

CHRISTOPHER
COSMOS

ARCADE PUBLISHING · NEW YORK

First Paperback Edition 2022

Arcade Publishing books may be purchased in bulk at special discounts for sales promotion, corporate gifts, fund-raising, or educational purposes. Special editions can also be created to specifications. For details, contact the Special Sales Department, Arcade Publishing, 307 West 36th Street, 11th Floor, New York, NY 10018 or arcade@skyhorsepublishing.com.

Arcade Publishing® is a registered trademark of Skyhorse Publishing, Inc.®, a Delaware corporation.

Visit our website at www.arcadepub.com.
Visit the author's site at christophercosmos.com.

10 9 8 7 6 5 4 3 2 1

Library of Congress Cataloging-in-Publication Data is available on file.

Cover design by Brian Peterson

Print ISBN: 978-1-956763-07-2
Ebook ISBN: 978-1-5107-5713-4

Printed in the United States of America

The dedication for this book is shared between four people:

For Michael John Lechner, keeper of secrets, sharer of experiences, my best friend, the best brother.

For Margaret Kelly Cosmos Ryan, an indomitable mountain of strength, the most beautiful person I know, an ageless treasure of this world.

For Elizabeth Helen Cosmos, who gave me everything, and made me anything that I am today, I'm so proud to even be a small part of you.

And for my *Papou*, who I never met,
but who gave me these stories,
that were his stories . . .

This is for you.

ONCE WE WERE HERE

THE PHOTOGRAPH

July 27th, 2014

I'M HAUNTED BY MY HISTORY.

My life has always been a life of stories, ever since I can remember, ever since I was very young and growing up on my grandfather's lap where he would tell me the great stories of his people, the stories of powerful and flawed gods and the daring deeds of the heroes they favored in faraway lands, and I think perhaps that's why I've always loved the morning and the rising sun, because when I'm alone in the stillness of the dawn the stories feel less distant, and when the mist rises above the concrete of my neighborhood and the dew is still fresh and speckled on the flowers that my wife plants outside our house it seems like the light that's about to come will touch everywhere, not just the places that I've been or that I know, but *everywhere*, and for a brief moment before the day begins the idea of real means something else entirely, and it's during those moments that I have no doubt why we're alive.

My life has been a life of stories, as all our lives are, and I study mine often, crossing and re-crossing the intersecting lines, trying to make sense of who I am through history and blood, the only way that I know how. And it was a story that came from high above, and fell slowly at my feet, on an ordinary day, late in an ordinary summer, that would lead me to finally realize, as I held the greatest history of my life in my hands, and slowly rubbed my thumb across the old and worn surface of it, perhaps something that I've known and felt all along—

I didn't know who I was.

I've spent the hottest and most important days of my summers at Papou's cottage on Lake Michigan since before I can remember, and that summer was no different. As soon as we pulled into the driveway and the car stopped, our two boys jumped out and ran into the house, David struggling to keep up with William, his big brother determined every year to be the first inside and the first to the beach and the first in the water and the first to do everything else. Stephanie and I unloaded the car and made our way behind them, arms full of bags of groceries and toys for the beach, and when we walked in I saw Yia Yia smiling and waiting for us.

"Papou took the boys down to the beach."

"Already?"

"They didn't want to wait. It's a great age, isn't it?" she said as I went forward and gave her a kiss on the cheek. "They're growing so fast."

"Every week, it seems," Stephanie answered, smiling as she gave my grandmother a kiss, too. "I've had to buy new shoes for William twice already this year. He keeps growing out of everything."

"He's going to be tall. That's good. Men should be tall."

I looked out the window to see my two boys hurrying with Papou down the long, winding staircase that leads to the beach, the tall marram grass lining the path all the way to the lake. Papou was more than ninety years old now, but he was still spry, active, healthy, able to keep up with his great-grandchildren. It's remarkable when you think about it, but I never did because he was Papou—he'd always been a giant, and I could never imagine him slowing down.

"What's wrong, Andrew?" Yia Yia asked, watching as I stared out the window. "You know I can always tell when there's something on your mind, right?"

"I found something, while I was packing this morning," I said, as I turned back to her. "It fell out of the boxes that you and Papou moved into the attic last summer."

"What did you find, Andreas?" she asked, using the Greek form of my name, more intimate, more personal.

I took the creased photograph out of my pocket and slowly handed it to her. It was in black and white, a soldier standing next to a woman, and while I recognized Yia Yia, the man in the uniform next to her wasn't Papou. He was taller, his nose was different, and so were his eyes.

She looked down at the picture for a long time, silently studying the faces without speaking, and I was surprised to see tears come to her eyes.

"What's the matter, Yia Yia? What is it?"

"Nothing. It's just something from a long time ago."

"Something that you'd forgotten?"

"No, Andreas," she said, as she looked up, and I saw that she was smiling sadly. "It's not something I could ever forget."

"I don't understand—I thought you and Papou left before the war began. That's what you always told me."

"That's what we told everyone."

"Why?"

"Because it was too hard for us to talk about it," she said simply.

"What happened?" I took her hand in mine so that she knew I didn't want to cause her any pain. "I'm sorry, Yia Yia, but I'm curious . . . why don't you want to talk about it? Did you have a brother?"

"Don't be sorry, Andreas. It's a part of us, and so it's a part of you, too. Which means that it's your story as much as it's ours." And she looked at me as she spoke, into my eyes, as if she was searching for something, and finding it inside me gave her strength. "Maybe it's time you learned about who your Papou really was."

"What do you mean?"

The door opened and my boys come back in, followed by my grandfather, and Stephanie came out from the back so that the whole family was in the living room when Papou saw the picture that his wife was holding. Yia Yia handed it to him and he took it, looked down at the worn image, rubbing his thumb gently across it, remembering a time long past.

"I'll take the boys on a walk down to the pier," Yia Yia said, looking at me. "They've always enjoyed that." My boys smiled and yelled with excitement as they scrambled to get themselves ready: they know that a walk to the pier always means a stop for ice cream at the Dairy Treat, which they'd been waiting for all summer.

"I'll go with them, too," Stephanie said.

"Of course," Yia Yia nodded to her, in love with the woman that I'm in love with.

"Grandma, you don't have to leave."

4

"Yes, I do."

She saw the look on my face and she smiled to try to make me feel better. I've seen my grandmother smile many times, but this time it wasn't a look that I could read—there was sadness, and there was hope, but there was something else, too.

"I think maybe this is a story best told between men," she said as she stood on her toes to kiss my forehead. "It's time that you knew. It's time that you learned about your family. I'll see you when we get back, *Andreas-mou.*"

I watched in silence as the boys came back in their swimming suits and left with Yia Yia and Stephanie and then, when they were gone, Papou finally turned to me—

"It's something that's hard for your Yia Yia to talk about, you see."

"Because it was during the war? What happened? Did you fight?"

"Yes. We fought."

"Where?"

"Let's go outside, Andreas. It's such a beautiful day."

We walked outside together and sat on the chairs on the patio, facing out towards the water in front of us—when the wind's up the waves get large enough that the whole lake is dotted with surfers, but today it's calm, the water has the look and color of smooth glass, and it's beautiful. In the distance my wife and my grandmother walk with my boys down towards the pier and I can't help but smile, seeing them there together, my boys out in front, kicking up water as they run through the surf. Then I turn back to my grandfather, and when I look at him I see an unfamiliar look in his eyes, and at first I think he's just trying to remember the story that he's about to tell me, but then I see that it's not his memory that he's searching for at all, but his strength.

"I'll tell you this story once, Andreas. Your grandfather's story. And then when you've heard it, it will be yours, and yours alone. To do with it what you will. Do you understand?"

"No, Papou. I don't think I do."

"You will. Trust me, Andreas. You will. Now, where to begin ..."

He closed his eyes, thinking back to a time long past. I can see the emotion in wrinkled and worn lines on his face, then after a moment he opened his eyes, looking directly into mine, as he took a large, deep breath full of purpose—

"The story begins on a beautiful day, in a beautiful city, in the most beautiful country in the world ..."

PART I

"Hitler always faces me with a fait accompli. This time I am going to pay him back in his own coin. He will find out from the papers that I have occupied Greece."

—Benito Mussolini, speaking to Count Ciano

October 28th, 1940

THE TOWN OF AGRIA SITS BELOW a large bluff, nestled
against the radiant azure waters of the Aegean Sea,
not far from the great eastern port of Volos. It's a fishing
village, and everything about it is dedicated to the water
and maritime life, as so many of the Hellenic cities and
islands are and have been since before anyone can remember. Alexei's father was a fisherman, as his father was before
that, and his father before him, so Alexei learned to cast a
fishing net when he was very young, before he was even six
years old, and his sun-tanned arms were strong enough to
pull in a full haul of *marides* or *lavraki* before his thirteenth
birthday. He was a boy who grew up slowly beside the sea,
in a corner of the world where everything was carefully
crafted out of beauty and full of an ancient history as sto-
ried and rich as time itself.

It was a few months past Alexei's eighteenth birthday,
and though he'd been fishing with his father for some years
by then, he'd recently been trying to make as many excuses
as he could to take their boat out alone. When he was

younger, Alexei's father seemed as large as Zeus to his son, a great bear of a man, a god amongst all the other ordinary fathers that Alexei knew in their town, and someone not destined to suffer the same fate as other mortals. Iannis was only five foot nine, three inches shorter than how tall his son stood now, but there was once a time when Alexei thought he'd never reach his father's height. It wasn't until years later that he realized that sometimes it's how a man lives his life that makes him seem taller. Iannis had left Greece and travelled the world at nineteen, going to college in Paris before returning home to fight in the Great War, taking a bullet in the leg fighting with the Greek Army against the Bulgarians when they invaded Thrace in 1918. Alexei used to ask his father many times for stories from the war, expecting feats of daring and heroism, tales to rival those of Homer and Aeschylus, but all he used to say to his son was—

"We won, Alexandros. That's all you need to know."

Iannis' response became a mantra, the same word always following the same word, each syllable pronounced exactly the same way. It wasn't until Alexei was older that it occurred to him what he might have been asking his father to relive. But what Alexei did know is that in the last few years Iannis' leg started bothering him more and more, to the point where Alexei saw his father, the Greek god, the man he'd thought of as Zeus, someone to rival Achilles himself in the eyes of a young boy, start walking with a slight limp that had become more noticeable with each passing year. He would never admit it, a proud and stubborn man, but a son who spent so many mornings on a boat with his father could see the toll the work was beginning to take on him. But it was as it should be. Old men are meant to slow down, and young men are meant to take up for them, and Alexei was happy to do his part. So Alexei learned to make excuses to wake up early and go out on the boat alone, telling Iannis that he needed to practice by himself, without a father there telling a son everything that he was doing wrong, anything Alexei could think of to keep him at home at least a few more days a week instead of out on the sea where he'd been since he was a boy.

And it was on one such morning, when Alexei had taken the boat out alone, that the entire world changed.

That fall had been particularly good for fishing, in a way that some falls are and it's impossible to explain, and Alexei had already filled three nets before the sun was high enough in the sky to signal that it was midday.

That summer he'd started diving for sponges, too.

He'd found a cove up the coast to the north of Agria where they were still plentiful because no other fishermen had found it yet, and after he collected them he could sell the sponges for 50 drachmae apiece in the agora. Alexei enjoyed the days when he could strip off his clothes and dive into the ocean, going as far down as his lungs would allow, which day after day was getting progressively deeper and longer. He'd gather the sponges off the rocks and load them into a special sack that he'd woven just for the task, then come bursting back up to the surface, and it became his favorite part of the day when he'd climb back onto the boat and allow himself to lay still for a few moments as the hot Mediterranean sun would bake the leftover salt onto his skin. It felt like youth to him, and like freedom. He was an adventurer alone on the open sea, the hero of his own story, the same as all the other heroes he'd grown up with. Achilles, Odysseus, Alexander ... the men he thought about when he lay in his bed at night. The great men whose stories they still told. These moments alone with himself and his dreams were innocence before Alexei ever really knew what innocence was, and certainly long before he knew how easily it could be taken.

But the coming fall would be sure to change that forever.

As Alexei came back to shore, his nets full with fish, which would make his father happy, and with a sackful of fresh sponges, he looked into the distance and saw a figure on the beach, standing next to the small and narrow dock and waving his arms wildly, calling out his name:

"*Alexei! Alexei!*" the words carried across the water.

Constantinos had been Alexei's best friend since before either of them could remember. They were both born on the exact same night, within hours of each other during the greatest storm anyone in Agria could recall. It lasted for six hours and killed ten people, and after the storm had finally passed each of their families found that they'd been blessed with two healthy baby boys, and their mothers had decided for them that their histories were certainly already irrevocably intertwined, that fate had already chosen them to be best friends, and so far their mothers had proven to be right. The local priest said any newborns that were able to survive that storm were destined for greatness, and while Costa and Alexei didn't care for any of the stories from their mothers or the priest, they'd both been obsessed since they were very young with finding out who was born first, and thus older, something that they knew they'd never be able to prove—Costa's father had died before he was born, and his mother had gotten cancer when he was six years old, leaving him an orphan—so they couldn't ask them about his birth, but it had become a point between them to try to speculate and unravel the mystery that they knew could never be unraveled.

"What's wrong, Costa?" Alexei called back to him.

"It's the Italians," he said, spitting the word out of his mouth like poison. "It's Mussolini."

"What about him?"

Alexei pulled the boat up to the shore and Costa grabbed hold of the wooden side, helping Alexei tie it off against the dock, something they'd done so many times together that it seemed as familiar to the son of a fisherman and his friend as tying the laces of a shoe.

"He called Metaxas and offered him an ultimatum. It's been all over the radio since it happened."

"What kind of ultimatum?"

"Unconditional surrender. Or he invades Greece with all the troops he has in Albania. Athens has three hours to respond. He laid it on the table thirty minutes ago."

Alexei paused, thinking about this—

"Metaxas is a German sympathizer."

"But this is the Italians. No Greek worth anything would ever surrender to the Italians."

"So you think it's happening, then? That we're going to fight?"

"Is there any other way? You should see the city. People started bracing for the worst as soon as they heard—saving their food, stockpiling their water, burying their valuables."

"What about the Germans? What about Hitler?"

"There's been no mention of the Germans. It seems Mussolini might be acting alone. Hitler's never cared about us, or seen us as any kind of threat, and he doesn't want to come this far south . . . not when he's busy getting ready for Russia."

Alexei and Costa both stood together in silence, the weight of the news between them, knowing what this would mean for them, for all the young men in their village and their country. Then Alexei picked up his sack of sponges and the fish that he'd caught and he started walking down the dock away from Costa.

"Where are you going?" Costa called after him.

"The agora."

"She already knows." Alexei paused, turning back to Costa, waiting for him to tell the rest. "I saw her, she was there with her father. He was discussing it with the other men."

"And what did they say?"

"That this would be the end of Greece."

Alexei was silent for a moment—

"How long did Mussolini give Metaxas to respond?"

"Three hours."

"What do you think he'll do?"

"I think he'll fight."

Costa's answer hung over them both, knowing that either way their hand would be forced, and their lives would be changed forever in the coming months. Alexei nodded to his friend, and then turned back towards town again.

"*Alexei* ..."

Alexei turned back to Costa one more time. Their eyes found each other, and something unspoken passed between them, a sharing of strength between two boys both born of a great storm.

"Good luck."

The road into town winds along the top of a bluff—mountains on one side, and the Aegean on the other—until it descends into the small valley where Agria and its beautiful harbor, one of the best in Greece, is nestled against the sea. Because of its proximity to Volos, the largest major port on Greece's eastern coast between Thessaloniki and Athens, the agora was filled daily not only with locals selling their wares, but foreign merchants as well, bringing products from the islands, from northern Greece, and even as far away as countries like Turkey, Lebanon, and sometimes even Egypt. The marketplace is normally boisterous and loud, men shouting, bargaining against each other, raising their voices for no other reason than to yell and be heard.

But not today.

Today the whole city was filled with an eerie silence and calm like Alexei had never seen or felt before. Walking down the street he could hear radios tuned loudly inside every house, but there was nobody talking, everybody was listening, waiting for the words that would come and change their world and send all of them spiraling into the abyss of another war that had no end in sight.

The dust on the road that was left over from the dry summer covered Alexei's old sandals as he went past a small hotel, and then the butcher shop and bakery, heading towards the town square. He could hear more radios with every step that he took, but he didn't stop to listen, and he soon came to the square, in the center of the city, lined with ancient olive and fig trees, and looked across at the café where a group of men were taking their afternoon coffee. The largest of the men, holding his familiar place in the middle of all the others, was Giorgos Karras—he was imposing, with an ample gut and the dark, harsh eyes of one who's used to always getting what he wants.

If Giorgos was there, then she couldn't be very far.

Alexei looked around, searching the marketplace, checking all her favorite shops and stalls until the crackle of the radios finally caught his attention, and the men at the café sat up a little straighter to hear the news that had finally come—

"Prime Minister Metaxas has made a decision for all of Greece. Mussolini gave him three hours, but he only needed three minutes to respond. He sent a telegram back to Rome with only one word on it—'Oxi.'"

It was a simple word, with the simple meaning just of "no," but the way that it would soon change Alexei's life in every way that a young life can be changed was anything but simple.

As soon as it came across the radio, young men spilled out into the streets with chants of *"Zito Hellas, Zito Hellas! Hail Greece!"* Their mothers and sisters and wives wept, knowing how the fate of an entire generation would now be defined by Metaxas' firm and proud declaration, and while the young men celebrated in the streets, the old men simply grunted, neither in compliance or disapproval, but because they had been young once, too, and even through all the death that they knew was sure to come, they also knew that fighting for your country is the most noble thing a man can do, even with the great price that it brings.

Alexei pushed his way through the mass of people in the streets, still spilling out of houses, shaking their fists with pride, no longer quiet because they knew now what their fate was going to be, and they were glad. He kept searching, pushing his way through the people, until he finally found her: she was across the square from him, next to a crooked olive tree, where she had walked out of the cobbler's shop, carrying her father's freshly polished shoes. Alexei pushed harder, making his way through the crowd, until he was finally almost next to her.

"Philia!" he called to her through the crowd—she didn't hear, so he yelled again, *"Philia!"*

She turned and saw him—

"Alexei, what are you doing here?"

He finally stood facing her, both of them knowing that nothing would ever be the same now, but neither of them wanting to admit it, not even secretly, not even just to themselves.

"Meet me," Alexei said quietly. "At the dock, tonight, after dinner but before the sun starts to go down. There's something I have to show you, and no one will see us. Promise me."

"Alexei, please ..."

Alexei squeezed her wrists, and his eyes found her eyes. "Promise me, Philia."

"I can't."

"I'll wait all night. I won't leave until you come."

She looked across the square and saw her father standing, looking around for his daughter—

"I have to go."

She gave Alexei one more look, then turned and left, and Alexei watched as she walked away from him, back across the square, the sun reflecting off her dark hair as she joined her father at the café where he'd been discussing the coming war with the other men. She hadn't said that she would come, or anything else at all, but Alexei knew Philia, and he knew the look that was on her face, and that she couldn't stay away, not from him, and not from an adventure.

Alexei's mother had made souvlaki for dinner.

Every meal in Greece has either lamb or feta and this one had both. The family ate in silence, chewing slowly and thoughtfully. Many families ask each other about their days at mealtimes, but Alexei's family never did because in their small village every day was always the same: they woke in the morning, they went to work, then they came home for dinner. But that night Alexei could feel his mother's anxiety next to him. Iannis was silent, not because it was dinner, but because he already knew what was going to happen.

Eleni put more cubes of lamb onto her son's plate—souvlaki was her specialty, and giving him more food was her excuse to start the conversation that hung over everything.

"Have you thought any more about school, Alexei?"

"School, Mana?" Alexei asked.

"University. Somewhere that you could put reading the books you always read to good use. You've talked about Thessaloniki. The new campus is supposed to be one of the best."

"The world's at war now, Mana. Universities are shutting their doors."

"Why? That doesn't make sense. Even if there's a war . . . we still have to keep learning."

"Because there'd be nobody to come. No teachers, no students . . . no staff to teach them."

"Somewhere the war hasn't touched, then. Switzerland, or maybe even Canada or America. It'd be more expensive, but we could talk to the bank. You've always loved to read so much, and hear stories of faraway places, you could go to one of them."

Alexei looked at his father, who kept his eyes down on his food, his leg rocking nervously under the table, the one that he'd injured. When he walked it caused him to limp. When he sat still, it ached and needed constantly to be moved, stretched, massaged.

"Enemies are coming to destroy our homes, Mana," Alexei said, turning back to her. "I'm not going to let them. I'm going to fight, like everyone else, to help protect our country."

"No, Alexei. Please. Young men are so quick to go to war. It's suicide . . . a small country like Greece in a war like this? Hitler took France in six weeks. How long do you think tiny Greece can last against an army like that? That's not war, Alexei."

"Then what is it?"

"It's just men dying."

"Every young man in this village is going to enlist tomorrow, to help defend our freedom. And it's not the Germans that we're fighting. It's the Italians. It's Mussolini. We've beaten them before, and we can beat them again." Alexei looked at her. "Would you want your son to be the only one that stayed behind, Mana? The only one that didn't fight or do his part? Would you want to take that from me?"

"If it meant that you were the only one that lived."

"Mana ..."

"Help me, Iannis," she said as she looked over at her husband, who hadn't looked up from his plate. "Help me talk sense into your son."

Iannis was quiet, and then he finally turned to Alexei, his eyes finding his son's, and his son seeing the pain in them. "He's right, Eleni. There's no family in this entire country that will be spared what's about to happen, and we'll be no different than any other family."

"Who'll help you with the traps and the nets if he leaves?"

"I can manage the traps and the nets."

Eleni turned back to her son, the tears starting to come now—

"Is this really the choice that you're making, Alexandros?"

"I'm sorry, Mana. But it's not a choice."

Alexei stood and took his dish to the sink, and before he left he went to his room, where he opened one of the drawers to his desk, moving aside books and papers that he'd stacked there to grab a pen, a knife, and a jar of ink. There was somewhere that he needed to be, someone that he needed to meet, and the sun was already starting to sink in the sky. But before he walked out he paused, because he could hear his father in the dining room, still sitting at the table with his mother, still talking to her, trying to comfort her.

"He's already made up his mind," Alexei heard Iannis say. "There's nothing that we can do."

"He's our son. He's our only son. You need to say something to stop him."

"What would you have me say?"

"Forbid him to go."

"I can't."

"You're his father."

Iannis was silent for a moment, and Alexei couldn't see his father, but he knew that he was staring down at his hands, the scarred and worn tools of his craft—

"You know nothing of what it is to be a man," Iannis

said quietly, barely more than a whisper. "We have to let him go."

"Why, Iannis?"

He stayed staring at his hands—

"Because it's the only way he'll come back to us."

It was still hot as Alexei made his way down to the dock.

It was a walk that he'd made more than a thousand times, but this time was different. He was nervous, which was something new. He could feel his pulse, just behind his ears, anxious about what was to come, and what he knew he was going to have to do, but also excited by the possibility of it, the possibility of the great things that were waiting for him.

He untied the boat from where he'd left it earlier that morning with Costa, and then he sat down to wait. It was past the time when he'd told Philia to meet him, the sun even lower in the sky now, but Alexei knew that she would come. He'd seen the look in her eyes, and he'd known her almost as long as he'd known Costa, so he knew what that look meant. But unlike Alexei and Costa, Philia hadn't been born in Agria—she'd been born in Athens. Her father was a merchant, one of the wealthiest in the city, and all of Greece even, though he hadn't always been. He started a shipping company when he was a young man, and he grew it to be the third largest in the country. Her mother had been an aristocrat, the oldest daughter of a family who had been wealthy and powerful for so long that nobody could remember why, and she had died while giving birth to Philia. After her death, Giorgos suffered in Athens for a few more years, alone with his child, and then made the decision to move them up the coast to Agria.

It was close enough to Volos that Giorgos could continue with his business, but it was small enough that he could raise a child in the way that a child should be raised. When Philia would ask her father later in her life why they left Athens, he would say things like, "Why be the third largest shipping company in Athens, when we could be the largest in Volos?" But Philia would see the emotion in his eyes when he spoke of Athens, and she knew that he left because he could no longer stand living in the same city and walking the same streets where he had once been so happy with his wife.

Alexei was playing with Costa in the street when he first saw her in the agora, holding her father's hand, dressed in a simple white dress with the bottom of it just above her ankles and blowing in the fresh salt breeze coming off the sea. Alexei didn't know what it meant to love a woman then—that would come later—but he did know that he wanted to talk to her, to be near her, and somehow a part of him also knew that everything that was going to matter in his life had just begun.

The first day they met, he took her everywhere.

He took her through all the stalls in the market, especially the ones that sell sweets, where his father's friend Thanos gave them free samples of fresh *baklava* and *loukoumades*. With the honey still sticky on their fingers, he showed her the secret alley behind the city hall that led to where they could climb down to the harbor. The way down was steep, but Philia never hesitated, not even to ask where they were going. He showed her the harbor where the fishermen were coming in with their catches, and some of the locals were diving and pulling octopus out of the shallow waters and selling them to the restaurant owners, haggling over their prices as Greeks always do. He told her with pride that his father was also a fisherman, like the men down in the harbor, and that sometimes his father would even let him pull the nets in during the summer when he didn't have school, and as soon as he was old enough he was going to be a fisherman, too. Philia smiled and told Alexei that his summers and his father sounded wonderful, and with her words in his heart, Alexei stood a little taller as he took her up to the cliffs above Agria, where everything they'd just seen was laid out beneath their feet, and that's when he told her the great stories of his city.

He pointed into the distance to where Volos was visible down the coast and he told her how it had once been called Iolcos, and how this coast had been the home of the great hero Jason, who was once king of all the lands as far as they could see. And that it was from the harbor below them that Jason had set out with his Argonauts to search for the Golden Fleece, and bring glory back to Greece, and take his rightful place as king. Alexei kept talking, telling her how the great Mount Pelion that rose to the north and east behind them had been home to Chiron the Centaur, the tutor of Achilles and Theseus and Jason, too, and how it was there on those rocky slopes that the great heroes had learned all that they knew, all that they carried with them to Troy, and Crete, and Colchis, and beyond. Alexei kept talking, summoning even the most obscure stories that he could think of, because he didn't want the day to end, he didn't want to leave Philia, and he was still talking when with a shiver they both realized that the sun had gone down and they were still high up on the cliffs.

As soon as they realized how late it'd gotten, Alexei quickly brought Philia back down from the mountain to her father's house where police were waiting and told them about the search parties that were out looking for them. Alexei watched the panic disappear when Giorgos laid eyes on his daughter, the only person left in this world that he loved, and Alexei would always remember how beautiful it was when he held her. And then, as they moved apart, and Giorgos sent his daughter into the house, his eyes found Alexei's, and for the first time in his life Alexei saw how harsh they could be, and also for the first time Alexei truly knew fear.

He smiled at the memories, as he sat on the dock for awhile longer, waiting for Philia, and his mind continued to wander until he saw her making her way down the mountain towards him, carefully picking her path along the dirt road that led to the sea. Alexei stood as she got closer. She was dressed in white again, her hair pulled back behind her ears, the linen contrasted against her tanned skin from the summer. She stopped when she reached the dock, and they stood there, facing each other.

"How are your parents?" she asked. "Do you think they're scared?"

"They'll be alright."

"What do they say?"

"My mother says that she doesn't want me to fight. My father says nothing at all."

"My father thinks this will be the end of Greece."

"We're no strangers to fighting against the odds, and we're stronger than Mussolini gives us credit for. We took Troy when nobody said we could. We defeated Persia, the greatest empire the world had ever seen not once but three times. Alexander conquered the whole world."

"That was a long time ago, Alexei."

"We're still the same people."

She smiled at Alexei, seeing his pride bristle.

"That's why I love you . . . you know that, right?"

"Why."

"They say that pride is a sin, but I don't believe that it is. Not always, at least. And your pride in us gives me pride in us, too. Now what is it that you wanted to show me?"

He took her hand and started guiding her towards the boat. "Let's make it out before the tide," he told her, as he helped her step into it, and then waded out from the shore, pushing the boat against the soft waves until they were far enough and he pulled himself over the side and started the engine.

The dull roar cut through the silence of the peaceful evening as Alexei turned the nose of the boat to the north.

They sailed up the coast until Alexei saw the distinctive shape of a peak off the shore that looked like the hooked beak of a bird, and that's when he turned east, away from the peak, and further out to sea. It was fifteen minutes of nothing—just Alexei and Philia and the sea and the waves—until an unmistakable shape appeared in front of them, a rocky crag of land jutting harshly up in the distance.

"What's this?" Philia asked, looking out towards the land that was getting closer in front of them, the island.

"It's what I wanted to show you."

"What's its name?"

"It doesn't have one."

"Really?"

"This sea is filled with islands . . . some that people know about, and some that they don't. This one is mine. We can call it whatever you want."

"Who else has been here?"

"No one. Just me."

"Not even Costa?"

"No," Alexei smiled. "Not even Costa."

He steered the boat clear of the rocks near the surface of the shallow water and into the natural harbor where he tied the boat off and got out, then helped Philia make the step over the railing and onto the land.

She looked around, taking it in.

The island was small, a person would have been able to walk from one side to the other in under ten minutes, with a secluded beach next to where they'd docked in the harbor, and there was a rocky mountain in the middle that rose to about a thousand feet.

"How did you find this place?" Philia asked, taking in the natural beauty around them, the beauty that she was a part of now, too.

"I stumbled on it when I was fishing one day. Come on . . . up this way, we have to go higher."

Alexei took her hand and led her along a pathway up the mountain, following the route that he always followed, and soon they came to the entrance of a small cave. Alexei ducked inside, pulling Philia in after him, and again she didn't hesitate, like the first day that he met her, even though the cave was deep and very dark, and as she crossed the threshold she saw that it was large and spacious, too. But the thing that Alexei loved most about his cave was how high the ceiling was, and the sense of immensity that it created, and also the intimacy, as if the people that were inside were shut off from the world in a place that could be theirs, nobody else's but theirs, and that's what he wanted to share with her.

"Do you like it?"

"It's amazing."

"Turn around."

They turned back to the entrance, which faced west, the way that they'd come, and far in the distance the sun had nearly completed its descent, setting slowly and full of bright and distinct color painted over the mountains and valleys of the land where they'd been born.

"It's beautiful," Philia said. "I've never seen anything like it."

"It's my favorite place in the whole world."

They kept watching in silence as the sun cast its soft orange glow over everything that was in front of them, getting closer and closer to disappearing behind the peaks in the distance. Then, with the sun sinking in the sky, almost gone, Philia turned back to Alexei, and he could see the worry that was in her eyes.

"What's going to happen tomorrow, Alexei?"

"Could you really love a man that's not willing to defend his home?" he asked. "Because that's not a man at all."

"Men search for pain. They search for pain because they don't know who they are without it."

"You know that's not what this is."

"Then what is it?"

"Philia, look at me," Alexei said, and he used his thumb to turn her cheek until she was looking directly into his eyes. "I love you, Philia. That's what this is. And while I don't know what's going to happen in the days to come, the one thing I do know is that's never going to change. That's the *only* thing that's never going to change."

"I'm scared, Alexei. I don't want to be, but I don't know what else there is left."

"I'll come back to you. I know that in my heart, more clearly than anything I've ever known. I'll come back to you."

"How do you know?"

He looked at her, and she looked back at him, and he hadn't planned this, but he was in love with the woman in front of him, and he knew that he wanted to do everything in his power to make her as close to him as he possibly could, for the rest of both of their lives.

"Marry me," he said.

"What?"

"Marry me, Philia. I want to make you my wife."

She put her hands over her mouth as the tears came to her eyes. "Alexei, I love you more than anything in the world, you know that . . . but you can't ask that of me."

"I'm not asking."

"We're too young."

"Too young for what?"

"My father . . . you know what he'll say. How could we be a family without his blessing?"

"Don't you want to be with me?"

"Of course I do. But you can't make me choose between you and him. You can't ask me to do that."

"I'll talk to him."

"You've tried that before. We both know that he won't listen."

"The world's changing, Philia. Your father can change, too. I'll talk to him. I'll make him understand."

"Alexei . . ."

"Come here."

Alexei sat down on a rock at the front of the cave and made room for her next to him as he took out the pen, knife, and ink that he'd brought from his desk.

"What are you doing?"

"Watch."

He took the knife in his right hand, then turned over his left, so that his palm faced the sky and his wrist was exposed, waiting for what was about to come.

He dug the knife into the soft flesh just where the wrist meets the hand, and the first drops of blood slid down his arm and into the dirt. He worked slowly, carefully cutting perfect and straight lines, and when he was done he reached for the ink and dipped the pen into it, black liquid gathering on its tip, before using it to trace back over the tender skin uncovered by the knife, using the pen to set the ink into the exposed flesh. He worked carefully, and when he was done he held his wrist out to show her what he'd created. It was four letters, perfectly drawn, embedded and inked with permanence into his flesh—φιλια—her name written in Greek.

"Now you'll always be with me."

She looked at it for a moment, then took Alexei's hand in hers and started to trace her fingers over the letters—

"Careful," he said. "The ink needs to set."

She raised his wrist to her mouth and gently pressed her lips against it, softly kissing his skin.

"I want you to do it to me now."

"There's not enough room," Alexei smiled. "My name's too long."

"Just your initial, then."

"No."

"Don't tell me no."

He turned and looked at her—

"Are you sure?" he asked.

"Yes."

"It'll hurt."

She looked back at him, and he could see the strength that was in her eyes, the strength that was in her soul, and he had no doubt why he loved her—

"I know," she said.

After they were done, and the ink had set, and the sun had disappeared behind the mountains, Alexei led her back into the cave to where two blankets waited for them. He lit the candle that he kept next to the blankets, and he took her hand and they gently lay down together.

He looked into her eyes.

"I love you, and I don't ever want to love anyone else. And when I come home I want you to have my children, and I want us to raise them here, where we were raised, in the fields and hills where we grew, in the city that we made ours, and teach them to love their country the way that we do. That's what I want, Philia. That's *all* that I want."

She looked back at him.

He traced his fingers along the lines of fresh ink on her wrist, and he could feel her heart beating against his. He kissed her, his dry lips rough against her smooth skin, their bodies begging for each other, but once again they would deny what their bodies asked. They'd never spoken of it, but they hadn't made love, and it was their silent agreement that their first time would be on their wedding night, the way that it used to be so many years ago.

So they lay there and held each other, Philia's eyes watching the light as it flickered and danced across the walls of the cave.

"I'm scared."

"I'm scared, too. But I'm right here."

He looked at her, the most beautiful girl in the world, and this the most perfect moment that he could possibly imagine—

"I'm right here, and I'll never leave you."

2

October 29ᵗʰ, 1940

THE NEXT MORNING THEY LEFT THE cave just as the sun was beginning to rise in the distance, early enough for Philia to slip into her bed before her father woke and discovered that she hadn't come home.

Alexei never went to sleep.

He stayed awake all night, memorizing every line of Philia's face, every wrinkle in her skin, the way that her hand felt in his hand and the way that her body felt against his body, how perfectly they fit together in every way.

It was what he was going to take with him.

When they finally went down from the mountain, back down the trail towards the boat that would take them home, Philia stopped and looked behind them, up towards their cave.

"You said this place has no name?" she asked, still taking it in, committing it to memory. "Because a place as beautiful as this needs a name."

"What do you want to call it?"

She thought for a moment, looking back to where they'd just spent such a perfect night together—

"*Eudaimonia*," she said.

Alexei smiled at her choice.

The word had many meanings, some going as far back as Socrates and Aristotle and Plato, but in this case the most common was the most fitting, and he was glad to hear her in her own way call the cave "happiness." He helped her into the boat, the pre-dawn breeze starting to pick up as he pulled the engine alive and they started back and away from the island, both of them silent, not wanting to change a single thing about what was already perfect.

After they returned and pulled next to Alexei's dock, he helped Philia out and over the railing just as he'd helped her in, and she gave him a small kiss and brushed his cheek with her fingers, lingering as long as she could, before she knew she had to leave. Alexei watched as she walked away from him and towards the road that would take her back towards her house, knowing that he would see her again very soon, and when she was gone Alexei finished tying off the boat before heading towards his own home to speak with his father.

As Alexei walked up the path towards his house, he saw that even though it was very early, Iannis was already awake and sitting on the porch in the back, overlooking the sea, the place where he always took his coffee in the morning. Alexei walked over and sat down next to him, Iannis smoking a cigar with his right hand, holding his worry beads in his left, flipping them through his fingers. Alexei smiled at the familiar *clack clack* the beads made as Iannis expertly twirled them and they struck together.

"You're up early, Papa."

"I haven't been to bed."

"No coffee today?"

"No. Not today."

Iannis and his son were silent for a moment, and Alexei looked down at the worry beads that he was still spinning in his hand, and he knew why his father hadn't been to sleep—

"I'm going to be alright, you know."

"Maybe you will. Maybe you won't. It's war, Alexei. It's a very dreadful thing."

"Are you going to tell me not to go? That you went, and that it broke you, and that you came back, but when you did nothing was the same?"

"No," Iannis took another puff of his cigar, slowly exhaling, still working his beads with his other hand. "A young man should fight for his home, and for his country. I wouldn't take that from my son. And besides, I don't think I could, even if I wanted to. Young men like to fight too much, blinded by that thing they call passion, until they're old enough to understand what it really is."

"And what's that?"

"You'll know when you're as old as me."

Alexei smiled as they sat in silence together a little longer, and then Iannis set his cigar down and put his hand on his son's shoulder, and in that moment Alexei saw how frail his father looked, the great man, the man who had once been Zeus to a little boy, who now looked so old, so infirm, and so suddenly mortal.

"Did she say yes?"

"What, Papa?"

"Make sure that she says yes. One thing that I learned in my time is that the men who return from war are the ones that have something to return to. She'll give you that. A reason to keep fighting, when the rest of the world will surely give you a million reasons not to."

Alexei looked at Iannis, and for the first time realized how much a father can know his son, how much they share of their own bodies, and that mystical understanding between two generations of the same man. Alexei reached into his pocket and took out a handful of drachmae that he'd been saving from the sponges that he'd sold.

"Here, Papa," he said. "I want you to take this."

"Where did my son get such a fortune?"

"It's not a fortune, Papa," Alexei smiled back, knowing his father liked to tease him. "I've been gathering sponges all summer, like I told you, and I've been selling them at the agora. Here, take it."

"Why?"

"Because I want to buy one of our goats from you."

Iannis reached out and instead of taking the money he gently closed Alexei's fingers around the coins and squeezed his son's hand into a fist. "Keep your money, Alexei. Take whichever goat you think will make him the happiest. Remember, you must make sure that she says yes. Give your mother something to plan, and to keep her busy while you're gone. That'll be the best thing that you can do for her. Women don't understand war, but they do understand weddings. My god, do women understand weddings."

Alexei sat for another moment with his father, neither of them sure when they'd be able to share a time like this again, a moment free of care between a father and his son with the sun rising above the waves in front of them in the land where they were born and had also been made. Alexei didn't want to go, to let a moment like this slip away without staying longer to appreciate it, but he knew that he had to. So with the sun almost over the mountains, he finally stood and patted his father on the hand, where he held his worry beads, and then walked towards the enclosure where they kept their goats. He looked at all of them until he found the best one—the youngest and healthiest—and slipped a rope around its neck to lead it out of the enclosure and down the dirt road towards Philia's house.

In so many of the books that he loved, he'd read about moments in people's lives. Moments when what they did mattered, because it changed everything else, for one way or the other. And that's what our lives are built on, these choices, and these moments. English doesn't have a word for it, but the Greeks have a word for everything.

Kairos.

As Alexei walked into the sun, he felt something inside him that he'd never felt before, and he knew.

This morning . . . this was a moment.

Alexei knocked on Giorgos' door.

He waited for a moment, and then it opened. Giorgos stood on the other side, and took in Alexei on his porch, holding a goat on a leash next to him.

"Are you lost?" he asked.

"No, sir."

Alexei could see Philia in the house, behind her father, sitting at a table eating breakfast. Giorgos followed Alexei's eyes and saw the look that they shared, so he stepped outside, closing the door shut behind him.

"Philia's busy today," he said. "She can't see you."

"I didn't come to see her, sir. I came to see you."

"What's this on the leash?" he nodded towards the goat. "I thought your people were fishermen."

"We are. It's for you," Alexei said, trying to hand the

leash to Giorgos, but Giorgos made no effort to take it, instead just folding his arms firmly across his chest.

"If you came all this way to give me a goat, then I'm afraid you've wasted your morning."

"I came to talk to you."

"Well, then. Talk."

"You know that Philia and I have loved each other for a long time now. Tomorrow I'm going to join the army, like every other young man in this country, and I'll head north to fight for Greece."

"That's brave of you. But what does that have to do with me?"

"I came to ask for her hand in marriage before I leave."

"No," Giorgos said, without any hesitation.

"Just no?"

"You'd make my daughter a widow before she's even twenty years old? That's what you've come to ask my blessing for?"

"No. She won't be a widow. I'm going to come back."

Giorgos was silent for a moment, narrowing his eyes as he looked back at Alexei—

"You're too late. She's promised to someone else."

"That's not possible," Alexei said shaking his head. "She can't be. She would have told me."

"She doesn't know. She hasn't met him."

"You'd give your daughter to a stranger?"

"No. I'd give her to a man that can keep her safe when there are foreign soldiers wandering these hills. A man that can offer her more than you can."

"The Italians won't get this far south."

"No. They won't. But the Germans will."

Alexei looked at Giorgos, realizing for the first time how

far ahead he was thinking, and he saw clearly for the first time the cunning that had made Giorgos the businessman that he was.

"If the Germans come, then who could protect her? Who here would have that power? If the Germans reach Agria, then it's the end for all of us."

"One of my old associates in Athens is a government minister. He has a son, a young lawyer from a good family with the connections and the ability to protect her when the Germans come."

"What would he protect her with? A dusty collection of books and law journals?"

"No," Giorgos smirked. "His money."

Alexei paused, realizing that he couldn't compete with the influence of a rich man from a powerful family in Athens, at least not in the eyes of Giorgos, and panic started rising in his chest and his throat—

"You'd marry her to someone that doesn't know her? That doesn't know her favorite color, or what she likes to eat, or how to make her laugh on the days when she needs to smile?"

"If that's what it takes to keep her safe."

"Even if this man has no love for your daughter?"

"Since when have we ever had the luxury of marrying for love?" Giorgos asked as he turned back to his house, and opened the door, almost back inside when Alexei called after him—

"You loved your wife, sir. I know you did."

Giorgos stopped and slowly turned back—

"And how could you know that?"

"Because I see it in your eyes, every time you look at Philia."

Giorgos stood in his doorway and faced Alexei, the young fisherman's son armed with nothing but a goat and a passion that Giorgos now saw wouldn't ever expire or burn out, and Alexei could see Giorgos change. It was in his eyes. They'd softened at the mention of his wife.

"I've asked people about you, sir," Alexei continued. "In the agora. About how you made your fortune."

"Is that right? And what do the people say?"

"They say that you were a man born to nothing. A man that gained everything through the sheer power of strength and will. That you started as an oil trader in the north, near Thessaloniki, with no parents to speak of, and nobody to help you in your business. You were my age when you started, and soon your business grew until you were able to move to Athens and rent a stall, and then soon after you saved enough money to buy that stall, the best in the whole agora. And then soon after that you made enough money to buy half the agora, before a few years later buying the whole thing."

Giorgos looked at Alexei, hearing the young man repeat back to him his story, and Giorgos heard it differently coming from someone else's mouth, and Alexei continued—

"Everything you have you built for yourself. Surely there's more to be said for that man than the one who's born rich and handed his fortune? I may come from nothing, but that means I come from the same as you, and I'll do what you did. I'll *build* a home for your daughter."

Giorgos looked at Alexei for a long time after he was finished, and Alexei knew that Giorgos' decision was going to define the rest of his life, the rest of *both* their lives. And then, when Giorgos finally opened his mouth, Alexei held his breath, waiting—

"You have the courage of your convictions," Giorgos said, "which is a rare enough thing for a young man in this world, and there's more to you than I've given you credit for, I'll accept that. But a father's only job is to make sure that his daughter is provided for, and there are a thousand men in Greece more suited to that than you are. I'm sorry, Alexei. But that's the way of things."

"Sir ..."

"The promise of a home isn't a home. There's a woman out there that you're going to make very happy, when this is all over, but it won't be my daughter. I know that it's not the answer that you came here looking for, but still . . . it will be my answer."

"What can I do to change your mind?"

"You can't. But take it from an older man," Giorgos said. "What you're feeling right now . . . in time it will fade."

"Has it faded for you, sir?"

Giorgos looked back at Alexei, the younger man's eyes blazing with something powerful, and Giorgos spoke slowly as he answered, with respect now, but not a change of heart.

"Take care of yourself, Alexei. War changes men, and very often not in the way that we'd like."

"So that's it?"

"I'll tell her that you said goodbye."

And with that, his final word, Giorgos went inside and shut the door behind him, leaving Alexei alone. Alexei waited, thinking that Giorgos might still return, that he might come out and tell him that he'd had time to think about it, and that he'd been moved by Alexei's passion, but the door never opened and Giorgos never came back. Alexei stood there in the same place for the rest of the morning, not moving a single inch, and as he did he lost track of time and many hours passed with the muted colors of day slowly turning into the pastels of afternoon and finally the blackness of night.

Nothing happened.

But still Alexei waited.

And after he'd waited in the darkness for well more than an hour, he finally turned and left the same way that he'd came, determined not to leave Agria until he'd come up with a new plan to change Giorgos' mind.

"And that was it?"

"Yeah."

"You just stood there like a statue, waiting for him to come back outside?"

"What else could I do?"

"We're *palikari* now, Alexei. Warriors. A warrior would have broken down the door and carried his girl off to his bed."

"We're not *palikari* yet."

"Well, no matter what we are you should have broken down his door and taken your woman."

"It's not that easy."

"Sure it is."

"You haven't seen their house. Giorgos has a very strong door."

Alexei and Costa were sitting outside at the taverna in the town square, their first bottle of ouzo empty on the table in front of them, Costa filling their glasses from the second that was already half-empty: it was their last night in their hometown as free men before they left to join the armies of Greece, and they were drunk, and talking about women, and the future, as men do when they drink too much.

What Alexei didn't know at the time, but Philia would tell him later, was what had happened when her father had come back inside after speaking to Alexei on his porch. When Giorgos had turned and left, and shut the door behind him, leaving Alexei out on the porch, Philia saw a look in her father's eyes that she'd never seen before, and she couldn't place it.

Was it anger?

Denial?

Something else?

She opened her mouth, and he knew the question that she wanted to ask, and before she could ask it he sent her to her room so sternly and suddenly that she didn't protest, but she only went to the top of the stairs and watched as Giorgos stayed standing in the living room, in a place where he had a clear view out their window. Giorgos could see Alexei, still on his porch, waiting, always waiting, but Alexei couldn't see him. Giorgos watched as Alexei stood there through the whole morning, and afternoon, and into the night.

Giorgos didn't move an inch.

Neither did Alexei.

At dinnertime, Philia came down and begged her father to reconsider his decision, and though he didn't give his daughter the answer that she was looking for, or any answer at all, she saw his eyes and could finally place the look that she saw in them earlier.

It was respect.

And it made her smile.

Because she knew her father, and so she knew what came next.

Alexei was still sitting with Costa in the square when he heard a deep voice behind him—

"Have you had too much to drink?"

They turned to see Giorgos, still dressed in the clothes that he'd been wearing when Alexei saw him last.

Alexei stood to face him—

"I'm sorry," he said. "If I'd known you were coming—"

"Don't apologize," Giorgos nodded. "A man should have too much to drink before he leaves for war."

Then Giorgos' eyes flicked to Costa, who also stood, and he recognized Giorgos' look, and that he wanted to speak to Alexei—

"I'll go get us another bottle," Costa said. "It looks like we're going to need it."

Then Costa left, and Alexei and Giorgos were alone together, outside the taverna in the empty town square. The breeze picked up. Alexei could smell salt in the air, coming off the sea.

"It's going be a new world when this war is over, Alexei," Giorgos said. "A new world that you'll be coming home to."

"Yes. It will be."

"I'm not sure that I'm going to recognize it. And it seems that no matter how much I wish it were otherwise, you hold the key to my daughter's happiness. I want to be clear, I'm not giving you my blessing," he paused, looking deep into Alexei's eyes. "But what I am offering you is a compromise."

"A compromise?"

"If you come home from this war, then you'll build a home for my daughter, as you promised you would. And if you don't come back, then she marries the lawyer from Athens."

"I'm . . . very grateful."

"Good."

"Can I ask you what changed your mind?"

"You did."

Alexei tried to hide the smile that came to his lips, but the smile was true, and from a place deep within, and there was no amount of will that was going to stop it no matter how strong a man he was.

"There's one more thing," Giorgos said.

"What's that?" Alexei asked warily.

"We're men. And we've just made a deal," Giorgos paused, looking back at Alexei. "So now we'll drink to it."

Giorgos poured two glasses of ouzo and handed one to Alexei as they raised them in a toast—

"To my daughter."

"To Philia," Alexei answered.

"*Yassou*," Giorgos said.

And they drank.

Alexei set his glass back down, and then with one more look and a last nod of approval, Giorgos turned to leave, but before he'd gone very far he paused and looked back—

"Oh, and Alexei ..."

Alexei stopped and met his eyes, worried that Giorgos might have changed his mind already—

"Sir?"

Giorgos waited another moment, and then he finally smiled.

"Get your damn goat out of my yard."

And Alexei smiled, too.

When Alexei told his mother, she fell to her knees and offered prayers of thanks to God, while Iannis stood behind her with a knowing smile and a nod of approval and pride in his son. It was a moment of great happiness that Alexei would remember for the rest of his life.

Then, when Eleni stood, she pulled Alexei back towards her bedroom.

She took him into their room, and from under her bed pulled an old dusty chest made of cedar wood. Inside there were many things—an old wedding dress, a crocheted cloth detailing a complicated and long family lineage, and finally a small and intricately designed jewelry box, which Eleni took out with great reverence, and inside found what she was looking for.

And, before she gave it to her son, she told him her story . . .

Eleni explained how she could trace her family back over two thousand years, to the time of the Romans and the New Testament, and the last age of miracles on earth. Her people were from the mountains, in the north, from a place once called Macedonia, and they lived in the hills where Alexander had spent his childhood before he left to march east and conquer the world and the rising sun.

And that's where her story began.

There was a young woman, unable to conceive a child, and a weary traveler, walking the Egnatia Road, who stopped in the ancient city of Veria looking for a drink of water on a hot summer day. The traveler had walked a long ways, and he didn't know why he stopped at the city other than it was on his way, and the sun was hot, and he thought he'd like a drink of water before he continued to Thessaloniki. He walked through the streets of Veria, and as he neared the well in the town square, he heard the soft sounds of crying, and saw that it was a beautiful young girl that was weeping.

Adonia had loved Myron since before she knew what love was.

Their parents had been friends for many years, and were each from important families in the city, and Adonia and Myron had been promised to each other since Myron was thirteen, as a way to bind the two powerful families together, with Adonia's eighteenth birthday marking the date that their long engagement was finally to be fulfilled, and it was a day that could not come soon enough for either of them.

Their wedding was huge, an event that was talked about in the village for many years, and that night Myron took Adonia to the wedding bed that they would share, and they tried to conceive a child. They tried that night, and many nights after. And soon those nights turned into weeks, which turned into months, which turned into years, and still to their disappointment there was no child. By the time Adonia was twenty years old, she was still trying to give her husband his first son, while some of her friends were already having their second and third. Myron never chastised her, nor was anything but supportive and respectful, but she knew that their inability to conceive was driving a wedge between them, and that a family with no children was no family at all. And then one day while she was shopping in the market, and she couldn't stop thinking about how kind Myron had been to her, through all these struggles that she blamed on herself, and how he was such a good man, and deserved a son, she was overwhelmed with emotion and couldn't stop the tears that came.

Her face was buried in her hands when she felt a shadow

over her, and then heard a voice: "It's a very beautiful day for such a pretty girl to spend the whole of it crying by a well."

Adonia looked up.

She had lived in Veria her whole life and knew every man in the city, but she didn't recognize the stranger that was standing before her, his body and head silhouetted by the sun behind him.

"Who are you?"

"Might I trouble you for a cup of water?" he asked.

She dried her tears, and then reached the cup down into the well, and when it was full she handed it to him and he drank deeply.

"I've travelled much of the world," he said, after he drank. "And this is some of the best water I've ever tasted. Would you like to try some?"

"I've lived here my whole life. I drink this water every day."

"Try it again today," the stranger said.

She reached the cup back down and filled it with more water, then when she was about to bring it to her lips, the stranger reached out and gently touched her hands, stopping her. They stayed like that for a moment, her hands wrapped in his, and she felt a strange and sudden warmth.

Then he nodded, and she drank.

From the moment the water touched her lips she knew that she'd never tasted anything like it before. As she'd told him, she'd drank at this well every day since she was a little girl, yet the water had never tasted like this: it was sweet like nectar, and she could feel it nourishing her body. She looked back at this stranger, and asked him again, this time with more curiosity—

"Who are you?"

"May I sit?"

She nodded and he sat next to her.

"My name is Paul," he said.

"I'm Adonia," she answered, taking in the state of his clothes. "Have you travelled very far, Paul?"

"I have travelled very far, yes. All the way from the East."

"From where in the East?"

"A city called Jerusalem."

"Is that far?"

"Quite far, yes."

"What are you doing here in Greece?"

"I'm bringing a message."

"A message to whom?"

"A message to all."

Adonia sat back and regarded this strange man who had come to their village, and the way that he looked at her, almost as if he was looking *through* her, asking a question and then finding the answer himself, without her needing to speak or reply.

"I've answered your questions, now you can answer mine," he said. "Tell me . . . what brings such a pretty girl to cry here in front of a well on a day as beautiful as this one?"

She looked back at him for a few more moments, but she knew she'd already decided to trust him.

It was because of his eyes.

"I've been married now for more than two years, and the thing I want more than anything is to give my husband a son. I love him so much, and I want to make him happy, but as much as we try I haven't been able to conceive. We haven't been able to make a child."

"What have you done about it?"

"What do you mean? We've tried, as much as we can, but we've had no luck."

"Have you asked for help?"

"Who would we ask for help?"

"What is the most sacred place in your country?"

She thought for a moment, then she told him—

"The Oracle, in the mountains at Delphi. Pilgrims have been making trips there since before the beginning of time."

"Then go there. Ask God for help, and believe that he will deliver that which you ask him."

"And what if he can't? Or if he's not listening?"

"He will be."

"How do you know?"

"Because in this world, we must walk by faith, not by sight."

"What is that?"

"Something I heard once, long ago. God parted a sea for Moses. He split stone for Joshua. He delivered David from the monster of Gath, and sent his only son to earth to suffer and die for our sins. God is powerful, Adonia. And he is always listening."

She understood now—

"You're a Jew."

"I was, once."

"And now you're not?"

"Now I'm what they call a Christian. A follower of the man that you call Christ in your tongue."

"And that's what he taught?"

"That's what he lived."

And then Paul stood abruptly—

"Thank you for the water," he said.

And then, with one more smile, as suddenly as he had

come, he was gone again. It wasn't until years later that Adonia learned of Paul's fate, when she heard the story of one of the Apostles of the prophet Joshua Bar-Joseph, whom his followers in Greece called Jesus Christ, and how Paul had travelled as far as Rome, spreading Joshua's message of faith and love, and was arrested on orders from the emperor Nero and crucified, upside-down in front of the Senate. After his crucifixion, Paul was beheaded, and his remains buried outside the city walls, where there now stands a church dedicated to the memory of his martyrdom which is visited by thousands of pilgrims every year who retrace his route from Jerusalem through Veria and Greece, and finally ending at the church in Rome, his last resting place on this earth.

Adonia made dinner for her husband that night.

They ate in silence, and she said nothing to him about the stranger that had come to Veria and talked to her beside the well, because she didn't want to let herself hope, at least not yet, in case the path that Paul had given her didn't lead anywhere. Instead, she told Myron that she wanted to visit a relative in Athens, and he gave her his blessing and the coins that she would need to make the trip south, and she left the next morning.

It took her three days to get to Delphi.

The oracle is located high in the mountains of Attica, on a jagged plateau set against the rocky peaks of central Greece, and pilgrims have been coming to the oracle, a place that Greeks believed to be the center of the earth, for as long as memory holds. And while the oracle had changed hands and patrons many times, in the year 49 AD it was a place where the old gods and the new were worshipped side by side.

As Adonia made her way up the mountain, just another woman in the crowd of pilgrims on their way to the shrine, she was stopped by another traveler, an old woman peddling her wares. Normally Adonia wouldn't have paid attention to a woman selling things that she didn't want, begging for gold and promising great deals that wouldn't be found anywhere else, but there was nothing normal or ordinary about this trip.

"Trinkets, just ten drachmae," the women called. "Trinkets that will bring all your heart's desires!" Then the woman saw Adonia, and she looked at her with almost a look of recognition, a look that if you were to study closely would reveal this as a moment the old woman had been waiting for a long time to come to pass.

"You," the woman said, focusing on Adonia. "What's your name?"

She hesitated, then—

"Adonia."

"Come here."

"I'm sorry, I'm not interested."

"I want you to take this," the old woman said, picking out a ring from a collection, a beautiful piece of jewelry fashioned out of silver with a cross etched across the top of it.

"I'm sorry, but I can't pay. My husband has only given me enough money for the trip."

"What is money? I'm asking for none. Here, take it," she said, pressing the ring into Adonia's hand. "It's yours."

"What do you mean?"

"Exactly what I said. It's meant for you. For your daughter."

"I don't have a—"

"Shhh. It's a gift, my girl. Just take it."

Adonia was moved by this old woman, and her kindness, and the peace that she felt when the woman gave her the silver ring and their hands grazed against each other and touched.

"I don't know what to say."

"You don't need to say anything."

"Thank you."

"You're very welcome, dear. Now go. Up the mountain, to find what you're looking for."

Adonia paused for a moment, but the woman turned away and went back to peddling her wares to the pilgrims passing by, and so Adonia kept walking up the mountain, leaving the old woman on the street behind her, until she finally reached the top and the shrine that was there. She stood in front of it, and looked up at the famous words of Apollo carved over the entrance, which have been gospel to Greeks through the centuries—

Know Thyself.

Nothing in Excess.

Be.

As Adonia looked at the words, carved into stone above her to stand the duration of time, she slowly made the sign of the cross over herself. When she thought back about it many years later, she didn't know why she did it, because she never had before, she only knew that it felt right.

She walked inside.

The shrine was cold, that was the first thing that she noticed, and it was dark, the entire structure lit only by a single torch. She waited in line with the other pilgrims, and when it was finally her turn to see the priest, she walked forward and knelt before him.

"Please, don't kneel," the priest said. "We're all equals here before God."

"Are you not his priest? His representative on earth?"

"I am, but I'm also a man, and God is God. I'm fortunate that he speaks through me, but it's just a man here before you that he's chosen, flesh and blood, the same as all other men."

"I've come far," Adonia said. "All the way from Veria, a city high in the mountains to the north."

"Your sacrifice and your pilgrimage pleases God, but he already knows why you're here."

"He does?"

"Of course. He knows all. Especially what we hold deepest in our hearts."

"Then what am I to do?"

"Do you want this?"

"Yes. More than anything in the world."

"Then it will be so."

"That's it?"

"Live a life of love, a life in his image, as he sent his son to show us, and you'll have everything that's in your heart."

The priest made the sign of the cross over Adonia, and then he touched her on the forehead. "Go now, and have a safe journey home," he said. "A safe journey back to your city high in the mountains."

It wasn't long after she returned to Veria that she became pregnant with her first child, and her husband rejoiced, as did their family, and the whole village, such was their happiness. She would have eleven more children after their first, and that's the story of how it came to pass that the girl who was worried she would never conceive a single child at all came to have the largest family in Veria, and also how she became a Christian.

When Alexei's mother finished her story, she was looking at her son as he processed everything he'd just been told.

"She had twelve children?"

"She did. Every one of them a blessing from God."

"That's a lot."

"She prayed very hard."

"And what happened to the ring?"

"She gave it to her first daughter, as the woman on the road to Delphi had told her that she would. And then her daughter passed it down to her daughter, and so on through their family, so that every first-born daughter would receive the ring and with it the memory of Adonia, and the blessing that she was given by the Apostle Paul."

"That's a wonderful story."

"It's yours."

"What?"

Alexei watched as his mother opened her hand and took Adonia's silver ring and handed it to him. Alexei looked at it, turning it over in his hands, running his fingers over the cross on the surface, feeling a connection deep inside him that he knew would never fade.

He looked up and saw tears in Eleni's eyes—

"Mana ..."

"Give it to her. Make her yours."

"I will," he nodded.

And there were tears in his eyes now, too, and this time he didn't hide them from her—

"I will."

3

October 30th, 1940

HOW DO YOU PREPARE FOR WAR?
How does a man prepare to take another man's life, or have his taken from him?

The morning before Alexei and Costa shipped out they woke early and went running down the coast. It was something they used to do every day as kids, though they hadn't in a long time, and neither of them knew why they decided to do it again that morning.

It started as a game.

When they were young, and before they knew that there were such things as soldiers that earned glory on the battlefields of Europe and Asia, young boys in Greece dreamt of going to the Olympics to represent their country in the games that they'd created and brought to the world, and Alexei and Costa had both settled on long distance running as the event that would be their best shot, and so they started to train together.

They were good, and they practiced every day, even during the grueling heat of the Greek summers, but as they got older, they soon came to realize that while they were good, there was no place for "good" at the Olympics, and they would never be fit enough to compete with the best athletes in the world. They were each blessed with many things in their lives, but neither of them had been given the lightness of build to be a world-class distance runner.

But that morning neither of them cared.

The sun was rising in the distance, and the cool breeze off the sea was soft against their faces, blowing through hair as they ran and ran and ran, each of them not chasing each other, or an elusive time, but instead a moment, a youth that was long gone and never to return again, no matter how fast they paced themselves, or how much distance they covered.

"Have you thought much about it?" Costa asked as they ran.

"Thought about what?"

"Is there anything else?" he asked. "The war, Alexei. The war. At least there's no chance you'll die a virgin now."

"How's that?"

"You're engaged, aren't you? So it's happened."

"What's happened?"

"The *consummation*," Costa said the word with a smile at his own formality as they ran.

"You don't consummate an engagement," Alexei laughed.

"What?"

"You consummate a marriage."

Costa shook his head, trying to understand—

"So are you going to war a virgin or not?"

"Yes."

"Jesus," Costa gave Alexei a shove. "You're going to

stick out from a mile away. You're not going to stand a chance . . . you're going to be the first Greek killed."

Alexei laughed again.

They kept running.

Costa had lost his virginity at fifteen, but he'd been desperate to lose it long before that, almost since before he could remember. He'd tried for years until he finally got his chance when a travelling circus came to town. The circus was just passing through on its way from Thessaloniki to Athens, and the man who owned it decided to stop so they could feed and water the exotic animals that comprised his many different acts, and while they were in Agria he decided to put on an impromptu show to make some extra money and pay for their lodging and food. And that's when Costa laid his eyes on the owner's beautiful daughter.

She was older than Costa, nineteen years to his fifteen, but that only made her more attractive to him.

And he was relentless.

He brought her flowers. He brought her gifts. He knew that he only had twenty-four hours to impress her, and he was determined to not let a single second of that time go by wasted. She rejected him, laughing and calling him a boy, telling him that he was too young, but she didn't know Costa, and so she didn't know that instead of giving up it would only make him try harder. Eventually, he wore her down, and she took him into the back of one of the tents amongst the empty animal cages while the show was going on and he finally convinced her to make him a man, long after she'd already decided that she would, but wanted to make him work for it. They both had their pants around their ankles when her father, who was conducting the show, accidentally ripped a small hole in his uniform and made an unexpected trip backstage to change into a spare, and when he saw Costa and his daughter he went into a blind rage and chased Costa out of the tent, and Costa, the runner, did what he knew how to do best . . .

He ran.

Even today, they still tell the story in Agria of the naked boy sprinting through the travelling circus, dodging giraffes and bears and elephants, and the angry animal tamer chasing after him, screaming as loud as he could scream for the blood of the boy who had dishonored his precious daughter.

After that night, flush with confidence, Costa set out to continue his conquests. It didn't hurt that puberty was kind to him, sharpening the muscles in his arms and chest, and filling out his face to give him a strong and powerful jaw that even the most conservative of men would be hard-pressed to call anything but handsome. And he chased any girl that would have him, as young men do when they first discover what Costa had discovered and think of nothing else. First, it was the girl that sat next to him in school, then it was one of their classmate's older sister, each of his partners more interesting than the last, until the culmination of his desire led him to a continued affair with a thirty-six-year-old widow and mother of two who had hired him for the summer as a laborer and fell in love with the boy that she paid to keep her yard clean.

Costa had always teased Alexei about being a virgin, ever since that night he had run through the circus naked, and Alexei had eventually gone home to find him waiting at his house, a bottle of ouzo already in his hand, ready to celebrate and tell his friend all about what had happened, and what Alexei was missing, and every time Costa teased him from that day on Alexei always had the same answer ready for him.

"Girls are just girls to you, Costa," Alexei would say.

"So?" Costa would ask him. "What's Philia then?"

"She's the mother of my children."

"You don't have any children."

"Not yet. But we will."

"Then why not get started now?"

"Because it's something worth waiting for. It's something worth doing the right way."

"The right way? You read too many books. There's only one way, and if only you knew how pleasurable it was then we wouldn't be having this conversation at all."

"You sleep with too many women."

"There's no such thing, Alexei," Costa would laugh back. "Once you sleep with Philia, the first time, the time that everything changes, then you'll realize, too . . . there's no such thing."

Alexei and Costa ran the rest of the distance together in silence, and if they'd known how much that morning they spent running together like they used to when they were boys would have meant to them, that it was something that they'd never be able to do again, surely they would have never stopped.

But they did.

They didn't say goodbye to each other.

They didn't need to.

So they nodded, like they usually did, and went their separate ways, Costa heading back towards town, while Alexei turned and went in the opposite direction, back towards his house, down the long dirt road next to the sea that would lead him home.

He opened the door and kissed his mother on the cheek as he walked in, then went to the bathroom where he stripped off his sweaty clothes and got into the shower to rinse the sweat from his hair, and it was during that shower, the last one that he would take in his home for a very long time, that the crushing reality of what was about to happen came, the realness of what he was going to do, where he was going to go, and what would be asked of him.

It all finally hit him in that moment.

The endorphins from the run and the blind confidence and optimism they always brought were gone, and all that was left was the water pouring over his head and the nausea brought on by the overwhelming feeling of knowing that one day very soon he was going to be asked to take another man's life. Another man like him. Too young to be fighting in the war that they were going to be fighting. Maybe he'd even have a girl like Philia waiting for him at his home, and parents like Iannis and Eleni, and a friend like Costa.

He couldn't help but wonder.

Alexei didn't know everything that going to war would entail, but he knew enough to know that even if he did make it home, like his father had warned him, there was no reason to expect that he would come back in the same way, or that he'd be able to take the things that he was going to see and that he was going to do and be able to leave them behind.

Should he be scared?

No, he thought.

Because this was his chance to do great things.

Alexei stood thinking about this, and wondering about the new man that war would make him into, and as the water continued to pour over his head and wash away the feelings, a boy became a man, and the nausea that he'd felt turned into pride, a deep pride in his country, and in his people, and he asked for forgiveness as he stood naked under the water, forgiveness from whoever might give it to him because he realized that it wasn't fear at all that was in his belly, but an overwhelming sense of duty and honor, and he was glad that this war had come to Greece. He was glad that this great moment was going to happen in the time that he was alive, and he relished the thought of what was about to come, and the stories that would be told, and that he was going to be a part of them.

He smiled as he thought about it.

There's a reason we're all only allowed to be young once.

Alexei said goodbye to his parents that night.

Eleni cried and hugged her son, and he let her hold him as long as she needed because he knew this was the hardest thing that she'd ever done. And as he stood there with her, he realized that it was the first time in his life that he'd wished that he'd had a sibling—a brother, or a sister—not for him, but for his mother. To stay with her and hold her and tell her that everything was going to be alright, that as soon as she'd realized Alexei was gone it would be nothing until she'd next see him walking back down the road towards their house because the war was over, and they'd won, and Alexei was a hero, and no matter whatever happened in the future he wouldn't ever leave his home again.

Iannis didn't shed any tears.

He simply walked forward and shook his son's hand,

then pressed a small box into his palm. Alexei opened it to see a 1917 DWM Artillery Luger, a standard-issue German pistol from WWI.

"I took it from a Bulgarian," was all that he offered in explanation. "It's old, but it's better than anything that you'll get in Greece. It's the manufacturing, the engineering. It's not regulation. So keep it somewhere out of sight otherwise they'll take it from you."

"I will," Alexei nodded.

"Stay close to Costa. Take care of each other."

"I'll be thinking about you both every day."

"Don't think about us. We don't exist anymore. Think only about the men next to you, and the men across from you. Think only about staying alive."

Alexei nodded again.

Saying goodbye to Philia was harder.

Alexei already had a whole lifetime spent with his parents, but his life with Philia had only just begun. He stood next to her, and he could feel her strength. He gave her his mother's ring, and Philia cried when Alexei told her its story, and how it had come to them, and after he was finished and slipped it on her finger neither of them were surprised when it fit perfectly, because that's how stories like these end, or maybe it's how they begin. Philia looked down at the ring for a few moments, admiring its beauty and simple elegance, feeling the history that she was now a part of, and then she turned and looked back at Alexei—

"Will you miss me?"

"Only when I'm breathing."

"Come back to me, Alexei," she said. "There is no me without you." Then she reached out and touched Alexei's wrist, where her name was set into his skin with ink, and then her own wrist, where Alexei's initial was marked. "There's no Philia without Alexandros."

"Live then, child of my heart, and until the day that I return know that all human wisdom is contained in these two words: wait and hope."

"What's that from?"

"Dumas."

"Maybe you do read too much," she smiled, because she knew it would help her not cry. "Maybe Costa's right."

"Wait for me. Hope for me."

She touched Alexei on the chest, her hand right above his heart, her eyes looking into his eyes—

"I'll be right here, Alexei. Waiting for you. Hoping for you."

"S'agapo."

"S'agapo moro mou."

She leaned in close, whispering into his ear, filling his soul—

"I love you," she said. "Come back to me."

The trains that would take Alexei and Costa north along with the other young men from Agria would come at dawn, and that night before they left Alexei lay alone in his bed, unable to sleep, his hands wrapped tightly around the pistol that his father had given him and he studied it, learning what it felt like to hold a weapon in his hand. The steel was cool and powerful against his flesh. He felt the handle, wondering who else it had belonged to, and then his hand moved further down the barrel, and he wondered where it had come from, and how many men it had killed, and what battles it had seen.

Where would Alexei take it?

What story would he contribute?

What part of him would live on after he'd died?

Alexei counted the last minutes he had in his room, this place that had made him so much of who he was, until outside the sun began to rise, the first rays of light peeking through his window, telling him that it was time to get up from a rest that had never come, the last that he would spend there, in his home, in his bedroom, as a boy of those lands, and of that city.

He rose and slowly dressed, looking outside at the calm waters of the Aegean that he'd fished so many times, and as he stared at the sun, gently rising above the peaceful surface, he knew that it was finally time for the only thing he had left to do.

It was time to leave.

PART II

"On the 28th of October 1940 Greece was given a deadline of three hours to decide on war or peace, but even if a three day or three week or three year period were given, the response would have been the same. The Greeks taught dignity throughout the centuries. When the entire world had lost all hope, the Greek people dared to question the invincibility of the German monster, raising against it in the proud spirit of freedom."

—Franklin D. Roosevelt, President of the United States of America, in a letter to the Ambassador of Greece

4

November 9th, 1940

THE GREEK SOLDIERS WERE SHIPPED NORTH by trains.

The whole village came to see them off at the station outside Agria—men, women, and children smiling, waving, yelling "*Zito Hellas*" at their young men as they left their homes to go do the work of heroes.

People were already calling October 28th a national holiday, and while the Prime Minister Metaxas had been unpopular and a known Nazi sympathizer before the war, even now the staunchest of opponents were hard-pressed to find fault in the man who had dared to stand so tall and act so courageously. Even as far away as America, an image of a Greek soldier, standing at attention, in an act of defiance, as he's called to arms, a bugle at his lips, was put on the cover of their *Life Magazine*, for all the world to see.

There was pride in the air.

There was pride in the mountains.

There was pride in the flowers that spread across the rocky fields.

And it was a deep pride that was born from how they'd

answered the world when they'd been called upon to show strength, and in the way that they were now going to honor the legacy of their ancestors—the great men like Achilles and Jason and Odysseus and Alexander—the men whose stories are still told, even now, so many years later. The whole world tells the stories of those heroes, Alexei thought, as he rode the train north.

And soon the world would tell theirs, too.

The Greek soldiers had no training.

Alexei and Costa thought there would be someone to show them how to shoot their weapons, give them basic instructions on how to work together as a team, and establish some semblance of a line of command and order amongst them. But instead of anything formal or organized, the army was simply divided into those who had been soldiers before "Oxi Day," and the young men with pride in their hearts who had enlisted and become soldiers in the days after.

As Alexei and Costa rode north, an officer came into their car and read them a speech by Metaxas that had aired on the Greek radios answering the question that Metaxas knew the soldiers would be asking as they travelled towards war and uncertainty. Metaxas told his people that as Greeks they had been warriors as far back as time could remember, and it was a part of who they were—a part of their blood—whether they'd been aware of it before that moment or not. It was a part of a legacy they had inherited from their parents and grandparents, and all the others who had come before them. Thus, it wasn't something that they needed to learn, or train for, and Metaxas reached back to antiquity, like so many Greeks can't help themselves from doing, ending his broadcast with a quote from the great dramatist Aeschylus:

"The time has come for Greece to fight for her independence. Greeks, now we must prove ourselves worthy of our forefathers and the freedom they bestowed upon us. Greeks, now fight for your Fatherland, for your wives, for your children and the sacred traditions. The struggle now is for everything!"

Alexei looked outside the window of the train and saw the landscape begin to change—they were rising through craggy foothills, heading towards large and sharp mountains in the distance ahead of them. Mussolini's men were in Albania, so the fighting was going to be in the Pindus Mountains, which ran as a border between northwestern Greece and Albania. The Italian plan was to hit Greece swift and hard, and when the thin lines that were defending the northern passes buckled, they'd march into the mainland and down to Athens. *Il Duce* had loudly proclaimed to anyone that would listen that the Italian flag would be flying over the Acropolis by Christmas.

Alexei and Costa saw their first action at the Kalamas River.

It was the natural border separating Albania to the north and Greece to the south, and it's at the river where the Greek High Command had decided to make a stand to halt the Italians from coming any further south, because if a single enemy crossed over that river, then the first footfall they'd be making on the other side would be on soil that wasn't theirs, and that's what Greek men were giving their blood to protect.

The battle had already started by the time Alexei and Costa got there, and the first thing they noted about battle was the noise.

Cannons being fired across the water.

The sudden harsh explosion of grenades.

Staccato gunfire piercing the night sky.

And that's all that Alexei and Costa had in the beginning, just the sounds of battle, and the screams of dying men, because as young and untested recruits they were held back from the actual fighting. The battle dragged on through day and night as Alexei and Costa and a dozen other new soldiers were tasked with running ammunitions from the Greek camp to the soldiers at the front, where they'd dug in at the small mountain city of Kalpaki, along the river, defending a bridge that spanned across from Albania to Greece.

And the fighting was the most intense on the third day.

Alexei and Costa were bringing pieces of bread with small bits of meat wrapped inside them to the soldiers who hadn't left the front since the fighting began, and that's when an Italian counter-attack caught the entire Greek line off-guard, and the fighting came right up to the area of the wall where Alexei and Costa stood, and their eyes got wide as they saw for the first time lives in front of them ending very violently and suddenly, the soldier standing five inches to Alexei's left going down with a shot to the gut, another next to them being shot in the head, and after his initial shock Alexei fell to the mud to protect himself.

But Costa didn't.

Italian soldiers jumped from behind cover to take advantage of the surprise and confusion they'd created by charging up the mountain. The Greek soldiers reacted instantly, firing blindly down beneath them into the dark, and while Alexei's reaction was the same as most soldiers during their first deafening moments of battle, Costa stayed standing and pulled his rifle off his back as he ran to the wall and fired shots into the dark at the Italians with the rest of the Greek soldiers.

Bang bang bang!!! Bang bang!! Bang bang bang!!!

The sound of the Greek answer rang through the mountains, and there were screams from below, letting the soldiers know that bullets were finding marks, and so they kept firing.

Alexei crawled to the wall, and reached up and fired into the night, too.

Because of the darkness it was impossible to tell whether Costa or Alexei had actually hit anyone, but the next morning there were three dozen bodies laid out in front of the Greek lines where the attack had come. And while the task of deciding which bullets had taken which lives was impossible to determine, in Costa's mind there was no doubt that he had just drawn his first blood in this war, and he grew a few inches that night.

After the fighting had died back down, and they had gone back to camp, Alexei realized that he couldn't get his hand to stop shaking. He thought about the shots that he'd taken, and the men that he may have killed.

Did they have families?

Did they have a father like Iannis, and a mother like Eleni, and a woman that they loved like Philia?

His hand kept shaking.

Costa had gone to the barracks to request more ammunition and tell anyone who'd listen what had happened at the front, and what he'd done, while Alexei sat with a bowl of soup and small piece of bread to dip into it, his first meal of the day, trying to calm his stomach.

And while he ate, he overheard a conversation between two officers.

The assault that they'd just fought back was actually little more than a distraction so that the Italians could try to get a courier through the mountains to their reinforcements on the other side. In a bit of miraculous luck, a Greek soldier who had walked away from the battle lines to relieve himself just moments before the attack saw the courier, and in a daring feat that had required more than a little bit of courage, the Greek soldier ran the Italian down, and from the letters that the courier was carrying, the Greeks had learned the exact date and location of the next Italian attack. The Italians didn't yet know that they'd lost their element of surprise, and that the reinforcements they were sending for wouldn't be there to meet them when they'd requested.

For the Greeks, it was their chance.

The Italians still had significantly more soldiers, but perhaps more importantly they had 170 tanks with them, with tanks being a luxury of modern warfare that the Greek Army did not possess, and was seen by the Italians as being a fatal flaw in the Greek resistance, one that no amount of courage or pride or bravery could overcome.

The two Greek officers smiled to themselves.

They knew how important the information that had been intercepted would be to the war they were fighting. And Alexei smiled, too, knowing that everything was about to change—a soldier from one army having to piss at the same time that a soldier from the other was trying to sneak by the spot he'd chosen would change everything.

But, then again, wars have been decided by less.

There wouldn't be much rest that night.

Alexei and Costa and the rest of the Greek soldiers were briefed and told to get ready for the fiercest fighting yet, as the Italian offensive would be coming in less than a few hours.

And they didn't need men running supplies any more.

They needed soldiers now.

So Alexei and Costa were sent to the barracks to get outfitted.

They stood in line and waited until it was their turn and they were given ammunition for their rifles, standard-issue pistols for their hips, a small knife in case they were caught in hand-to-hand combat, and two grenades that they were told to use with extreme judiciousness because every kind of ammunition was becoming scarce, especially grenades, and there's nothing worse than fighting a war without anything to fight it with.

As they got outfitted with their weapons, Costa looked over and saw Alexei's hand still trembling. Costa didn't know what he was supposed to do, but he knew that he needed to do something, so he reached out and held his friend's arm. They looked at each other. It was the same way that they'd looked at each other on the dock, when they'd learned of Mussolini's ultimatum.

"They die easy," Costa said, trying to soften his voice, to be as reassuring as possible.

"Everyone dies the same way."

"No, they don't."

"What do you mean?"

"Did Achilles die the same as Agamemnon?" Costa asked. "Did Theseus die the same as Minos, or his beast?"

Alexei looked back at Costa, and a smile gradually came over his face, and he was grateful for having a friend that knew him the way that Costa knew him. And he was also grateful that they were there at this war together, during what was surely to be the most important days of their lives, and that neither of them would have to face what was next alone.

Alexei slowly nodded.

His hand stopped shaking.

"It's going to be alright, isn't it?" he said.

Costa smiled—

"It's going to be more than that," Costa answered with his steady eyes, and belief in the words he spoke. "It's going to be a day that makes our fathers proud."

And Alexei finally smiled, too.

The Greek soldiers lay in the dirt.

They were settled behind the line that the Greeks had built at the top of the mountains. A few soldiers stayed standing to make it seem to the Italians like nothing had changed, like it was just another day that they would fight again, the same as the last three days had been.

Costa glanced at the position of the sun.

"It's past noon now."

"Yeah," Alexei said, absently fingering his rifle, feeling it in his hands, preparing himself.

"When are they coming? The letter said noon, right?"

"The Italians are never on time."

"They have been with Mussolini."

"They're still Italians, and Mussolini's in Rome."

Costa tried to settle back in and wait, but he'd never been good at waiting. More time passed, though how much or how little neither of them would be able to tell, and then they heard a rumbling in the distance.

"Tanks," Costa whispered.

They both held their weapons a little tighter, as did the rest of the soldiers around them, and they each had time for one last thought. This is it. This is what everything's led to. This is the rest of their lives.

And then the bullets started above them—

Bang bang bang bang bang bang!!!

The peaceful evening was shattered by the sound of gunfire erupting from both sides now.

And then mortars from the Italians.

Kaboom kaboom kaboom!!!

They lobbed them at the Greek lines and there was nothing that Alexei and Costa could do except lay in the dirt where they were and pray that the mortars didn't come near where they were waiting. The first two missed—one short of the Greek position, and one too far—and then the third hit the Greek line a hundred yards from them, and they looked over as screams filled the air and Greek bodies were torn apart and blood spilled across rocky soil.

They still couldn't move yet.

They couldn't stand to fight back, or run to help the soldiers that lay wounded with missing limbs and in terrible pain, because they needed the Italians to be drawn closer, and then the Greek officers would give the signal for them to stand and join the attack so that they could keep the element of surprise that the Italians thought was theirs.

Alexei closed his eyes.

He said a soft prayer and held the orthodox cross that he wore around his neck as he imagined the clear azure water of the Aegean where he grew up, and the feeling that he loved of the sun baking the salt from the sea onto his skin after he'd gone diving for sponges. He imagined Philia next to him. How she felt. Her soft skin against his rough and calloused hands. He imagined the children that they'd have together when this was over. What color hair would they have? What color would their eyes be?

Costa stared at the man next to him.

He'd been hit by a mortar or shrapnel, and half his leg was gone. He was writhing in pain on the ground, without saying a word, his teeth gritted until blood spilt from his torn cheeks as he choked back his screams. Costa didn't think of Agria or his home. He thought of the man that was dying next to him, and his eyes hardened as he gripped his rifle even tighter, allowing the hate to fill him because he knew he was going to need it now.

And then they heard the Greek officer shout.

Alexei and Costa looked at each other to make sure it was what they thought it was, and then they rose in unison with the rest of the Greek soldiers that had been hiding behind the wall and fired down at the Italians that were advancing up the mountain towards them.

Bang bang bang bang bang!!!!

Alexei's hand started to shake again but he kept firing.

Bang bang bang bang!!!

A great volley of bullets flew from the Greek side, and the Italians were close enough for Alexei and Costa to see the surprise on their faces as they watched the Greek forces triple and then hope drain from their eyes as enemy bullets tore through their flesh.

Alexei and Costa didn't even have to aim.

There were too many Italians.

They just fired below them into the mass of soldiers coming closer and closer and closer and knew that they were doing what they were supposed to be doing, and didn't stop to think about it any further, because they didn't need those thoughts now.

They expected the Italians to retreat, but they didn't.

They kept coming with more men than the Greeks had anticipated, and a few yards away from him Alexei saw a Greek soldier drop his rifle and pick up stones that he started throwing at the Italian lines.

"What's he doing?" Alexei shouted over all the noises that had surrounded them.

Costa looked to where more soldiers had dropped their guns and started throwing rocks, and he remembered what the arms-master in the barracks had told him.

"They're out of ammunition," Costa said, and he turned to Alexei. "How much do you have left?" They each checked how many bullets they had between them and there weren't many.

Costa looked back up.

"They're getting closer."

"And they're going to keep coming."

"If they're able to get their tanks up the mountain, then they're into Greece on the other side."

"I know."

And that's when Alexei felt the first raindrop hit his forehead. He looked up, into the clouds, searching the heavens.

"Did you feel that, Costa?"

"What?"

"*Rain*."

"So?"

"It'll turn the roads to mud."

Costa looked up now, too, and they watched as larger and darker rain clouds swept towards them from the west, over the tops of the mountains, the peaks piercing the clouds, and opening them, and as the scattered drops soon turned into a downpour, Alexei and Costa knew that they were going to be saved.

There was shouting below them.

They looked over the wall to see Italian tanks getting stuck in newly made mud, just as Alexei had said they would. There were officers screaming at soldiers, but there wasn't anything any man could do, Italian or otherwise. Alexei and Costa smiled as they watched, just as every Greek fighting in the mountains that day smiled.

They'd been delivered.

The Greek soldiers shouted battle cries and fired every last bit of ammunition they had, and cheered even louder as the Italian line finally broke, and their enemy started running back to the north in retreat, leaving their tanks behind, and as they ran the Greeks shot as many Italians as they possibly could.

After they'd fired their final bullets, and caught their breath, the last Italians disappearing through the mountains in front of them, Alexei turned and looked at Costa next to him.

They nodded their heads, slowly.

"Alright," Costa said.

Then they turned and looked below them into the valley where more than fifty tanks and armored vehicles had gotten stuck in the mud, so now the Greek Army had its very own armored division, a luxury that they hadn't had when the war began. Alexei and Costa and all the rest of them would drink too much ouzo and wine that night and celebrate until dawn, knowing that the whole of Europe was sure to be doing the same, because what they had accomplished would be on the front page of every newspaper in the world in the morning.

It was the first Allied victory in the whole war.

November 19th, 1940

B RIGHT FLAKES DROPPED FROM THE CLOUDS.
That winter was the first of many things for Alexei
and Costa, including the first time they'd ever seen snow so
close, and on the morning it came Alexei opened the flap
to the tent they shared and looked out to see white covering everything as far as they could see.

He yelled to Costa.

They both went outside, not even bothering to dress or
bring their coats, even with the sharp and bitter cold in the
mountain air. Instead, they bent down to touch the snow,
to let it run through their fingers, to feel the way it was wet
and melted against their skin, and how beautiful it was.

They smiled at each other.

A new discovery.

It was a certain type of natural and ordinary magic that
had come to save them, even if only for a few moments,
from the killing and death that was their lives now, as all
the soldiers yelled and laughed and threw snowballs and for

one morning forgot where they were and what they were doing.

Alexei and Costa received their new commission a few hours later.

They were being sent east towards Macedonia, higher into the mountains, along with the rest of the inexperienced soldiers, to where they would see less combat. It was a city in the Albanian mountains called Pogradec that they were charged with holding, nestled amongst craggy peaks and next to a large and deep blue lake that was called Ohrid by the natives. The lake was on the eastern side of the city and wrapped around to cover its northern side as well, while the western and southern sides were bordered by snow-capped mountains, rising up steeply from the edges of the city.

Because of the geography, the Greek soldiers wouldn't be able to see any Italians coming from the city itself, so the garrison was split in half—one unit was sent to the peaks, up to the highest points, to be able to look out across the countryside and keep watch over everything around them—while the other half stayed in the city. Each day they would switch, so every Greek soldier only had to stay in the cold and mountains for one night at a time, and the next they got to sleep in a warm bed in the city.

Alexei and Costa would spend many long nights in those cold hills, with nothing to do but stare into the distance and rub their hands together, trying not to look at their breath as it froze in the air in front of them. Most of the soldiers kept to themselves, because it was too cold to do anything else, most of the soldiers except one, who walked up to Alexei and Costa on a particularly cold night while they were sharing a cup of coffee, each of them taking as small of sips as possible, trying to make it last.

"Either of you got a smoke?"

Alexei and Costa looked up and saw the stranger standing over them: he looked to be about the same age as they were, and had mischief and fire in his dark eyes.

"We don't smoke," Costa said.

"What about you?" the stranger asked, jerking his head towards Alexei.

"He doesn't either."

"He always talk for the both of you?"

"Only sometimes."

The stranger smiled and stuck out his hand. "My name's Constantinos," he said.

"Well, that's going to be a problem," Alexei answered.

"Why?"

"Because there's already a Constantinos here," Costa told him, patting his own chest. "What's your full name?"

"Constantinos Koukidis."

"We'll call you Koukidis, then," Alexei said.

"You can call me whatever you like if you have a cigarette."

"Whatever we call you, the answer's still the same. We still don't have a cigarette."

"You don't smoke. Right."

Koukidis sat down next to them anyways, blowing into his hands, trying to do anything in his power to keep them warm.

"You'd think there were no cigarettes in all of the Greek Army," he said. "I've looked everywhere, asked every damn soldier I could find, and it's all the same. That's fine. It's too cold to smoke anyway. I think my dick's about to fall off."

Alexei and Costa smiled, and Koukidis stayed with them and kept talking, and Alexei and Costa were glad to listen because it meant that they didn't have to say anything and they could instead concentrate all of their energy and thoughts on staying warm.

And so they listened as Koukidis told them his story.

He told them how he had come from the hills outside Athens, and that he'd enlisted and travelled to the front with three other men from the small city where he lived, but in a stroke of ill fate all the other men were killed when a mortar exploded next to them at Kalpaki. For some reason—nothing short of divine will and intervention, according to Koukidis—he was spared from the mortar. Even though he was standing closer to the shell than any of his friends, somehow all the shrapnel had missed him completely. He'd spent the next days trying to make sense of what had happened and why, until he finally had to accept that at worst war never makes sense, and at best he was spared because there was still something important left for him to do. Either way, all that he could do was keep fighting, to honor the memories of his friends, and that's how he carried himself now, and he lived his new and borrowed life as a man who'd faced death and come away with life.

A city in the midst of a war is a strange thing.

People go about their lives and daily activities with as much normalcy as possible, but there's an aura of lawlessness that hangs over everything, especially the streets, men and women looking over their shoulders, glancing warily at soldiers carrying rifles across their backs and pistols at their hips. Not long ago Pogradec was Albanian.

Then, soon after, the Italians came, and for a time they held the city. Now it'd been liberated from the Italians and was controlled by the Greeks. Tomorrow might very well bring back an Italian occupation—or, everyone's greatest fear, the Germans. So the people hoarded bread and water. They boarded their windows and doors. They tried to find ways to blend in and not be noticed by the soldiers that were on their streets, and this was something that was especially true for the women of Pogradec.

Koukidis was also single, the same as Costa, and so on the days that they were stationed in Pogradec, and not in the mountains, they started chasing the local girls together, both of them claiming that the war had already caused them to spend more time away from women than any young man should ever have to face or endure. It wasn't natural, they said, and amongst all the barbaric things that had happened in those northern mountains, that had so far been the cruelest.

Costa and Koukidis went to the only taverna in town that was still open.

Single women still came looking for men, and while most spoke Greek, Costa and Koukidis quickly learned the words they needed in Albanian for the ones who didn't. Back up in the mountains, with the glow of discovery and intimacy still fresh, Costa and Koukidis would pass the time by regaling Alexei with their exploits, each of them giving more and more details, embellishing everything that happened, sparing nothing, because it was warmer to think about than the snow that swirled around them.

"These girls in the north," Costa would say, "they're not like girls from back home, Alexei. They're barbarians." And he said the word in this sense as a compliment of the highest form, and Koukidis nodded in agreement, and Alexei smiled.

"It's true," Koukidis would confirm. "They know things that no Christian girl should ever know. And I'm so glad that they do."

"Maybe they're not Christian."

"What are you talking about? Of course they're Christian. The Turks never came here."

"How do you know?"

"Because the Turks don't go where it's cold. Everyone knows that."

"Maybe you shouldn't use these girls the way that you're using them."

"Oh, what's that . . . you're a priest now, Alexei? Concerned for our mortal souls?"

"He's a virgin," Costa explained to Koukidis. "He doesn't understand what we're talking about. He doesn't know what he's missing."

"What do you mean? I thought he was engaged?"

"He is, but they don't have sex yet."

"Strange," Koukidis smiled. "I wasn't sure that's how that worked."

"We're guests here, and this isn't our city," Alexei said as he blew into his hands.

"And they're showing us Albanian hospitality, treating us as liberators should be treated."

"They're just trying to stay alive."

"It's war, Alexei," Costa said. "We're all just trying to stay alive."

"And lighten up," Koukidis added. "This isn't Kalpaki. The fighting isn't coming here. The Italians don't want to leave the coast and their supply line from home. They'll stick with their stupid plan of trying to go south through the mountains where all the rest of us are waiting, defending the quickest route to Athens."

"So you're Mussolini's general now, too?"

"No. I just know that the Italians haven't had an original thought since the Caesars."

"Mussolini's telling everyone that he is a Caesar."

"Yeah. And I'm Alexander the fucking Great," Koukidis scoffed.

The conversations continued, and as much as Alexei tried to dissuade Costa and Koukidis from their nighttime exploits, it was good for everyone that they didn't listen to him, because in the end it was the women of Pogradec who would save them all.

They'd been in the city for a few weeks before Costa met Adelina.

She was young, beautiful, and had a temper so fiery that Costa was completely smitten and swore that he'd seen his future and could love no one else and that this girl would be the end of him. The problem was, however, that he already had loved someone else, and after their first night together Adelina came into the taverna to see another girl talking to Costa and she grabbed the girl, threw her halfway across the room, then slapped Costa twice across the face, harder than he'd ever been slapped before, and without a single word turned and left.

The whole room was silent.

"God help me, I think I might be in love," Costa said, breaking the silence, and the men around him smiled, knowing exactly what he was feeling, and then Costa ran out after her.

Nobody knew exactly what he said to her, but by the time Alexei and the rest of the men followed them out onto the street, Costa and Adelina were already kissing like the world was about to end. All of the men started to clap, and Costa lifted Adelina off her feet and carried her through the city and back to their bed and they didn't leave until the next morning.

And that was the end of Costa's nights at the taverna.

Costa and Adelina became inseparable on the days he wasn't in the mountains, and she didn't let him sleep during the nights he was back in the city, though he always left her apartment rejuvenated and with a smile on his face, as if he was fit and ready to run a marathon. And it was on one such night, after they'd made love and were lying in her bed together, keeping each other warm, that Adelina told him her secret.

Before the Greeks had come to Pogradec, the Italians had stationed a garrison in the city while they still controlled Albania. And after six months of courting and bringing flowers, of playing a violin and singing, and perhaps most importantly, the many gifts of food, Adelina had finally taken up with an Italian soldier named Ciro. After Metaxas rejected Mussolini's ultimatum, and the Greek Army headed north, Ciro and the Italian division that had been in Pogradec were called back west to help where the fighting was going to be the most fierce, and both sides would need every soldier available to them. When it came time for Ciro to leave, it was a tearful goodbye, and Ciro promised Adelina that he would come back for her when Italy had won and defeated the weak and gutless Greeks. The Italians had such an advantage over their enemies, he said, that it wouldn't take them long, and that when he did come back he would make her his wife. But as she watched him walk away, she doubted in her heart that she'd ever see him again, and that his flowery language was only just that—words, and a promise made to the wind. After all, this was war now, and war doesn't make families, war only makes orphans and widows. And as a child of Pogradec, Adelina was certainly no stranger to war.

So she carried on with her life.

She heard about the Italian defeat at Kalpaki and wondered if Ciro had been killed or captured, if he'd survived and escaped or if his corpse was lying face-down in the mud, lost and forgotten. And if he had survived, how much longer would he continue to? How many more battles would there be before the fighting was over? The war even now had already gone longer than he'd promised her it would. She thought about it all, then forced herself to put it from her mind. Even if Ciro had lived, he would never come back to her—she was just a moment in his life, a spoil of war, a story to tell his friends when he returned home and they asked about what had happened while he was away and he'd drink too much and tell them every intimate detail that they'd shared. These were the thoughts that Adelina had as she met another handsome soldier, and took up with him, and that's when she received her letter.

It was from Ciro.

It was short, but the message very clear.

The Italians were coming back to take Pogradec again, and he had volunteered for the unit that was on its way to the city.

"Wait for me," he wrote. "Wait for me, because I'm coming back to you, like I promised I would."

She read the letter three times, each time wondering

what she should do. If she didn't tell Costa, it would surely mean his death. But if she did, it would mean Ciro's. In the end, she decided that the only way she could live with herself was to show Costa the letter and then let God decide who would live and who would die in the fighting that was sure to follow.

"The Italians are supposed to be staying in the west," Costa said as he read what Ciro had written.

"Sometimes people don't do what they're supposed to."

"Why did you show this to me?"

"Because I don't want you to get killed."

"Even if it means that I kill him?"

She was silent for a moment—

"I don't want either of you to die. But if God's decided that one of you must, at least it can be a fair fight."

He sat there for a moment longer, then kissed her with great passion before jumping out of bed and pulling his pants on and running out the door as fast as he could. He sprinted down the street, pulling one shoe on and then the other as he went, buttoning the final buttons on his shirt before he finally reached the officer's quarters that had been set up in the town hall.

He rushed in, not waiting to be announced, and told the officers what he'd learned, and that though they hadn't seen any enemies yet, or heard anything, the Italians were most assuredly on the move . . .

And they were coming to Pogradec.

November 20th, 1940

"I TOLD YOU I HAD A PLAN all along."

"You had no plan."

"Sure, I did. And it's lucky for you and the rest of Greece that I know how to talk to a woman. A lesser man would have been turned down by Adelina, and we'd all be dead tonight."

The Greek soldiers were hiding in Albanian houses as they waited for the Italians to come. Alexei and Costa were placed in a small ground floor apartment shared by a man and his wife and their three young boys. Alexei kept watch by the window, while Costa played with the boys on the floor, and the man's wife finished cleaning up after dinner. The Greeks had brought them leftover meat and vegetables and she'd made it into a stew. Costa was smiling and the boys were laughing until their father came and told them it was time for bed, and they each hugged Costa, and he hugged them back, and the wife smiled from the kitchen and then came to carry them to their bedroom. Alexei kept his eyes trained outside, waiting for any signs of their enemies in the darkness on the other side of the glass.

"Do you have everything that you need?"

Alexei turned back to see the husband watching him—

"Stay in your bedroom with the boys," Alexei told him, with much more confidence than he felt. "The fighting will be in the streets. You'll be safe if you're out of the way."

"Thank you for the stew," the husband said.

"Your wife is an amazing cook," Costa answered.

"Why do you think I married her?" the husband replied, smiling. "We don't marry for looks in Albania, we marry for skill in the kitchen. If I could teach young men like yourselves one thing, that would be the lesson. Beauty fades. Skill in the kitchen lasts forever."

"We'll keep it in mind," Alexei said, and the husband smiled, and he nodded and took his leave, walking to his bedroom where his family was waiting for him. When he was gone, Costa picked up his rifle and went to where Alexei was sitting by the window.

He looked out.

"When do you think they'll come?"

"Probably not for awhile yet. They'll want to wait until they think we're asleep."

Costa nodded.

They held their rifles tighter and settled in to wait.

It was going to be a long night.

They weren't sure how many hours had passed when Alexei looked outside and saw the shadows moving and he gently shook Costa awake next to him: it was well into the night, the moon high above the city, casting its glow over the old cobblestone streets.

"What is it?" Costa rubbed his eyes.

"Look. There."

He turned to where Alexei was pointing across the road and saw ten Italian soldiers moving in the darkness, black pitch smeared across their faces, making their way quietly through the streets and looking for any Greek soldiers that they could find. Costa chambered a bullet in his rifle, but Alexei reached a hand out to stop him—

"They need to get further into the city," he whispered.

"We can take them now."

"Not yet. Not until we hear shots first."

Costa swallowed because he didn't like it, but he knew Alexei was right, so he lowered his rifle but kept the bullet where it was in the chamber. The Greek plan was to wait until as many Italians as possible had made their way into the city, and then when they'd reached the town square, where they thought the Greek soldiers were camped, the Greeks would make their move and come out of all the houses behind them, and Alexei and Costa and the rest of the soldiers had been told to hold their fire until they heard shots first.

That's how they would know it was time.

The next minutes crawled by as they watched more and more Italians come into the city. Their fingers hung over their triggers, bracing themselves, waiting for the signal, sweat beading on their foreheads even though it was the dead of night and the middle of winter. The stirring inside them was stronger than the elements. They continued to watch until the Italian soldiers passed, and the street outside the house was quiet again.

Then, they heard it.

Bang bang!

Gunshots in the distance.

Alexei and Costa looked at each other, knowing what that meant, so they slowly opened the door and walked outside, their rifles ready. Alexei gestured to Costa to head in the direction of the Italians that they'd seen—they could take them from behind, hopefully still unawares, and so they turned, starting to make their way towards the city, when—

Blam blam!

Two shots blasted against the wall of the house next to them and they dove for cover into an alley as pieces of stone exploded and fell in showers around them and even more bullets flew over their head towards where they'd been just seconds before.

Blam blam blam!

"Are you hit?" Costa yelled.

"I'm fine!"

Alexei fumbled with his rifle as Costa swung his around and returned fire across the street—*blam, blam, blam*—killing one of the Italians that was firing at them, before he ducked back behind cover.

"I got one."

"How many are there?"

"Six."

"Shit."

Costa reloaded his rifle—

"Cover me," he told Alexei.

"I can't see anything. It's too dark."

"They're by the bench. Just shoot in that general direction. I've got to get a better angle."

Alexei didn't ask any more questions.

He cocked his rifle, turned, and started firing into the

darkness towards where the bench was and he could see the outline of the soldiers that were firing back at them. Costa waited for a moment, then when the Italians ducked down and away from Alexei's volley, he ran out and further down the street to take cover behind the building next to them, closer to their enemies, giving him a better shot at them.

More rifles sparked and fired, and bullets flew into the night as Alexei dove back to cover again and the wall above him exploded and rained more bits of rock and debris down on them.

Behind his building, Costa took note of where the bullets were coming from, then dropped to one knee and fired.

Blam blam blam blam.

Four more shots. Two more screams. The Italians scream louder than any other soldiers when they die.

"There's three left!" Costa yelled.

They spoke in Greek, knowing the Italians wouldn't understand—

"Are you sure?"

"Of course I'm sure!"

"They've seen where you're at. You draw their fire now and I'll take the shot."

"You're a terrible shot."

"I won't be tonight."

Costa looked back over at Alexei from his hiding place and he could see Alexei's eyes through the darkness and saw the truth in them.

"Alright."

Alexei nodded, and Costa nodded.

Then they both chambered more bullets into their rifle as Costa began to silently mouth a count for them, going backwards from three, and when he reached one he jumped up, firing three quick shots then ducking back behind the building as bullets exploded once again where his head had been moments before.

Then, Alexei fired—

Bang bang bang bang!

He aimed in the darkness towards where he saw the Italians expose themselves, trying to shoot Costa, and he smiled when he heard two more Italian screams come from the distance.

"Four shots, two bodies," Costa yelled. "Not bad, Alexei."

"There's one still left, then."

There was a noise across from them—

"What's that?"

Alexei thought Costa was talking about the rifle shots coming from the city center, the battle that the rest of them were fighting—

"More fighting."

"No, not that. Listen."

There it was again.

This time Alexei heard it, too. A click. Metal against metal. Costa knew what that meant.

"He's out."

"What?"

"He's out of ammo. He's reloading."

"So?"

Costa jumped up—

"Cover me."

"Where are you going?"

But Costa didn't wait to answer.

He sprinted across the street to where the last Italian

94

hiding behind the bench in the park almost had his rifle reloaded.

The Italian looked up and saw Costa running at him.

He saw Costa's rifle raised and about to take the clear shot that would end his life, and as Costa aimed, ready to pull the trigger, the Italian grabbed a knife from his boot and threw it as hard as he could.

It spun through the air and struck Costa in the face.

The blade didn't cut him, but when Costa fired, it caused his shot to go wide.

Seeing his opening, the Italian soldier jumped up and charged.

Costa was already reeling backwards when the Italian tackled him to the ground, Costa's head hitting the hard cobblestones of the road beneath them and knocking him out cold.

The Italian grabbed a rock and raised it over his head.

He was about to smash it down into Costa's skull when he heard something. He looked up to see Alexei standing in front of him, his rifle trained directly on his chest.

They stayed there, just like that for a moment, looking into each other's eyes, then the Italian spoke.

"No," he said. "*Per favore. Ho una moglie.*"

Alexei didn't speak Italian, but it didn't matter, because he didn't care what the soldier was saying, or what his words meant. It was all going to end the same way.

Bang!

Alexei's bullet tore through the soldier's chest and came out his back.

He stayed kneeling on Costa for a moment, blood coming out of the hole in front of him, streaming down onto them both, then his body slumped to the side, falling to the ground, more blood pooling out and around him now and across the snow that was covering the street.

Alexei took a deep breath.

There had been no great moment or ceremony that went with taking a life so intimately: the Italian soldier was simply there and breathing one moment, his hand raised, about to kill Alexei's friend, and then the next he wasn't. And now he was sprawled across the street, a pile of paling flesh and spilt blood, just another dead body in a forgotten city high in the mountains.

Then, another noise, softer, coming from directly behind Alexei—

He whipped around, rifle at the ready, and scanned the dead bodies and found the source of the noise that he'd heard. It was gurgling through a punctured neck. Blood filling lungs. A young soldier suffocating.

Alexei walked over and looked down at the man who was not yet dead. He was too young to be there. Probably fifteen years old. And he wheezed every time he tried to take a breath.

Alexei stood over the young soldier.

The soldier tried to speak, but all that came out of his mouth was more blood. But his eyes met Alexei's, pleading with him, and Alexei knew what he wanted. He raised his rifle and aimed again. With the very last bit of his strength, the Italian soldier weakly made the sign of the cross over his body—his left shoulder before his right, the opposite of the way that the Greeks cross themselves—and when he was done, Alexei swallowed heavily, then—

Bang.

The soldier's head snapped back, a bullet through his

skull, one more shot echoing into the black night. Alexei looked down at him for another moment, the blood pooling out of his head now, and then Alexei's hand started to shake violently. He had to set his rifle down, as he tried to control it, then he turned away and went back to where Costa lay in the street.

He was still out cold.

Alexei slapped him on the face, and Costa didn't move. Alexei slapped him again, even harder, and his eyes shot open, darting around, taking everything in—

"What the hell happened?"

"You got your ass kicked."

"What? Not possible."

"You got hit in the head."

"Bullshit."

"You went after the last one," Alexei said. "You charged him and were about to take the shot and he threw his knife. He slammed your head onto the street."

"Where is he now?"

Alexei jerked his head next to them, and Costa turned to see the soldier who'd tackled him with his chest torn open, then he looked further and saw all six of the Italian bodies around them, foreign blood spread across foreign snow.

"Jesus. We got all of them."

"It could have just as easily been us."

"But it wasn't."

Then Costa saw Alexei's hand. It was still shaking at his side. Costa nodded towards it—

"Are you alright?"

"They didn't hit me."

"That's not what I asked."

Alexei thought about it, and what he knew that Costa was asking, the worry that was there in his friend's eyes, but those weren't the thoughts that Alexei needed then. The sun was starting to rise over the mountains in the east, the beginning of the coming dawn that would stretch across the streets of Pogradec, but the night wasn't over.

"Do you think we're winning?" Alexei asked instead, voicing the question that was on both of their minds.

"I don't know."

Alexei picked up his rifle.

Costa did the same next to him.

Then they looked at each other—

"I suppose it's time we went and found out."

They made their way back through the city, looking for any Italian soldiers that might still be alive in the streets. Certain blocks looked so normal, so innocent, as if only the city hadn't woken up yet. Then other streets were littered with bodies, left where they'd fallen, the snow under them stained black now with dried blood, and the putrid smell of death hung over everything, everything, everything, cutting through the cold dawn air.

Alexei and Costa walked in silence.

They held their rifles ready.

Most of the bodies they passed were Italian, but there were Greek soldiers scattered throughout as well, and they would stop to look down into the faces of their countrymen, but there were none that had fallen that they recognized or knew by name.

Then, Alexei saw Costa looking down at one of the Greek dead, and Alexei came to stand next to him—

"I think he was with us at Kalpaki," Costa said, still looking down at the fallen soldier.

"What was his name?"

"I don't know."

Alexei looked at the body that Costa was looking at and didn't recognize the man. Then Costa knelt down beside him.

"We'll come back to bury them when it's over," Alexei said.

Costa reached out and closed the soldier's eyelids, so that he was no longer staring blankly up at the world, and maybe he could find some rest, some of the peace that he deserved and gave his life for.

Then, Costa stood—

"Let's go," he said.

And they continued on through the city, the air starting to warm as the day came, the red morning sun climbing up and over the high snow-capped mountains in the distance.

They were cautious, but they didn't need to be.

There weren't any Italians left alive in Pogradec.

When Alexei and Costa made it to the Greek camp at the town hall, they saw all the surviving Greek soldiers making their way back from their respective posts in the city and gathering together. They saw Koukidis, leaning on his rifle, enjoying the cigarette that hung from his lips, a look of pure satisfaction on his face, and they went to stand next to him.

"You both lived," Koukidis smiled. "Good."

"Finally found yourself a cigarette, have you?" Costa asked.

"Apparently they have no shortage of cigarettes in Italy. I found a whole box on one of them over there in the street," he jerked his head towards a pile of Italian bodies. "How many did you kill?"

"Six," Alexei answered.

"Each?"

"Total."

"I killed eight by myself."

"Fuck you," Costa laughed.

"It's true!"

"That's a lot of Italians," Alexei said. "How could you possibly kill that many on your own?"

"I was in the second story of a building, thinking I was going to be a sniper. You know I'm the best shot in the army, right? Well, I am, and you can ask anyone about that. So there I was, lining up a shot, when I heard something beneath me and I looked down to see a whole squadron right there. So I put my rifle aside and dropped a grenade into the middle of them. You should have seen it. It was amazing."

"Where'd you get a grenade?" Alexei asked suspiciously. "I thought there weren't any left."

"I saved it from Kalpaki. Anyways, the Italians heard it fall next to them, and they looked around, each asking the other what that noise was. The next question they ask they'll be asking directly to God. Or the Devil, I suppose. It was all over very quickly, actually. One moment they were there, and the next only pieces of them were. I never even had to fire a shot, which was a shame. I would have liked to have tested myself. Kept my eye sharp."

"So I guess we know that our grenades work."

"And that as soldiers the Italians are as clueless as we are."

"We're not clueless," Alexei said.

"Alexei believes we all still have some of Achilles and Alexander left in us," Costa explained to Koukidis.

"Don't be stupid," Koukidis said. "We're not warriors. We're farmers and fishermen that were handed rifles. It takes a lifetime to train for war. That's why the Germans have already conquered Europe. They spent their whole lives preparing for this, while the rest of us have been busy doing other things."

"You think the Germans are going to win?" Alexei asked, surprised.

"Did I say that? I don't think they're going to win. I just said that they've been training for this for a long time, and that I don't think it's us that's going to beat them."

Then they were silent for a moment because in front of them the Greek officers had gathered and were meeting on the steps of the town hall, discussing points of strategy, animatedly talking and pointing over the mountains to the west. They could see the officer's faces. They didn't look like men who had just won a victory.

"What's happening?" Alexei asked Koukidis, nodding towards the officers and the dark looks on their faces. "Didn't we just win?"

"Of course we won. I wouldn't be standing here with you smoking this beautiful cigarette if we hadn't."

"So where's the wine? The ouzo? The celebration?"

"You haven't heard, then."

"We just got back," Alexei said. "We haven't heard anything."

"That was just the advance guard that they sent into the city, trying to make quick and quiet work of us before the rest of them came."

"The rest of them?"

"The entire Arrezzo Division is a half-day behind."

"How many men is that?"

"That's what they're discussing right now, I'd bet."

Alexei and Costa looked at each other—

"So what does that mean?"

Koukidis made a great show out of finishing his cigarette, smoking it all the way down until it was surely burning the tips of his fingers, then he dropped it onto the street, and stepped on it with his boot, before turning and looking back at them—

"It means, my friends, that we're surrounded."

7

November 21st, 1940

A MAN'S NEVER BEEN TRULY DESPERATE UNTIL he's been hungry.

Not the type of hunger that comes with going a day without food, or even a few days. That's not hunger. It's not real hunger until you can feel your body caving in on itself, your cheeks getting gaunter, and the soul-crushing despair that comes with not knowing when or where you're going to find your next meal. That's the type of hunger that the Greeks had.

The type of hunger that breaks men.

The day after the Italian advance guard had been defeated, the Greek garrison of Pogradec met the main force of the Italian Arezzo Division in the mountains above the city.

Once again, like at Kalpaki, the Greeks held the high ground.

The first bit of fighting was fierce, lasting most of the day, with the Greek forces raining down calculated fire whenever an Italian came into range between the snow-covered rocks, and the Italians in turns lobbing mortars at the Greek position so that every Greek, even when talking to each other, kept their eyes trained to the skies above them, watching for incoming shells. The most casualties occurred in the initial surge when the Italians tried to take the summit on their first assault, and after the Greeks pushed them back, the fighting evened out until the Greeks realized that the Italians were just testing them, keeping them awake and hungry, and not trying to make it to the other side of the mountain, knowing that in time the Greeks would run out of ammo, and out of food, and then they'd take the city when it would cost them less men.

The Italians cut off all lines of communication and supplies, so the Greeks couldn't send to their main army for reinforcements or aid, and as far as the Greek Army knew, nothing at Pogradec had changed.

The Greeks would try to send out small groups to look for food, wood, anything that could be of use—logs, berries, vegetables, even the occasional pheasant or grouse—and they'd inevitably be met by an Italian patrol and would have to fight to defend whatever they'd scavenged.

It was during these skirmishes that Alexei and Costa really learned how to fight. They figured out how to walk through the snow silently, following in each other's tracks to make less noise, learning how to blend into the forest, and that marching with distance between each man made them harder targets to hit if they did happen to be found by enemies. Costa learned that he had a gift for shooting—steady hands and a sharp eye that resulted in superb marksmanship—and Alexei learned that he really had no particular skill for war at all, at least not as far as weapons and guns went.

But he found that men listened to him.

The other soldiers valued what he had to say, and in many instances his words were often the final ones that would be heard before a decision was made or actions were taken. It was a different type of gift than Costa's, but still a gift, and the men got used to seeing the two boys from Agria venture out of the city into the snow together.

It was on one of these trips into the forest between the armies that Alexei looked down and saw something in the snow that made him pause. Costa was marching behind him, and he must have been day-dreaming about Adelina, or warm *avgolemono*, or something else, because he didn't see Alexei stop and he walked straight into his friend's back.

"Ach, Alexei. What is it?"

"Look."

"What?"

"There."

Costa looked into the snow near them and saw what Alexei was staring at—there were hoof prints, single-pronged with two toes, the hind legs larger and heavier than the front.

"Boar," Alexei said.

"They're fresh. It's probably still close."

"Let's track it."

"Track it? We can't do that."

"Why not?"

"What are you going to do when you find it? Catch it with your bare hands? As soon as we fire a single round we'll have every Italian soldier in these mountains down here and around our necks."

They stayed looking at the tracks for another moment,

both thinking about the taste of warm meat, and how long it'd been since they'd had any, and then Alexei turned to Costa, both of them shivering now because they'd stopped walking and their blood began to settle—

"I can't remember how long it's been since I've had something real in my stomach," Alexei told him.

"I can't either," Costa answered. "But this is crazy. Even for me this would be crazy, and I'm supposed to be the crazy one. You're the rational one, remember? That's how it's always been."

"I can't be rational all the time."

"You can if the decision is between a hot meal and a box in the ground. What do you think Philia would say?"

"She wouldn't say anything. She'd ask me how I was going to cook it, and then when I'd told her, she'd let me know that I was planning on doing it all wrong, and kick me out of her kitchen."

They stood there and looked at each other for another moment, and then Costa's mouth turned up into a small smile.

"You're insane," he said. "You know that, don't you?"

"No," Alexei answered. "I'm just hungry."

So they tracked the boar.

They followed the hoof-prints to a dense undergrowth filled with thorns and brambles where it had made its roost for winter. When they got near, they inched their way over the last few feet, not wanting to startle it, inspecting the shrubs in front of them as they looked to the small opening where the boar had dug through the snow underneath the weeds.

Costa nodded towards it—

"We can't go in there. The opening's too small."

"No."

"I'll go around back and flush it out," he said. "Then you take it when you have the shot."

"Alright," Alexei said, nodding.

"And then we run like hell. Faster than either of us have ever run before."

"Don't worry, I'm not planning on sticking around," Alexei said, unslinging the rifle that he carried across his back, chambering a bullet, sliding the lever back and forth to clear the action and make sure that it wasn't sticking in the cold, the way that it sometimes did during the winter when the temperatures dropped.

Alexei braced himself and took aim.

When Costa saw that he was in position and ready, he started rustling the branches, but nothing happened. He called out, as loudly as he dared call out, knowing that Italians had to be close somewhere.

But still there was nothing.

He looked at Alexei over the growth in front of them, raising his hands as if to say, "What now?"

"Stand back," Alexei said.

"What?"

"If they're gonna hear one shot, then two won't make a difference."

And before Costa could say anything else, Alexei took aim and fired into the undergrowth—

Blam blam.

Two piercing shots echoed through the mountains.

And the shots did their job.

The boar broke cover.

With a loud squeal it burst from its den and directly towards Alexei, who carefully took aim as it ran, coming straight at him, knowing he'd only have one shot to bring it down—if he didn't, the boar would gore him, and it wouldn't matter if the Italians heard or not, because he'd already be dead.

His finger hovered over the trigger.

He aimed in front of the boar's nose, trying to calculate and take into account how fast it was running, then—

Bang!

One more shot rang out and the boar stumbled and crashed to the ground in a large pile of snow and blood. Alexei ran to it and knelt down beside the animal. It was a clean shot: the bullet had gone straight through its neck and into its heart. Costa then ran up and looked down at the boar, too, seeing that it was dead.

"Good shot," he said, a little surprised.

"It was right in front of me. It was impossible to miss."

"It's bigger than I thought it was going to be. It's going to be hard to get it back."

"So let's hurry."

They both quickly strapped their rifles across their backs, and Alexei grabbed the boar's hind legs. Costa grabbed the two front legs and together they started running back towards Pogradec. They struggled with the boar between them. It wasn't easy to run.

"Did you think it'd be this heavy?" Costa asked.

"It just means there'll be more to eat when we get it back."

"I suppose that's one way to look at it."

Sweat poured down their foreheads even in the deep

cold as they struggled with the awkward and heavy weight between them.

And they hadn't gone far when the Italians caught them.

Bang bang bang!!

Bullets flew past their heads and they stumbled and fell to the snow when they heard the shots.

"Shit," Costa swore under his breath. "That was sure fast."

"There's only five of them," Alexei said, squinting into the distance behind them, counting the number of soldiers running through the trees.

"Only?"

"It's better than six, isn't it?"

They reached for their rifles, but Alexei stopped Costa.

"Keep going. I'll hold them off."

"Are you joking? There's five of them, like you said. That's way too many. Besides . . . I'm a better shot."

"You're stronger, too. Which means you can run faster while you're carrying it."

Alexei turned and fired three shots back at the Italians, causing them to stop and hide behind the trees, before he turned back to Costa again—

"I'm eating this boar in the city tonight, and we can't fire back at them if we're both carrying it between us. We need to keep some bullets on them, otherwise their next volley won't go over our heads. And remember . . . they don't want to die out here, either. It's easier for them not to be heroes."

"They're probably hungry, too."

"No. They're not the ones cut off from supplies. They have rations from the army."

Costa was silent a moment, then he stood and fired two quick shots himself before he knelt back down next to Alexei.

They both knew that it was the only way.

"Run fast," Alexei said. "I'll be right behind you."

"Don't try to be a hero today."

"I don't want to be a hero," Alexei said. "I just want dinner."

And with one more nod, Costa jumped up and grabbed the hind legs of the boar and started pulling it through the snow with every bit of strength that he could summon.

Alexei found a large-trunked tree to hide behind and unloaded a volley of bullets on the Italians, keeping them pinned where they were as Costa ran, getting closer towards Pogradec, foot by foot. Alexei retreated to a tree further back, reloaded his rifle, then fired again. He smiled when he saw red in the snow next to his enemies and heard a distant scream and knew that he'd connected with at least one of his targets.

It was one less Italian to come after them.

Alexei quickly reloaded again, and then ran to the next tree that he'd hide behind.

Blam blam blam.

He didn't hit any more Italians, and they were getting closer now. Alexei checked his ammo. Three shells lefts. He should have taken Costa's gun from him, or at least some of his bullets. He looked behind him to see that Costa was far enough away to be out of range.

There was only one thing for Alexei to do.

He turned and fired his last three shots to slow the Italians as much as possible. He hit one of them, but there were still four more coming after him. It was a very small moment of satisfaction, before he slung his rifle back over his shoulder and started to run through the trees as fast as he possibly could.

He zig-zagged as he ran.

It made him a smaller target.

And the Italians opened fire.

Bang bang!! Bang bang bang!!! Bang bang!!!

The air around Alexei exploded with bullets.

Bark burst off trees.

But none of the shots hit him.

The Italians were running themselves now, as they shot, getting closer, and it was only a matter of time before one of the bullets would find Alexei's flesh, and Alexei closed his eyes as he heard a fresh volley, closer to him than the rest had been, and he stumbled to the ground, expecting the worst.

But the worst never came.

Then Alexei realized the shots hadn't come from behind him.

He opened his eyes to see Koukidis running towards him with ten other Greek soldiers, firing at the Italians who stopped in their tracks and tried to return fire, but it was no use, and all four of them were shot and cut down were they stood in the snow.

The Italians had heard gunshots in the forest, but they weren't the only ones—

The Greeks had heard them, too.

"Did you miss me?" Koukidis asked, a big grin on his face as he walked towards where Alexei lay in the snow.

"Not until now," Alexei said. "Are you hungry?"

"Of course I'm hungry. What kind of a question is that?" Koukidis reached down and grabbed Alexei's hand to help pull him to his feet. "Let's get back to the city before more of them come, though."

"Sounds good to me."

The Greek soldiers helped Costa with the boar, and with ten men taking turns carrying it the way back to the city was much easier, and as they returned the whole army put up a cheer when they saw what Alexei and Costa had brought back with them. They tore apart a gardening cart to use the wood to make a large fire, and they roasted the boar on a spit over the flames in the middle of the city, and for each of them for a single night it was the closest they'd felt to being back home since they'd come north. Alexei and Costa were heroes for what they'd done, but one boar doesn't last very long when there's an entire army to feed, and they were all hungry again by morning.

But, for one night, they were happy.

In the days that followed, Alexei and Costa stayed in the city, not wanting to press their luck any further as more and more Italians gathered around them, but their skirmish over the boar had the opposite effect on Koukidis.

He wanted more Italian blood.

He started going into the woods by himself, and would dig cover under the snow and hide, waiting for Italian patrols to come by. And when they were sleeping, or relieving themselves, or sitting by a fire, he'd come on them unawares and he started murdering Italians by the dozen. They came up with a nickname for him—*volpe inverno*—which meant "winter fox," and they put a one million lira reward on his head.

When he found out, he was warming his hands next to Alexei around a fire they'd built from tearing more wood from unused buildings on the edge of town, and he laughed, wondering why the reward wasn't more.

Costa was with Adelina, so it was just Alexei and Koukidis at the fire.

"You're the only one of us with a price on their head at all," Alexei said. "That's got to count for something."

"I suppose. But the reward should be higher. Much higher. I guess I'll just have to kill more *italianos*," he said, pronouncing the last word like it was a putrid acid burning his tongue, much the same way as Costa had done standing on Alexei's dock when they had discussed the same thing, and all that would soon come, all that they now were living.

There were shots in the distance, at the edge of the city.

The Greeks didn't even bother to fire back.

They knew what this was by now. The Italians would get close enough to just fire into the darkness, as their plan was to starve the Greeks by day, and then keep them awake at night, and if they could get them to waste precious ammo by firing back into the darkness, then it was all the better.

Alexei and Koukidis kept their attention on the fire in front of them, and Alexei asked Koukidis how he'd gotten so good at killing Italians. Because by the time he'd arrived in Pogradec, he seemed to be a soldier in a way that none of the rest of them quite were. Koukidis looked at Alexei curiously for a moment, after he'd asked the question, and then turned his attention back to the fire in front of them before answering—

"I pretend they're Turks," he said softly.

"Turks?"

"Yes. And that's why I take such pleasure in killing them."

"I don't understand."

And that's when Koukidis told Alexei the story of his childhood.

Koukidis had been a boy in Asia Minor, and he was in Smyrna when the war between the Greeks and the Turks ended. All Greeks know about the atrocities committed in Smyrna, and while Alexei had read all the literature, and had heard all the stories, he'd never spoken with someone who had actually been there, and who had suffered so directly at the hands of their centuries-long oppressors and mortal enemies.

Koukidis had been very young, but he told Alexei how the smoke had smelled that night, a putrid and choking stench that buried itself deep in his nose and snaked its way down to his lungs. He told Alexei how that was his first memory, his mother holding him in her arms and telling him that it was just smoke in the air that night, and that he was going to be alright. But, before long, the armies came, and his father told his mother that it was no longer safe in their home, and they needed to leave the city.

"Where will we go?" she asked her husband.

"I don't know," he answered. "We just need to leave."

Koukidis' mother carried him in her arms, while his father led his older brother by the hand. Koukidis thought that it was dawn and the sun was coming up, but he later realized that it was just the blaze that was sweeping through the city—the fire that the Turks had started—burning everything in its path and bringing a terrible and unnatural light to the dark night. They tried to make their way out of the city as a family, but the Turkish Army was already there, waiting for them, herding all the families that came and tried to leave back inside the walls.

So, like everyone else, they went to the docks.

There was a giant mass of them—Greeks, Armenians, anyone else in Smyrna who didn't kneel and pray to the crescent and star—and when they got to the docks, there was already the smell of death in the air.

And that's when the Turks started firing.

Not aiming, just firing.

The panic carried Koukidis and his mother onto one of the boats while his father and brother were still trapped on the docks. They stood screaming as men and women and children were shot and thrown into the harbor and the water that had very quickly turned red. And Koukidis watched with his mother from the deck of a Japanese freighter filled with refugees as his father and brother were thrown into the harbor, too, and how they disappeared beneath the surface of the water and never came up again. The freighter sailed to Piraeus carrying what refugees it could, but nobody on that boat ever really left Smyrna.

One hundred thousand innocent lives were taken that night.

When Koukidis finished his story, and he'd sat in silence with Alexei for a little bit longer, Alexei stood and found the last drop of brandy they had left and he split it into two copper cups with bent handles. He offered one of the cups to Koukidis, who took it and stared down, searching for comfort in the dark swirling liquid, but finding none.

"Sometimes I lay awake at night and wonder what Turkish general is living in my house," he finally said. "The house where my parents raised me, and my brother. The house where we'd been so happy together."

They sat in silence for a moment longer because there wasn't anything that Alexei could say: they both could feel

Koukidis' story, and his pain, deep in their souls, and so Alexei raised his glass.

"For our families," he said. "And our blood."

Koukidis waited another moment, still staring into his cup, then he turned and looked up, meeting Alexei's eyes—

"For Greece," he finally said.

"For Greece," Alexei said, too.

And they drank.

8

November 25th, 1940

THE ITALIAN PLAN WORKED.

The Greek soldiers starved in the cold.

They ran out of everything, even the most meager scraps to eat.

Everyone in Pogradec grew up more than they wanted to during those long, hungry days and nights, and in that month they all had enough winter and cold to last an entire lifetime for boys that were used to the sea and the sun. They looked around at each other, the soldiers next to them, across from them. They knew they wouldn't last another week. There was desperation and lost hope wherever they went.

And that's when the officers called the army together.

The army all gathered in front of the town hall where their officers stood in front of them and told the gaunt and hollow faces that looked back that rations were being cut even more than they already had been. The soldiers didn't even have the energy to react, or to protest, or anything else: they'd learned a long time ago to save everything that they could, and anger required energy.

The officers started the process of marking everyone's ration cards to reflect the announcement, and Alexei and Costa stood and waited for the officers to reach them, to make the change that was surely the signal that the beginning of the end was upon them. Alexei didn't see Costa walk towards the town hall where the officers were standing.

"We can't do it," a voice said, and Alexei looked up to see Costa facing the officers, the rest of the army behind him.

The Lieutenant who was in charge looked up then, too, and found Costa staring back at him—

"We can't do what?" the Lieutenant asked.

"We're already half-starved. I'd rather get shot out there in the snow than die here in the city and take none of them with us."

"If you'd rather get shot, then you know where the Italians are. I'm sure they'd be happy to oblige you."

The Lieutenant went back to the ration cards, but he didn't know Costa, so he didn't know that Costa wasn't finished—

"If we could get word to the rest of the army," Costa continued, "and they came here, even if it was just one more company . . . then we'd be able to push the Italians back. We could trap them in the mountains and we could beat them."

"The rest of the army doesn't know that they're here. They don't know that we need their help."

"But what if they did?"

"That's not possible."

"Why?"

The Lieutenant paused again, narrowing his eyes—

"Because there's a lot of Italians between us and the rest of the Greek Army."

"So we run."

"We *run?*"

"We can do it in pairs, two soldiers each. A runner and a spotter. We use the main army to create a distraction. Some kind of false offensive to draw them away. Then each division sends a runner west. These hills have many places to hide. One of us is bound to get through to the main army."

"It's suicide."

"No, it's not. It's suicide to stay here and starve. It's our only chance, is what it is. And I'll be the first to volunteer."

Before he knew what he was doing, Alexei walked forward to stand next to Costa—

"No, he won't, sir," Alexei said. "I'll go from our division. Costa can spot me. He's a better shot."

"Is that right?"

"It is. We grew up racing each other," Alexei explained. "So we both know that I'm faster than he is. Any day of the week. Even on an empty stomach."

"That's bullshit," Costa turned to Alexei. "He hasn't beaten me at anything since we were six."

"He'll shoot and cover me," Alexei said. "Costa doesn't miss. Ask anyone."

"You're crazy, Alexei. It was my idea, so I'm—"

The Lieutenant cut them both off—

"Where are you boys from?" he asked.

"Agria," Alexei told him. "Near Volos."

"They make them different in Agria, then, is that it?"

"What do you mean by different, sir?"

"I was being polite. I meant crazy."

"It's only crazy if we get shot. If we make it through, then we'll all be home for Christmas, and Greece will be ours."

The Lieutenant was silent for a moment—

"If you don't make it, then you'll be dead, out in the forest, and we need every soldier that we have here, defending the city, which was our charge. Do you really think that you can make it?"

"Have you seen the Italians that are out there, sir?" Alexei asked.

"Of course I have."

"They fire at us every night, and they haven't hit shit."

"So?"

"Yeah. I think we can make it."

There was one more moment, the Lieutenant looking back and forth between them, then he nodded. "Alright," he said, and he pointed to Costa. "You'll run, since it was your idea, and your friend can cover you. I'll be with the army, and we'll see if we can't give you the distraction you're looking for."

"Yes, sir."

"Is there anyone else who wants to volunteer?"

Immediately, every hand went into the air.

"Well, isn't that something."

The soldiers smiled. The Lieutenant smiled, too. They were proud of themselves, and what they now knew they were made of.

And they had their plan.

Night came to the city.

The Greeks decided to stagger the runs into the mountains, and they'd go under cover of darkness. Six teams were chosen, and they'd leave from different points around the city. All the runners and spotters chose their marks and routes and where they'd leave the safety of the buildings.

The main army would make their diversion soon.

Alexei and Costa walked down the street towards the southern edge of Pogradec. That's where Costa had chosen to make his run, and Alexei would cover him. They thought it was the best position because it was the nearest to where the forest came almost to the edge of the city, and a soldier in the forest was harder to hit because there were more places to hide.

Alexei had two rifles slung across his back, and tried to protest one more time, that it should be him that would go, and that Costa should cover for him. He reminded Costa of how many times he'd told Alexei that he was the best shot in the whole army.

But Costa just smiled at his friend—

"We don't need to hit them, Alexei. We just need to shoot in their general direction, to keep them pinned down so that they can't shoot at me. Or at least won't want to."

"What do you mean? Of course they're going to want to shoot you."

"We're not fighting a bunch of heroes. You're the one that told me that, remember? These are men that just wanna get out of here, with their lives, the same as we do. Nobody wants to die up here. Especially the Italians, who aren't even sure what they're here fighting for in the first place."

"You know that we're equal as runners. We always have been."

"That's not true. I'm a better runner, and I'm a better shot," Costa said. "And besides . . . you have Philia waiting for you back at home. And your parents. And all the children that you're going to have, that you're always going around and talking about."

"And you have, what . . . nothing at all?"

"No," Costa said, and he turned to look at Alexei. "I have you."

Alexei stopped walking, and they stood in the street, looking at each other, and Alexei tried to swallow his emotion—

"Costa . . ."

"Do you have enough ammo?" Costa didn't let him finish what he was going to say.

"I think so," Alexei nodded.

"I don't want you running out on me and shooting blanks."

"I have enough."

"Good. Let's go, then. It's almost time."

There was a belltower in front of them, and that's where they'd decided that Alexei would hide and cover Costa as he made his run.

"Now remember," Costa told him one more time, "just shoot in their general direction to keep them pinned. When they hear your rifle, they're going to be more worried about getting shot than anything that I'm doing, so they're going to duck until the firing stops."

"Make sure that you zig-zag when you run," Alexei said. "Like when we got the boar. Don't run straight, so they can't hit you."

"Anything else?"

"Stay alive."

They faced each other and clasped arms—

"The next time I see you," Costa said, "I'll be marching over those mountains with an army at my back."

Blam blam blam.

Kaboom kaboom.

Gunfire in the distance. The false offensive. It was the diversion from the Greek Army.

"That's the signal," Costa said.

"Yeah."

"It won't keep them busy for long. It's time for me to move."

They both nodded one last time, then Costa went to wait in the shadows at the edge of the city, staring out into the forest, up towards the mountains, as Alexei climbed the stairs into the belltower.

When he reached the top, he knelt by the window and unslung the two rifles from his back. He propped one against the wall, then took the other and rested it on the edge of the window, taking aim towards the forest. He took a deep breath, then crossed himself, three fingers to his forehead, then his right shoulder before his left—it was the orthodox way, that the Greeks used, the ancient way.

Then, Alexei settled in to wait.

The sound of the offensive got louder in the distance.

Below the belltower, Costa crept out of the shadows and towards the forest, and when Costa reached the end of the outskirts of the city, the end of his cover between the buildings, he turned and looked above him.

He nodded once.

Alexei squeezed the rifle tight against his shoulder.

Then Costa started to run, and he'd almost made it across the distance between the city and the forest, almost to the safety of the trees that were there, and that's when the first shots came—

Blam blam blam.

They were close. Urgent. Coming from the north.

Alexei couldn't see the shooters amongst the dense growth of forest, but he fired at the general sound of them, just as they'd talked about. Costa started to zig-zag as he ran, altering the path of his route as he sprinted between the trees, and Alexei kept firing as many rounds as possible.

Blam blam blam blam blam!!

He shot as many bullets through the trees towards where he thought the Italians might be as he could possibly fire, shooting rounds as fast as his rifle would allow him to shoot, then—

Click click.

He was out of ammo.

He tossed his rifle aside and grabbed the next one.

He fired more rounds into the trees.

There were shouts from the Italians and the faint sounds of words that he did not understand, but he didn't care about any of that. He didn't know if he'd hit any of them, and that's what they were talking about, or if they were just telling their friends to wait and keep cover, none of that mattered at all because it was working.

They'd stopped firing at Costa while Alexei fired at them.

Blam blam blam!!

Costa was getting further and further into the distance.

And then Alexei felt his trigger jam.

He pulled as hard as he could, but he couldn't squeeze it back anymore. It was stuck. Frozen in the cold. He ripped the action back towards him and an empty casing flew out and sizzled as the hot metal hit the snow at his feet. But he couldn't jam the action back into place. He tried as hard as he could, again and again, strength in his desperation, until he ripped the entire bolt from the barrel and the rifle came apart in his hand.

There were more shouts from the Italians.

Then they started shooting again.

Bang bang bang bang.

"Shit," Alexei muttered under his breath.

He looked into the distance and saw Costa stumble and fall, and he didn't know if he'd been hit, or if he'd just tripped. Then, Costa got up and kept running, and Alexei could see the bullets hitting the snow around him, making him dance as he ran.

Then, in the distance, Alexei saw one of the Italian soldiers kneel, taking careful aim at Costa. He took his time. Lining up his shot. And even from the distance that he watched, Alexei could tell by how this Italian held his weapon that he knew how to shoot and that his bullet was going to find his friend, and there was nothing that Alexei could do about it.

"*Costa!!*" Alexei yelled, but his words were lost in the wind.

Below him, the Italian was ready to fire.

Then, like a thunderbolt straight from God, Alexei remembered the pistol that his father had given him. He didn't need to hit the Italians. He just needed to shoot at them.

He grabbed the pistol from where he kept it strapped to his lower leg, beneath his pants and just above his boot, and then he stood tall in the window and fired—

Bang bang bang!!

The Italian sniper heard the shots and dropped to find cover just before he was about to take his shot.

Costa kept running.

Bang bang bang!!

Alexei fired the rest of the bullets he had and then heard the hammer of the pistol click against steel and he sat back down, staring into the distance, grateful at what he saw.

Costa had disappeared over the mountains in the distance.

There wasn't anything left that Alexei could do to help him.

The rest was now with God.

Costa would later tell the story of what happened over the next three days.

When he'd stumbled and fell in the snow, it was because one of the Italian bullets had hit him in the back of his hand. He'd smile when he showed it to Alexei and tell him how fortunate he was that it was just his hand, and that they didn't hit anything that he needed to be able to run. And also how the cold had stopped it from bleeding much at all, and so it was just a flesh wound that soon had healed itself shut.

Costa made it through the forest, and once he crested the mountain and was on the other side, he couldn't see any more Italians, no matter which way he looked, but he still didn't stop running. He put his head down against the stiff wind and kept going until he saw the sun starting to rise in the distance and he knew he needed to look for shelter.

He found a small farm.

The entire place was empty, as far as he could tell, and there was a barn on the far side of the property which looked like the perfect place to hide for the day, until the sun started to set again and he could continue on under the cover of darkness.

He stayed in the barn all day, and left again at night.

He ran through the darkness, until the sun rose again.

Then he found another farm, with a farmer just getting up to go about his morning tasks, and Costa raised his hands in peace as the farmer put down his tools when he saw Costa approach and then led him towards the house.

He lived with his wife and two daughters, who were cooking breakfast, and they invited Costa to join them as they ate, and he gladly did, not having had any food in a very long time, as the farmer went back outside.

They were at the table, and just about finished, and that's when Costa heard the roar of an engine outside and he went to the window to see a truck full of Italians approaching, and he knew the farmer had betrayed him. He couldn't blame him. The man was Albanian, and likely just wanted to be left alone. He didn't care who was Greek or Italian or anything else, as long as they left him and his family to their crops and their lives. And the Italians had promised death to any Albanians who harbored Greek soldiers.

So Costa picked up his rifle and ran.

He went out the back door, and across a wide field, Italian shots echoing behind him now, as he made it to the forest in the distance.

The Italian vehicles couldn't follow him through the trees, and while some of the Italians tried to run after him, none of them were even going to come close to catching the Greek boy from Agria who'd grown every day of his life with dreams of being an Olympic runner.

Costa stayed in the forest for the rest of that day, away from all the roads, and as high in the mountains as he could go, where the Italians couldn't bring their armored vehicles. He had some food in his belly from the farmer's wife, and he continued on for another day and a night, keeping his cover in the trees, knowing that was his survival, until the next morning he finally walked out of the forest and found himself on the other side of the mountains.

He went to the edge of the peak, the sun rising over the hills behind him, and looked down into the gorge below. He smiled when he saw the jeeps and the tents and the flags in the valley.

Then he began his walk down the mountain.

Because he'd found what he'd been looking for.

9

December 3rd, 1940

ALEXEI WAITED FOR THREE EXCRUCIATING DAYS. None of the soldiers in Pogradec knew if any of the runners had made it through the forest, and if they had, did they survive the night, and the rest of the Italian soldiers patrolling the hills and mountains?

Were they still alive?

Was any help coming?

The men that had brought worry beads held them tighter in their hands. Alexei had found a pair and wrapped them around his palm as he sat in the cold with the rest of the Greek soldiers and anxiously flipped them. There was nothing else for them to do but wait.

Then, there were shots in the distance.

Blam blam blam.

The Greek soldiers stood.

But the shots weren't near the buildings.

They were further than that.

They were in the mountains.

Alexei quickly slung his rifle over his shoulder and ran

all the way to the edge of the city, and he climbed the same belltower from where he'd covered Costa, and when he was at the top he looked out past the buildings as far as he could look.

And what he saw in the distance turned his lips into the largest smile he could remember.

It was the entire Greek 3rd Army.

They were coming over the peaks in a glorious fury of exploding cannons and fire and steel, bringing death to the Italians across from them.

Bang bang!!! Bang bang bang!!!!

Then, mortars—

Kaboom kaboom!!!!

Alexei watched for another moment as the battle took shape in front of him, then he turned and yelled to the soldiers below him in the city.

He told them what was happening.

For a moment, everyone's hunger was forgotten, and so was the cold.

Because they knew they'd been delivered.

The fighting in the mountains didn't last long.

The Italians were surrounded, and overwhelmed, and they soon surrendered before most of the Greeks from Pogradec were even able to join the battle. The Italians that didn't surrender ran north towards the town of Elbasan, and Alexei watched them flee into the distance, but he didn't chase after them. There were other soldiers that would do that.

Alexei was too hungry.

He was too tired.

And there was something else that he needed to do first.

He pushed his way through the Italians, with their hands raised in the air, as the newly arrived Greek soldiers walked amongst the prisoners, collecting their weapons and disarming them. Alexei looked through the army, seeing many fresh young faces, but not the one that he was searching for.

Then, there was a voice behind him—

"I told you I'd run faster."

Alexei turned to see Costa standing there. He was smiling, with snow starting to fall around them.

"It took you three days," Alexei said. "I would have done it in two."

"Nobody could have done it in two."

"Pheidippides made it from Marathon to Athens in thirty-six hours."

"There aren't any mountains between Marathon and Athens, or snow, and there especially wasn't anyone shooting at him. And, besides, that's just a story."

"So that means it's not true? Everyone said Troy was just a story, too."

Costa laughed, then held up his bloodied hand with a bandage wrapped around it for Alexei to see—

"What's that?"

"First wound of the war. Something to remember it by."

"As if we could forget."

Alexei crossed the distance between them, and embraced his friend.

"I'm ready to go home," he said.

"I am, too," Costa answered.

And Alexei held on to Costa longer than he ever had before, the snow falling around them, collecting in their hair, and on their coats, and he didn't hold his friend because he thought it was going to bring them any greater comfort, or that he felt either of them needed it.

It was simpler than that.

He held him because he didn't want anyone to see the tears that were in his eyes.

10

January 19ᵗʰ, 1941

V ICTORY DIDN'T FEEL THE WAY THAT Alexei thought it
would.

The Greek soldiers were shipped back south by train, the
same way that they'd come. After the 3ʳᵈ Army had made it
to Pogradec and liberated the garrison, Alexei learned that
the main Greek forces had just beaten the Italian Army deci-
sively, and except for a few small skirmishes in the mountains, as the Italians retreated back north, the war was over.

And the Greeks had won.

Alexei sat on his train, looking out the window, as Costa
slept next to him, his body rocking gently back and forth
along with the motion of the tracks. Alexei watched the
countryside start to flatten as they came out of the mountains, the snow receding further and further behind them
the closer they got to Agria, until soon there wasn't any
left at all. And as the snow disappeared, and everything
around him started to look more like home, Alexei started
to think about what was waiting for him there when he
returned.

Philia. His parents. The future.

He felt his father's pistol that he still kept in his boot, and the metal no longer felt strange against his skin.

Then he heard a voice behind him.

He turned in his seat to see a young soldier—he couldn't have been more than eighteen years old—talking to another soldier sitting next to him. The young soldier wore thick glasses, and had a very slight frame. He looked strange in his uniform that he didn't even come close to filling out.

And he was talking about his glasses.

He'd had them since he was eight years old, he told the soldier, and without them he couldn't see at all. Not people. Not landscapes. Not anything. Without them, he could only tell a tree from a building by the colors and approximate size and shape.

Alexei frowned.

Why was he telling this story?

The young soldier continued and explained that he'd always wanted to be a scientist, because he was so grateful for the technology that allowed him to see, otherwise he wouldn't have had any sort of life at all. Without his glasses, he would have been confined to a house, essentially blind, but the glasses had given him a perfectly normal existence, which he would have never known without them. He had been more grateful for his glasses, he said, than for anything else in his life, until now.

And now he wished he'd never had them.

"Why?" the soldier next to him asked, not understanding.

The young soldier was silent for a moment, staring into the distance, and when he spoke again, his voice was different, pitched low, and filled with pain—

"Because, without them, I wouldn't have seen what men can do to other men," he said softly.

And then he was silent.

Alexei turned back around in his seat.

He sat there and thought about what the young soldier had just said, and he wondered if he felt the same way, and after a moment of consideration he decided that he didn't. He decided that the soldier behind him was wrong, and that he wasn't a soldier at all. Because, Alexei decided, he was glad that he'd seen what he'd seen in the mountains. He was proud of what they'd done, and what he'd been a part of, though he was also glad that he didn't enjoy it, as he'd heard some men do. He'd been made hard in places that hadn't been hard before, and where he'd been broken he knew he'd now be stronger.

He'd done what men do, he told himself.

He sat there in silence for a moment longer, then he told himself again.

He'd done what men do.

It wasn't long until they reached Agria.

Alexei and Costa said their goodbyes to Koukidis, and Alexei told him there would be a wedding soon, and that he should stay, but Koukidis had business in Athens, and it couldn't wait.

They shook hands.

Alexei asked for his address, or any way that they could contact him, but Koukidis just smiled—

"We'll meet again," he said. "Don't worry. This war's not over. Not yet. And when you need me . . . just turn around, and Koukidis will be there."

Costa rolled his eyes, and then they were at the station,

and Koukidis nodded to where Philia was standing on the platform, waiting for the train that was bringing the soldier who would be a husband home to her.

"Is that her right there?" Koukidis asked.

"She's beautiful, isn't she?"

"You'd better get down there before she takes up with some other soldier."

"Fuck you," Alexei laughed.

"Enjoy your wedding."

"Are you sure you can't come?"

"Get outta here," Koukidis smiled back with his eyes. "Go make that girl your wife."

Alexei shook his hand one more time, then Costa did the same, saying his own goodbye, and the two boys from Agria grabbed their bags and got off the train. Before they were out of the car, however, Costa stopped, just for a moment, putting his arm out against Alexei's chest.

"What is it?" Alexei asked. "What's wrong?"

"Do you smell that?"

"Smell what?"

Costa took a deep breath and closed his eyes.

Then, Alexei did the same.

They breathed in the air, coming from the windows, filling their lungs, tasting it on their lips.

"Salt," Alexei said.

"Home," Costa answered.

And they smiled.

Alexei would never forget the way that Philia looked that morning.

It was a picture that he'd carry with him for all of the days that he had left. And when she saw him, dressed in his pressed uniform, her breath caught in her throat, as Alexei went to her and lifted her up, held her as tightly as he could hold her, and whispered softly into her ear, through the tears on her cheek, that were on his cheek, now, too—

"I told you I'd come back to you."

"I never stopped hoping."

"*S'agapo.*"

"*S'agapo moro mou.*"

Iannis and Eleni waited at a distance, respectful of the new life that their son was about to start, and the place that Philia was going to take in it, and so they hugged Costa first, who was their son, too.

Then Alexei set Philia down, and he went to them.

When he saw the tears in his father's eyes, he knew that neither of them would be able to say anything. So he embraced each of them in turn, and he was happy because he knew that they could feel everything that he wanted to say, and he didn't need to find the words.

Then Alexei saw Giorgos in the distance.

He walked to where Philia's father stood at the back of the platform. The older man sized up the young soldier in front of him. He looked him up and down, every inch, from head to toe. Then he looked into his eyes. And he nodded at what he found.

He stuck out his hand, and Alexei shook it—

"Welcome home, son," he said.

And so it would be.

When a Greek village prepares for a wedding, it's a beautiful thing.

Everybody has a job, and they go about everything with a smile on their face, and the work they do together allows them to share in the joy of the bride and groom. And that spring, everyone in Agria had so much to be thankful for. They'd fought against their enemies, and in spite of the odds, they'd won, and their sons had come home.

Alexei felt invincible.

Everything that had haunted him in the mountains had faded—the moments of indecision and uncertainty, the lives that he'd taken, and his hand that shook—and he felt like he was so much larger for having experienced what he'd experienced and returned from it.

It was a beautiful feeling.

He couldn't stop smiling as he watched his mother and Philia sitting at their kitchen table, choosing fabrics and flowers and preparing place settings. Alexei was leaning against the wall, watching them work, when Iannis came up behind him and whispered softly into his son's ear so that Philia and Eleni couldn't hear.

"Is this something that you feel like sticking around for?"

"Not particularly. Was there something else you had in mind?"

"Join your old man in a boat?"

Alexei smiled, as he followed Iannis out the door, a boy born of the sea not needing to be asked twice if he cared to return.

Alexei and his father walked down the path to the dock together.

It was the same way they used to take when Alexei was a boy, but this time, after having been away for the longest he'd ever been away, each step they took meant more to him.

They silently untied the boat from the dock and climbed

in, pushing it away from shore to sail into the calm waters, and Alexei looked around, as far as his eyes would take him, and he smiled.

These were his waters.

He felt that now.

Then when they were far enough out they loosed their nets, letting them sink to the bottom of the sea, and when the nets were full Alexei strained his biceps to haul them in, pulling them up and over the side of the boat, using muscles that he realized he hadn't used in the months since he'd been gone. He grunted as he pulled up net after net into the boat, sun glistening across azure water, and Iannis began to sort through their catch. Father and son worked silently, like they always did, ever since Alexei had been a boy, and when they were done Iannis sat back, watching Alexei with a small smile.

"What's the matter?"

"Does it look different?"

"Does what look different?"

"Your home."

"Not really," Alexei said, looking around. "The water's the same. The air. The birds. Why do you ask?"

"Because it should. You've changed, so the things around you that you know . . . they have to change, too."

"You think I've changed?"

"I know you have," Iannis said. "You forget. I've been to war, too. And it's right there in your eyes, Alexei. It's the only part of ourselves that we can't hide, you know." And Alexei was silent, because foolish as it was he hadn't thought that his father might know what his son had known, and Iannis continued, his voice lower now, more comforting. "It's alright, though," he said, giving Alexei's shoulder a little shake. "We can't become men until we've seen what the world can do to men, and that's not a bad thing."

Alexei sat back in the boat, because he finally realized what he felt, what he'd brought home with him. They were silent for a moment, each looking down at the fish below them, then Iannis spoke again—

"Was it very difficult up there?"

"Yes, Papa. It was."

"And are you proud of what you did?"

"Yes," Alexei said, meeting Iannis' eyes. "I am."

Iannis could see the truth in his son's eyes, and he was glad, because it was a truth that a soldier returning from war needs.

"That's good, Alexei," he said. "That's very good. That's all that matters."

"That's not *all* that matters."

Alexei looked at Iannis, and then he smiled, a boy again, out in the boat with his father, out in the boat with Zeus—

"We won," he said. "That matters, too."

January 22nd, 1941

Alexei married Philia in the Agios Georgios church where he'd gone every Sunday of his life until the war began, and they were married by the same priest who had baptized Alexei, given him every communion he'd ever received, and had been patient with him as he learned where to go and how to stand when he was young and had served in the altar with Costa and all the other boys in Agria until they were sixteen.

Eleni had invited the whole village to the wedding, and the whole village came.

They wanted a reason to celebrate.

After a war, they *needed* a reason to celebrate.

Costa stood next to Alexei during the ceremony as *koumbaro*, and Alexei saw Costa suppress a smile as Alexei and Philia were crowned with the *stefana* and Costa had to hold the ring of flowers in place and walk behind them as Alexei and Philia were led around the altar three times in the symbolic unending journey of husband and wife. After the ceremonial walk, the crowns were removed, and the priest blessed Alexei and Philia one more time, joining their hands together in a reminder that they belonged to each other now, and from that day forward, they could be separated only by God.

After the ceremony, they went up the hill to Giorgos' great house.

Alexei and Philia led the procession through town, with the priest next to them, and the rest of the village followed. When they got to Giorgos' house, they saw prepared the most lavish feast and party that had ever been seen in Agria. And they were glad, because it was needed. It was very needed. The smiles. The dancing. The laughter.

The first thing Alexei did was look for Giorgos.

He found him talking to an old business associate from Athens, and when Giorgos saw Alexei standing near his shoulder, he quietly excused himself so he could speak to his new son.

"What is it, Alexandros?" Giorgos asked. "Is everything alright?"

"Everything's perfect," Alexei said. "I just wanted ..." Alexei met Giorgos' eyes as he swallowed, gathering himself. "I just wanted to say thank you."

Giorgos looked back at him for a moment, then he said softly—

"You deserve it. You did what you told me you would do. You came back, and you came back a hero. Now I'm doing what I said I'd do."

"I appreciate it. That's what I wanted to say."

Alexei smiled at Giorgos, and Giorgos smiled back, and Alexei was happy as the older man patted him on the shoulder and then watched as he rejoined his guests and the conversation that he'd left. And then, just past

Giorgos, he saw Philia, watching him from across the mass of people, and he knew that she was happy to see her husband and her father speaking in the way that she'd just seen them speak.

Alexei went to her, through their guests, no one in the world mattering to him the way that the girl in front of him did, and he took her in his arms and kissed her deeply. She kissed him back. He felt her hair tickle as the wind blew it against his cheek. He felt her lips as they parted softly around his lips for the hundredth time that day.

She tasted of sweet salt and spring flowers, he thought.

No, that's not right.

Then he found it.

She tasted of home.

And then, after the sun went down, the dancing began.

Too much dancing can be counted on at all Greek weddings, and not just from the young and those at the ceremony that were looking to find their own love. The men dance. The women dance. The children dance. Eleni had once told Alexei that Greeks learn how to dance before they learn how to walk, and Alexei couldn't remember the moment that he'd learned, it was just something that had always been with him, as far back as he could remember, and so he was sure that his mother must be right.

Men jumped and twisted.

Their bodies flew through the air.

Each of the young men was trying to do better than the young man next to him. Each of the old men watched them and remembered what it was like to be young. They stood in a circle and clapped as dancers twisted and flew, and then the tempo picked up, and they spread into a larger circle in Giorgos' magnificent yard. Alexei and Philia were in the middle of it all, and together they danced the *kalamatiano* more than two dozen times, and it still wasn't enough.

They kept dancing.

Greeks are some of the few people who still dance today the same way that they danced in ancient times—and so there they were, all the people of Agria, dancing high on a cliff the same way that Plato had danced, the way that Aristotle had danced, the same way that the great kings like Leonidas and Alexander had danced. They were dancing the same way that their ancestors had danced on foreign beaches when Troy fell, and when Persian ships collapsed in the waters at Salamis, and when Darius' line finally broke at Gaugamela, during that long summer when the whole world changed.

And it was the same way they danced that night.

It would all go on well into the dawn, but it was sometime after midnight and before the sun came up that Giorgos got the attention of his guests to let them know that the bride would be leaving with the groom to spend their first night together.

"Where are they going?" a man who'd had too much to drink yelled from the crowd.

"To make my first grandson," Giorgos shot back at him, not missing a beat, and the crowd laughed as Philia blushed and Alexei looked at the ground, not wanting all of the guests that were gathered to see the smile and the joy that he couldn't hold back. He took Philia's hand in his and they left the applause and laughter behind them.

He took her in his strong arms.

They were in the bedroom they would share in Giorgos'

house, and though Alexei had been between these walls a million times, and knew every inch by heart, tonight it was different. Tonight this room was a temple, and the girl standing in front of him its goddess.

That's all there was, and all there needed to be.

She was breathing heavily, her chest rising and falling in anticipation of what was to come.

She shivered.

He held her closer.

And then she slowly stepped backwards, her eyes never leaving his, Alexei watching as she slipped the straps of her dress over her shoulders and let it fall to the floor in a puddle of white silk. Alexei looked at her, bathed only in the moonlight, and then he picked her up in his arms and carried her to the bed. He lifted his shirt over his head and tossed it aside. He unbuckled his belt, and his pants fell to the floor. And when he moved on top of her, and leaned his lips down next to hers, his voice was a whisper in her ear—

"I love you so much."

"You're everything," she answered, looking into his eyes. "You're everything, and it scares me."

"I'm yours," he said, and then he repeated it, because it was the truth, and the truth shouldn't be hidden. *"I'm yours . . . I'm yours . . . I'm yours,"* he whispered to her.

"Then take me," she said. "Make me your wife."

He looked down at her.

He traced every inch of her with his eyes, because he knew that it was something he would return to, then he slowly moved so that he was between her legs.

He leaned down and kissed her as he entered her for the first time, and with the promise that their bodies made in that moment, he knew that one of his lives had faded away and another had begun.

They made love as moonlight poured through the window.

Time had ceased to be anything.

They finally finished, and Alexei lay next to his wife, still holding her as closely as he could, and they knew that things could not have ever possibly been more right in the world than they were at that moment. They made love many more times that night, and before either of them knew it the sun was starting to rise outside the window where the moon had been so many hours ago, before everything had begun.

Alexei looked at Philia, silhouetted against the light behind her. She saw him, and knew how he felt, because she felt it, too.

"They'll be wondering why we're not at breakfast," she said.

"They'll know why we're not at breakfast."

"I didn't sleep at all. But I'm not tired. Maybe it'll always be like this."

"Of course it will be," Alexei said as he leaned over to kiss her. "You're only tired when you're bored. And how could this ever be boring?"

She reached out and touched his cheek, pulled his arm towards her, and he knew what she wanted, and he wanted it, too.

They made love again.

The sunlight was streaming in through the window, warm on their naked bodies, intertwined, meant for each other, promised to each other, the dream that they now shared.

Alexei lay naked on the bed.

The sheets were tangled on the floor, long forgotten.

He watched as Philia dressed in front of him, and he learned that morning that watching a woman get dressed is easily one of the greatest pleasures in life, an invitation into a mystery of ritual and preparation that men know nothing about, and this was the first time that he'd been invited to witness the intricacies of zippers and buttons and strange garments that before that moment he hadn't even known existed.

She spoke to Alexei without turning around—

"Do you think I'm pregnant?" she asked.

"If you're not, it won't be for lack of trying."

"I think I'm pregnant."

"It doesn't always happen the first time."

"That's not what mothers tell their daughters. But then again, nothing about it was like they said it would be."

"How was it?"

"It was better."

She was dressed now and brought Alexei's clothes to him—

"Here. Get dressed."

"I don't want to."

"You have to."

"Why?"

"Because I'm hungry."

"You're supposed to make me breakfast. That's how this works."

"I know."

"Then why do I have to get dressed?"

"Because I don't want you to ever be out of my sight again. Not even while I'm downstairs, making you breakfast."

Alexei smiled and sat on the edge of the bed and kissed her one more time, until she moved away and handed him his pants.

She checked herself in the mirror one last time before she turned to leave, and that's when Alexei grabbed her hand, stopping her, wanting this moment to last just a little bit longer—

"What is it, Alexei?" she said, looking at him.

And he looked back at her. At her eyes. At her beautiful eyes.

"*Kalimera*," he said.

She waited a moment longer, then she smiled, too, as she kissed his lips, and looked deeply into him—

"*Kalimera*," she said.

12

February 26th, 1941

T HEY WERE HIGH UP ON A cliff.

It was the place where Alexei had chosen to build the home for Philia that he'd promised her, and it was down the road from his parent's house, not far from the spot where he'd brought Philia the first day that they'd met.

That was her idea.

"We'll continue at the same spot where we started," she'd said.

The practicality, though, was that it was within walking distance from both Giorgos' and Iannis' houses, and the view of the Aegean was one of the best in all of Agria. If eyes could only see a little bit further, on a clear day it might even be possible to find Eudaimonia in the distance across the gentle waves. But even though they couldn't see the island from where they'd live, they knew it was still there, just out of sight, and they'd smile at the memory that they shared, and then they'd look down at their reminder, together, the ink that was set deep into their skin.

Alexei started building soon after the wedding.

Costa helped him everyday, and the structure of the house was just beginning to take shape as they worked. Neither of them knew how to build a house, or had done it before, but Alexei didn't care. He didn't want someone else to build his home. And after what they'd done in the mountains against the Italians, how could he possibly fail at something so simple? He'd learn later what that feeling was called.

Post-war optimism.

He'd also learn that it doesn't last.

Alexei and Costa sat in front of the house.

They were taking a break for lunch, the Mediterranean sun beating against their skin, even though it was only February. They drank fresh spring water and ate peasant salad from a large bowl and argued over what they'd accomplished that morning and what they still had left to do.

"You don't want any windows to the north, Alexei," Costa said.

"Why's that?"

"Because there's nothing to see. You need windows to the east, and windows to the west. Sunrise, sunset. That's all there is. Everything else is useless. Just empty glass."

"The bedroom faces north."

"So?"

"I don't want to have a bedroom without windows."

"Why not?"

"Because I don't."

"But *why*."

"I like windows."

"What do you want to look at out there?" he waved to

the north, in the direction the window would face. "It's just dirt and hills. Tell me what you want to look at out the window."

"I don't want to look at anything. I just want the window."

"C'mon, *malaka*," Costa said. "You have to trust me on this."

"Why's that? How many houses have you built?"

"How many houses have *you* built?"

"You're just trying to get out of doing it."

Costa was silent for a moment, then he tackled Alexei off the steps and put him in a choke-hold but Alexei pushed back and threw Costa off. They rolled around in the dirt, until Costa finally got the upper-hand and pinned Alexei to the ground.

"Get off me," Alexei said.

"Not until you give up."

"We're putting the window in."

"You want a window to stare out at nothing? Fine. We'll take an extra two days and you'll have your window to stare out at nothing. But don't blame me when Philia wants to tear this whole thing down."

Then they both smiled.

They knew Philia would want no such thing.

Three hours later, with the sun beginning its descent, they looked up to see Philia coming down the path towards them. Costa wiped his hands on his pants, then nodded towards her—

"Is she pregnant yet?"

"I don't know. But if she is, don't tell her."

"Why?"

"Because I don't want to stop trying."

"I told you it was great, right?"

"You act like you're the first person to ever discover it."

Philia finally reached them, and she saw their smiles, and the looks on their faces.

"What are you guys talking about?"

"Nothing," Alexei said.

"Love-making," Costa smirked.

"Is that all you talk about up here?"

"Costa rarely thinks of anything else."

"Alexei jokes," Costa scolded him, "but it was my lust that saved us at Pogradec."

"Is that right? I didn't hear that story."

"My lust saved the whole of the Greek Army up there in the mountains. Without my charm and appetite for beautiful women we'd have never known that the Italians were coming."

"Is that true?" Philia asked, looking at Alexei.

"No."

"*What??* Tell the truth, Alexei. Tell your wife what happened."

Philia shook her head, having had enough already—

"I guess I shouldn't have expected anything different leaving you two up here alone. How's Thalia, Costa?"

"Things are delicate right now."

"Delicate?"

"This morning Nico asked if I was moving in. I think I may have spent the night too many times."

Since coming back from Albania, every girl in Agria had seen the scar from the Italian bullet on Costa's hand. He'd taken to wearing a glove when he went out, so that girls would ask him about it, and he could tell them every detail about the wound he'd gotten saving Greece. The girls would coo, and hold him in their arms, and stroke his hair to comfort him, not realizing they were already halfway into his bed, and after a week of being home Costa had loudly proclaimed that getting shot was the greatest thing that had ever happened to him.

After sleeping with all the girls that were the same age as him, he'd moved on to different targets and different conquests, until the one that had finally took hold of him in a way that was more than just fleeting was a woman of twenty-seven with a regal and proud bearing, and her eleven-year-old son Nicandro. Thalia's husband had died in an auto accident shortly after their son had been born, when he was walking down a road and was struck by a driver who hadn't seen him, and so Nico had never known what it was like to have a father.

Costa had met her in the market.

He was a man who'd been born with the gift of being able to walk up to a beautiful woman and know exactly what to say, something that so many men wish they had but most can only watch with envy. He saw her, and couldn't take his eyes from her, and when she looked up and their eyes met she ignored him, and that's when he fell in love with her.

She drove him crazy.

She didn't care about his scar, or that he was handsome, or his charming smile and invitations for drinks and picnics and trips to the countryside. He kept pursuing her, though, through every rejection, and every denial. He started bringing her flowers at all times of the day, but she wouldn't let him into her house. Alexei told Costa that he was crazy, and he agreed, but he also found that he liked how it felt.

Then on one chilly night when he'd brought dozens of bouquets and fruits and any other gifts that he could think to bring her, she finally let him in, and offered him a cup of warm tea. When Alexei asked Costa later why he chose her instead of the scores of other girls that he could have had, his answer was very simple:

"It's experience, Alexei."

"Experience?"

"I'm sick of having to teach them the tricks. I want to be taught, too. I want to find someone who knows how to do things that I've never done before, things that I've never even thought of, pleasures that haven't even been invented until that very moment that we invent them. I've forgotten girls, Alexei, because I've finally discovered a woman."

He also fell in love with Nico, every bit as much as he'd fallen in love with his mother. Costa had always been good with kids, and with Nico he found someone to rescue from the same fatherless childhood that he'd had. Thalia worked as a waitress in Volos during the day, and she would bring Nico with her to work, sitting him in a corner of the kitchen while she waited tables out front. But then, when her relationship with Costa had started, and she finally trusted him, and could see how much Nico worshipped him, she started to leave Nico with Costa when she went to work.

Everyone in Agria had gotten used to the sight of them together.

Costa taught Nico how to play soccer in the town square. He would take him swimming in the sea when it was warm. He showed him how to build a fire with nothing but twigs and flint. And even young as he was, Costa taught him how to haggle with vendors in the market, with haggling being a time-honored Greek skill and rite-of-passage, and after Nico brought down the price of a watermelon by more than half, his first great deal-making victory, Costa took him to the café for a gelato, though while they sat in the sun and licked their sticky fingers he made sure that the boy knew that what they'd just finished eating was the only good thing to ever come out of Italy.

Nico laughed, and so did Costa.

Everyone could see that Costa had completely transformed, and such is the mystery of life that it can change so quickly with the simplest addition of something that one never even knew had been missing.

Then, one morning, Costa decided that he wanted to teach Nico how to fish.

Alexei brought them out on his boat, and they showed Nico how to hold the nets, and how to throw them, and cast them out, even though the boy wasn't strong enough yet to do it by himself.

"All Greeks need to know how to fish," Costa told him. "It's something that's in our blood, and it's time that you learned about your birthright as a boy of these waters."

"Why?"

"I don't know. It just is."

Nico wrinkled his nose at the smell of the catch filling up the bottom of the boat.

"It doesn't smell great."

"No. It doesn't. I'll give you that. But you'll get used to it," Costa winked. "You can ask Theo Alexei about that."

And then Alexei showed Nico how to identify each of the fish that they'd caught by their fins and the marks on their backs, and then how to sort them accordingly, and once they'd found which ones were good and that they could sell at the market, they threw the rest back into the water for the other fish to eat and get bigger so that they could come back for them another day. And after Costa and Alexei had set Nico to work, sorting the fish on his own, they each lay back in the boat, enjoying the morning and the sun and the soft waves that gently rocked them back and forth.

"It's nice, you know," Alexei said, nodding to Nico in front of them. "What you're doing for him. You should see the way he looks at you."

"How's that?"

"Like there's been something he's needed his whole life, and has only just been found, and now everything in the world's right again."

Nico kept counting and sorting the fish as Alexei and Costa watched him: the boy was making sure that he did it the right way, the way that Alexei had showed him, and he worked with all the enthusiasm of a young boy included for the first time in the world of men. And, in a rare moment of complete vulnerability, as Costa sat there watching Nico, he turned and looked at Alexei, and spoke again, but this time very quietly, very differently, with his voice pitched low—

"You know . . . boys shouldn't grow up without a father, Alexei."

"No," Alexei agreed, thinking of his own father, and how much a part of him he was. "No, they shouldn't."

Thalia and Nico had both together changed Costa, which was something that had become more than clear, and it was also the reason why Philia had wrinkled her nose when Costa had said that things were currently delicate between them.

"You like her, don't you?" Philia asked.

"Of course I do," Costa said.

"So what's the problem?"

"She wants to know that I'm serious. She says it's more complicated when there's a child involved."

"It is more complicated when there's a child involved. But that's not necessarily a bad thing, either."

"So what do I do?"

"You show her that you're serious."

"I've tried everything, but she said that the only thing that can show true commitment is time."

"It sounds like she's a smart woman, and she knows who she's dealing with."

"I know. That's the problem. That's why it's delicate, and why I'm up here building a house with your husband every day. And then, of course, there's the other thing."

They all knew what the other thing was.

It was the cloud that hung over the heads of every single man, woman, and child in Agria, as well as all the rest of Greece. Even the hills and trees and waters around them seemed to be bracing themselves, gathering and saving all of their strength for the storm that was surely about to come. The Italians had been defeated, of course, but there would also be retribution for the Greek victory. Because the war thus far had made one thing very clear, and that was that Hitler didn't like to be embarrassed, and so everyone knew that it was very likely only a matter of time before the Germans would come sweeping down into their peninsula.

"That's why I came up here," Philia said. "I knew you were both alone, and didn't have a radio, so you wouldn't have heard the news."

"What news?"

Philia turned and looked at Alexei, and when he saw the darkness that was behind her eyes he forgot about the house that they were building. That would come later, he knew, if it came at all.

Because he knew what her look meant.

"It's the Germans," she said.

And so it was that war would intrude on paradise once again.

Alexei and Philia left Costa, who went to go find Thalia and Nico, and Alexei held her hand as they walked down the dirt road until it became worn cobblestone streets near the town square. Neither of them spoke as they walked because in front of them was a scene that they'd seen before, and had hoped to have never seen again.

Stores were empty.

People weren't out on the streets.

There were no children laughing.

There were no men arguing.

It was a city that had fought one war, and now knew that it had to prepare itself to fight another. "Why are we going to fight again?" Philia asked Alexei. "Italy was Italy, but this is Germany. What chance do we have?"

Alexei turned to her.

He'd followed all the details of the war very closely over the past month, so he explained it to her.

The great battle in this war was going to be fought in Russia—all the Allies already knew that—but they also knew that before that battle was ever fought, the outcome of it would be decided in Greece. Because the only way that the Russians could defeat the Germans would be with their age-old ally, that they'd relied upon since the beginning of time: the harshness of their winter, and the inhospitable conditions that it brought against an invading army. It was only February, so the Allies needed Greece to fight and delay the Germans for as long as they could, so that the Germans couldn't invade Russia during the long European summer.

It was their only chance.

And so, once again, the Greeks would fight.

Churchill was already mobilizing British soldiers to come to Greece's aid. Other Allied soldiers would also come from around the world to fight with them and Alexei knew, along with the rest of the men, that the fate of the world would be decided on their peninsula.

"Don't go, Alexei," Philia said, after she'd heard what he told her. "You've already fought. You've already done your part. Let someone else go this time."

"There is no one else."

"Then let the Germans come and do what they will."

"It's our home, Philia. We have to fight for our home."

"But for how long?"

"For however long it takes."

She was silent for a moment, searching Alexei's eyes with her own, looking for anything that she might hold onto—

"Don't go," she said again, softer this time. "Please don't go."

"Do you want your husband to be the only man in Greece that doesn't fight? You know that's not who you married."

She bit her lip, because they both knew that Alexei was right, even though neither of them wanted him to be.

"Do you remember the first day that we met?" she asked.

"Of course I do. We were down there by the market. I asked your father if I could show you the city."

"I saw you before that. When we first arrived. You were walking into town by yourself, carrying a net of fish that you were going to sell, and there was something about the way the sun was reflecting in your eyes that I knew I couldn't turn away from, and I didn't want to, either. Not with the look that you had that day."

"What look?"

"It was like you had a secret. A secret that I wanted to share."

"I don't have any secrets, Philia. Not from you."

"Yes, you do. You just don't know it. But I'll tell you. Your secret is that you're stronger than anyone I know, and that you feel more than you ever let yourself admit. Do you want to know what my secret is?"

"What?"

"That I wish you weren't."

They were silent for a moment as they stood there together in the agora, then Philia took Alexei's hand and placed it on her belly, underneath her shirt, his skin soft against her skin. Then she moved his palm until it was exactly where she wanted it.

"Do you feel that?" she asked him.

"What?"

"You can't feel him yet . . . but that's your son."

Alexei looked up and met her eyes—

"I'm pregnant," she said.

Philia's news changed everything and it changed nothing.

Alexei still had to go north. He still had to fight. All the

Greek soldiers that were on leave were called back, and so he'd go with his countrymen to protect their borders for as long as they could, and kill as many of their enemies as they could take with them. They decided that Philia would live with her father while Alexei was gone, and they went to speak to Giorgos together.

He was sitting at his large desk in a room that overlooked the Aegean. He clicked off the radio when he saw Alexei and Philia, and they gave him the good news first. He was overjoyed when Philia told him about his grandchild, but the celebration was overshadowed by the darkness that had settled over everything and what they all knew would come next.

Alexei and Philia walked down to the beach together.

They didn't talk, Alexei holding Philia's hand again, studying the way that it felt in his, and they continued. They were content just to be with each other, because they knew that it couldn't last.

Alexei looked out towards the sea, the islands dotting the distance, the breeze picking up off the water.

And he sighed.

"I wish I could have finished the house," he finally said, breaking the silence between them.

"The house doesn't matter."

"Another month and we could have been close."

"Who needs a house if there's not anyone to live in it."

"Make sure you check on it," Alexei continued. "Maybe once a week. The stone will be fine, but I don't want the wood to dry out too much."

Philia looked down at her hand in Alexei's, at her name set in ink on his wrist, and she rubbed her thumb against it.

"Do you think he'll have your eyes?" she asked him.

"I guess I haven't thought about it."

"You haven't thought about what he'll look like?"

"Have you?"

"My father still has all his hair. That's where the gene comes from . . . the mother's father. So at least he won't have to worry about going bald. Did you hear what happened in Denmark?"

"No," Alexei said. "What happened?"

"Germany went there, too, and before there was any fighting the Danish King surrendered and gave his crown to Hitler's motorcyclist. Before the German troops even came. Before they even tried to fight."

"So?"

"So they're all still alive."

"We're not Denmark."

She stopped walking and turned to look at Alexei—

"Everyone in this country thinks that they can be heroes because we were once. But that was so long ago. We used to rule the world, but that's not our place anymore. That's not who we are now."

"Just because we haven't been heroes for a long time doesn't mean that we can't be again."

"I just wish that it didn't have to be you."

"No, you don't. You don't wish that."

"Yes, I do."

"Then you're not the woman that I know you are."

"How's that?"

"You'd rather be married to a coward? A man that didn't love his country?"

"No."

"So if it wasn't me that left to fight, and others like me, then who would you have go in our place?"

162

"I don't know, someone else. Anyone else. Someone who doesn't have what we have."

"Wars are fought by fathers and husbands, too. Not just childless men with nothing to lose."

They stood there longer.

Alexei thought about the times that he'd been born into, and the strength that he knew now he'd been given, and how all these great events in the world had intruded on them and turned their lives into the same type of lives that he'd only ever read about in books before.

He wondered what it all meant.

Then he saw that Philia was looking up at him. She was looking into his eyes, and the way that the sun and the sea and the clouds reflected off the deep, soft blue that was behind them, and she thought of the first day she met him. And the secret that he kept. Then he held her as close as he could, her head against his chest, his heart beating against her heart.

A pelican cawed in the distance as it dove into the water.

"It's going to be alright," he said.

She was silent for a moment, then she answered him, without taking her head from his chest.

"I hope he has your eyes," she said.

Alexei went to see his parents alone.

He sat at the table with his father, a glass of ouzo in front of each of them. His mother had gone back to their bedroom. This was a conversation between men, she'd said. Though the truth was that she knew she wouldn't be able to keep herself from crying if she'd stayed.

"When did you get taller than me?" she asked Alexei before she left.

"A long time ago, Mana," he said. "When I was ten."

"That's right. What a wonderful summer that was."

"It was the first summer Papa let me fish alone."

"You're right," she said, and she smiled. Then she kissed him on the cheek as Alexei sat down with his father.

They sipped their ouzo.

"They're saying on the radio that the Germans are in Romania," Iannis said, without looking up from his glass. "So I suppose it won't be long now."

"No. It won't."

"And the Bulgarians will join them."

"Yes."

"And then the Italians will come back. So there'll be two fronts when the Germans get here. The Italians coming from Albania again, and the Germans next to them, coming from Bulgaria."

The words hung over everything because they both knew what it meant for Alexei, and what it meant for Greece. Alexei looked at his father, who in that moment looked so frail, so mortal, and he wondered how a boy could have ever looked at him and seen an invincible god.

"What will you do?" Iannis asked him.

"I'll do what they ask me to do."

"So you'll fight again."

"I'm a soldier now, Papa. I have to fight."

They were both silent for a moment, staring down at their hands, and when Alexei looked up and saw his father he knew that he was speaking from his soul now.

"This is a very ancient land that we live in," Iannis said slowly, "but it's also a cursed land. It's a land that's been made fertile with blood that's been spilt for more years than anyone can count, in too many wars that have been wars to end all wars, but there's always another. When does it stop?"

"*The continuation of war is man's religion and his unceasing faith.*"

"What's that?"

"Something I read once. I didn't understand it until now."

"Who wrote it? He speaks like a young man."

"He was a young man. But that doesn't make it less true."

"You have a wife now, Alexei. A family. You can't afford to be a young man anymore."

"Papa..."

"If they come, and you don't fight against them, they won't kill us. They don't care about killing us. They just care about conquering us, since the Italians couldn't, and they want our ports. That's all that this is about. They have no grudge against us."

"You don't believe that."

"How do you know what I believe?"

"Because I'm your son."

"So?"

"We're the same flesh. The same blood."

Iannis was silent for a moment.

It was a very difficult time for him to be so proud of his son, and he chose his next words very carefully, because he knew how important they would be.

"Leave this place, Alexei. I'm begging you now. You've already done more than your part. Take your wife and leave. Go west, go to America, go somewhere untouched by the war that's surely going to destroy this land."

"I can't do that, Papa," Alexei said quietly, looking down at his hands.

"Why?"

"Because this is my home. This is *our* home."

"We're a people too haunted by our own history. Make somewhere else your home. Forget your pride. Just slip away in the night with Philia. No one would ever see you go."

Alexei was silent for a moment, then he spoke in a soft voice—

"No, they wouldn't," he said. "But I would see myself."

Iannis was silent for a long time after that, and when he finally spoke again, Alexei realized that his father was a broken man, and that it was him, his only son, that had broken him. Alexei knew he'd remember the pain he heard in his father's voice for the rest of his life—

"It's Germany now, Alexei. You can't win. You know that, in your heart. It's suicide to fight against them."

"We don't need to win, Papa. That's not what this is about."

Alexei looked up and met his father's eyes—

"We just need to fight."

PART III

"For the sake of historical truth, I must verify that only the Greeks, of all the adversaries who have confronted us, have fought with the boldest courage and highest disregard of death."
—Adolf Hitler, Chancellor of Germany, Speech to the Reichstag on May 4, 1941

"I am sorry, because I am getting old, and I shall not live long enough to thank the Greek people, whose resistance decided WWII. You fought unarmed and won, small against big. We owe you gratitude, because you gave us time to defend ourselves. As Russians and as people we thank you."
—Joseph Stalin, leader of the Soviet Union, in a speech following the victory of Stalingrad

13

March 13th, 1941

THE WAR WOULD BREAK THEM THAT spring.

Alexei and Costa went back north again, the same way that they had before, by train, but this time there was no cheering or celebration at the station when they left. Instead, the platform was filled with old men, and women, and children, and everyone was somber, dressed in dark clothes, crying and embracing loved ones, knowing that there was a great chance that the embraces they shared that day might very well be their last.

No one was speaking.

No one was chanting "*Zito Hellas.*"

Alexei had been to many funerals in his life, but there was nothing he'd ever seen, nothing he'd ever felt that compared to the darkness of that moment. The looks on the faces of the women that stood there on the platform, wishing that there was something they could do, or something that they could say, that would change this tide of men.

But there was nothing.

Alexei was surprised he was able to leave at all.

He kissed his mother first, and held her for too long, her body frail and small against his own. Then he shook his father's hand, unable to meet his eyes, knowing what he would find in them if he dared to look. Then he finally stood in front of Philia. He knelt down and kissed her belly, hoping in that kiss that their child could feel what was in his heart, and that he would carry it to his mother, the words that Alexei couldn't find to bring her comfort, to bring her peace, as she watched her husband go off to war again. Alexei stood and held her one more time, and when he looked down into her eyes, he tried to make her feel the ten thousand *I love you's* that they'd already said, and the ten thousand more that would come as they grew old together.

He looked into her eyes and held her as long as he could.

Further down the platform, Costa was with Thalia.

He knelt in front of Nico and handed him a small package.

"What is it?" the boy asked.

"Open it."

Nico opened the box and took out a pocket-knife: the blade was shiny and polished, the handle carved from imported ivory.

"It's from Athens," Costa told him. "The blade's steel. If you keep it clean it'll never rust."

Nico looked back at Costa with worship and innocence in his young eyes—

"When are you going to come back?" he asked.

"I don't know. That's why I'm giving you the knife. So that you can keep things safe while I'm gone, alright?"

"I will," he said, nodding.

"Bravo."

"*Costa* ..." Thalia said, above them. "He's too young."

"A boy should have a knife."

"He's only eleven."

"It doesn't matter how old he is," Costa said. "It'll be alright. I showed him how to use it. He's responsible." And Costa put his hand on Nico's shoulder as she bit her lip and he stood.

"How is it that you always know what to say to him?"

"Because I was a boy once, too."

"So what about me? Is there no hope?"

"You're his mother. You'll always be everything that's most beautiful to him."

Costa moved his hands to Thalia's hips and pulled her closer to him until they were touching.

"Everyone leaves," Thalia said softly. "Everyone always leaves."

"I'm going to come back."

"I don't know what I'll do without you."

"I do. You'll be strong."

She looked back at him. His voice and his words made her *feel* strong, even if she wasn't sure yet whether she was or wasn't. He bent down and kissed her for as long as he could. Then he looked at Nico standing next to them and he spoke to the boy as he'd speak to another man.

"Make sure you look after your mother, alright?"

"Alright."

"Keep the dirty old men away from her while I'm gone."

"I will," Nico smiled back as Costa ran his hand through the boy's hair one more time, then winked at Thalia, before he turned and found Alexei standing with Philia, not wanting to leave her.

But they both knew that it was time.

The shrill whistle of the train filled the air around the station.

Around them other soldiers said their final farewells to their families, and Alexei and Costa took their place with them, walking across the platform and onto the train, loading the gear that they were carrying into the racks above their seats.

They sat down together.

They looked outside to where Thalia now stood next to Philia and Iannis and Eleni and Giorgos, with Eleni bending down to hand Nico a sweet from her purse, and Alexei's breath caught in his throat at the beauty of what they were leaving behind. He took a picture of that moment in his mind, knowing that wherever he went, whatever he did, whatever happened to him, that moment would never be very far away. The Germans could come, and they could take many things, but they could never take that feeling.

They could never take that beauty.

The ride was long, and nobody spoke the whole way, not even Costa.

The soldiers had been briefed on their destination.

Before he'd died a few weeks earlier, the Prime Minister Metaxas had ordered a fortified line of defenses built across the Bulgarian border. The French had designed a similar system of fortifications along their eastern border—the Maginot Line—and the Germans overran them in the summer of 1940 with an ease that shocked so much of Europe into capitulation. The German plan was to overrun the Greek fortified defenses in the same way, and that was where the Greek Army would make its stand.

All of the soldiers knew the odds.

There was no secret.

And that's also why there were no words spoken.

When they finally arrived in the north, and saw Metaxas' line, they knew how hopeless it really was, and how doomed they were all going to be. The line was hastily built, only a few feet off the ground, and the forts along it were spread too far apart. And the wall itself was too short to do anything except make a man have to step over the top of it, and it didn't even continue the entire length of the mountain range. They realized that it was a wall that was built to be more symbolic than anything else, and not to be able to actually repel the full wrath of Hitler and the Nazis.

Alexei stood with Costa.

Along the length of the line, there were troops that had already started to dig themselves in for what they knew was coming.

"How long do you think until they're here?" Costa asked.

"Nobody's saying."

"Which means it's probably shorter than we all expect."

They looked up and down the line with eyes that had been trained from their time fighting the Italians. They assessed everything.

Their numbers.

The size and length of the wall.

The terrain in front of them.

"We won't last a week up here," Alexei said, putting all

their calculations together. "They'll flank us as soon as they come, and then it'll be over."

"So what the hell are we doing?"

"What we've been ordered to do."

Alexei picked up two shovels and handed one of them to Costa.

"So let's start digging."

They worked hard under the hot sun.

They dug foxholes to shoot from the places where there wasn't any wall. And from the places where there was a wall, they tried to raise the height of it however they could. They dug tank barriers into the hills. They tried to do everything that they could think of, use every trick that they'd learned to make their position as strong as they possibly could in the limited time they had before the mountains and hills in front of them were filled with tanks and soldiers speaking a foreign language and carrying a foreign flag.

They were digging a tank barrier in the valley, creating a shallow trench and burying in the trench triangular pieces of cement pointed upwards—"dragon's teeth," they learned that they were called—when Alexei stopped to wipe the sweat from his brow. He looked around them, into the distance at the mountains with the snow still on their peaks, then down at the sloppy mud and dirt that was under their booted feet, and then Alexei sat heavily on the ground.

"What's the matter?" Costa asked.

"Nothing," Alexei said. "I was just thinking that I don't want to die up here. That's all."

"Did you have somewhere else in mind?"

"*Thalatta*, Costa," Alexei said, echoing the famous Greek word spoken by Xenophon after his impossible march back across Asia had finally come to an end in the sands of Asia Minor. "I want to at least die somewhere where I can smell the sea. The same way that we were born. Not in the mountains. And not in the mud."

"We might not have a choice."

"They're going to overrun us. And when they do, we need to retreat. That's how we'll live."

"*Retreat?*"

"The battle's not going to be fought here. Well, not the *real* battle, at least. They have the artillery. They have the men. But we have the hills, and we have the sea. That's where we'll fight them, after they come pouring over the wall. We'll make them earn every single step they take towards Athens."

"That's good. But we still need to hold them here as long as we can."

"Yes. And we will."

"And then what? The Germans will keep coming."

The sun beat fiercely down on them together—

"Yes. They'll keep coming. And we'll keep fighting."

14

April 6th, 1941

"*Cannon fodder.*"

Those were the words that Costa used to describe what all the Greek soldiers that were manning the walls that spring were going to be, and they all feared that he would be proven right, though regardless of the sense of doom, everyone continued to work hard, just the same.

Whatever happened, in the coming weeks, they'd do the best they could.

Alexei and Costa spent their days working with a group of soldiers to add more "dragon's teeth" next to the holes that they'd already dug in front of the wall, and they hoped that the concrete blocks would do what no other soldiers had yet figured out how to do and at least slow the advance of the German Panzers. They worked every day in the hot sun, both of their shirts off, sweating as they rolled the concrete blocks down the hill and into position.

And they talked as they worked.

"Did you ever think we'd spend so much time in the mountains?" Costa asked, looking around them.

"At least they're Greek mountains."

"I suppose that's true."

"Did you know that there used to be lions up here?"

"Lions?"

"Big ones. As big as the ones in Africa."

"Here in Greece?"

"They're in all the art. Herodotus wrote about them. In the time of Achilles and Odysseus, they used to be everywhere, even out on the islands. Later, by the time of Rome, there were less of them, but they were still up here, in these mountains where Alexander was born. He used to hunt them when he was a boy, with Hephaestion."

"And now?"

"There's none left."

"What happened?"

"The same thing that always happens. They were driven from here by time and by man."

"Better them than us. A bullet's one thing, and it's a quick death. But can you imagine being eaten by a lion?"

"Nero used to feed Christians to his lions in the Coliseum."

"I'm not saying I wouldn't watch. I'm just saying I wouldn't want to be down there with them."

Alexei smiled as they paused from their work and wiped the sweat from their faces. Alexei drank from one of their canteens then poured some of the water over his head before handing it to Costa who did the same. After he drank, they just sat there for a moment, the sun shining through the clouds above them, down on their faces, and they surveyed everything around them where they'd make their stand against the Germans.

"I suppose it's not all worthless. With the high ground we'll be able to take a lot of them with us," Costa said.

"It'll be our Thermopylae, if nothing else," Alexei replied. "They'll make motion pictures about it in America."

"Let's hope not. Thermopylae was a massacre, and everyone died. I want to live."

"I do, too."

"Then what the hell are we doing up here? There's going to be too many of them."

"Because only we, contrary to the barbarians, never count the enemy in battle."

"What's that . . . Shakespeare?"

"Aeschylus."

"Who?"

"Didn't you pay attention to anything in school?"

Everyone in Greece grew up reading the plays of Aeschylus, the greatest of the Greek dramatists, alongside Homer, which is why Alexei knew his friend was joking.

"Girls," Costa said with a smile, as he got back up and started shoveling again, "I paid attention to girls."

They both laughed because it'd been a long day and they knew that it would likely be the last moment for a long time where they'd be able to laugh together. Then they looked out across the mountains to the north.

"When do you think they're going to come?"

"I don't know."

They kept looking out across the mountains—

"I guess we should keep digging then."

It wouldn't be long until they'd receive their answer.

Greek scouts came running back to camp to tell the officers that they'd spotted the first German soldiers approaching their position. It was nighttime, and they could see the moonlight reflected off the metal of the Panzers in the distance as they drove down roads that weren't theirs, and through ancient hills that had seen many foreign armies march through them. Fighting would certainly be coming at dawn, the scouts said. The Germans were just there, in the distance, they waved into the dark, towards the north, and it didn't look like they had any intention of slowing down.

Not a single soldier would sleep that night.

And the Germans came at first light, as the scouts had promised.

The first thing that the Greeks heard was the high-pitched whine of the Luftwaffe planes as they broke through the clouds above them. Alexei looked up and saw the swastikas painted on the tails as they flew overhead. They dropped bombs on the Greek position, but the Greeks didn't return fire, not even as they were rocked by explosions and the first screams of their countrymen began to fill the air. Their bullets were too precious, and they knew they wouldn't pierce the sides of the planes, not at the altitude they were flying.

So they stood their ground as the planes circled back.

And then they felt the ground shake under them.

Costa peered over the top of the section of the wall that they were hiding behind and saw the Panzers climbing the mountains in front of them.

"How many?" Alexei asked him.

"Too many."

"Let's set it up."

They had a 120MM mortar cannon between them that they'd been shown how to aim and fire. Alexei loaded a shell into the barrel while Costa held it in place and made his calculations: it was spring powered, and Costa flexed his muscles as he pulled the trigger down towards the ground, settling on the distance and range that he wanted, and then he let go.

Thunk.

The mortar went flying high overhead and they watched as it sailed through the air and landed on a Panzer—*kaboom!*—and the whole Greek Army cheered as the tank exploded in flames.

"Holy shit."

"I hit it."

"Yeah."

And then from overhead—

Kaboom!! Kaboom!! Kaboom!!

The wall was rocked by bomb blasts from the Luftwaffe that had circled around again, and Alexei and Costa were both blown off their feet and thrown heavily to the ground, their ears ringing, and they looked at their arms and legs and saw that everything was still intact, so they painfully crawled back towards the wall and their cover where their cannon lay behind the barrier.

They started loading it again.

They launched ten mortars and hit three more tanks before the day was over, but their small victories were short-lived because when darkness came the Germans didn't stop their attack. They shelled the Greek position throughout the night, and for the second straight evening none of the Greek soldiers were able to sleep.

Then, dawn came.

And the Germans kept coming.

The Greeks had run out of mortars and artillery so they couldn't stop the Panzers any more. All they had were rifles and pistols and not enough bullets for either. And it was on the second day that the Germans launched their strongest offensive.

Alexei and Costa shared a canteen of water, taking small sips so that their supply would last, their faces caked with dirt and mud and every piece of their bodies aching with pain and exhaustion.

And then there were more explosions.

Kaboom kaboom kaboom!!!

More screams filled the air.

Costa looked down the wall to his right and saw part of it get blown away by a tank blast, and then there were German soldiers with swastikas patched onto their arms pouring through the breach.

Costa grabbed his rifle, about to fire, when—

"Costa!"

He heard Alexei shout and turned back to see more German soldiers coming at them, over the wall, directly on top of where they were. One of them raised his rifle, taking aim at a Greek soldier, but—

Bang!

Alexei dropped him with a single shot as another German launched himself from the wall to tackle Alexei.

Costa ran towards them.

Alexei rolled on the ground with the German as his

adversary pulled a knife and Alexei struggled against him. The larger German was quickly overpowering him—he got a punch in to Alexei's face—then raised his hand that was holding the knife.

Costa knew he had no other choice.

He dropped to one knee and took aim—

Bang!

The shot found its mark and the German's head exploded in bright pieces of bone and flesh across Alexei's face.

"Are you alright?"

"Yeah?"

"Are you sure? You're covered in blood."

"It's not mine."

Costa looked further down the wall to where more Germans had breached the defenses and the Greeks were fighting back. There were more German bodies than Greek that lay in the mud.

Then, the Greeks let up a cheer.

The Germans were retreating.

"Come on," Costa said.

And they crawled towards their part of the wall. They peered over to see the German soldiers running back to hide behind the safety of their tanks, and Costa and Alexei loaded their rifles.

Bang bang bang!

They shot Germans in the back as they ran.

Bang bang!

More Germans fell.

Soon, the rest of the German soldiers that had survived all made it back behind the Panzers, and out of range, and then they retreated further back down the hill. Alexei and

Costa were breathing heavily. They were covered in even more dirt, and mud, and blood.

But they were alive.

They smiled.

They'd beaten the odds, once again, and they'd won the day.

That night Costa built a small fire.

They sat around it at their section of the wall and other soldiers came to warm their hands. In those mountains it was hot days and cold nights, and so the fire was especially welcome, even though every hour the Germans would lob more shells at their position to make sure that no one slept for another night.

And then, when the dawn came again, more death came with it.

The Germans attacked at first light, and their offensive was stronger this time, reinforced by more troops that had made their way from the north, the full force of the German war machine bearing down on Greece now.

For twenty-four hours there wasn't a single moment not marked by a violent explosion. The air smelled of burnt powder and putrid flesh. The dragon's teeth and pits that the Greeks had dug stopped the tanks temporarily, but without any mortars or artillery left, Alexei knew that it wouldn't last for very much longer. Every so often they cautiously peered over the wall and fired their rifles whenever they could see a German. They didn't hit many, but they kept the German soldiers pinned behind their tanks and below the position the Greeks were holding at the Line.

At least for the moment.

"Look," Costa said.

"What?"

"There."

They looked over the wall to see a company of Germans running across the battlefield. They nodded and jumped up along with the other Greek soldiers next to them.

Bang bang bang!

They fired at the Germans as they ran, and two of them stumbled and fell. They were reloading, when—

Bang!

A shot rang out and the soldier next to Alexei flew backwards, lifted off his feet, and Alexei looked down and saw the bullet in his skull.

"Get down!"

Alexei grabbed Costa and pulled him to the ground.

"What happened?"

"They've got a sniper."

"Where?"

"I don't know."

"We have to find him."

"We barely have any ammo left. Let's just stay down for awhile."

Costa bit his lip, then he saw something—

"What's that?"

Alexei followed Costa's eyes to where he was looking in the distance. There were more German soldiers behind them where there shouldn't have been German soldiers.

Then the air exploded in gunfire—

Bang bang bang bang bang!!!

"Shit!" Costa and Alexei swung their rifles around along with the rest of the Greek Army to fire on the new enemy that was somehow behind them now, too.

But it wasn't going to be a battle.

Because it was already a slaughter.

Alexei saw a Greek commander giving the orders for surrender as Greeks were being cut down everywhere, the brown mud turning red and sticky underneath their feet.

"Down!" Alexei yelled to Costa.

"What?" Costa yelled back, his ears ringing from the guns and the canons.

"Put your rifle down!" Alexei said. "It's over!"

Costa either couldn't hear him or he just didn't care so he kept shooting at the Germans until Alexei grabbed the rifle from his hand and threw it to the ground as far away from them as he could.

"What the hell are you doing?" Costa yelled.

"Look around! It's over! They've taken the wall!"

Costa looked to see the Greeks dropping their arms and putting their hands in the air. He was breathing heavily. This wouldn't be easy for him. It wouldn't be easy for any of them.

He slowly put his hands in the air, and Alexei did the same.

Soon the whole army had surrendered and the gunfire stopped.

"We could have held them longer. We pushed them back yesterday. We could have held our ground."

"They were just waiting, I think, because they knew that the rest of them were behind us."

"How'd they get behind us?"

"I don't know."

Five Germans soldiers walked towards them.

They pointed their rifles at Alexei and Costa and yelled something in German that neither of them could understand.

"Surrender," Alexei said in English, the universal language of war.

He gestured towards their weapons that were on the ground in the distance, and repeated himself, saying "surrender" again. The Germans understood now, and the one who was their leader nodded towards them.

"Surrender," he repeated.

The Greek survivors were herded into the middle of their camp.

Alexei and Costa watched as their general Konstantinos Bakopoulos met with the German Field Marshall in front of both armies. Bakopoulos stood before the German, bowing and formally surrendering their position. Alexei looked next to him and saw the bodies of his countrymen lying where they'd fallen, not very far from where Bakopoulos now stood, and Alexei couldn't stop staring at all the lifeless faces around him.

Next to him, a soldier was crying.

And then more soldiers started to weep.

Alexei was nineteen years old, and it was the first time that he'd ever seen grown men cry, and he cried with them.

The German Field Marshall turned to the Greek survivors.

He told them in a loud voice how bravely they'd fought. He told them how he'd already marched through all of Europe and fought against every type of soldier that had stood in his way, and the Greeks were the only adversaries that hadn't panicked and broken their lines when the Luftwaffe had flown overhead of them. He told them with truth in his eyes and the tenor of his voice that of anyone the Germans had fought against, the Greeks were the most fierce, the most courageous, and the most noble of them all. And he told them that their courage would be rewarded, and that the Germans had respect for the pride of Greece.

Alexei and Costa looked at each other.

They wondered what that meant.

Then the Field Marshall gave an order and the German soldiers came forward to inspect the Greek survivors. They were all exhausted, their skin caked with dried blood and dirt, and Alexei and Costa watched as the Germans walked down their lines, passing over each soldier they walked in front of until they came to one in particular and started to roughly haul him away.

"What are they doing?" Costa asked.

Alexei knew the soldier they'd pulled out. He remembered talking to him while they worked on the wall, before the Germans came. They'd been digging the pits, their shirts off, and Alexei remembered the Star of David that he wore around his neck.

"Take your cross out," Alexei said.

"What?"

"Your cross."

"Why?"

"Just do it."

Even in 1941 the whole world had heard the rumblings across the continent about the Germans and the racial war that they'd waged on their own people and the people that they'd conquered. Alexei reached under his shirt and took out the orthodox cross that every Greek wears on a gold chain around his neck, and Costa did the same.

Alexei let his cross hang on the front of his uniform.

His cross had belonged to his father, and Iannis had given it to him when he was thirteen years old, and had told Alexei to wear it until he had a son of his own, and when his son turned thirteen he'd give it to him in the same way.

Alexei hadn't asked any questions, he'd just nodded.

The Germans pulled out five more Greek soldiers before they reached Alexei and Costa. When the Germans stood in front of them, Alexei and Costa watched as they examined their ears and noses. They saw Alexei and Costa's clear, sapphire eyes, their fair skin, their soft features, and the crosses that hung around their necks.

"Good," the German said in accented English, patting them firmly on the chest. "Very good."

Three more Greek soldiers were pulled and sent towards the German lines. The rest of the Greek soldiers were held as prisoners for seven days until word came from Hitler himself that the Greeks were to be treated with the utmost respect. On his orders, the Greek officers were given their side-arms back, and the rest of the Greek soldiers were released and given a crust of bread and allowed to leave the mountains and go back home in peace. Hitler respected the way the Greeks had fought, he said, and he thought that the Greeks had been broken now, and that like everywhere else he'd conquered, they would submit to his occupation without any further question or struggle, but he'd underestimated them. He saw their courage and their pride in the history of the land that they fought for and defended, but he didn't recognize just how deep it went, and how far they'd go.

He didn't realize the Greek resistance was only just beginning.

15

April 10th, 1941

I T DIDN'T TAKE LONG FOR NEWS to reach Agria.
Philia was at home when she heard. Her father had
tuned the radio and she listened to the broadcast describing
the Greek defeat and how the Germans had overrun the
Metaxas Line and her breath went from her and she had to
sit down. She asked her father what it meant, and he told
her that the Germans would now make their way south,
and soon they'd be in Agria. It was a port, and a good one,
and the Germans needed as many Mediterranean ports as
they could take.

And so soon Agria would cease to be a free city in a free
land.

The worst thing, though, Giorgos told her, wouldn't be
the loss of freedoms, but the lack of food: the Germans
honored wartime conditions for the enemies that they
respected, and they had all heard how Hitler had respected
the Greeks in their bravery fighting and beating the
Italians, and how their soldiers didn't cower before the
Luftwaffe like every other German opponent had, but even

with that respect, when an army occupies a city, they take all the food.

"What about Alexei?" Philia asked.

Giorgos told her that any soldiers that survived would be taken prisoner, and they'd be held by the Germans until they decided what to do with them.

Would they release them?

Giorgos didn't have that answer.

But he could tell that no matter what he said, his daughter was going to hold on to hope that one day soon she'd wake up and see her husband walking down the small dirt road that they'd walked down together so many times, coming back to her, bloody from the war and perhaps wounded, too, but still alive and still whole and still hers.

Soldiers soon came to Agria, as Giorgos said they would.

But when Giorgos walked out of his house to see the soldiers marching past, he saw that it was the British who had arrived before the Germans did.

They were bloody.

They were covered in dirt.

But they were proud, and they still marched with their heads held high.

Giorgos told Philia to stay in the house, and he followed the soldiers as they marched straight down to the harbor. The merchants of Agria that kept their boats in the city watched as the British came to take them. They protested, Giorgos among them, but how much could they protest against armed men with rifles pointed at them?

The British officer came forward to explain.

They'd fought the Germans at Thessaloniki, and their lines had broken there, and the Germans came flooding into the city and then up into the mountains *behind* the

190

Greek Army fighting at the Metaxas Line, which is what had finally broken the Greek ranks, and won the day for the Germans.

So the surviving British made their way south.

Their orders from Churchill were to evacuate to Crete at any cost. They'd keep fighting from there, he promised, they'd continue helping the cause by keeping the Germans pinned in Greece for as long as they could, but Churchill wanted his men to avoid the slaughter that was now sure to come to the mainland.

That was why they needed the boats.

So the men of Agria could do nothing but watch as the British loaded everything they could and sailed out of the harbor, and once they were a ways out, they turned and headed south, towards Crete and the islands.

Philia didn't listen to her father.

She left the house and walked the dirt road to town. But before she left, she went upstairs to where Giorgos kept a large pile of drachmae for any emergencies that might arise and she took all the money. If food was going to be as scarce as her father had told her that it was going to be, she'd find whatever was available for her to buy.

But the agora was empty again that day.

Stores were locked up.

The taverna was closed.

She looked down towards the harbor where Giorgos and the other men were watching their ships sail into the distance. She felt the large sum of money in her pocket that she'd taken from their house, knowing that before all this it could have bought her half the city. But now money was useless because you can't eat gold or paper. It was amazing, she thought, the way that things can change. Her father, who had once been the richest man in the city, had been reduced to the stature of a commoner in a matter of a few hours.

Everyone in Agria was the same now.

"Philia?"

She turned, when she heard her name, to see Thanos standing behind her, the baker who'd given her and Alexei sweets on her first day in Agria.

"How are you, dear?" he asked with a smile.

"I don't recognize my own village," she answered, with a sad look.

"Neither do I," Thanos said. "And I've lived here longer than you have. Much longer. What brings you into town?"

"I came to see if I could buy any food," she gestured around them. "And I think I've gotten my answer."

"No. There's been no answer. Not yet, at least. Let's see what we can find around here."

"But everything's closed."

"Not everything," he smiled. "Follow me."

She followed Thanos down to his stall at the end of the agora and watched as he opened the small door and went inside. He came back moments later with a small package wrapped in waxpaper and carefully tied around the top, and he handed it to her.

"Thanos . . . no."

"Take it."

"I couldn't."

"For the daughter-in-law of my greatest friend? Of course you could. It would be my honor."

"There's not going to be anything left soon."

"You're going to need to eat if the small one's going to

grow up strong enough to haul in the nets like his father and his grandfather," Thanos said, smiling at Philia's belly.

"News travels fast."

"Only the good news," the old man said. "Good news certainly travels the fastest."

"Let me at least pay you," she said, taking the money out of her pocket, but he stopped her, his fingers wrapping around hers, holding her hand closed before she could offer him anything.

"No, dear," he said. "But you should go home now. It won't be long before the rest of them are here."

"I will," she nodded.

"It was good to see you," he smiled. "Say hello to your father for me."

He turned and started to walk away, and Philia watched him go, rooted to the same spot, moved by this old man's kindness.

"Thanos ..."

He stopped and turned back to her—

"*Efkaristo*," she said, and meant the word more than she'd ever meant it before. "Thank you."

"He's going to be alright up there," Thanos said with a nod of reassurance that made her somehow believe that he and he alone knew the truth about Alexei.

"I've prayed for it," she said.

And then, with one last smile, and a last nod, Thanos turned and continued on his way to wherever it was that he was going. Philia stood and watched until he was gone, and she couldn't see him any more.

Then she looked around.

She was alone in Agria.

She sighed as she turned and finally started on her way

back to her house. She'd think about that day many years later, and smile when she did, because if nothing else, she'd always know that she'd lived in a town full of good people.

That night Philia sat with her father at their great oak table.

She told him what she'd seen in town, and Giorgos said nothing, and she knew that he'd seen it, too. She unwrapped the neatly tied package from Thanos and set four pieces of perfectly made baklava on the table. Giorgos had calculated that depending when the Germans came, they'd have enough food to be comfortable for about a week, and enough to stay alive for two, as long as they hid some of it so that it wouldn't be included in the rations that the Germans would surely levy from the people. She knew all of this as she watched her father stare down at the baklava in front of them.

"We'll keep two of them, and take the other two to Iannis," Giorgos said. Philia looked up at her father, and he added simply, "They're our family now, too. And we honor that."

"Of course," she said, smiling, and glad of his decision.

She stood and walked to the kitchen to find something to wrap the two pieces in to take them to Alexei's parents. She found an old newspaper and carefully set the sweets inside and pulled the edges of paper around them. Then she walked to the door, about to leave, when her father spoke again from behind her, from where he still sat at the great oak table, staring ahead at nothing in particular.

"Philia ..."

She turned back to look at him.

"Yes, Papa?"

Then she saw his eyes, and the darkness in them—
"Hurry back, alright?"

Philia felt the Germans before she saw them.

Iannis had been out fishing so Philia sat and had a cup
of strong dark coffee with Eleni. Neither of them said much
that afternoon, but they found comfort in each other's
company, because they were two women who were both
praying for the same thing. Eleni was looking at Philia's
ring, resting there on the table, and as she looked at it on
Philia's finger, she realized that it was the first time that
she'd smiled since her son had left.

"Iannis will be sorry that he missed you."

"I can come back again tomorrow."

"Only if you want to, dear. You really don't need to
worry about us. We'll be just fine."

"It's not a problem. I can't stay in the house all day long
waiting. I'll go crazy. I need to get out and stretch my legs."

"It's the baby that makes you restless. It was the same
when I was pregnant with Alexei. Just wait . . . in a few
months, it'll do the opposite, and you'll be so glad to be off
your feet."

Philia was quiet with her thoughts again, and Eleni
watched her.

"What is it, dear? What's the matter?"

"I was thinking about when I was in town earlier."

"What about it?"

"Nothing, it's just . . . a town without young men is a
very strange thing."

"They'll be back before any of us know it."

"I hope you're right."

"I know that I'm right."

"How?"

"Because I've asked God for it."

They were silent together for another moment, and then Philia finished her coffee and stood—

"Thank you for the coffee," she said.

"Thank you for coming all the way down here. The baklava looks delicious. I'm glad that you ran into Thanos."

"He's a good man."

"They all are, aren't they? All the men that we have here in our little town. It's the sea breeze, you know. It keeps them calm. It keeps them calm, and it keeps them good."

Eleni walked her to the door and Philia left.

And then, when Philia was some ways down the road, to a point where the mountains opened and she could see into the distance, north across the low rolling hills, she heard the first rumbling. At first, she thought, it was an earthquake, until she remembered that she was living in a nation that was at war now, and that's when she knew what it really was.

She looked across the hills.

Then in the distance, the first German Panzers crested the peaks in front of her. She kept watching and saw the German infantry soldiers in their grey-dark uniforms following behind the tanks.

She was frozen.

Rooted to the spot where she'd stopped.

The sight in front of her was like nothing she'd ever seen before.

She watched the lines and lines of soldiers and tanks and artillery and kubelwagen jeeps that seemed to last as far as the horizon itself. The enemies of Greece were finally here, and they were marching in a long and steady stream south towards her home. She continued to watch as they got closer—close enough for her to be able to read the numbers on the sides of the tanks, and see the swastikas—and when she heard the buzz of the Luftwaffe overhead it finally broke her from the moment that had cast its spell over her.

She remembered what her father had said.

"Hurry home."

So she cast one last glance over her shoulder, then turned and pulled her skirt up over her knees as she began to run, silently whispering a prayer as she went to any God, new or ancient, that might still be listening.

16

April 13th, 1941

THERE WAS A LIGHT SNOW THAT swirled through the mountains the day the Greek soldiers were released. It was late in the season for snow, even at the elevation that they were being held, and so many men considered it to be an omen of sorts, though an omen of what no one knew.

There was no great ceremony.

One day the Greek soldiers were being kept under guard in their camp, and the next they learned that the Germans had received orders from Hitler and they were to be released. Before they left, the Germans took their rifles and told them that if they didn't pick up any more firearms they wouldn't be treated as enemy combatants, but rather as citizens of an occupied nation, the same as the rest of Europe. The Greeks smiled and nodded and the Germans didn't know what was behind those smiles.

Alexei and Costa left together.

They headed south, the same as everyone else, and with no other choice in front of them but to walk.

"Do you think the Germans will keep their word?" Costa asked.

"I don't know. They could have just killed us. That's what they did to the French. They didn't have to let us go."

"How are we going to get home?" Costa looked around them. "The train will be closed, of course. The Germans will be using it for supplies and for men, the same as we did. And the roads, too."

"So I guess that leaves us our feet," Alexei said.

"I was hoping you weren't going to say that."

"What were you hoping I was going to say?"

"That you had another idea. A smart idea that was going to get us back to Agria much quicker."

"There's no other way."

Alexei stopped and studied the hills in front of them, the landscape and terrain that they'd have to cross, and Costa watched his friend curiously as he studied the distance—

"We have to run."

"What?"

"Like we used to, every morning. We'll get home three times as fast as if we walk. And we can keep going through the night, too."

"Are you serious?"

"Think about what we're going back to," Alexei said. "And think about what it means. They held us for seven days, which means that the Germans are already at Agria, and that also means that there's going to be Nazis sleeping in Philia's house, in my parents' house, in Thalia and Nico's house. They'll be sleeping in our beds. Next to our families. In our city."

Costa watched as Alexei started stripping off his jacket

and all the unnecessary clothing that he wasn't going to need in the warmer weather to the south.

"You're right," Costa said, nodding. "We have to get back as quickly as we can. Thank God we're fast. That's good at least."

"Nobody we know would be able to run it quicker."

Costa took his jacket off, too, and any other clothes that he wouldn't need, and left them on the ground.

"Ready?" Alexei asked his friend. "Because it looks like our war's about to begin."

"Ready," Costa answered.

They nodded at each other once more with dark and worried eyes, then they started to run south, over the rolling hills in front of them, keeping a stiff pace that they hoped would soon bring them home.

They came to the hills outside Kozani on the second day.

They'd kept a steady pace running through the first afternoon and night, watching the morning sun rise in the east, but they needed food. They saw the town in the distance, but they didn't want to risk approaching it in case the Germans had stopped there, and left a garrison.

Then they saw a large farm in front of them.

It was an old but proud farmhouse, made of wood and stone, with a stucco roof, set on a wide expanse of land in the hills around the city, and there was a low barn behind the property.

They slowed their run to a walk as they came to it.

"What do you think?" Alexei asked.

"It looks abandoned."

"That'd be good if it was."

They made their way down the road to the front door.

As they got closer, they saw no signs of the family that lived there.

"Do you think they left?" Alexei asked.

"I don't know."

"If they're here, what are we going to say?"

"That we're soldiers coming from the front, and we're looking for any food that they might be able to spare."

Alexei felt an uneasiness in the depths of his stomach, but he knew that they had to risk it, because they couldn't go much longer without anything to eat.

Costa knocked on the door.

They waited but no one answered.

Alexei looked around until he spotted tangled vines of grapes planted in neat, orderly lines along the hillside behind the barn, set to face the sunrise so they could get as much light as possible during the growing season.

"Look," he said.

"What?"

"Grapes."

"So?"

"Let's take some and leave. There's nobody here."

"Where do you think they went?"

"Maybe south. Maybe the Germans killed them. Who knows, let's just take some grapes and go."

"Don't you want more than that?"

"Like what?"

"Like whatever they've left behind. We can't make it all the way home on just grapes."

Before Alexei could protest any further, Costa pushed the door open and went inside: the floorboards creaked as he made his way into the house and went to the living room, looking around.

"Hello?" Costa said, waiting for a response. "Is there anyone here?"

Silence.

"It doesn't look like it," Alexei said from his place behind Costa, whispering in case the owner of the house was there waiting with a rifle, not caring which army the soldiers standing in his house fought for or against.

Costa kept walking.

"Where are you going?"

"The kitchen."

They went through the dining room and then a study and down a hallway, eventually coming to the kitchen tucked away in the back of the house with a panoramic view facing the mountains. Then they saw the dining table and there was a neatly prepared meal that had been laid out—a hastily made moussaka with fresh bread, olive oil and an assorted plate of small green Amfissa olives sprinkled with feta.

"It's like they knew that we were coming," Costa said as he walked towards the meal, popping the olives into his mouth. Alexei went to the loaf of bread and held his hand over it.

"What's the matter?" Costa asked, seeing the look on Alexei's face.

"It's still warm."

"Shit."

They both knew what that meant—

"Let's just take what we can carry and get out of here."

"Alright," Costa nodded.

He went to the counter and grabbed the bread as Alexei quickly wrapped two pieces of moussaka in an old newspaper on the table, and as soon as they were done they went back down the hallway and through the study again towards the front door where they'd entered.

Then, just as they were almost to the door, ready to walk out—

Click, click.

"*Stoppen,*" a voice said behind them.

They turned to find a group of German soldiers with pistols pointed at them, the soft clicks that they heard the hammers being cocked back and ready. Alexei and Costa didn't speak German, but they didn't need to in order to know what the soldiers were telling them.

They put their hands in the air.

The Germans said something else that Alexei and Costa didn't understand, and Costa shook his head as he answered them.

"*Nein. No sprechen sie Deutsch. English, maybe?*"

The German Leader stepped forward.

"No English," he said. "But I speak Greek. Where are your weapons?"

"We don't have any," Alexei said. "We're coming from the front. They took them before they let us go."

"I see," the German Leader responded with a look that was hard for them to read. "And you haven't picked any up along the way?"

"No. They told us not to. We're just trying to make our way back home."

"There are Greeks still fighting in these hills."

"Not us."

"And where is home for you?"

"Agria. To the south."

"Ah. I know of your home. A very beautiful city by the sea."

"That's right. How do you know Greek?"

"I studied Classics before the war, at the *Universitat Berlin*, the greatest university in the world."

"What a coincidence," Costa said. "Alexei studies Classics, too. On his own time mostly, though. He's very strange."

"You talk too much," the German Leader said, a look of contempt on his face as he studied Costa. "In Germany we say that is the sign of a small mind."

"Then I guess everyone in Greece is stupid."

The German Leader motioned to two of his soldiers and they pushed Alexei and Costa in front of them.

"Let's go."

"What?"

"Out back. There's something I want to show you."

"We told you we don't have any guns."

"I know. And that's very good."

The Germans led Alexei and Costa through the kitchen and out the back door, their pistols still trained sharply on them as Alexei and Costa kept their hands over their head and went outside.

The Germans pushed them towards the barn, and as they got closer they were hit by a putrid and rotting smell. Then they saw a large hole. There were flies swarming above it.

The German Leader smiled as they saw it.

"Go on," he said. "Walk to the edge, and then *stoppen*."

There were guns pointed at Alexei and Costa and so there was nothing else they could do except what he asked. They went to the edge and when they looked down they saw the mutilated bodies of the farmer, his wife, and their three sons.

"What did you do?" Alexei asked, a look of horror on his face.

"They resisted," the German responded evenly, allowing himself no emotion, no pleasure or remorse, just a man going about his day.

"They told us that Hitler said civilians weren't to be killed," Alexei said. "And that the soldiers that were released from the front were to be given safe passage back to their homes if we laid down our arms."

"You're right. The Fuhrer did say that. But do you see the Fuhrer here?" the German smiled broadly. "No. There's only Jurgen here. And Jurgen knows the truth of war . . . that every unarmed Greek soldier that he kills is one less Greek soldier that can pick up arms to fight against Germany again. Killing you might save one of my friend's lives. Killing you might even save Jurgen's life."

"And what about honor?"

"What about it?"

"You murdered these people. Those are just kids in there."

"It's war," he said with a shrug. "Many terrible things happen. Sometimes even to small children."

Then Jurgen pulled the pistol from his waist and cocked the hammer back, pointing it at Alexei and Costa as they stood at the edge of the pit, facing the Germans.

"They did do one thing for you," Jurgen said. "They've already dug the hole. They did save you that. They were very tired when they died. To go that way, it looked very … *unpleasant.*"

Alexei and Costa looked at each other.

Then Costa reached out and held Alexei's arm.

If they fell, at least they'd fall together. If they died, at least they'd die together.

But Alexei wasn't ready.

There was still so much left.

Jurgen walked towards them, his finger hovering over his trigger, just as Alexei found his voice—

"Wait," he said.

"What is it?"

"Can I say a prayer first?"

"Is it very important to you?"

"Yes."

"Fine, then. Make it quick."

Jurgen holstered his pistol and took out a cigarette.

One of his men was quick to pull a lighter from his pocket, shielding the flame against the wind with his hand as he lit his superior's cigarette in a gesture that Jurgen liked very much.

Alexei bent over, reaching down towards his boot when Jurgen raised his gun again towards him.

"What are you doing?"

"I'm getting my cross."

"You don't wear it around your neck?"

"I put it in my boot to keep it safe. When we were at the front."

Jurgen waited for a moment, then he nodded and went back to his cigarette, inhaling and blowing smoke through his lips, as Alexei's eyes caught Costa's. Costa knew that Alexei wore his cross around his neck. That he never took it off. Which meant that Costa also knew what Alexei was about to do.

Alexei reached into his boot and felt cold steel.

It was the German Luger that his father had given him,

that he'd kept with him through all these months of war, as if it were a part of him.

Costa tensed next to him.

Jurgen still smoked his cigarette.

Then Alexei whipped the gun out of his boot and—

Bang bang!

Two bullets ripped into Jurgen's chest.

The other German soldiers whipped their guns up, but—

Bang bang bang!

Three more German soldiers fell.

There was only one left.

Costa dove towards the remaining soldier and tackled him to the ground. They struggled against each other as the German's gun slipped out of his grasp, both of them reaching for it in the dirt, just past their outstretched fingertips, when—

Bang!

The German's head snapped back, and he lay still on the ground, Costa's face covered in strange and foreign blood. Alexei walked over and pulled Costa to his feet and he brushed himself off.

Then Alexei turned back to Jurgen.

He walked to where he was laying on the ground, the two bullets having pierced his chest, and he was breathing in short, painful gasps, and Alexei didn't need to be a doctor or know much about anatomy to know that the bullets had punctured his lungs.

There was blood speckled on his lips.

He was crawling painfully through the dirt, trying to reach the spot where his gun had fallen, but Alexei came to him first and when he stomped down on the German's hand he screamed in pain. Alexei kicked him across the mouth and saw several teeth break loose.

Jurgen lay on the ground a slobbering mess.

He finally turned himself over and looked up at Alexei.

"*You said . . . you didn't . . . have any weapons,*" he said weakly through the blood that was pooling in his mouth.

"I lied," Alexei said.

"*You . . . lied?*" It seemed to surprise him.

"It's war," he answered. "Many terrible things happen. Sometimes even to German officers."

Then Alexei brought his pistol up so that it was only inches from Jurgen's skull. There was one shot left in it. The German saw that it was a Luger that was going to take his life, and he almost smiled.

"Good craftsmanship," he said.

"You deserve worse."

"I suppose God will decide that."

Bang!

The German's head snapped back, and then he lay still, and the farm was quiet again. Costa came to stand next to Alexei, and they looked down at the bodies at their feet.

"You hit all your shots."

"We've gotten better at killing."

Then, in the distance, they heard something.

A deep rumbling, and an explosion.

They waited and there was another one, and then another, and then another still. They walked to the edge of the farm and when they looked out across the valley they saw an entire German Panzer division approaching Kozani, lobbing shells into the streets as they came. They could hear the screams in the city, even at the distance that they were standing.

"That's the whole 9th Division down there," Costa said squinting his eyes as he looked towards the battle.

"We have to go," Alexei said.

He walked among the German corpses, and Costa watched as he took their guns from them now, tucking the pistols into his belt, slinging a rifle across his back, filling his pockets with their ammo.

"What are you doing?" Costa asked.

Alexei grabbed another rifle and tossed it to Costa.

"Take as much as you can carry."

"They'll kill us if they see us with rifles."

"I think we've seen that they'll kill us either way," Alexei said. "And I'd rather take some of them with me."

Costa hesitated, but he knew that Alexei was right, so he bent down with him to search the Germans for anything else that might be useful. When they had as much as they could carry, Alexei looked over to the pit where the farmer's body lay with his family.

Then he walked to the barn and returned with a can of fuel.

"Gasoline?" Costa asked.

"We don't have time to bury them."

"No. Not if we want to stay ahead of the Germans."

"So we'll do it the ancient way."

Costa watched as Alexei poured the gasoline in the hole that the farmer had dug, covering their bodies, soaking through their clothes. Then after he'd doused them, he set the can down and went to one of the German soldiers and searched through his pockets until he found the lighter that he'd used to light Jurgen's cigarette.

He took the lighter and walked to the edge of the hole. He looked below him, and then after a solemn moment and an urgent, whispered prayer, he sparked the lighter and dropped it into the hole and watched as the bodies caught fire and flames quickly spread, consuming innocent flesh.

"It's time to go," Alexei said, his eyes not leaving the flames.

"What about them?" Costa gestured towards the German bodies in the dirt behind them.

Alexei turned to look at the faces of their enemies, on the ground behind them, frozen in death. Nothing about him changed as he looked at the bodies. His voice was steady when he spoke.

"Leave them to rot," he said.

And then they turned and left.

17

April 14th, 1941

F ood.

It was all Giorgos could think about.

The first thing that the Germans did when they reached Agria was go through every house and take every last bit of food that they could find. Feeding an army isn't easy, and there's no better way to subjugate a city than to break the people by weakening them with hunger, and so Giorgos knew now that his only job was to find a way to feed his daughter and the grandchild that she was carrying. He hadn't been a desperate man in some time now, but in his heart he was still a boy from the streets—in his heart he was still hungry, as he'd always been—and now he was afraid again, too.

He didn't push the feelings away.

He knew he'd need them again now.

It was afternoon when Giorgos stood outside with Philia and watched an armored kubelwagen jeep with a red swastika painted across the hood drive to their house. The doors opened and soldiers got out, and the commanding officer, a tall German with slick blond hair and piercing blue eyes, came forward until he was standing in front of Giorgos. There was a polished Knight's Cross hanging from his neck where a tie would have been for a gentleman, and Giorgos knew that this denoted him as a Nazi of distinguished deed or rank.

"Is this your house?" the German asked Giorgos.

"Yes."

"It's very large."

"Surely not as large as many in Germany."

"No. But we're not in Germany." The officer looked around, taking in the rest of the grounds. "The Fuhrer has issued a decree that any food in your possession belongs to us. Do you understand?"

"All of our food?"

"Yes. Everything."

"What will we eat?"

"That's not the Fuhrer's problem. You have two mouths to feed. He has an entire army, and much of Europe now."

Giorgos knew there was no choice, so he nodded—

"I'll gather what we have."

"No. You'll stay here with me. My men will go in and have a look around themselves."

Giorgos bowed his head—

"Of course."

The German Officer nodded, and his men walked past them and into the house, heading to the kitchen to take any food they could find, or anything else that they wanted.

The German Officer stayed outside with Giorgos and Philia.

"My name is Meinhard," he said, extending his hand to Giorgos.

"Giorgos," he said, and they shook.

"And who is this?"

"My daughter."

"She's very beautiful," he said, his eyes scanning every inch of Philia's body, and she didn't wilt under the practiced gaze that he'd developed to discipline and intimidate his soldiers.

"Yes, she is."

"You must be very proud of her."

"I am. As proud as a father could be."

Meinhard looked at her for another moment, then he turned back to the house.

"Is this the largest house in Agria?" he asked.

"I don't know. It might be. There might be others that are larger."

"You're being modest. We've already seen most of Agria, and some of Volos, and it is not a very rich place, is it? At least not compared to Germany, as you've said. This is the largest house in the city," he said, nodding his head, as if he was convincing himself.

Behind him the men came back out, carrying boxes of all the food they could carry, and they started piling it in the back of the jeep. Giorgos watched with a blank look. It wasn't as if he hadn't expected it.

Then Meinhard spoke again.

"We'll be staying here in your city for the foreseeable future," he said. "So we'll be housing soldiers in your people's houses."

"I've heard."

"I like your big house," he said. "It's much too big for a regular infantryman, and your daughter is too beautiful for the company of a common soldier. So I think I'll stay here."

Giorgos swallowed.

Then Meinhard turned to Philia, and his eyes didn't leave hers.

"I have business to attend to in the city," he said. "And then I'll be back tonight. See to it that you make your house presentable for an officer of the Reich. I'll take the largest bedroom."

"Of course," Giorgos nodded.

Meinhard stayed staring at Philia for another moment, and she held his gaze as only a woman of her strength could, and he liked that. Then, when he was sure that she knew his intentions, and what he wanted, he turned and walked back to the jeep, where his men waited for him.

Giorgos and Philia watched them drive away, and they both knew that there was nothing that could be done except what he'd told them. They went back into the house together to see everything that they owned thrown onto the floors and destroyed, and every piece of food that they had was gone. They stood there together, the war finally touching them in a way that it hadn't until that moment, and Giorgos put his arm around his daughter's shoulders.

"It's going to be alright," he told her.

"How do you know that?"

"I'm your father, so at least let me say it."

"And then what? Now that you've said it?"

"Go upstairs and get my room ready for him. Change the sheets and take anything valuable and bring it back down here. We'll bury it in the backyard until they leave."

"I can help you here."

"Save your energy. You're going to need it."

"Papa ..."

"You need to save your strength."

"I'm fine."

"I know you're fine. It's my grandson that I'm worried about."

He leaned down and gave Philia a kiss on the forehead, and then she finally nodded and he grabbed a bristled broom and a bag to use for the trash. Philia glanced at her father one more time as he started to clean the kitchen, his proud shoulders slumped as he began to sweep, and with a heavy heart she left him and went upstairs to do as he'd asked and prepare his bedroom for a German officer.

Meinhard came back that night, as he'd promised he would.

Giorgos saw the lights of his vehicle flash through their windows and he looked to Philia—

"Go to bed."

"What?"

"Now. Go to your room and lock the door."

Philia didn't argue. She stood and went upstairs to do as her father had told her. Giorgos waited until she was gone, then he went to the door to greet Meinhard. As soon as he looked at the German, and saw his eyes and the way that he was walking, Giorgos could tell that he was drunk. And Giorgos had seen the way that he'd looked at Philia earlier, and so Giorgos also knew that there would be no sleep while this man stayed in his house. Men who drink are dangerous. But men who drink and can't handle their liquor are fatal, especially when they're powerful in the way that Meinhard was powerful.

"You're still awake," Meinhard said.

"Yes."

He walked in and looked around—

"Where's your daughter?" he asked.

"She went to bed."

"Already? It's still early."

"She was tired. It's been a long day."

Meinhard narrowed his eyes, and Giorgos read his look. He knew that this excuse would work for tonight, but it wouldn't work forever.

"Would you like me to show you to your room?"

"Has it been cleaned?"

"Yes. It's been made ready for you."

"Very good."

Meinhard followed Giorgos up the stairs to the largest bedroom in the largest house in Agria, and Giorgos opened the door to show him in. Meinhard walked through and looked at the perfectly made bed, the smartly decorated dresser and mirror, simple and plain, crafted for a man's taste.

"This will do well," Meinhard said.

"I'm glad," Giorgos bowed his head. "We'll see you tomorrow."

Giorgos started to close the door, when Meinhard reached out, holding it open, stopping him—

"Yes?" Giorgos asked.

Meinhard held Giorgos' eyes for a moment, and Giorgos could see that Meinhard's hand had gone to his pistol. Giorgos couldn't tell if he was drunk or lucid, and for the first time since this German had showed up on his doorstep, Giorgos couldn't read his intentions. They stayed like that for longer than Giorgos expected, until Meinhard finally spoke again.

"Nevermind," Meinhard said.

Then he turned and walked to the bed, and Giorgos left and shut the door behind him, and after he did he stood in

216

the hallway by himself, leaning against the wall, breathing heavily, scared of this man who was now an interloper forced into their home.

When his body finally settled, and he'd come back into himself, Giorgos walked further down the hallway to where Philia slept and he took a key out and used it to gently unlock and open the door to her room, being careful not to disturb her.

He saw that she was already asleep.

He stood there for a moment, looking down at his daughter, wondering what the next days were going to bring for them, and how hard they would be. And then, knowing that the night wouldn't give him any of the answers that he was looking for, he went to the large chair that was in the corner of the room and sat down. He shifted his body, making himself as comfortable as he could as he settled in for the night to watch over his daughter as she slept.

18

April 15th, 1941

A LEXEI AND COSTA KEPT RUNNING.
They ran through the night, their stomachs filled
with the moussaka and olives and bread that they'd found,
and they had strength for the first time since they'd left the
front.

It felt good in their bellies.

But they knew it wouldn't last long.

As they ran through the darkness, they saw more mortars exploding in the distance, fired from tanks, and they
wondered about the battle that was just beginning in the
hills, and the young men like themselves that were surely
fighting and dying there.

They kept running.

Sweat poured down their foreheads.

They're a resilient people, Alexei told himself, and
they'd faced occupation before. This wasn't the first time
they'd seen their churches and monuments destroyed. Or
had their food taken. They'd seen their women carried

away to foreign lands and foreign beds, and watched as their boys and men were taken as slaves. That's why they didn't even for one moment let themselves fear that they wouldn't survive and make things right again. They knew that in the future there would be a dawn that would soon come where they'd wake and realize that everything that had happened was a distant memory.

But in that moment it wasn't.

So they kept running.

Dawn came again to the hills, as they ran through them, and they saw a small creek and stopped for a drink of the water that was rushing down from the northern mountains.

As they drank, they discussed their route.

"If we continue directly south, we'll come to Larissa," Costa said.

"I know."

"That'll be the first place the Germans will want to take, which means that they're probably already there."

Larissa had the only airfield in central Greece. It wasn't important for the Greek Army, because their air force was non-existent, but it was critical for the Germans because the backbone of their fighting force was the Luftwaffe, and they needed a place for their planes to be able to stop and refuel. And Larissa would also be the best staging point for their invasion of Central Greece, and then the capital, Athens itself.

"It'll be more dangerous," Alexei said. "But it's also the quicker route."

"What if we run into Germans?"

"We'll stick to the mountains and the forests. Like we have been. Away from all the main roads. Places that their tanks and vehicles can't go."

"Alright."

They nodded.

They had their plan.

They stood and put their heads down and started running again, picking up their pace as they kept going through the hills.

They came to more mountains.

The slopes were rolling and rocky and they ran towards the high pass over the top of them and started their way back down the other side, carefully picking a path through the stones. They knew that a twisted ankle meant death. Alexei was staring down at his feet, concentrating on the ground in front of him, when he heard Costa next to him.

"What's that?" Costa asked.

Alexei looked up and saw that the forest was ending, and with it so was their cover. There was a gap in the mountains in front of them, and a swift river running through it, with a wide stone bridge spanning the rapids. They studied the bridge from a distance and saw that it was large enough for armored jeeps or trucks to pass over—maybe even a full-sized Panzer, too—which was extremely rare to find in the countryside, away from the cities.

"Do you see anyone?"

"No. But let's be careful."

They snuck forward as quietly as they could, until they were to the edge of the forest and there wasn't any cover left in front of them. If they went any further, they'd be exposed and easy targets if there were any Germans watching.

"We have to cross it," Costa said, glancing at the bridge, and then at the peaks that were bottling them in. "We can't go around. We'd lose an entire day and maybe more."

"Dammit."

"What?"

"Anyone in this valley is going to be able to see us."

"Maybe there's no one here."

"Look at the size of the bridge. It's huge. Reinforced. It's probably the only one for miles that could handle anything more than just men and horses."

"We have to do it."

"I guess we do."

"Alright. I'll go first."

"It's a bridge, Costa. It can hold both of us."

"You think?"

"Shut up, *malaka*."

"If you say so," he said, and smiled as they both stood up, unslinging their rifles from their backs.

They inched their way out of the forest.

They scanned the hills and mountains, looking for any signs of movement or glint of metal in the bright sun, the way that they'd been trained to find snipers.

"Do you think we should run across?" Alexei asked, his voice pitched low in case there was anyone listening. "We'd be harder to hit."

"I don't know. Maybe. What do you think?"

"Let's just walk across like we're supposed to be here."

"Alright."

They walked to the bridge.

They started across like it was the most normal thing in the world, like it was a time before war had come to these hills, and there was nothing to be scared of, or worry them in any way, but it only took one word to shatter their confidence, and they were in the middle of the bridge when they heard it ring out, echoing all around them—

"Stop!" the word came.

"Shit, run!" Alexei said.

"No, wait," Costa grabbed him.

"What? Let's go!"

"It was in Greek."

"So? Jurgen spoke Greek."

"There wasn't an accent."

Alexei paused, looking at Costa, realizing that he was right. Then Costa called back to the hills—

"We're Greek!"

There was silence for a moment, then a response—

"If you're Greek, then prove it!"

"Can't you tell by our accents?"

"We've heard plenty of Germans speaking the holy language of the Bible and God, the language that Jesus Christ spoke when he blessed his Apostles at their final supper."

"Then how do we prove that we're Greek?"

There was more silence, then—

"What's the question that your mother asks you most . . . morning, noon and night? The question that she never tires of?"

Alexei and Costa shared a look. Then Alexei turned back to the hills, and smiled as he called out—

"She asks when she's going to be a Yia Yia."

He was sure that he'd answered the question correctly, but there was more silence, and then Alexei felt the butt of a gun dig into his back. Was this it? And then he heard the voice of the man holding the gun, and this time he recognized it.

"I told you when you needed me you'd turn around and I'd be there. I promised you that, didn't I, *malaka*?"

Alexei and Costa turned and smiled when they saw their friend holding the rifle behind them.

"Koukidis," Alexei said.

"Did you miss me?"

"Not even for a second."

"You always were a shit liar, Alexei. Not blessed with a forked tongue like Costa."

"Why'd you have to wait so long?" Costa shoved him across the bridge as Koukidis laughed.

"You should have seen the looks on your faces."

"I thought we were going to die."

"It was their idea," Koukidis said as he gestured up towards the mountains. Alexei and Costa looked and saw there was a group of Greek soldiers that had come out from their hiding places, not one of them older than their early twenties, smiles on their faces.

"What the hell is this?"

"What do you mean? You haven't heard?"

"Heard what?"

Koukidis wrapped his arm around Alexei's shoulder, pulling him closer and whispering in his ear—

"We're the Resistance."

They all sat around a small fire.

Koukidis and the rest of the men were grilling cubes of lamb skewered on spits, holding them over the flames until the meat turned a dark and tender pink, juices dripping off that they were catching in a pan and that they'd use to flavor the crusty bread they'd found to go with the souvlaki. As they waited for lunch, Alexei looked around, taking in the small camp. They were high in the

223

mountains, above the bridge, obscured from the sight of anyone passing below. Someone gave Alexei a canteen and he drank deeply, then splashed some of the water on his face, washing off the dirt, before he passed it on to Costa.

"What are you planning on doing up here?" Alexei asked Koukidis.

"Isn't it obvious? We're killing Germans."

"There's not very many of you," Costa said, pouring some water over his head and shaking it from his hair.

"What do you mean?"

"You expect to take on the Germans with what . . . twenty men? That's not much of a resistance."

"There's only eighteen of us. But now with you it's twenty. Twenty is a better number, don't you think?"

"It's still just eighteen," Alexei said. "We can't stay."

"What, you have somewhere more important to be?"

"We have to get back to Agria. We've been running for two days straight trying to get there."

"You haven't heard?" Koukidis looked between them. "The Mountain Division took Volos the day before yesterday. I'm sure they took Agria some time before that. It was their first objective after the Line fell. They sent all the special units straight to secure the ports. The British had already been there, but they left right before the Germans arrived."

"How do you know all that?" Costa asked.

"We found a German. I put my knife under his balls and he told me everything I wanted to know."

"It just means that we need to get home quicker," Alexei said. "We saw the Germans shelling Kozani on our way."

"They took Kozani this morning, and now they're on their way here."

"*Here?*"

"Well, Larissa. They want to take the airfield. And the only way to move heavy artillery through these mountains is across this bridge."

"What are you going to do?" Costa asked him. "It's a whole army, and you're just a few men."

"We're going to make it difficult for them. The more Germans that we kill, the better the world will be."

"But there's only eighteen of you."

"There's twenty now."

"I told you. We can't stay."

"Alexei, look at me."

Alexei paused and looked at him—

"The Germans are already to Agria. There's a whole unit of them stationed there. What do you think you're going to do against them alone?"

"He's not alone," Costa said.

"So there's two of you. What do you think you're going to do against such odds?"

"Probably about the same as you trying to hold this bridge."

"*Hold* the bridge? Who said anything about holding it? We're going to blow it up."

"Then why don't you just do it?"

"Because I want to wait until there's Germans on it first."

Alexei and Costa paused and looked at each other. They were at a crossroads, and they each knew it.

"Stay and fight with us," Koukidis said, and then they turned and looked at him. "You're going back to Agria for your family, yes? The ones there that you love? Stay here and fight with us, and after we blow this bridge, and kill as many Germans as we can, we'll go to Agria with you."

"Why?"

"Because we're in the business of killing Germans. And it doesn't matter where we kill them. If there's Germans in Agria, then Agria's as good a place as any for us. And more importantly, it'll help my friends."

Alexei looked at Koukidis, then back down towards the bridge that was below them.

"How are you going to destroy it?"

"We have the whole thing wired with explosives."

"Explosives?"

"The British left them behind. The British love their explosives."

"So that's your plan?"

"We wait until the advance guard is on the bridge, and then we blow it up, taking as many of them with us as we can. They'll lose three days having to travel around this pass instead of over it. And every step they take from here to Athens, they won't know if bullets are going to be raining down on their heads or not, or if any other bridge or town is rigged with explosives in the same way. You've heard Papagos, Churchill, Stalin, the American Roosevelt . . . it's not easy to occupy a country when you're being shot at from the hills and the streets. That's what the French didn't understand. And that's why France fell so easily. But Greece won't. Because there's men like us that are here. Doing our part. And I hope that you'll stay with us, and do your part, too."

Alexei looked at Costa, and they both knew what they had to do.

Costa nodded towards the mountains that were around them.

"So we shoot at them from up here," Costa said. "And then when they realize what's happening, they'll start shooting back. And there's more of them than us. A lot more. So what do we do then?"

Koukidis smiled—

"Then, my friends ... *we run.*"

19

April 16th, 1941

THALIA HAD SENT WORD TO PHILIA that they needed to speak.

They met in the agora and then walked down towards the harbor where there was less noise and they wouldn't be overheard. It was a strange sight, a harbor with no boats.

But it was a time for many strange things that hadn't been seen before.

The wind kicked up and blew through their hair, and the sun beat down, heavy and warm on their faces. Philia told Thalia about Meinhard, and how he'd come and taken their food and her father's bed, and she asked Thalia about the soldier that was staying at their house.

"For once, it's a blessing to have a small house," Thalia said as they walked. "None of the soldiers wanted to stay there, so they assigned it to a private. He's very young. When I asked him how old he was he wouldn't answer, but he looks like he couldn't be more than sixteen. He doesn't even need to shave in the morning."

"That certainly makes things easier for you. Having a man before he's really a man."

"It has been. He tried to get Nico to play soccer with him yesterday, but Nico just stared at him. He was standing there in his uniform in our yard with the ball at his feet, and Nico just turned around and went back into the house."

"A little warrior."

"He told Costa before he left that he wanted to fight with him. That he wanted to do his part."

"It seems like war is all men want to do."

"I brought you something," Thalia said, and she took a small piece of bread from her dress. "We've both been saving our rations."

"You can't, Thalia. You need that."

"It's for your son."

"Keep it. For yours."

But Thalia ignored her, and wrapped Philia's hand around the bread as they walked, and Philia sighed.

"People can't keep taking care of me like this."

"Why? They want to."

"We'll share it," Philia said, and broke it in half, handing the larger piece back to Thalia. "Now, tell me what it is that you wanted to talk about."

"I got a letter from one of my cousins in Rhodes. He wants me to come stay with him. He says the war won't reach that far into the sea, and he sent a ticket for me and Nico to leave from Athens."

"That's wonderful."

"I don't want to leave Agria. But I look around and I don't know what else to do. A city occupied by Germans is no place to raise a boy."

"No. It isn't."

"I've heard stories of others to the north. There are some villages that are so hungry they've been forced to eat the soles of their shoes."

"The soles of their shoes?" Philia shook her head, not understanding.

"Shoes are made of leather."

Philia took this in, feeling the desperation of the entire country that was hanging over them in that one thought and image.

"I want to wait for Costa," Thalia continued. "I want to wait for him more than anything, and be standing here watching as he comes marching back over those hills, with Alexei, the same as you, it's just ..."

Philia looked at her.

She knew exactly what Thalia felt, because she felt it too, and she finished the sentence for her.

"You don't know if he's coming back."

Thalia looked at Philia and they were both quiet as they fought against the pain they carried.

"I'm sorry," Thalia said quietly. "I want to be strong. Like you are. But I have Nico."

"Do you have enough money?"

"Money doesn't mean anything in Greece now."

"Will you be able to make the journey?"

"The Germans aren't to Athens yet. They're not even past Volos. So if we're going to go, it needs to be now. Before they get any further."

"How do you know where they're at? That they haven't made it any further south?"

"The boy staying in my house told me. He stays up late at night and watches me clean."

"He may be young. But they're all still men, aren't they?"

"I think he was trying to impress me with how much he knew of the German plans and strategy."

They stopped walking and turned to look at each other—

"When are you leaving?" Philia asked.

"Our bags are already packed."

"So this is it, then."

Thalia held back her tears.

"You'll tell him, won't you? You'll tell him that I wanted to stay? That I wanted to be here?"

Philia nodded.

"Of course I will."

"Thank you."

"God protect you on the road."

"And you here."

They looked at each other one more time, then Thalia finally left, going back towards her house and her son and her packed bags, but after she was a few paces away, she turned and looked back at Philia, and spoke with a very clear truth—

"He's going to come back, Philia. They both are. I can feel it. I've asked God for it, as many times as he'll listen."

"I have, too," Philia said. "So I'm sure that he'll listen."

And with one final smile, Thalia turned and crossed the rest of the length of the harbor towards her house, while Philia went the opposite way, back towards the city behind them.

"Philia ..."

She was walking past the agora, in front of the city hall, when she heard her name called out. She turned to see Meinhard smoking a cigarette on the steps and watching her. His eyes devoured every inch of her body as the sea breeze caused her loose dress to cling to her.

"How are you today?" he asked.

"I'm fine, thank you," she said, putting her head down, trying to walk past him, but he reached out and stopped her.

"How about this breeze?" he spoke again. "We don't have any breeze like this back in Germany."

"It's very nice."

He finished his cigarette and let it fall to the cobblestones. "Where are you going?" he asked.

"I'm going home, sir."

"You don't need to call me sir. I want you to call me by my name."

She tried to push past him, and continue on her way, but he held her by the elbow, stopping her.

"Try it out," he said. "Call me Meinhard."

She hesitated as she looked at him, trying to gauge his intentions, but he just stared back at her with his blank and dark German eyes, and she was scared, though she didn't want to be.

"Meinhard," she finally said, very softly.

"I like it when you say my name," he said. "Now ask me why I like it."

She hesitated. He still held her elbow.

"Why do you like it when I say your name," she said, trying to look away from him.

He put his fingers underneath her chin and turned her face so that she was looking into his eyes. He stood over her and looked down, and he was much taller than she was.

"It's because of the way it makes your lips move."

She hesitated for a moment, looking back at him, and then she tried to pull herself away.

But he held her arm.

He held it a little bit longer, just to let her know that it was his decision to let her go, and not hers. He wanted her to know that everything that would now happen would be his decision.

"Where are you going?" he asked.

"I told you. I'm going home."

"How come I never see you there? You're always sleeping, and I'm left awake with your boring father."

"I go to bed early."

"Don't tonight."

"What?"

"I have much to do here, so I'll be back late. But I want you to be there, waiting for me, when I come back."

"Why?"

"So that we can talk. If I'm going to be staying at your house, I'd like to get to know you. You can go to sleep if you'd like. But I think it'll be better for you if you stayed awake."

She met his eyes and swallowed, then walked past him, and this time he let her. The breeze picked up again and whipped her dress low across her legs, and around her waist, revealing her figure.

They don't make girls like that in Germany, Meinhard thought.

Then he smiled to himself.

They don't make girls like that in Germany at all.

Philia told her father what had happened in town, even though they both knew there was nothing that could be done about it. She would wait for Meinhard, and she would talk to him. She'd do as he asked.

Giorgos didn't want to leave his daughter alone with this man, not even for a single moment, so he'd decided that he'd listen to their whole conversation from the other side of the wall.

There was nothing else for them to do.

They waited, and soon night came.

Meinhard was drunk again, when he came back, like Philia knew that he would be. She was waiting at the dining room table, a glass of warm water with lemon squeezed into it in front of her, and he walked past the threshold and smiled as he sat down.

"I was hoping that you had sense enough to listen to me," he said.

She was silent.

"Don't you want to ask me how my day was?"

She hesitated, then—

"How was your day?"

"It was very good. I destroyed three boats with English soldiers in them, and executed two Resistance fighters that we found in the hills. And then we discovered some fishermen, who were trying to keep their catch for themselves, which the Fuhrer has of course forbid, and so we killed them, too. So it was a good day."

He saw the look that passed across Philia's face and was pleased that he'd surprised her. She hadn't been ready for such an honest answer.

"What's the matter?" he asked, smiling.

"Is that what you wanted to talk to me about?"

"No," he looked across the table at her. "No, it's not."

He stood and crossed the distance between them so

that he was above her again, and looking down. Then he reached to his neck and took off the Knight's Cross that he wore there.

He set it on the table in front of her.

"Do you know what this is?"

"Yes," she said.

"It was given to me by the Fuhrer himself. After I conquered a city in France, that was very difficult to conquer, with very few German casualties, and very many French ones. I know that this cross might not mean very much to you here in Greece, but it means very much to me. In Germany, it means that I'm a very important person."

"I know."

"How do you know?"

"Because you give orders to the men, and they listen."

"That's right. That means I'm a powerful man," he touched her hair, running his fingers through it. "And during war, women need powerful men to protect them."

"I have a husband."

"Where is he? I don't see him here."

"He was fighting."

"Fighting where? At the Line?"

"Yes."

"And you know what happened at the Line, don't you?" Silence.

"Answer me. What happened?"

"We were defeated."

"That's right," Meinhard said. "You were defeated. And many Greeks were killed. Where do you think your husband is?"

Philia didn't answer, but Meinhard smiled when he saw the damp corners of her eyes.

"I'll tell you where he is," Meinhard said cruelly. "He's dead. He's dead, and he's not coming home to you."

"You don't know that."

"Do you care to wager?"

"No."

"I see the look in your eyes, and I know that you think I'm an animal, but I'm not, Philia. I'm a realist. You know that, don't you? You know that what I'm telling you is the truth."

Philia didn't respond.

Meinhard reached into his uniform and took out a small parcel wrapped in cloth, which he set on the table in front of her. He slowly unwrapped it and when the package had revealed its secret, Philia saw a perfectly cooked steak sitting in front of her.

"You must be hungry, right? Of course you are. You haven't really eaten in some days now, have you? Trust me, I know. Nobody in Agria has."

"And you'd bring me extra food?"

"You know it's illegal to have more food than we give you. But I can bring you many things. Though, of course, I don't bring gifts for nothing in return."

"How much do you want? My father can pay you."

"Money means nothing."

"You're fighting a war. Wars are expensive. Everyone needs money during war."

He laughed.

"For what . . . to buy guns from America? To buy wheat from Russia? I believe those ships have already sailed, as the saying goes. What we have, and what we need, we've already taken from our enemies. Strength is the only currency that matters during war."

"Then what do you want?"

"I want you."

She swallowed.

He looked down at her. Then tilted her head up towards his, and leaned in towards her lips, but she turned away.

Meinhard stayed there for a moment, looking down at her.

"You know that I could force myself on you."

"Yes."

"And still you'd turn away from me?"

"Yes."

"Why? There's nobody here that would see you. Nobody would ever have to know."

She remembered words that Alexei had said to her once, and she almost smiled as she spoke them herself—

"No. There would be nobody that would see us," she said very softly. "But I would see myself."

Meinhard looked at her for another moment, deciding what to make of this woman in front of him, then he roughly grabbed her chin and she wondered if he was going to rape her, right there, on top of her dining room table, like he said he could.

But then, after a moment, he let her go.

He picked up his Knight's Cross and went back to his seat across from her. He reached out and pulled the steak towards him.

"The Fuhrer's ordered us to treat the people of Greece in a certain way, and I honor what the Fuhrer commands. I won't take you unless you want me to. Do you understand my offer?"

"Yes."

"Good. Now bring me a plate and a knife. I've just eaten, and I'm very full, but I think I'll eat again."

Philia nodded and went to the kitchen.

She returned and set a plate in front of him, laid utensils on either side, and tucked a napkin into his shirt collar, right over where he'd returned the Knight's Cross at his neck.

"Thank you," he answered with decorum and formality.

She sat back down across from him, and even though her stomach was eating itself and her unborn son cried out for nourishment, too, she watched stone-faced as Meinhard ate the entire steak and even the grease and juices left on the bottom of the plate. When he was finished, he stood and walked upstairs to his bedroom without another word.

Philia breathed relief as he left.

And behind the wall, where he'd been waiting ever since Meinhard had first stepped through his door, Giorgos finally allowed himself to relax, loosening his grip on the knife that he'd been holding ready at his side.

20

April 17th, 1941

THE GERMANS CAME TO THE BRIDGE at dawn.

Alexei and Costa had stayed up all night with Koukidis and the rest of the Greeks, waiting for their enemies to arrive. They were shivering through the cold darkness, not able to make a fire because it would have given away their position. But they were soldiers now. They'd beaten the elements in Albania, and then again at the Metaxas Line.

They were used to being cold.

They were used to not sleeping.

The sun was finally beginning to rise in front of them as they ate leftover souvlaki and drank cold coffee when they saw the small stones around where they were sitting begin to rattle in the dirt. Then, ripples started in the middle of their coffee, too.

They looked at each other.

They knew what those ripples meant.

"Tanks," Koukidis said.

They took their positions. The strategy had already

239

been decided the day before—they would space themselves across the mountains to make it harder to hit any of them individually, and it would also confuse the Germans with bullets coming at them from as many directions as possible.

They'd each fortified their own position where they were going to hide.

They'd spent the afternoon amongst the rocks, piling them to make makeshift turrets and cover. It was hard work in the sun, but a little more sweat was better than taking a bullet.

And it wasn't long until they saw the tanks that they'd already felt.

They came down the long road that led to the bridge, from the opposite way as the forest, the way that Alexei and Costa had come, and as soon as the Greeks saw the tanks, each man hurried to their position and hid so that the Germans wouldn't see them.

Alexei was next to Costa, and on the other side of Costa was Koukidis. He had the trigger for the explosions with him, and when he detonated them . . . that would be the signal to begin their attack.

The Germans stopped when they came to the bridge.

The Greeks could see the Officers discussing, pointing up towards the mountains.

"They've heard of us," Koukidis whispered, and when Alexei and Costa looked at him, they saw that he was smiling.

In front of them, the Germans looked at a map, and after seeing there was no other way around, they must have decided that crossing the bridge would be worth the risk. They sent their young soldiers out first, to see if there were any trip wires or land mines laid under the foundation.

And Koukidis waited.

He wanted more than a few teenage casualties.

The young soldiers soon reached the other side, and waved back towards the others. The Panzers roared to life, and the Officers walked behind the tanks, as the entire group started across the bridge.

Alexei heard Koukidis whisper—

"*... three of them . . . I want three of them ...*"

They looked below to see the first Panzer already almost across, and the second Panzer inch its way onto the bridge, and still Koukidis waited.

"*Koukidis ...*" Costa whispered.

"*Shhh,*" he replied.

The third Panzer started to move.

He waited longer.

The first Panzer's tracks were halfway off the bridge.

Koukidis still waited.

Finally, the third Panzer was a quarter of the way onto the bridge.

They saw Koukidis' muscles tense, and Alexei and Costa held their rifles at the ready, just as—

Kaboom!!!! Kaboom kaboom!!!! Kaboom!!!!

The bridge exploded in a mess of wood and stone and metal.

The second Panzer, which was in the middle, fell to the river below and crashed against the rocks.

The third Panzer, which was only part of the way onto the bridge teetered there on the edge for a moment, before finally pitching forward and slipping down the bank to where it crashed into the river near the second, destroying them both.

But the first Panzer made it across.

The back of its tracks were still on the bridge when it exploded, and the explosion knocked the tracks off so that it couldn't go any further, but it was on the other side of the bridge.

The Greeks jumped up from their hiding spots.

Bang bang bang!!! Bang bang!!! Bang bang bang!!!

They fired on the Germans and cut down more than a dozen in their first volley. Some fell off the bridge, their bodies tearing apart on the rocks below, and some dove to try to find cover, but there was no cover to be had.

Not where they'd been caught.

They gathered themselves.

They hid behind the Panzer that they had left.

Then smoke cleared so they could see, and they returned fire—

Bang bang bang!!!

The Greeks ducked back behind their rocks, taking shelter as the hills around them exploded with enemy bullets, and two of them found their mark, and two Greek soldiers fell.

The Greeks fired back.

Bang bang!!! Bang bang!! Bang bang!!!

More Germans screamed, and the Greeks hid behind the rocks again after they fired.

Their element of surprise was gone, so they knew it wouldn't be long that they could hold out, because it was eighteen Greeks now against an entire army of Germans, but it was Costa that saw the end first.

"Shit!" he yelled.

"What?" Koukidis answered as he returned fire, then dove back behind his cover.

He turned to look where Costa was pointing and saw

the Panzer that had made it on to their side of the bridge. The tracks were blown off, so it couldn't move forward, but the turret was rotating on top, spinning around until soon the large barrel of the gun was pointed directly at where the Greeks were hiding in the mountains.

"Shit," Koukidis said, echoing Costa, but it was too late.

Kaboom!!!!

The explosion rocked the mountain and blew the Greeks off their feet. Alexei looked through the smoke and dust and saw five dead bodies, limbs torn from freshly made corpses.

"We have to go!" Alexei yelled to Koukidis and Costa.

Beneath them, German soldiers were starting to wade across the river.

"One more volley!" Koukidis yelled.

They loaded their rifles.

"Now!"

Bang bang bang bang!!!

They shot the Germans that were wading in the river.

Then, the Greeks turned to run.

They sprinted up the mountain, to start heading south on the other side, as Koukidis lobbed two British-issued grenades below to give them as much cover as possible.

Boom boom!!!

The Germans returned fire through the smoke and dust, firing in the general direction of their enemies, though not able to see them.

They hit one more Greek soldier.

The bullet caught him in the back, just below the armpit, and Alexei saw him fall. The wound itself wouldn't have killed him, but it knocked him off-balance, and his footing gave out as he slipped and his body went tumbling down the mountain, gashed by all the sharp rocks, and Alexei knew that by the time he reached the bottom he wouldn't be recognizable as anything other than something that had once been a man.

The rest of the Greeks got to the top and safety.

They were protected from the German fire now.

Alexei looked around as they caught their breath. Costa and Koukidis had both made it. There were eleven Greeks total that had survived and climbed to safety.

One must have been hit that Alexei didn't see.

But it was still victory.

They'd killed almost a hundred German soldiers, destroyed three Panzers, and set the German advance back by days.

"Not bad," Koukidis smiled as they gathered themselves.

Alexei walked to where Costa stood waiting and they found each other's eyes once more.

It was time to run again.

"Ready?"

"Ready."

They shouldered their rifles, pulling them tight across their backs, and then they turned to Koukidis.

"We'll see you in Agria," Alexei said.

And then they started to go.

They set a stiff pace through the rocky slopes.

Costa checked behind them after they'd gone a short distance and saw the rest of the Greeks start their run, Koukidis leading them, and then Costa looked back to Alexei—

"How long do you think they'll be able to keep it up for?" he asked him. "They look pretty slow."

"They're faster than the Germans. That's all that matters."

"You're right."

"We're not far now, you know."

"No, we aren't," Costa agreed.

Then they looked at each other again. Both of them knew what the other was thinking. That was their gift. Two boys both born in the same village, on the same day, with the same heart. And the thought of Agria and what lay in front of them gave them a powerful new strength.

They put their heads down and locked their jaws.

They picked up their pace even more, matching long strides.

They wouldn't stop now until they were home.

April 18ᵗʰ, 1941

THALIA HAD DECIDED THAT THEY WOULD leave Agria by night.

There wasn't strictly speaking any rule that said the villagers couldn't come and go as they pleased—the rules were clear, and they were limited to restricting food rations, the carrying of firearms, and allowing the quartering of German troops in Greek homes.

But she still didn't want to take any chances.

So she waited until the young soldier staying with them went to sleep.

Thalia peered into his room, checking the rising and falling of his breathing, and once it had become even—rhythmic and steady and deep—she was satisfied that he wasn't going to wake until morning and that it was time for what she knew they had to do.

They snuck out of the house and into the dark night.

Nico had explored every inch of Agria on his afternoons with Costa and he showed his mother a secret way out of the city. They walked down towards the Aegean and onto the rocky beach past the harbor and kept going until they came to the end of the sand, and then the beginning of the mountains that now closed them in.

"What are you doing?" Thalia whispered to him. "This is a dead end. There's nowhere to go."

"Yes, there is," he said. "This way. Costa showed me."

And then the boy led his mother to the hidden path through the mountains that Costa had showed him, and the shortcut saved them hours on their journey, and allowed them to leave Agria without being seen.

They walked through the night in silence.

Nico felt like a man, because he'd been important, and as they walked he held the pocket-knife that Costa had given him in his hand. He thought of how Costa had told him that he needed to protect his mother, and he knew that he would, though he didn't know what was waiting for them out there in the darkness.

They kept walking.

It was hard for either of them to tell how much time had passed, or how far they'd gone.

Then, they saw lights.

They were on the road in front of them, heading towards where they were walking, and Thalia made a quick calculation—

"Hurry," she said to Nico. "We need to get off the road."

"Where?"

"That way. Go."

She pulled Nico off to the side of the road where she saw a group of low bushes and they hurried towards it and got down on their stomachs to crawl underneath and hide as best they could.

The lights on the road got closer.

And Thalia's heart sank when she saw them stop.

There were two kubelwagen jeeps, with swastikas painted on the hoods, and then a pair of well-polished boots that stepped out.

German boots.

She watched the heels of the boots grind against gravel on the road, then turn towards where they were hiding and walk until they were right in front of them.

"We saw you on the road," the German voice said. "You can either come out, or I can shoot you where you are, and drive away never knowing who it was that I killed."

Thalia looked at Nico.

She made another calculation.

She mouthed the words *"stay here"* to him, and then pulled herself along the ground, and stood up. She faced the German and saw the polished Luger that he was pointing at her and the way that the moonlight above them was reflecting off the barrel.

"I'm sorry," she said. "I shouldn't have been on the road. I was just going back home."

"Tell the boy to come out, too," the German said evenly.

"There's no boy. It's just me."

He pulled the hammer on his Luger back.

Click.

But Thalia didn't move.

She just stared back at him.

And then he smiled.

"I like that," he said, then moved the Luger so that it

wasn't aimed at her anymore, but at the bush she'd just crawled from under. "But lying to me isn't very smart."

She quickly moved so that she was between the pistol and the bush, her hands raised.

"Please, don't," she said.

"Then tell the boy to come out."

She closed her eyes.

She waited for a very long moment, then—

"Nico ..." she finally whispered.

And when he heard his mother's voice, Nico came out and stood next to her, and they faced the German in front of them together. More German soldiers got out of the jeeps and walked towards them.

"What's your name, boy?"

"Nico."

The German nodded, and then he turned to Thalia next to him, and he asked her, too.

"And his mother? What's Nico's mother's name?"

Another long moment, then—

"Thalia," she said softly.

"Good," the German said. "Very good. My name is Franz."

Franz turned to the other soldiers that had joined him, and they switched to speaking in German—

"What do you think?"

"She's too old for you, Franz."

"Do you reckon?"

"Look at her boy. He has to be at least eleven."

"Sometimes I like them old. It makes them more . . . grateful."

"Something tells me this one won't be," the soldier said with a devilish grin, and when Thalia saw that grin, even if

she didn't understand their words, she knew what her fate was going to be that night.

She thought only of Nico now.

"*Bring them with us,*" Franz said to his men. "*Perhaps this night won't be quite so boring after all.*"

"*Sir,*" they said, saluting Franz, their Captain.

Then they came forward and roughly grabbed Thalia and Nico, leading them back towards the road and where their vehicles waited.

That same night, under the same moon, Giorgos and Iannis had made a plan. Philia was pregnant with their grandson and she needed more food than the Germans gave them. The two men had heard the same stories that Thalia had heard, and they vowed that no grandson of theirs would have to chew on the leather soles of worn shoes for his first meal.

Giorgos had snuck down to the dock to speak with Iannis.

It was late afternoon, and the sun was still hot when Giorgos told him of his worry about his daughter, and Iannis didn't waste a moment coming up with an idea—

"We'll bring her fish," he said.

"Don't the Germans watch what you catch and bring back home?"

"Yes. They do. And they take all of it for their men. But they can only take what they see."

"What do you mean?"

"I mean that they only see me during the day. If I go out at night, and sail far to the south, where there still aren't any Germans, I'll be able to fish without anyone seeing what I'm doing."

"And then what? Won't they see when you come back?"

"You'll meet me on the beach, to the south, and I'll unload what I catch. Then, when I come back, and pass through the harbor, there will be nothing for them to find. And they don't check men walking back into the city for fish."

Giorgos nodded.

It was a good plan.

"Fish is good for women when they're pregnant."

"When Eleni was pregnant with Alexei she didn't want to eat anything else."

And so it was settled.

Both men smiled and shook hands—

"Tomorrow night, then."

"Tomorrow night."

The next day passed, and Giorgos didn't say anything to Philia, because he knew that his daughter was strong, and that she'd insist that he didn't go, she'd insist that there was too much danger for him, and for Iannis, but he was her father, and he knew that he needed to do this.

Giorgos snuck out of the house before Meinhard came back that night.

Meinhard would be drunk and wouldn't miss him.

He went through the town and a few miles south of the city to the spot on the beach where he'd arranged to meet Iannis. He knew the area well. It was where many of the locals went during the hottest months of summer. He had never been someone that went to the beach—he'd never had time for it, not as a boy or as a man, and he didn't care to lay out in the sun—but he'd come down to pick up his daughter many times when she was younger, and so the path was not new to him.

He came to the spot where they'd arranged to meet.

He looked into the distance and didn't see anything.

He'd buried his watch along with a pair of engraved cuff-links and his wedding ring in a box in the backyard behind his house, before the Germans had come, and so without his watch he wasn't sure if he was early or late.

He checked the position of the moon, but it meant nothing to him.

He hadn't done outdoor things with his father, that other boys had when they were young, and so he didn't have those skills. He hadn't had a father. He'd been poor, and the purpose of his life since before he could remember was to not be poor. His entire world had revolved around making as much money as he possibly could, and he smiled at the irony, thinking about how successful he'd been at that, and how it now meant nothing.

It didn't matter. He'd make himself again.

Then, there was a soft whistle in the darkness.

A small boat approached, and Giorgos waded into the water to meet Iannis, and took hold of the side of his boat as he got closer.

"Fancy seeing you here tonight," Iannis said with a smile.

"I was worried I was late."

"How much can you carry?"

"How much do you have?"

Giorgos peered over the edge of the boat and saw the bottom nearly full with *lavraki*, so he took the newspapers that he'd brought and used them to start wrapping three of the fish, and then searched for places to hide each of them in his jacket and tucked them away. He patted his clothes as straight as he could, so that there weren't any bulges or lines that might betray him, or give him away to the Germans.

When he was finished he turned back to Iannis—

"How do I look?"

"Like a man out for a midnight stroll."

"Perfect."

"Grill them with butter," Iannis told him. "And a few capers, if there are any left. Then squeeze a lemon on top before it cools."

"Thank you."

"Send her my love."

"I will."

"She's lucky that you're her father," Iannis said.

"She's lucky that you are, too," Giorgos answered.

Then Giorgos pushed Iannis' boat back out against the waves, back towards the open sea, as Giorgos returned to the beach and walked the whole way back to Agria without seeing another soul.

He crept into his house and silently went upstairs in a way that was so silent that he was sure that he wouldn't wake Meinhard, sleeping off another drunken night. He softly opened the door to where Philia slept and went inside and looked down at his beautiful daughter for a moment, before he shook her awake.

"What is it?" she asked.

"I have a surprise."

"What surprise?"

He smiled—

"Are you hungry?"

The Germans put Thalia and Nico in two different jeeps.

They drove through the night for some time, and Thalia was blindfolded so that she didn't know in which direction, or how far they'd gone. Then the engines stopped.

She heard more German voices. Then, the Germans in the jeep responded to them.

A door opened and shut.

Her blindfold was taken off.

One of the Germans, who wasn't Franz, stood in front of her.

"Let's go," he said.

"Where?"

"To see the Captain."

"Where's my son?"

"You'll see him soon."

The German pulled her out of the jeep and she saw that they'd been brought to the middle of a German camp. She tried to look around, for any sign of Nico, but the soldier pushed her in front of him, forcing her to walk quickly.

"The Captain doesn't like to be kept waiting. So we should hurry. You'll like him better when he's not angry."

They went to the far side of the camp where Thalia saw that they'd come to a tent that was larger than the rest of the tents in the camp. The German soldier pushed open the flap, and then he looked back at her, from where they stood just outside of it.

"Go on," he said. "He's inside."

"Where's Nico?"

"He'll be waiting for you when you come back out."

She bit her lip.

The German's hand moved to the Luger at his hip.

She didn't have any other choice—not when they had her son—so she bowed her head, and walked inside. In the center of the tent she saw Franz standing with his back to her.

When he heard her behind him, he turned and smiled—

"Ah, Thalia. Very nice of you to join me."

"Where's my son?"

"He's safe. With the other men."

"I want to see him."

"Do you?"

She looked at him, and she knew that he was playing with her, and that he was enjoying it.

"Would you like a drink?" he asked her. "I'm going to have one."

"No."

"I'm going to pretend that you didn't say that."

He walked to a small table and poured a glass of whiskey for himself, then took an already-opened bottle of wine and poured a large glass.

He went to her, carrying both drinks.

"I'm going to pretend instead, that when you opened your mouth, you said, 'Yes, Master Franz. I'd love to have a drink with you.' And then after you accepted my generous offer, we'd have a drink together."

He handed her the glass of wine.

"I don't like women who drink liquor," he said, explaining. "In fact, I insist that they don't. It's something that I find most vulgar. There's some things that should be left just to men, don't you think? And whiskey is certainly one of them."

He raised his glass in a toast—

"To the Reich."

She hesitated, and then held her glass up, and took a very small sip to please him.

"Are you married?" he asked her.

"I was."

"He left you? The boy's father?"

"He died."

"And you haven't found another man?"

She hesitated—

"It's alright. You can tell me the truth. It won't change anything that's going to happen tonight."

"Yes. I've found someone else."

"And does he treat you well?"

"He does."

"Where is he?"

"He's fighting in the war."

"Ah, yes. The war. The great war, that we're all fighting in. The reason why we're here tonight, right? And do you know my favorite thing about war?" he asked as he finished his whiskey and set his glass down.

"No."

"It's the conquest," he said, licking his lips. "In peace, there are certain rules, certain civilities, laws that we create in order to prevent ourselves from acting on our most basic and primitive instincts and desires. But why should we do that? Why shouldn't we behave the way that we wish to? Why shouldn't we be able to take what we're strong enough to take? That's why I love war. In war, the only laws that we make are our own. The only rules that are enforced are the rules that we're strong enough to enforce. It's refreshing, don't you think? It's more real. It's more genuine."

He paused, searching—

"It's more . . . *primal.*"

"Where's my son?" she asked him again.

"He's safe, like I told you. But whether he stays that way is up to you."

"How?"

"It depends on what you do tonight."

"I'll do whatever you want."

"I want you to take your clothes off."

He said it so calmly, as if he was just asking for directions, that for a moment Thalia looked back at him and didn't know if he was serious, or if she'd heard him correctly.

"What?"

"I want you to stand facing me, and then I want you to take your clothes off, while I watch, and I want you to let them fall to the floor in front of you. And I want you to make sure that you do it slowly. That's very important. We're in no hurry tonight."

"Hitler . . . he said . . . about the women in Greece . . ."

"I know what Hitler said. But he's not here, is he? And I am. And so is your son. So the best thing for you, and for Nico, is to listen to what I'm saying to you. Do you under-stand?"

She swallowed—

"Yes."

"Good. Now, go on. Take off your clothes. And make sure that you do it in a way that I will like it, otherwise this will become much less pleasant."

She waited for one more moment.

She closed her eyes, so that he wouldn't see her tears.

Then she turned her face away from him, as she reached up and gently tugged at the strings around her neck, unty-ing her dress, letting it fall down to her feet.

"Good," Franz said. "And now the rest."

She was shaking.

She reached up and pulled the sheer slip she wore under her dress over her head as Franz stared at her body.

Her pure, naked body.

He drank in every inch of her.

Her breasts, the curves of her hips, her legs, what was between them.

"Good," he said. "Very good."

He stood and walked closer to her. He put his face next to hers so that she could smell the whiskey on his breath when he spoke. He touched her, to make sure that she knew she was his.

"If you want your son to live then you're going to do exactly what I tell you," he breathed. "Do you understand me?"

She tried to search for the strength that Costa told her she had inside.

"Yes."

"I want to make sure that you understand."

"I understand."

"Because if you don't make this the best night of my life, then neither of you are going to live to see the sun rise again."

"Please don't hurt him."

"Turn around and bend over until you touch the ground. I don't want to see your face."

She did as he told her.

He walked behind her and unbuckled his pants with one hand and pulled a knife from his belt with the other. As he spread her legs further apart he held his knife underneath her throat.

It pricked against her skin.

"If you try anything, I'll kill you. Do you understand?"

She nodded—

"Good," he said.

He kept the knife at her throat as his pants slid all the way to the ground and she gasped in pain as he entered her and started thrusting. She cried. She didn't want to, but she couldn't help it, and as she cried he started thrusting harder, with each of her sobs pushing himself deeper and deeper inside of her.

He worked himself into a fever.

He turned himself into something far beyond an animal.

He kept thrusting, and she kept crying, and he didn't notice as her sobs turned from shame to terror and then pain and finally something else altogether. He didn't feel the blood that was seeping down his wrist, or realize that the sobs had stopped now, and her body had rolled to the side and fell to the floor, and then he saw that he hadn't kept his knife steady at all, but had cut across her throat, severing her vocal chords and several of the arteries in her neck.

He looked down at her body at his feet and let out a sigh.

He hadn't meant to kill her.

Nico sat at the campfire with the soldiers from Franz's company.

They were passing around a bottle of liquor, and when it came to him, they offered him some. He took the bottle and pretended to drink, and when he did they cheered and clapped him on the back thinking that it was great sport. This young boy was fast on his way to becoming a man, they said, thinking that he was young enough that he didn't know what was happening to his mother that night. They were drunk, and talking, and laughing, and they thought that Nico might even be thinking of them as friends now.

They couldn't read the look on the boy's face.

They were far enough from Franz's tent that Nico couldn't hear his mother's screams, or her sobs, but he was old enough to know what happened to women during war, and he'd always known that his mother was beautiful. The soldiers continued to pass the bottle, and a second cheer went up when Nico asked for another drink.

"Are you sure that you're not German?" one of them asked.

"You certainly handle the drink like you're a German," another told him, and slapped him on the back again.

Nico smiled because he knew that they'd like that, and then he asked if he could go to the forest to take a piss. The men laughed as if they all shared the same secret now, and one of them jerked his head at another telling him to go with Nico and keep an eye on the boy while he took his piss among the trees.

They went to the edge of the forest.

Nico unbuttoned his pants as he stood next to a tree.

The German soldier who'd walked with him waited patiently as the boy relieved himself, and the soldier was drunk and looking at the moon rather than the boy so he didn't see Nico take the knife that Costa had given him from his pocket and hide it in his sleeve.

Nico finished, and buttoned his pants.

He turned back to the soldier with a smile that the German returned, and as they started to walk back towards the fire, Nico let the soldier go ahead of him, and then Nico came behind and stabbed his knife clean through the back of the German's throat.

The German tried to call out, but his voice would never be his voice again.

As soon as he fell to his knees, Nico pulled his knife from the soldier's throat and then stabbed him in the chest, finding his heart, and watching the man die. Then when the soldier's eyes were finally frozen, he looked behind them, towards the fire.

The men were still laughing.

They were still passing the bottle back and forth.

So Nico stole away into the night, sneaking through the camp towards the tent where they had taken his mother.

He had little trouble finding Franz's tent.

But instead of opening the front flap, and walking in, he went around to the back. He gently lifted the bottom and peered under it to see that Franz was standing, still naked, his back to Nico, washing Thalia's blood off his hands. Her body was still warm at his feet.

It didn't shock Nico the way that he thought it would. Somehow he'd already known that his mother would be dead, and that he wasn't going there to save her.

He was going there for something else.

Franz was softly humming and very pleased with himself so he didn't hear anything as Nico snuck towards him, until the boy was close enough to stab his knife into the small of Franz's back, puncturing his kidneys. When Franz turned around, looking down at the wound, and then the young boy holding the knife, he didn't even scream as Nico pulled his knife out and slashed Franz across the stomach in a wound that they both knew would make sure that Franz never left his tent again.

Franz fell to his knees.

Nico caught him and put his hand over Franz's mouth to keep him from crying out as he suffered, and it worked. Nico watched the life slowly drain from Franz's eyes, and then Franz died, naked, at the hands of his enemy, who was no more than a boy, with no final words, nothing to remember him by, as his life bled out in a distant land that was very far from his home.

Nico stared at Franz's lifeless eyes.

It was over.

Then he went to where his mother's body lay on the ground.

He knew as he looked down into her eyes, open wide in the agony of a painful death, that there was nothing he could do for her, not if he didn't want to risk his own life.

He couldn't even bury her.

So he'd do the only other thing he could think of.

He found a blanket in the corner and used it to cover her body. Then he bent down and kissed her softly on the cheek, and used his fingers to gently close the lids of her eyes so that she had some peace, a small bit of the dignity and rest that she deserved. He looked around the tent again until he found Franz's clothes in the corner and he went to them and rifled through the pants until he found what he was looking for.

Two worn coins.

German Deutschmarks.

They'd have to do.

He went back to his mother and placed them on her eyelids, in the old way, as an offering to Charon to ensure her safe passage across the river Styx, and into the next life. He sat there for a moment, looking down at her, and he wanted to cry, but he couldn't.

He stood up again.

He'd wonder later why he couldn't cry in that moment, but it was probably all too much for a boy of eleven, and who knows the answers to questions that are beyond what we've been made to be able to endure?

He looked at her one more time.

He tried to feel as much as he could.

He wouldn't need the anger and the hatred now, so he'd tuck it away, because he'd use it later, he knew. The Germans had come, and he'd now seen what they were going to do, and also what they'd already done. There would be a time soon that he would need the anger and the hatred and he was glad to feel it burn deep inside of him.

There was nothing else left now.

After Giorgos had gone from her room, Philia pulled her nightgown around her shoulders, and quietly went downstairs.

She found her father in the kitchen, cooking two freshly cleaned fish on the stove, grilling them in a little bit of butter with a wedge of lemon next to him to squeeze over it when the fish was done cooking, the way that Iannis had told him to prepare it.

"What are you doing?" she whispered when she saw him.

"I thought I'd make a midnight snack."

"A midnight snack?"

"You need to keep your strength up."

"I don't need it, Papa."

"Fine. If you don't need it, I'm making it for my grandson, then. You can't deny him a little *lavraki*."

"Are you crazy? If Meinhard came downstairs …"

"He won't."

"He'll smell it."

"He drinks too much. He won't wake up."

"You're crazy."

"Maybe just a little bit."

He took the fish off the stove and put them on a plate and

squeezed the lemon over the top and the flaky meat in the center was still steaming and hot and it filled the kitchen.

"*Papa* ..."

"We'll be able to hear him if he wakes up, and I'll throw the plate out the window and deny the whole thing. It'll be fine."

Philia hesitated for another moment.

She looked at her father.

Then she finally took the fork that he offered with a smile and began to eat. It was certainly the best *lavraki* that she had ever tasted, she was sure of that, though she knew it couldn't be true.

Her father was good at many things, but he was a terrible cook.

Philia raised the fork to her mouth, and then again and again, savoring every bite, eating the fish expertly—since she had known Alexei for so long, she'd had much practice eating around the small bones, searching for them with her tongue before using her fingers to pick them out of her teeth.

Giorgos ate some of the fish, too, but not very much, he mostly watched Philia, and he smiled. It was such a beautiful moment, the two of them together in the kitchen, the thrill of doing what they were doing.

And then, there was a voice behind them—

"That looks quite delicious."

They both froze and turned to see Meinhard standing in the doorway, watching as Philia ate.

"Meinhard?"

"You're surprised."

"How ...?"

"What? You thought that you'd hear me on the stairs if I came down? You foolish man. You foolish, foolish man. We got a telegram from the Fuhrer tonight with new plans. I had to stay at the barracks very late. What, did you think that I was upstairs, asleep? Is this what you always do when I sleep?"

Giorgos stepped in front of his daughter—

"No, we—"

"*Silence*," Meinhard said.

And there was authority in his voice, and whether he was drunk or not, Giorgos and Philia could now see why he had been chosen to be a commander of men.

His look hardened, and he had no eyes for Giorgos anymore.

He spoke directly to Philia.

"I could have taken you if I wanted to. Any of the nights that I've stayed here. Your room was only feet down the hallway from where I slept, and I wanted you so badly. Do you know how hard that is for a man?"

"*I'm sorry ...*" she whispered.

"But some men have honor, and I followed the Fuhrer's rules. Even that night when you stayed up to talk to me. All that I asked in return is that you followed the Fuhrer's rules, too. And you betrayed me."

"*Meinhard, please ...*"

"Silence," he said again.

There was so much anger in his eyes.

"What can I do?" Philia asked him.

"Nothing. You can do nothing."

Philia opened her mouth, about to speak, to plead with him, to give him anything that he asked for, but before any more words came Meinhard pulled the Luger from the holster at his waist and shot her father in the head.

PART IV

"From henceforth we will not say that the Greeks fight like heroes . . . but that heroes fight like Greeks."
—Winston Churchill, Prime Minister of the United Kingdom, from a speech on the BBC

22

April 19th, 1941

ALEXEI STOOD HIGH ON THE BLUFF above Agria and looked down on his city.

The sun was above him, beating in waves on his already-tanned skin, and it was the smell of salt in the air that let him know more than anything else that he was home. The sun shed familiar warmth on his cheeks. The water of the Aegean was as clear as it had ever been. He breathed it all in. There had been so many nights that he'd dreamt of this.

Costa came next to him.

"Germans," Costa said.

They looked together into the valley at where the dark-grey Panzers were parked in neatly ordered lines outside the city, and then they looked to the town square where the grey-suited soldiers were walking through their village, past their buildings, and along their cobbled streets where Alexei and Costa had run and played when they were children.

"How many do you think there are?" Alexei asked Costa.

Costa squinted into the distance.

"It's hard to tell," he said. "It looks like they've taken over the city hall for their officers."

They stood there looking below them, each with their own thoughts. The Germans had made it to their village, and they needed to wait for Koukidis and his men to catch up before they could do anything. Two men against an entire army, as Koukidis had pointed out, was less than good odds. Then Alexei saw something in the distance.

"Look," Alexei said.

Costa turned, and he saw, too.

"It's a boy, I think," Costa answered. "It looks like Nico."

"What's he doing up here?"

"I don't know."

They glanced at each other. They both knew that whatever the reason, it surely couldn't be good.

They went to meet him.

And when they saw his face they saw how it'd changed.

His eyes were darker and sunken in. It was as if he'd aged ten years in as many days. He was a man in a boy's body now, because he'd seen things that only a man should have to see. He'd done things that only a man should have to do, if they have to even be done at all.

"Nico," Costa said walking towards him. "What are you doing up here? Where's your mother?"

Nico paused. He looked down into the dirt as he gathered himself. Then he looked up and met their eyes and told them what happened.

He told them how he'd left Agria with Thalia, and how the Germans had found them on the road. He told them about the German camp, and how the soldiers brought him to their fire while their captain had taken his mother to his tent. He told them how he'd killed the German soldier in the woods, and then snuck off and found the tent where the officer had his mother, and how he'd come to the tent too late. And then he told them how he'd killed the German officer who'd raped his mother, and after it was done how he'd found his way back to Agria, because he didn't know what else to do, or where else to go.

He went to Philia's house when he returned, he said.

Philia would know what to do.

But when he arrived at Philia's house, he knew something wasn't right there, too. There were too many people. Soldiers. Coming and going. Too much traffic for a normal morning. So instead of knocking on the door, or going inside, he waited and watched from a distance.

And that's when he saw them carry Giorgos' body out.

There was a hole in his forehead, Nico told them. He could see it, even from a distance. It was the size of a drachmae, a shot from close range. And there were too many Germans there, so he went back to the hills.

And that's when he'd seen Alexei and Costa.

They stood in stunned silence when Nico had finished his story, each of them processing their own individual losses in their own different ways.

Then Costa looked back down at Nico.

He knew that he was this boy's father now.

And not just his father, but the only parent that he had left in the world.

He reached out and put his arms around Nico's shoulders, pulling the boy closer to him.

"What are we going to do?" Nico asked, his head buried against Costa's chest.

And the question hung in the air.

"Have they seen you in the city?" Alexei asked him.

"We left last night," Nico said. "And I came back today. They don't know that I was ever gone."

"Good."

"What are you thinking?" Costa asked Alexei.

Alexei turned back to Nico—

"I want you to go back down to the city, Nico. They won't do anything to you. But I need you to find Philia, and tell her that we're here, and that there's more of us coming."

"More of you?"

"Other soldiers that we've fought with. And when you speak with her, make sure that there isn't anyone else around, so that she's the only one that knows. That's very important, Nico. The Germans can't know that we're up here. Tell her that I'll meet her at the old ruins at Dimini at midnight tonight. She knows where they are."

"Alright."

"And tell her to make sure that nobody sees her when she leaves the village. That's very important, too. Can you do that for me?"

Nico nodded—

"Good."

"Then what's going to happen, Theo Alexei?" he asked. "Are we going to fight back?"

"Yes," Alexei said. "We're going to fight back."

Nico stood there for a moment longer, and Costa ran his hand through the boy's hair, and then Nico nodded, and turned to head back down the mountains towards Agria.

Alexei and Costa stood next to each other and watched as the boy left. They stood in silence for a long time, until Costa finally spoke—

"Alexei ..."

"Yes?"

"Are you thinking the same thing that I am?"

"I don't know."

"I think you are, but you don't want to. Because you don't want to let yourself feel what you know you should feel. You want to keep your judgment. But we should let ourselves feel it, after what they've done to us. It's the only way that we're going to survive."

Alexei turned and looked at him, and when Costa saw his eyes, he knew that he was right. They shared the same anger. The same hatred, buried now, deep in their souls. It was the first time that they'd truly felt the fire that the hatred brings with it, and they both knew that they would need it now, all of it, if they were going to survive the days that were to come. That was all they could hope. That the pain and the anger could now be useful.

Alexei started to leave—

"Where are you going?" Costa called after him.

"Dimini."

"Alone?"

"Koukidis should be here soon. Tell him and the others what's happened. I'll be back at dawn."

Costa nodded. He'd wait for Koukidis.

"And Costa …" Alexei said.

"What is it?"

Alexei knew he didn't need to say it, but he still wanted to.

"Let's kill all of them, alright?"

Costa stared back at him—

"Yes," he said. "Let's kill every last one."

Alexei came to Dimini as the sun was sinking in the sky.

It was a three mile walk to the west of Agria before he

came to the well-preserved ruins of the late Neolithic city that sat on a low hill overlooking the Pagasitikos Bay.

Alexei went slowly as he made the journey.

It was the only bit of rest and beauty that he'd allowed himself in some time, and he realized that it was something that he needed. When he finally got to the ruins he stood on the hill that looked out over the sea and found himself thinking of his father. Was he out there, in his boat? Did he even still have his boat, or had it been taken by the Germans? How had the fishing been that spring? It was the longest Alexei had been away from the water in his entire life, he realized, and he missed it.

But that was all gone now.

He walked through the ruins by himself.

Alexei enjoyed the way that it felt, to be among such history. Had Agamemnon lived here? Had Jason sat in these halls, and walked these hills? Did Achilles stop here on his journey to Troy and immortality? Alexei was just a solitary man, he knew, a solitary man alone amongst the giants hidden in those old and ruined piles of stone, the ancient reminders of how great his people had once been.

And they had been great once, there was no doubt.

But could they still be great again?

If Agamemnon's palace could fade to dust and stone— the same dust and stone that was now under his feet—then what would their fate be? The fate of the men like Alexei and Costa and everyone else that had been born in this land, and were the descendants of those heroes, and the inheritors of their great legacy?

He didn't know.

Time passed.

Alexei sat on the cold stones of what had once been a wall, or perhaps the foundation of a house, and he realized that the sun had set, and the moon was large in the night sky.

And then he saw Philia walking towards him.

She was walking softly, picking her way between the ancient stones when Alexei stood to meet her. They didn't say anything as they moved together under the moon and stars above them, and they held each other longer than they'd ever held each other before.

"I told you I'd come back," Alexei said softly.

"It's all I've prayed for."

"I'm sorry, Philia. I'm so sorry."

"So am I," she said, and she started to cry, and Alexei held her even closer. She buried herself in his chest. She felt safe when he was holding her, and soon her tears dried, and she looked up at him.

"The funeral's going to be in three days," she whispered quietly. "I don't know what suit to dress him in. I don't know which was his favorite. Maybe you can help me?"

"Philia ..." Alexei said softly.

He knew this was going to be hard.

"What?"

"We need to be gone by then," he told her, as gently as he could.

"What do you mean? Gone where?"

"Away from here. Somewhere safe."

"I have to bury my father. I can't just leave him."

"There's no time for a funeral."

"And so we just leave his body to rot? I can't do that, Alexei. Children bury their parents."

Alexei thought about this, and he knew that she was right, but he also knew that he was right, too.

"We'll talk to my father. We can do it the old way, the way that the fisherman did it when there were people living here on this hill, and the way that they do it sometimes still."

"And how is that?"

"Burial at sea. My father will have no more need of his boat after this. There's not going to be any more fishing."

"And then where will we go?"

"First to Athens. Athens is still free. And we'll find something there. A boat. A way for us to leave."

"And then what?

"We'll go to any part of the world that hasn't been touched by this war. But we need to stay ahead of the Germans. They haven't made it to Athens yet. There's still hope, but we need to get there before they do."

"You haven't thought this through, have you? We'll just sail and sail until we come to something?"

"America. We'll go to America."

She was silent for a moment, then she bit her lip as she looked back at him in the darkness—

"I know that we have to go," she said. "I know that we have to do this, and that we have to leave. But it just seems so . . . final. Like an ending."

"It's not final, Philia. And it's not an ending. It's a beginning."

"The Germans in the city . . . they won't let us just leave."

"No, they won't. But soon there won't be any Germans in Agria."

She paused and looked back at him and saw the fire that was in his eyes, and she wanted to be closer to it, closer to that fire.

"What are you going to do?" she asked him.

"We're going to kill them."

"There's too many, Alexei. There's dozens of men in the city."

"Costa is with me, and our friend Koukidis, who fought with us in Albania, and his men. It'll be alright."

They were silent together for another moment.

"I wanted our son to be born in Greece," Philia said.

"So did I," Alexei answered. "But the world's decided for us, and there's nothing else to be done. He'll still be Greek, and he'll be ours, no matter where he's born. But if we want to live, and if we want our son to live, and to be free, then we need to leave here. As soon as possible."

"I want to make love to you," she said.

"What?"

"I want to make love to my husband."

"Philia, something terrible's just happened."

"I know. And I don't want to feel that anymore. I want to feel you. That's what I want right now, more than anything. I want to feel you inside of me, instead of this unbearable sadness."

She moved closer to him.

She took his hands and put them on her hips. She tilted her head up and kissed him deeply.

"I love that you're taller than me," she said.

And then she took her dress off, and his shirt and trousers next, and they were naked together in the moonlight of the ancient ruins and they used their clothes to make a soft bed on the rocky and uneven ground beneath them. He kissed her again, and gently laid her down before he lowered himself on top of her, moving between her legs, his breath catching in his throat as he heard her gasp when their love began.

They were in no hurry.

The night was finally theirs again.

They were as close as two people could ever be, and they took the time to bring each other as much pleasure as they could. He knew exactly what she wanted, exactly where she needed to be touched, and the way that she wanted him to do it, and she knew the same for him.

There was no concept of time.

He only knew her, the woman beside him, his wife.

But that night she wasn't his wife.

She was a princess, and he was a prince. She was a goddess, and he was a god. They both knew that there were other lovers in the world, but they also knew that there was no question that for one night the world belonged to them, and to them alone, and that it would always be theirs.

They never stopped. Not for the whole night.

It was something that they didn't even know was possible until that moment. When they eventually slowed they just lay there on the thin bed that they'd made and held each other. They held each other so close. They didn't need anything else. They lay there and held each other under the moon and the stars and the godless sky that stretched on above them forever.

23

April 20th, 1941

ALEXEI AND PHILIA WOKE AT FIRST light.

They dressed without speaking, then left the ruins, the sun rising in front of them, high over the Aegean, and they walked back the way that Alexei had come, towards the bluff above the city and the friends that were waiting there and the plans that needed to be made.

They knew that it was going to be a long day, and as they walked Alexei took in as much as he possibly could—the sights of his home, his youth, of every happy memory that he'd ever had—because he wasn't sure when he would see them again.

If he'd *ever* see them again.

When they got back to the bluff, they saw that Costa and Koukidis had allowed a small fire, and they were using the last of the warm embers to heat a small pot of coffee. They sat down on the rocks and Koukidis passed around cups while they discussed how they'd take back Agria.

Alexei was next to Philia.

Costa pulled Nico closer to him.

Koukidis sat with his men.

"Do we know where the main German armies are?" Alexei asked.

"We haven't heard anything more after the bridge," Koukidis answered him. "They should be to Larissa by now. Other than that, your guess is as good as ours. Do we know how many soldiers there are in the town?"

"Twenty-seven," Nico said, from his place next to Costa, and they all turned to look at him. "I've counted them," he added, with his young voice.

"Good," Costa said next to him, squeezing his shoulders. "Bravo."

"But that's just Agria," Koukidis said. "Do we know how many are in Volos?"

"It won't matter," Costa answered.

"Why?"

"Because we'll be gone by the time the soldiers from Volos get here."

"Philia is going to go back this morning," Alexei said, holding her hand, trying to give her some of his strength.

"It's not safe anymore," Koukidis turned to them. "It's better if she stays here."

"She has business with my father."

Koukidis saw the look in Alexei's eyes and knew not to ask anything further, and so he nodded, "Alright." And then he turned to look at Alexei and Costa both. "You two know the village better than anyone. Tell us how this begins?"

Alexei opened his mouth, about to speak, when Philia cut him off—

"The man who's staying at my home."

They all turned to look at her.

"His name's Meinhard," she said. "He wears one of the crosses at his neck, and he's very important to Germany. He's an officer. Their leader. Without him they won't have any orders."

"That's good."

"He comes home each night, just before midnight, and he's always drunk."

"I'll handle him," Alexei said, knowing what it meant to Philia, and that it was something that he needed to do personally.

"We'll send men with you."

"No," Alexei shook his head, and Koukidis saw the look on his face. "It's family business."

Koukidis nodded, understanding.

"My parents aren't far from Philia's house," Alexei continued. "After the German's gone, I'll find them and bring them up here."

"I'll get your parents," Costa said. "You won't have enough time." Then Costa put his arm around the boy next to him. "And Nico will go with me."

"Good," Alexei said, and he was happy because he knew his parents would be as safe with Costa as they would be with himself.

"So it's settled, then," Koukidis said. "Now what happens after you kill this German that's in your house?"

"It's close to the village. The rest of the soldiers will hear the gunshot, and they'll come to see what's happened. So we'll have to find somewhere to ambush them in the dark while they're on the way."

"That'll take care of half the garrison."

"Then we continue to town and take care of the other half."

"And leave before the sun comes up."

They all looked at each other.

"So we have a plan."

"We'll start as soon as it's dark, and we know that most of them will have gone to sleep."

Costa stood, and Nico stood with him.

"Where are you going?" Alexei asked.

"To teach the boy how to shoot," Costa answered.

Alexei watched as Costa and Nico walked into the distance towards the rocky hills above the city, and then Koukidis stood, too.

"It's going to be a long night," Koukidis said. "And then certainly a long day after that. I'm going to get some sleep. Someone wake me when it's dark."

Alexei was alone with Philia.

"What should I bring from the house?" she asked him.

"As much food as you can find."

"There's no food left."

"That's alright. We'll find some on the way, then."

"I know we will."

"We'll be safe."

"Our son will know nothing of the pain that we knew here. He'll only know how beautiful this land is."

Alexei realized they were finishing each other's sentences. It didn't matter who was speaking. It was all one.

"He'll have the best of everything that we've had," he said.

"He'll have a big backyard to play in. He'll smile a lot."

"He won't know anything of war."

"Except what he reads in books, a long time from now."

"We'll find somewhere near the water," Alexei smiled. "So that he can grow up the way that Greek boys grow up."

"He'll be happy, won't he?"

"And we'll be happy, too."

"It'll be beautiful."

They sat there together for another moment, Philia leaning against Alexei's chest, and he put his arms around her. In front of them the sun was already starting to sink. It was a moment, and they both could feel it.

"I have to go now, don't I?" Philia asked.

"Find my father," Alexei answered. "Tell him what I told you, and he'll know what to do."

"I will," she said, and she finally stood.

She kissed Alexei.

"I will," she said again.

Philia went to see Iannis and Eleni.

Eleni fell to her knees and wept when Philia told her that Alexei was safe and had come back to Agria, and Costa, too. It's all she'd prayed for, and her prayers had been heard, and answered. Iannis listened quietly as Philia delivered Alexei's message, about what they were to do, and then he nodded.

He agreed with his son.

It was the only way.

Then Iannis took Philia in his strong and sun-tanned arms—his dark fisherman's arms—and he held her, because she'd lost her father, but he wanted to make sure that she knew she still had a father. She apologized to him for the burden, and that he'd have to lose his boat, but he stopped her.

"Bring him to us here," he said.

"Thank you, Iannis."

"He was a great man, and we'll do him great honor."

"Thank you," she said again.

And she wiped away her tears.

She needed to be strong now.

Alexei sat next to Koukidis in the mountains at dusk.

He was looking into the distance as Koukidis polished his weapons and they were both watching as Costa taught Nico how to aim a rifle. They couldn't fire any rounds, because of the Germans in the city, but they were practicing without them. Alexei remembered himself at that age, but he had to quickly put it from his mind.

"Doesn't he seem a bit young?" Alexei said instead.

Koukidis looked up from polishing his rifle.

"You heard his story."

"I did."

"Maybe yesterday he was too young. Today he's one of us."

Costa showed Nico how to brace the butt of the gun against his shoulder and leverage the barrel to keep it steady. Costa looked like a father already, the way he was so natural with the boy. He'd have to ask him about it, Alexei thought, about his instincts, and how he knew what to do, and what to say. He looked much more comfortable than Alexei thought he was going to feel when his own child came, when the war was over.

When the war was over.

Whenever that would be.

Alexei took his rifle from where it leaned against a rock and began to polish it alongside Koukidis.

"It's too bad, isn't it?" Alexei said.

"What?"

"There's going to be so many more stories like his before

it's all over. There's still so much pain that has to be suffered. So many more mothers and fathers and brothers and husbands that are going to die."

"Try not to think about it."

"Why?"

"Because it's war," Koukidis said. "It's always beyond anything that we can imagine."

"There's going to be an entire generation of us marked and changed by what's happened."

"And the world will continue, as it always does, and as it always has, no matter what goes on in these hills. These won't be the first children to have seen horrible things in the dark, you know. There'll be scars. Of course there will be. But our children are strong, and we're strong, too."

Alexei looked at Koukidis, remembering Koukidis' own childhood, the story that he'd told Alexei on a cold night next to a fire in Pogradec. Then Koukidis nodded down towards Agria—

"Your wife is sure pretty," he said. "It's no secret now why you ran so fast to get back here. How'd she ever fall for an ugly *malaka* like you, anyways?"

"I don't know."

"Come on, tell Koukidis your secret."

"There's no secret," Alexei shrugged. "Agria's a small village. She didn't have many options."

Alexei looked back at Koukidis, keeping a straight face, and then he broke into a grin, and Koukidis saw that Alexei was making a joke, and he was glad.

"A joke, Alexei?" Koukidis laughed. "Costa was always the one making jokes, up in the mountains, and you were always so serious, sitting there in the cold with your books—your Hemingway and your Dumas—telling me that you didn't have any cigarettes. I always thought you were incapable of a joke."

"Maybe I was."

"What happened?"

Alexei took some of the grease that Koukidis was using and rubbed it across the barrel of his rifle, expertly polishing it to a bright shine, without even thinking about it.

Being the son of a fisherman was a lifetime ago.

"The world changes us, Koukidis," Alexei said.

He kept polishing his rifle—

"One day at a time . . . the world changes us."

They brought Giorgos' body to the dock.

Philia remembered the day that Alexei had taken her sailing to his island before he left, and she looked down at the ink that was on her wrist, and thought of the ink that was on his, and the promise that they shared between them.

How long ago had it been?

She couldn't remember.

Would she ever feel that way again?

She stared down at her father's body in the boat. Iannis had laid him out, and Thanos the baker had helped him, and come to bear witness. His arms were crossed peacefully over his chest. His eyes were closed. His lips were turned up into an almost-smile. Eleni had done everything that she could with her makeup, using every trick that she knew, but the small hole in Giorgos' forehead was still visible.

"It's time," Iannis said.

Philia nodded and walked forward to sprinkle flower petals that she'd picked around the boat and over the body.

Then she bent down next to him.

"Goodbye, Papa," she whispered into his ear. "I love you. I love all of you. Kiss your wife for me. Tell her how beautiful her grandson is going to be. Kiss your wife, and tell her that I love her, too."

She kissed her father on the cheek, for the last time, then walked away from the boat.

She nodded to Iannis.

He came forward with Thanos and they poured gasoline over the wood. When they'd poured all the gasoline, and set the can aside, Iannis struck a match and dropped it over the edge.

The flames began.

They rose above the edges of the boat.

Giorgos and Thanos pushed the burning boat out into the water, over the small waves, until they were up to their chests, and the current was stronger.

On the beach, Eleni stood next to Philia and put her arm around her daughter, to give her strength. They watched as Iannis and Thanos gave the boat one last push so that it would catch the current and float out to sea as it burned. Philia wondered where the current would take it. She wondered which direction it would go, and how far.

She wondered how her father had imagined his own end.

In the mountains, high above the city, Alexei and Costa and the rest of the Greek soldiers made their final preparations as the sun sank in the sky and disappeared behind the peaks.

Soon it was dark.

Costa would leave first, with Nico, to go to Alexei's parents' house. It was far enough out of the city that they could use the cover of darkness to not be seen by any Germans, and Iannis and Eleni knew that they were coming, so they'd be ready and waiting for them.

Alexei left next.

He slung his rifle over his shoulder and made his way quietly down the mountain alone, heading to Philia's house, and as he walked he realized that he wasn't scared for what the night would bring, but rather he was glad. He was going to kill the men who had brought suffering and death to his village, and to his family. He didn't worry if what he was going to do was right, or just, or deserved. It was just going to be. The Germans had already answered any moral questions the Greeks might have had, a long time ago.

"*No prisoners,*" Koukidis had said to each of them before they left, and then repeated it again. They couldn't afford to leave anyone behind, and they couldn't afford to take anyone with them. Not where they were going, and not with what they had to do.

Alexei kept walking.

He made his way through the darkness to the road that led to Philia's house, and he remembered a morning not so long ago when he'd walked this same path with a goat following behind him.

He remembered what he'd thought that morning.

Kairos.

And then he thought it again.

When he came to Philia's house he saw that she'd left the light on in the kitchen, like she'd told him she would. He went in the back, and Philia was waiting there to meet him.

"Is he upstairs?" Alexei asked.

"Yes," she said. "He's sleeping."

Alexei kept his rifle slung across his back and took the Luger pistol from his boot. He went to the stairs, where Philia stopped him. She put her hand on the Luger, and Alexei knew what she wanted. He saw the look on her face, and recognized the same look she had the night they spent together on Eudaimonia, when she'd asked him to ink her wrist, the same as he'd done to himself.

But this time he wouldn't let her get her way.

"No," he whispered.

"He was my father," she said. "And I was there. I want to do it."

"He was my father, too."

She hesitated—

"Please," Alexei whispered in the dark. "Let me save you from this. We're going to have a child to raise soon. Only one of us can have done horrible things here in the dark. It's no secret that taking a life breaks us, and only one of us can afford to be broken."

She saw his eyes.

And what she saw scared her.

Because for a moment she didn't recognize them.

Alexei gently took her hand from the gun, and she let him do it, and then she watched as he made his way quietly up the stairs, careful not to make any noise, something he'd learned in Albania.

When he was out of her sight, Philia looked around, at everything, and she realized that it wasn't her home anymore. Nothing in it was hers. Not a single thing. It was a museum now. A museum that would soon belong to someone else.

She waited.

Alexei crept down the hallway.

He came to Meinhard's bedroom and turned the knob as he gently pushed the door open. He looked in to see that Meinhard hadn't woken. Alexei crossed the room to stand next to him and then took the barrel of his gun and pushed it down between Meinhard's lips and past his teeth, and when Meinhard felt the cold steel in his mouth his eyes snapped open. Alexei was pleased to see the panic in them. He could have just killed Meinhard while he slept. But he hadn't. He wanted to break him first, because isn't death release?

"Who are you?" Meinhard asked through the barrel between his teeth.

Alexei didn't answer.

"I have money," Meinhard continued. "You don't have to do this."

"Yes. I do."

"Why?"

"Because you killed my father."

"No. I killed the father of the woman who lives here, which was my right. He broke the law."

"The woman that lives here is my wife. And eating our own fish from our own waters is breaking no law."

"You haven't thought this through," Meinhard said. "You can still walk away. My men in town . . . they'll come as soon as they hear the gunshot. When I shot the man who lived here, they were in the driveway within ten minutes, to see what had happened."

"I'm counting on it."

Alexei saw the recognition dawn in Meinhard's eyes,

that this was more than just uncalculated revenge, and that it had been thought through, and there were more Greek soldiers in Agria than just the one standing in front of him, and they had plans to kill Germans that night.

"How many of there are you?"

"Enough to kill all the Germans that will come."

"We have a lot of soldiers stationed here."

"You have twenty-seven soldiers. And soon there will only be twenty-six."

"You won't make it very far," Meinhard said evenly. "The rest of us . . . the armies that we have . . . all of Germany is coming to destroy every piece of this god-forsaken land."

"My wife tells me that you have no son."

"That's right."

"And that you were hoping to have one after the war."

"Yes."

"Then your name will die tonight, too."

Meinhard swallowed—

"Can I at least put my clothes on, so that I can die respectably? Would you at least let me have that dignity?"

Alexei swept the blankets that were covering him off the bed to see that he was completely naked underneath, and he had the distinct pale skin of the northern races that don't see much sunlight or allow themselves enough joy.

"No," Alexei said.

Let it be his final shame, Alexei thought. Let the men from Volos that would come find their commander stark naked and dead in the bed that he'd taken as his own.

What shame for a German.

What shame for a proud man.

Alexei thought all this in a split second and Meinhard must have recognized the look that he saw in Alexei's eyes and known that this was the end as Alexei squeezed his index finger and the barrel of the pistol exploded, a bright flash in the dark night.

Bang!

The shot echoed through the house as Meinhard's head snapped back against the bed, spraying bits of blood and skull and flesh across Alexei's sleeve and up his arm and onto his neck.

Alexei looked down at the body in front of him.

A proud German left dead and naked and already forgotten.

It was a fitting ending for such a man.

He turned and went back downstairs to find Philia waiting for him. She hadn't moved from the spot where he'd left her. She stared at the blood across Alexei's sleeve and up his arm, and he went to her and took a moment to hold her close, his heart beating rapidly, his body still flush with adrenaline.

Her head rested against his chest—

"Is it over?" she asked, and there was blood on her now, too, on her dress, and on her skin.

"It's over."

She stared at the dark red stains, her head still resting on her husband, and she realized—

"I can feel your heart," she said.

"We have to go."

They met Costa outside.

He was with Nico and Iannis and Eleni, and as soon as Alexei saw them he gave his mother a long hug. He held his arm to the side so that he didn't get any of Meinhard's blood on her. After she'd held onto him for too long, her body shaking with soft little sobs, he gently led her towards the hills and the path up to their camp in the mountains, where they'd be safe.

"We'll be right behind you," Alexei said.

"What do you mean?" Eleni asked.

"Nico knows where our camp is, Mana. He's going to take you and Papa up there, with Philia, to wait for us. We won't be long."

"What are you going to do?"

"Just one last thing."

Alexei looked to his father who walked forward and took his wife by the hand, squeezing as reassuringly as he could. "Come on, Eleni," he said. "Let's go with Nico, like Alexei says. They have to hurry now. We don't want to keep them. There'll be plenty of time to talk when we're on our way tomorrow."

She hesitated, and Alexei offered her the best smile that he could.

"We'll be right behind you, Mana," he said.

She still looked back at him, and didn't move.

"I promise," he said. "We'll be right behind you."

Alexei and Costa ran through the night.

Nico had taken Iannis and Eleni to wait at the camp above the city, and Alexei and Costa were going to meet Koukidis and the rest of the Greek soldiers on the road to Agria. They had business to take care of, and as they went around a bend in the road, they saw a hastily created blockade.

There were several boulders rolled across the road.

Then, a whisper in the darkness—

"Over here, *malaka*."

They turned to see Koukidis hidden in the undergrowth, his face rubbed black with tar, the same as the rest of his men, blending into the darkness and the night. Half of the men were on one side of the road, and half were on the other.

Alexei and Costa walked towards Koukidis.

"If we're lucky, the boulders will do most of our work for us," Koukidis said. "We'll only have to pick off the stragglers that survive the crash."

"If they don't see the boulders."

"They won't. They'll be driving fast. They'll be in too much of a hurry to find out who else Meinhard has killed. So get yourselves ready because it won't be long now. The Germans are nothing if not punctual."

Alexei and Costa nodded and joined Koukidis and his men in their hiding places and only a few moments passed before they heard a low rumbling in the distance.

And then there were lights on the road.

They saw the German kubelwagen jeeps driving towards them, and they held their breath as they got closer, and then they saw that there were three of them in total. Alexei chambered his first bullet. He looked at Costa. Then they nodded at each other.

Once more unto the breach.

"*Steady now ...*" Koukidis whispered.

They aimed their rifles as the jeeps came barreling towards them, around the corner, and they didn't see the boulders as Koukidis had said they wouldn't and they slammed on their brakes but it was too late, as—

Kaboom!!!

The first jeep plowed into the blockade and the other

jeeps behind ran into the back of the first jeep and there were huge explosions of shattered glass and twisted metal.

The men inside were dazed.

"Hold ..." Koukidis whispered again. "... *let them get out.*"

The Germans opened the doors and fell out of the jeeps—they were coughing, bleeding, staggering to find footing and trying to adjust their eyes to the darkness and figure out what had happened.

The Greeks waited.

Half the Germans were out of the jeeps.

Koukidis would give the signal.

More men stepped out.

Alexei and Costa took their aim.

Then all of the Germans were out of the jeeps and onto the road and Koukidis yelled into the night—

"Now!!!"

Bang bang!!

Rat-a-tat-tat-tat!!!

Bang bang bang!!!

The road lit up with bullets flying from both sides of it, angled backwards towards the Germans so that the Greeks wouldn't hit each other. In the first volley, six Germans were cut down immediately. The others dove for cover as soon as they heard the shots, reaching for their guns, but the Greeks kept firing, and it was a massacre.

There wasn't anything the Germans could have done.

The Greek soldiers were everywhere, on all sides of them, ghosts in the darkness, exactly what Koukidis had wanted, and they spared no thoughts for mercy, or prisoners.

Not after what the Germans had done.

Not after they'd each heard Nico's story.

When the last of them were cut down, and lay bleeding their lives out in the dirt, the Greeks came from their hiding spots and walked amongst the bodies. Some of them were still moving, not quite dead, and the Greeks put bullets in their skulls. Alexei looked at the bodies on the road and made a quick count.

"There's twelve of them," he said.

"That means there's still fifteen left."

"That's not so bad."

"Not so bad for us," Koukidis smiled. "But very bad for them."

"Let's be careful as we get closer to town. They'll be expecting us now."

They all nodded and slung their rifles across their backs and some of the men tucked new Lugers into their belts. They left the remnants of the kubelwagen jeeps in the middle of the road. It would be a reminder for the next Germans that came along that the Resistance had been there, and that if you were an enemy of Greece, then you weren't safe, not anywhere that you would go.

They turned and ran towards Agria.

The night was still dark, and they were going to finish the job that they'd started.

There was shouting in the streets.

The Greek soldiers crept quietly through the alleys of the city, staying in the shadows so they wouldn't be seen. They stopped at the edge of the town square, in view of the city hall, which the Germans had turned into their barracks. The German soldiers were outside arguing. They'd heard the first shot, at Philia's house, where Meinhard had been staying, and half their company had left to see what had happened. Then they'd heard more shots, from the distance, and now they didn't know what to do. Without Meinhard there was no clear chain of command.

And, for the Germans, that was a problem.

And the Greeks knew it.

"*Everyone spread out ...*" Koukidis whispered to the Greek soldiers as they got closer, "*... it'll make us harder targets to hit.*"

Alexei and Costa used their hands to point and show the Greeks where to find hiding spots around the square and still be able to aim at the building and their enemies in front of it. There were five Germans in the courtyard—two guards by the door to the city hall, and three more pacing back and forth and arguing. That meant that there were ten that were still left in the building.

"Can you hit them from here?" Koukidis asked Costa.

"I think so."

"We'll take out the two guards first."

"If we're lucky some of them in the building will come out into the courtyard," Alexei added.

"Yeah, and if they don't ..." Koukidis smiled, "then we'll have to go in after them."

"Alexei, do you want to give us a count?" Costa asked.

Alexei nodded as Koukidis and Costa checked the ammo in their rifles. Everything was so different than it had been even just a short time ago. This was something they were experienced with now.

War.

Killing.

And they were good at it, too.

Costa and Koukidis rested their rifles against the side of the building in front of them as they each took careful aim at their marks across the square.

"Do you want right or left?" Koukidis asked him.

"I'll take left," Costa said.

"Ready?" Alexei asked quietly.

"Ready."

Alexei began the count—

"*Five ... four ... three ...*"

Costa and Koukidis flipped the safeties off their rifles, lined their targets in the sights—

"*... two ... one ...*"

Bang bang!!!

The guards dropped dead with bullets in their skulls.

The other Germans whipped around as the rest of the Greek soldiers opened fire—

Bang bang bang bang bang bang bang!!!!!

There were quickly five corpses in the courtyard, and Germans came running out of the building to see what had happened, like the Greeks had hoped they would.

Bang bang bang bang bang!!! Rat-a-tat-tat!! Bang bang!!!

The Germans tried to return fire but they were cut down before any of their bullets could find marks.

"*How many??*" Costa yelled as he reloaded.

Alexei tried to make a quick count.

Rat-a-tat-a-tat-a-tat-a-tat-a-tat-a-tat!!!

The Greeks dove for cover as the Germans still left inside the building unleashed a hail of automatic fire from their MP40 machine guns and two of the Greeks were hit and fell to the ground, blood pooling onto the streets around them.

Rat-a-tat-a-tat-a-tat!!!

More automatic fire kept the Greeks pinned where they were.

"Eight bodies," Alexei said.

"That means there's seven left inside the building," Costa answered.

Rat-a-tat-a-tat-a-tat-a-tat-a-tat-a-tat!!!

More automatic fire from the Germans pelted the town square around where the Greeks were hiding, shredding bits of rock as bullets buried into ancient walls and stone.

The Greeks knew that they were out-gunned.

"We're not going to be able to do much against those MP40s," Costa said.

"How much ammo do you think they've got in there?"

"They're Germans," Alexei said. "I'm sure they've got as much as they need."

"I wasn't counting on the machine guns," Koukidis said.

"We can't afford to waste all our bullets here," Costa was thinking out loud. "We need to get them out into the square."

Then Costa thought for another moment, and he turned to Koukidis—

"Do you have a grenade?"

"What?"

"From the Germans we killed," he said. "On the road."

Koukidis reached into his pocket and took a grenade that he'd found on a dead German and handed it to Costa.

"You think you can make the throw?" Koukidis asked.

"No," Costa answered him. "Not from here. Alexei, can you cover me?"

Alexei nodded.

"What are you going to do?" Koukidis asked.

Costa smiled—

"I told you, *malaka*. This is my city."

Costa crept along the edge of the square, staying in the shadows and blending in with the night. The grenade that Koukidis had given him was in his pocket. Alexei and Koukidis watched Costa as he reached the point where he needed to be, and Costa looked to them and nodded as he made the sign of the cross over his chest.

He was ready.

Alexei and Koukidis loaded their rifles.

"Alright," Koukidis whispered.

Then they nodded to the rest of the Greek soldiers, spread around the square, and on Koukidis' move they all jumped up with their weapons, and—

Bang bang bang!!! Bang bang!!! Bang bang bang!!!!!!

Their bullets exploded against the sides of the city hall and the Germans ducked behind their cover.

The Greeks kept reloading and kept firing as fast as they could.

Bang bang bang bang bang bang!!!

Costa used the distraction to run through the courtyard towards the city hall. He went down a back alley behind the building that only he would have known was there because he knew every inch of those streets.

The Greeks kept firing.

Costa crept closer.

Soon he was next to the building, able to reach out and touch the wall, the Germans right above him.

Alexei waved at the Greeks to stop shooting so they wouldn't hit him.

It was the first quiet since the fighting had started.

The Germans, on their side, took deep breaths.

Costa knew that this was the only moment that he was going to have, and he quickly calculated timing and angles as he took the grenade from his pocket and above him the Germans started firing again, their bullets launching from just mere feet above his head.

Rat-a-tat-a-tat-a-tat!!!

The noise was deafening.

And then, with his calculations complete, in one motion Costa pulled the pin and threw the grenade inside the window above him, where the Germans were firing from.

There was German shouting.

Costa ran as fast as he could, back the way he'd come.

Kaboom!!!!!!

German limbs were torn from their bodies.

There was more screaming.

Smoke was pouring out of the building.

"Come on!" Alexei shouted.

The Greeks ran across the courtyard.

Koukidis ran into the building first, and the rest of the Greeks followed after him.

The Germans that weren't already dead were blind from the smoke and their ears ringing from the explosion and the Greeks pulled their knives to save their bullets and made quick work of them. Steel ripped into flesh, and Germans fell, and the floor was slick with their blood.

Alexei looked down and only counted six bodies at their feet.

He kept his rifle at the ready as he went further into the building, searching for the last soldier that should be there, covering the corners of each room that he went into, like he'd been taught to do.

Then he saw him.

The last German soldier was lying on the ground in a puddle of his own blood. It was coming from his face, and Alexei saw the fresh wounds that were across his eyes from the shrapnel, and he also saw that the soldier was now blind.

Alexei stood over him.

The German was young. Maybe no more than fifteen years old. Why would they do this? Why would they waste their youth in this way? Was all this so important that it meant sending children to die?

The German boy could feel Alexei standing over him.

He tried to speak in German, which Alexei didn't understand, but then Alexei saw the German's hand next to him, and it was reaching for something, a prayer card lying on the floor, slick with the boy's blood smeared across the picture of Saint Christopher.

"Here," Alexei said, as he bent down and picked the card up and put it into the boy's hand.

"*Danke*," the German said gratefully, his hands wrapping around the card, bringing it closer to him. "*Danke ... danke ... danke ... danke*."

The boy held the saint close to his chest, and began to whisper a hushed and final prayer, "*Vater unser im Himmel, geheiligt werde dein name, dein reich komme, dein Wille geschehe ...*"

Alexei stood again.

He aimed his rifle down as the boy prayed.

And then, when his prayer was finished, the boy nodded his head, softly, one last time, and—

Bang.

The boy's head snapped back, his face now frozen in death. Alexei looked down at him. And as he did, he realized something was wrong. He'd just killed a boy, a fifteen-year-old boy, and he felt nothing.

He wanted to, but it wasn't there.

And he realized that it hadn't been for some time. Not when he killed Jurgen. Not when they killed the Germans at the bridge. Not when he'd killed Meinhard, as he lay naked in Giorgos' bed, or any of the other Germans in Agria.

What had happened?

When did it happen?

It scared him.

He thought of the mountains of Albania, and the young Greek soldier who couldn't stop his hand from shaking after the first man that he'd killed. That was him, he told himself. That was me.

It had been.

Was it still?

"*Alexei* ..."

He turned to see Costa waiting behind him—

"Are you ready?"

He shook his head clear.

There would be time for worry and fear later, he knew. There would be time for many things once they were safe and away from there.

But they weren't yet.

So Alexei and Costa left together, walking back out into the night.

The Greek soldiers quickly made their way back up to their camp in the mountains. When they got there they saw Nico sitting with Philia and Iannis and Eleni around a small fire that they'd built, and Nico stood when he heard men coming, his rifle aimed and ready, the way that Costa had showed him to hold it. Then, he saw who it was, and he lowered it, slinging it back across his shoulders, and he nodded.

As they walked towards the fire, Alexei found Philia's eyes and he watched as she took in the state of their clothes—the fresh blood and dirt caked on them in layers, and the fact that the group that had been eleven when they left was now only nine.

And she could see the look that was in her husband's eyes. She could see that something had changed. That something had shaken him.

"*Alexei* ..." she said softly.

"I'm alright," he said too quickly.

"Are you sure?"

"It's done," Alexei said, as he looked around, and then he said it again. "It's done now."

Eleni came over and hugged her son, and Iannis followed, and he hugged Alexei, too.

"We brought some fish and cooked it over the fire," Philia told him. "Are you hungry?"

"We'll eat it on the road."

"Are the Germans going to be coming that quickly?"

Alexei looked at his wife and tried to talk with her as if he wasn't covered from head to foot in dirt and blood, and they hadn't just come from killing two dozen Germans.

"They might be," he said. "They're on the move, and we have to make it to Athens before they do. That's the only thing that matters now."

She nodded.

"Is everyone ready?" Alexei asked, turning to the others.

More nods.

They were ready.

Alexei went to the head of the group where he stood with Costa and Koukidis and they started to walk, setting the pace that they'd keep through the night, and the route that they'd take south. The rest of the group fell into step behind them—Eleni, Iannis, Philia and Nico, and the rest of the Greek soldiers.

Alexei turned and looked back at them. They had women, and children, and old men. He knew they'd have to go slower than he wanted, but he also knew there was no other way.

"What do you think?" Alexei asked Costa softly, turning to him, so that only they could hear.

"It'll be long, and it'll be hard," Costa said. "But we'll make it."

"As long as the Germans don't find us."

"As long as the Germans don't find us," he agreed.

They looked at each other one more time, and then they were silent as they started out on their final journey through their ravaged and war-torn country. They knew they'd need to save their energy. They'd need to save their words. They'd need to save everything that they could. The sun was just beginning to rise in the distance, and they had a long ways to go.

24

April 21st, 1941

THEY KEPT WALKING UNTIL THEY HEARD the sounds of another battle.

The sun was now peaking over the mountains to the east and the dawn just coming, and that's when they heard the large explosions in the distance and felt the ground tremble beneath them.

Tanks.

Then more gunfire.

The soft whine of approaching planes.

Costa looked above them, squinting against the morning sun.

"Luftwaffe," he said, seeing the swastikas painted on the tails of the German fighters as they flew over them towards the battle. "They must have taken the airfield."

They couldn't see the battle from where they were walking: there were too many hills that were between them and wherever it was happening, but there was surely fierce fighting taking place in one of the many valleys in the near distance.

"What do you think?" Alexei asked him. "Do you think it's some of ours that they're fighting against?"

"It doesn't matter. Greek, British, Australian, New Zealanders . . . whoever's fighting, it's still the same answer. We need to keep going."

"We should take a look. See how close they are."

Costa agreed, and they jogged away from the group and up to the top of a hill some meters away from where they'd been walking to see if they could get a glimpse of the fighting. The noise grew and grew as they went, and as it did they then knew that the fighting wasn't going to be in some distant valley away from where they were at, and then they reached the top of the hill and looked below them and that's when they finally saw the fierce battle that was being fought.

It was easy for them to identify the well-armed German Army on the northern side of the valley by the grey of their uniforms and the swastikas on the row of Panzers that were protecting their lines, lobbing mortars and shells across the field at the army to the south. And it wasn't hard to see the flag that was flying above the army that was across from the Germans, and the new flag that they were fighting against—

"*British*," Alexei said.

They watched as the German fire intensified, bombarding the British position with mortars from their tanks, and then the Luftwaffe circled back around to make another pass, laying down more machine-gun fire on the British lines, and Alexei and Costa watched as too many soldiers fell. The British had anti-aircraft guns that they used to send shells up into the sky at the passing planes as they dove at their lines, and Alexei and Costa also watched as one of the shells that they fired tore through the wing of a Luftwaffe plane and it spiraled out of control and then crashed down, down, down, until it finally exploded into the ground between the two armies.

It was a small victory for the British.

But too much damage had already been done.

Between the Panzers across the valley, and the Luftwaffe above them, it was very clear that the British wouldn't last much longer. To stay and fight any further would be suicide, so the British would retreat, and the Germans would keep pushing south after them, Alexei and Costa knew, further into Greece, further towards Athens, and along the same road that Alexei and Costa and the rest of the survivors would be taking also.

They both understood that.

And so they also understood that plans needed to be changed.

"Let's go further to the west," Alexei said to Costa. "Further inland. We'll find another way there. It'll take us longer, but it's better than running into the Germans on the road."

Costa nodded, and they agreed.

They went back to the group and told them what they'd seen.

Then they turned west together, and kept walking.

Alexei was worried about his mother.

It was a long journey, and a journey that they had to make too quickly. And he was worried about his father, too, and the limp that was still there in his leg, and had only gotten worse, his wound from the war that he'd fought, many years before this one that they were now fighting again. And then there was Philia, who was carrying their child inside her, and although she wore a brave face every moment that they were together, Alexei knew that she hadn't felt brave for some time now.

But no matter how much he worried, they had no other choice.

They had to keep going.

They had to reach Athens.

So they picked up their pace. Alexei fell back to walk with his mother, and it was no mystery to her why her son was walking next to her, with the look of concern on his face. She smiled for him, to try to show him that he shouldn't be worried, and he smiled back as he passed her some water and she drank, being careful not to have too much.

"You spoil me, *Alexei-mou*," she said, wiping her lips as she handed the water back to her son and watched as he put it away instead of drinking any himself.

"You spent your whole life spoiling me, Mana."

She nodded at the countryside around them that they were walking through—

"This is a beautiful part of the country, isn't it? Have I ever taken you here, Alexei?"

"On the train. When we went to Athens, when I was six."

"That's right," she said, thinking back and smiling. "That was a good trip. Do you remember what you said when you saw the Acropolis for the first time?"

"Of course," he smiled. "I asked you who lived there."

"And do you remember what I told you?"

"God lives there."

"You were such a beautiful little boy," she put her hand

on the side of his cheek. "You still are, you know. You're still very beautiful, and you'll always be a boy to me."

Alexei smiled—

"There's nothing more behind, but such a day tomorrow as today, and to be boy eternal."

"What's that from, Alexei? It's very beautiful, too."

"It should be. It's Shakespeare."

"I never did read much Shakespeare. But perhaps there's still time."

"I'll take you to America, Mana," he said. "And I'll buy you a big house because everyone in America has a big house. And you'll have all the time in the world to read Shakespeare or plant a garden or do anything else that you'll want to do."

"All I want is to play with my grandchildren. You know that just one isn't enough, right?"

"We'll give you as many as you want."

"I want four."

"It sounds like you've thought about it."

Eleni elbowed her son in the ribs, and he smiled again—

"Four would do," she said. "But five would be better."

They didn't slow their pace or stop to rest until Alexei and Costa were satisfied that they were far enough away from the Germans and their army, which had surely broken the British by now, and the route that the Germans would take.

Koukidis and his men had fanned out around the rest of them—some of the soldiers were ahead, and some were behind—and they were hiding in the hills on either sides of the road to keep watch in case there were any other Germans that might be in front of them, or coming from the other way, the way that they'd just walked from. If there were, the Greeks would fight, of course. But they didn't want Iannis and Eleni and Philia to be anywhere near where the fighting would happen.

Philia changed her pace so that she was next to Alexei.

"How long do you think it will take us to get to Athens?" she asked him as they walked.

"It should take four days," he said. "Or at least that's what I've calculated. But we need to do it in three. I don't know . . . we may even need to do it in two, if it comes to it."

"Do you think we'll be able to?"

"It depends on a lot."

"Like what?"

He turned and looked at her. He'd decided on honesty. They needed that now.

"It depends on how far the Germans have gotten," he said. "There's really no way to know. If they broke the British, they'll be right behind us, trying to make it to Athens as quickly as possible, and they'll be moving faster than we are. We think they'll take the other road, the one that we were on before, but we can really only guess and just hope that they take that one and not this one, and that they don't split their forces."

"There's thirteen of us here. The Germans have an entire army. Surely we'll make it to Athens before them?"

"They've conquered Europe because of how quickly they can move. They've been practicing it for years, and they can move faster than any army ever should be able to move. That's how they conquered Poland, Denmark, Norway, France, the Low Countries. And also . . . they only have soldiers with them," he added softly, meeting her eyes. "So they'll move quickly. They'll move very quickly."

"Do you think he'll make it?"

Alexei raised his eyebrows.

"Who?" he asked.

And he watched as Philia nodded to where Nico was walking next to Costa. He had a rifle slung across his back, and the large weapon looked even larger juxtaposed against his young shoulders, and he was trying to match Costa's long strides with his own. He'd been very quiet since they'd left Agria. In fact, he'd barely spoken at all since they'd found him in the hills above the city, after all that he'd seen, and after all that he'd done.

"He's strong," Alexei said, nodding. "And he has Costa."

"And what about you?" she asked, thinking back to the look that she saw, the one that was there in his eyes after he had come back from the battle against the garrison in Agria. "What about my husband?"

"Your husband's strong, too."

But she'd seen the change in him.

And as much as he tried, he couldn't hide his heart from her.

It's why they were what they were.

"What happened?" she asked him again, softly, so only they could hear.

"What do you mean?"

"In Agria."

He thought about it, and what he'd felt, and what he'd seen: the young boy, the much too young boy, and the bloody prayer card that he'd reached for.

He wasn't ready to tell her, he knew.

Not yet.

Then he saw something ahead of them in the distance, and he nodded towards it—

"Can you see that?"

312

"See what?"

"Stay here," Alexei said, and then Costa saw it, too, and they slipped their rifles off their backs as they went ahead again together. There was something that was on the road in front of them—a dark shape across their path in the distance that they couldn't identify. But as they got closer, the shape became sharper, clearer, and as they got closer still they then saw that it was the wreckage of a fighter plane.

They took note of the insignia on the wings and tail—

A red circle inside a large blue ring.

"British again," Costa said.

"It must be the last of the RAF."

And then as they got even closer still, they could smell the stench of flesh rotting in the sun. They pulled their shirts over their noses as they inched forward over the last of the distance and examined the wreckage.

The pilot was still in the cockpit.

Or at least what was left of him.

He had a massive gash across his forehead, and his face and body were badly burned from the engine exploding upon impact with the ground. Alexei went even closer and saw next to the gears and controls a picture of a woman clipped above the fuel gage: she was smiling, holding a baby in her arms, and somehow the picture had escaped the flames. Alexei took it and looked at the man's family, and then he heard Costa behind him.

"That stench is too strong for just one body."

"You're right."

"There has to be more."

"But where?"

They each looked around and then Costa pointed towards a small hill that was near them and they walked over and up to the top of it together and then saw scattered across the valley below them the wreckage of at least twenty more planes.

They were both British and German.

It was the remnants of a vicious battle that had taken place in the not too distant past. Germany would rule the skies, eventually, but not without a struggle. Greece and her allies were fighting back.

They wouldn't win.

But they were still fighting.

"It must have been some dogfight," Costa said quietly, and Alexei knew that he'd lowered his voice out of respect for the dead.

"Churchill kept his word."

"He's certainly determined to help us kill as many of them as we can."

"Let's keep moving," Alexei said, and nodded his head towards the mountains rising in the distance. "Let's see if we can make it to those mountains by nightfall."

"The mountains?"

"The roads and the countryside belong to the Germans now. But the mountains . . . they still belong to us."

Costa nodded.

And then they went.

They stopped and made camp soon after the sun went down.

They needed to rest, Alexei knew.

They'd already gone too far for Iannis and Eleni, and even for Philia, too, though none of them would ever admit it. They had too much pride, and they knew that there was too much at stake.

They weren't to the mountains yet, but they were close,

and they built a small fire in the sparse forest where they'd stopped. They didn't have much food left, either, and so Alexei had made the decision to eat only breakfast and lunch so that everyone had the strength to keep walking, but they'd skip dinner in the evenings, when they didn't need their energy.

It made for lonely and cheerless nights.

Iannis sat down next to his son and handed him a bottle of Metaxa.

"Metaxa?" Alexei said, taking the bottle from his father, looking at the label. "Where'd you get this?"

"I hid it before the Germans came," Iannis smiled. "I couldn't let them take everything."

"Papa ..."

"The old dog still has a few tricks, right?"

"I guess so."

"So have a drink with your old man."

Alexei smiled as he put the bottle to his lips and felt the familiar and welcome burn of the liquor. He passed the bottle to his father who drank also, and held the amber liquid in his mouth before swallowing. It felt good for them to have a moment to do something so simple.

Then Alexei heard a noise.

He grabbed his rifle and stood to face the darkness, where the noise had come from.

He waited ... his rifle at the ready.

Then Koukidis came out of the night, with the rest of his men following behind. They'd been out in the hills and valleys, scouting and trying to make sure that the roads had stayed clear ahead of them, and Koukidis walked straight to the fire and sat down next to Alexei. He took the bottle of Metaxa and tipped two-fingers down his throat before he said a single word, and that's how Alexei knew that he had news.

"What is it?" Alexei asked. "What's wrong?"

"The Germans," Koukidis said. "What else?"

"Where are they?"

"Not far, unfortunately. The British didn't last long, as we expected. They're all dead. Every one of them. They tried to retreat, but the Germans stayed on them. It looks like they're intent on pressing all the way to Athens, as quickly as they can."

"Which way did they take?"

"They're about twenty kilometers behind us."

"Shit," Alexei said.

There was silence.

Everyone had heard Koukidis' news.

"We have to keep going," Alexei finally said. "Right now. We'll have to walk through the night again. We have to stay in front of them until we get to the mountains."

They all nodded.

They knew there wasn't any other way.

Everyone stood to begin packing what they'd brought with them. It was habit by now, and they did it quickly. Alexei could see how tired they all were, and how badly they needed a night to rest, but with Koukidis' news they didn't have any other choice.

Alexei and Costa kicked dirt on their fire.

"We'll be alright," Philia said, standing next to Eleni, putting her arm around her mother.

"Of course we will," Eleni said.

The group kept walking through the night.

Alexei had heard Philia's words, speaking to Eleni, and

he wanted to believe her. Instead, he watched his mother as she walked, and he was angry because there wasn't anything he could do to help her. She was exhausted, and hungry. His father's limp was as bad as it had ever been. Then he looked at Philia. His wife who was pregnant with their child, their future, the dream that he'd dreamed so many times that it was now real. She should be in a beautiful home, their beautiful home, relaxing, laying on the couch, eating and building her strength, but there they were.

The world changes us, he'd once said.

And he felt it.

But now he felt something else, too.

It was a pit of uneasiness that was deep inside of him, lodged in his stomach, and no matter what they did or how far they walked or how much closer to Athens their journey took them, he still couldn't shake it. No matter what he did, it was never very far from him now.

Where had his confidence gone?

Where was the nineteen year old that had survived a dozen battles in the last six months, having had thousands of bullets dance around him in each one, but still knowing and holding so surely in his heart that none of them would touch him simply because it wasn't his time yet? Because he still had more to do. Or maybe his confidence had been blind, and maybe he'd lived his life believing that all of them that were there and on the side of righteousness in this conflict were greater than they really were.

Maybe, he thought, he wasn't as strong as he used to think he was.

Had Alexander ever doubted, he wondered?

Had Achilles ever been scared?

Had Odysseus ever questioned his way home?

He shook his head, trying to clear his thoughts.

But he couldn't.

Day by day, he hadn't felt anything change, but when he looked back, everything was different, and he knew now that it always would be. He knew now that this would never be a distant memory, as he'd once thought. And it was some time not long before dawn that he accepted that this new fear that he carried wasn't something that was going to leave. He'd changed. He'd felt it, as he stared down into the face of a young German soldier under his barrel in Agria, a German that was too young to die.

He finally let himself believe it now.

He had allowed himself to be honest, and when he turned inwards, what he found scared him. He'd found the part of himself that he'd kept buried, but he couldn't any longer, and so he knew now that he had to make room. He had to make room for the part of him that had lost the confidence that he'd carried through Kalpaki, and Pogradec, and the Metaxas Line, and the part of him that had ran with Costa on their way back home to Agria. And he had to now face this part of him that told him there was a chance that they might not make it, and he looked at Philia, walking next to him, and he was scared.

The night ahead of them was dark.

There was nothing else.

They kept walking.

25

April 22nd, 1941

They passed Lamia in the morning.

It was the last major city in Central Greece, and the gateway to the rest of the Attic Peninsula. They skirted around it to the west, staying in the foothills, and as they looked down below them they saw many of the buildings were boarded up, and there wasn't anyone in the streets. A village preparing itself for the worst was a familiar scene for the survivors of Agria, and then they heard mortar shells exploding further east, on the other side of the city, between Lamia and the sea.

Nobody had to explain what it meant.

They wordlessly picked up their pace.

The route they had decided on wasn't the quickest way to Athens, but it would take them through the mountains, which would surely be safer than any of the main roads where the Germans were going to be travelling very soon.

When Alexei had told his mother about which road they'd take, she'd smiled at him—

"You know where we'll pass through, don't you?"

"Of course."

"I imagine it's not far now."

"No," Alexei said. "We'll make camp there tonight."

They kept walking, and they could soon see Mount Parnassus in the distance, in front of them, the tallest and most distinct peak among a range of much gentler and more sloped mountains, the summits all still capped with ice and snow from the long winter. They would make their way along the southern edge of Parnassus, which would lead through the ancient city of Delphi, the home of the famous oracle of which there are only ruins left now. It had been the destination in Eleni's story about her family, and Paul the Apostle, and it was the city that had given them the ring that Philia now wore on her finger.

"I'll be glad to finally see it," Eleni said, and she smiled.

"So will I," Alexei said.

And he smiled, too.

They reached Delphi as the sun was setting.

Alexei and Costa went first, with Koukidis and his men next to them, their rifles at the ready, because they weren't sure what they were going to find.

They came to the city.

They walked through the streets, perched high on a cliff, overlooking the soft and rolling hills of Attica to the south, and found everything completely deserted. It was normally an area filled with busses and tourists, but it was now completely quiet, except for the few birds in the sky, who didn't seem to notice or care what was going on below them.

"Where do you think they all went?" Koukidis asked.

"I don't know," Costa answered.

Alexei looked around at the shops—

"Nothing's been taken," he said. "The stores haven't been looted or broken into. That means the Germans probably haven't made it here yet."

"That's some news at least."

They motioned for the rest of the group to follow, and they passed through the village, and up towards the ancient ruins.

Alexei slowed to walk next to Philia.

She touched the ring on her finger, rubbing it back and forth, as they looked in awe on the works of their people and what they'd done, so many years ago, the history that they'd made. The setting sun cast everything in a soft orange glow, and they were sure that there had never been anything in the world that looked as beautiful as the great ruins of Delphi did that afternoon. There were rows of long-abandoned ancient houses. There were large stone columns that reached up and up and up towards the heavens. There was the wide expanse of the arena where athletes had bled and sweat and given everything they had to give for their cities and their people and their pride.

Alexei and Philia breathed it all in.

They kept walking.

Each member of the group was mesmerized by the beauty, and wandered off on their own, or with a loved one, or someone else that was special, to experience their moment.

Alexei and Philia went through the Temple of Apollo, reaching their hands out to touch the stone columns that were still there standing, tall and proud against all time and elements. They climbed higher to the Delphic Stadium where the Pythian Games, a forerunner of the modern Olympic Games, had been held every four years, bringing together the tribes of ancient Greece to compete against each other in sport and fitness. They stepped through the empty benches of the amphitheater where Aeschylus and Euripides and so many others had first heard their words spoken and performed, and had first seen the power they had over their rapt audiences . . . the power of their stories.

Alexei and Philia breathed deeply.

Neither of them had ever felt so small before.

Alexei had walked with ghosts for as long as he could remember, and he was glad that they had come there, because he could now finally see those ghosts, for the first time, and he could see them very clearly. He could feel them all around. They were in all the ideas and words and memories of every great person that had come before them, and had once walked on those stones where they were now walking, and felt the same things that they were now feeling.

They went to the Tholos, the iconic circular sanctuary that had once been constructed out of twenty beautifully crafted and symmetric Doric columns, of which there were three that were still defiantly upright. Alexei and Philia walked through the remnants of the sanctuary until they stood directly in the middle of it.

"This is it," Alexei said quietly.

"This is what?"

"The *omphalos*," he said. "The center of the world."

They looked up. They looked around them. They breathed it all in and let it change them.

"It's beautiful," Philia whispered. "I don't know what else to say. It's enough to take our words from us, isn't it?"

"*But for the sons of Cronus, opened the earth with a thunderbolt, and hid the holiest of all things in these scared hills. They were angry at the sweet voice, because strangers perished away from their children and wives, but they hung their lives there on the honey-hearted words, and it was good."*

"Who said that?"

"Pindar. He stood here once and couldn't find words either, so he wrote a poem."

"It's beautiful."

"I think so, too."

Philia smiled as she stood on her toes to kiss Alexei—

"I'm glad that I'm here with you, Alexandros," she said.

"I'm glad that I'm here with you, too."

"Here, together, at the center of the world."

They built their camp among the ruins.

They made another small fire beneath the ancient columns that would keep watch over them throughout the night. They were hungry as they sat together in silence.

Alexei tried to calculate the rest of their journey.

They were close. If they made good time they could be in Athens by the day after the next. If they were lucky. And if they didn't run into any Germans on the road.

Then he saw a man running towards them.

Alexei stood together with Costa and Koukidis, but they recognized the man that was coming as one of Koukidis' younger soldiers, and they all relaxed. The young soldier was out of breath as he reached them and Koukidis stood forward and grabbed him by the shoulders, shaking him—

"What is it, man? Why the hell are you running so fast?"

"… *there's a group of them … on the road … heading this way …*"

"A group of who?"

"… *soldiers …*"

"How many are there?"

"... *looked to be ... around fifteen.*"

"Germans?"

"... *I don't know ... couldn't get close enough ... to see ... their colors,*" he shook his head, regaining his strength, "... *I saw them and ran straight back ...*"

"Good man," Koukidis said, slapping his shoulder. "Good man. Now someone get Pheidippides here some water."

A canteen was passed to him.

"You know you've already made that joke before," Alexei said, as the soldier drank.

"No, that wasn't me. That was Costa."

"What does it matter?" Costa said. "A good joke is a good joke."

Koukidis and Costa both smiled, and they picked up their rifles, and so did Alexei, and the rest of the men.

"Where are they?" Alexei asked the young soldier.

"The same road that we came in on," he told them. "Probably about three kilometers back by now."

Alexei turned to Costa and Koukidis—

"We'll go a little ways and find somewhere to meet them. They'll have gone more themselves by then, and it'll give us time to pick out a spot."

"Let's hurry, then."

Alexei nodded and went back to his things to find extra ammo to put into a pouch that was on his belt and next to his knife. He saw Philia, watching him with concern, and she came to where he was readying himself.

"Don't worry," he said to her. "I'm sure it's nothing."

"But what if it isn't?"

"Then we'll deal with it."

"How?"

"The same way that we did in Agria."

She bit her lip—

"Philia, we've been doing this for the last six months. Believe it or not, we've gotten pretty good at it."

She knew there was nothing left to say. There were enemies behind them, and they had to be taken care of.

"We've come so far …"

"We have."

"Don't take any chances, alright?"

He kissed her—

"I won't. We'll be fine. Trust me. We'll be back before you know that we were even gone."

Then Alexei left where he was standing with her.

He walked to where Iannis watched his son, with Eleni next to him.

Alexei paused for a moment in front of his father, then he bent down and took the Luger from his boot, the pistol that Iannis had given him before he'd left to go fight the Italians, the same pistol that had saved Costa's life at Pogradec, and then both of their lives at the farm outside of Kozani.

He handed it back to his father.

"Just in case," Alexei said, and their eyes met as Iannis took the gun, nodding at his son in return.

"Just in case," Iannis repeated.

Then Iannis watched with Eleni and Philia both as Alexei left and joined the rest of the men who were waiting for him. They turned and hurried back down the mountain, the same way that they'd come, ready to fight whoever it was that was chasing after them.

"How about here?" Costa asked.

"Looks as good a place as any," Alexei answered.

They were about a kilometer back down the mountain and they'd come to a place where the road narrowed along a bend as it cut between two tall walls of jutting rock on either side.

"Half of us on each side," Koukidis said. "The same way that we did on the road at Agria. And we'll make short work of them in the same way, too."

They nodded and spread out, taking their positions in the hills, hidden from view of the road but in places where they'd still have a clear aim and shot when the soldiers came around the bend.

They sat quietly.

They all waited.

They'd been in their positions for less than ten minutes when one of Koukidis' men who'd climbed higher than the rest silently waved back down, and they knew that meant that their enemies were approaching.

Alexei took aim.

He flipped the safety off his rifle.

The other Greek soldiers also took aim at the point in the road where they knew their enemies were about to appear.

They waited.

Then Alexei saw Costa raise his arm. He was motioning for them to hold their fire. Costa was at a spot further up than Alexei and had gotten his first glimpse of the men walking towards them and they weren't wearing grey uniforms with green collars and shoulder straps: these men were battered and bloody, and they all wore dark green collarless tunics and steel brodie hats.

They were British.

The Greek soldiers smiled and lowered their weapons

as Costa called out from behind the rock where he was hiding—

"Where are you boys heading?"

The British instantly fell into formation, rifles up and ready, scanning the hills around them—

"Who's there?" their Leader yelled.

"Easy, mate. We're Resistance," Costa called back down. "We're killing the same people."

"You're Greek?"

"Yes. We're coming out now, alright?"

The British lowered their rifles, as they kept looking around, and the Leader stepped forward as the Greeks came from their hiding spots and down to the road. Costa nodded to the state of their uniforms, the dirt and the blood that was caked on their clothes and skin—

"What the hell happened to you guys?" he asked.

"We ran into a few of them down the road a bit."

"Down the road where?"

"Thermopylae, if you can believe it. The Hot Gates. History repeating itself, and all that."

The British Leader extended his hand—

"John Worthington," he said, and shook hands with Alexei, Costa, and Koukidis in turn.

"Pleasure," Costa said.

"You fought them at Thermopylae?" Alexei asked.

"Yes. Well, the British and the Kiwis together, that is. Have you ever seen a New Zealander fight? Didn't know much about them before this, but bloody hell are they terrifying," he swallowed, and continued. "We held the pass for as long as we could . . . it's still the best route into southern Greece, the same for the Germans today as it was for Xerxes two thousand years ago. Of course they broke us there. We knew that we couldn't win, but we held them . . . by God did we hold them. Leonidas' spirit surely would have been proud, and I know that Byron was watching with a smile."

"And then what happened?" Alexei asked. "We're a long ways from Thermopylae."

"We fought the Germans outside of Lamia again this morning, but it was a slaughter. They're in Attica now, I'm afraid. They're on their way to Athens, and there's nobody left to stand in their way."

"Where are you headed?"

"It's just a race to Athens now. For everybody. We're trying to get there before the Germans, to find a boat to take us to the British base on Crete. That's where the RAF is now. We'll continue to fight them from there."

Alexei and Costa and Koukidis and the rest of the Greeks looked at each other—

"What is it?" Worthington asked.

"Well, Mr. Worthington," Costa said. "It looks like this meeting was meant to happen."

"How's that?"

"We're headed the same way," Alexei told him.

"Strength in numbers," Worthington said. "Bloody good."

He grinned back at them, and then shook their hands again—

"Bloody good, indeed."

26

April 23rd, 1941

THEY LEFT DELPHI AT FIRST LIGHT the next day.

Their group had grown now, there were more soldiers with rifles and bullets, but they still knew that if they met any Germans then it wouldn't matter how many of them there were, not even if they had all the Resistance fighters in Greece, and all the British soldiers that had come to help, because the Germans had an unstoppable army.

They went though the town again, and before they were gone, Eleni looked back at the ruins behind them.

She was next to Alexei.

"How come we never came here before?" she asked him.

"There'd always been more time before," he answered.

She thought about it further—

"I think I was afraid. I'd pictured it a certain way in my mind, and I didn't know if I wanted that to change."

"Well, you've seen it now."

"And I'm glad," she said, and she smiled. "I'm glad that

I saw it before we left. We might not have the chance ever again."

"Was it what you expected?"

"No," she said, with one last look over her shoulder. "It was more. It was so much more."

Alexei looked back at Delphi once more himself.

He was glad that he had come to the ruins later in his life, and not when he was younger. It meant more to him as an older man.

No, not older, he thought.

A man who'd been through all that they'd been through.

Because isn't that what age is, after all, an accumulation of experience, rather than time, and even though they were still young—him and Costa and Koukidis—they were old now. He'd once heard that a child dreams when a man doubts. He thought of his feelings on the road to Delphi, and he believed what he'd heard, and could see the wisdom and truth in it. Young men laugh at God, and fate, and all the other things that they cannot control, because they don't need them yet. There's time left, always still in front of them, always, always. It's not until a man becomes part of the world, and broken in the way that the world breaks men, that you need faith, and you start searching for God.

Alexei knew that's what he needed now.

And so, with the great monument of Greece behind them, and the sun rising in front of them, they continued to walk.

They made good time through the mountains, and once again, instead of heading down into the valley to use the main road to Athens, Alexei made the decision to push as far south as they could, until they were almost hugging the

Gulf of Corinth. It would be slower, staying in the mountains, but there wasn't any other way to avoid the Germans, especially after the information that Worthington had brought, which was really only confirmation of what they'd feared and in their hearts had probably known all along.

Alexei found himself walking next to Worthington. He took the chance to ask him about his family, about how he'd come to Greece, and where he was from back in England—

"Yorkshire," he said. "Up in the north. Famous for our terriers and our pudding," he added with a smile. "How about yourselves?"

"Agria," Alexei told him. "A small town near Volos."

"Coming from that far north I assume that you've seen your fair share of fighting."

"Yes, we've seen our fair share."

"Where?"

"In Albania first, against the Italians. And then we fought at the Line when the Germans came."

"Is that so? We all read about it in the papers, of course. London could talk of nothing else. They made it into a proper Greek tragedy, the old and ancient rising one last time in pride to fight against the unbeatable monster. Tell me how it really happened?"

And so Alexei told him their story as they walked.

He told him about the beginning of the war, and their first action at the Kalamas River, and then at Kalpaki, when they didn't know what they were doing. He told them how cold and hungry they'd been in Pogradec, and how Costa had saved them because of the girl that he was sleeping with and the letter that she'd received. Alexei couldn't recall the girl's name—how long had it been?—and then they walked a little further, and it came back to him.

Adelina.

He told Worthington how they went home after Pogradec, and he told him of his wedding to Philia, and the house that he'd started to build for her on the bluff above their city.

And then Alexei told him of the Metaxas Line.

He told him of how they fought there for longer than anyone thought they ever could have fought, and how maybe it was like the papers in London had said after all, and then he told him of how it had ended. Alexei told him of the journey back home with Costa, and of Jurgen, and the bridge outside Larissa, and all that they had seen in the Greek countryside. And then they finally reached Agria, and Alexei told him what they did when they heard of what the Germans had done to their families and their city.

Worthington listened to the whole thing.

They continued to walk together, in silence for a few more paces, and then when Worthington finally spoke, it was with great emotion.

"You should know that the whole world has watched your struggle," he said. "And you should also know that you've given the world courage when so many of us had none. You gave us our first victory, in the mountains in Albania. You fought the Germans at the Line, when so many others wouldn't have. You should have heard Churchill's broadcasts and everything that he said about the Greeks. They say that history is written by the victors, and that so often they get it wrong, but you and your people deserve everything they'll write about you when this war is over. You truly are the people sprung of Achilles and Alexander. I've never been more sure."

"And what about you?"

"What about me?"

"How'd you end up here, so far from home?"

"I volunteered."

"You volunteered?"

"Of course. How many of us are fortunate to live in a time like this? To be able to be a part of such great things?"

"You wanted to fight?"

"We spoke of Byron earlier. There's certainly a little bit of Byron in all of us that have come here from England. Why else would we be here, if not for the same reasons? It's history and courage that we admire, as humans and as men. That's the legacy that he gave us. And it's no different for you, Alexei. How you and your people still share the blood of Alexander and Achilles, your great heroes. If you don't think that still lives on in this land, then you need to look around again, and see all that you've done these last months. The odds that you've beaten. The courage that's inspired us all. People speak of blood as if it's distant, and it fades. But it doesn't."

Alexei heard these words, and he knew Worthington would never know how much they meant to him—

"*Pothos*," Alexei smiled.

"It's a Greek word," Worthington said, shaking his head. "What does it mean?"

"There's no word for it in English."

"What is it in Greek?"

Alexei paused, reaching back as he tried to think of the best translation that he could come up with—

"Desire, longing, passion, regret."

"That's all in the same word?"

"Yes."

"It sounds complicated."

"We're a complicated people."

"So it would seem," Worthington smiled, as he took out a cigarette and offered Alexei one, and when Alexei refused he put his own to his lips and lit it—

"Are you afraid?" Alexei asked as Worthington inhaled.

"Afraid of what?"

"Dying in a foreign place, halfway across the world, in a land that's not your own, so far from your home, your wife, your family."

"No. I thank God every day that I was brought here. I think of my sons. What would I tell them if I'd stayed home and tended the farm while others rode off to do the great things that every book and every poem and every song in all the world's been written about? I'd be trimming hedges and plowing fields while other men took their places in history. I want to be a part of that, too. My sons are young now, but when they're grown, they'll understand, and they'll be a part of it as well, like their father was, during whatever great times they're born into. That's the benefit of education, isn't it? It haunts us. The great journeys and deeds of others. It gives us so very much to live up to."

"So Byron's spirit lives on."

"It most certainly does," he said. "He was just one of us, but he was great, and here we are, so many years later, walking the same lands where he walked, fighting for the same things that he fought for. That's immortality, Alexei.

That's what we're all fighting for, and what we're either marching towards or away from."

Alexei thought about this, and finally a smile touched his lips, as Worthington gestured towards Philia in front of them, next to Alexei's parents—

"What are you going to name him?" Worthington asked.

"I don't know yet. We haven't talked about it."

"You haven't talked about it?"

"We haven't had time."

"Probably because there was a war on and all."

Alexei smiled at him—

"Probably."

"Think of a good name," Worthington said, as he finished his cigarette, putting it out under his boot. "A good name is important for a boy."

"It is."

"A good name will take you far in the world."

Alexei nodded, and Worthington fell back with his men, as Alexei went to his family, and they continued to walk.

It was midday when they first saw it.

There was a building in the distance, nestled amongst the mountains that they were passing through, and they decided to stop. The sun was high, directly above them, and it was hot.

Costa came forward to stand next to Alexei.

"What do you think it is?" he asked.

"I don't know," Alexei answered.

"It's too large to be a house."

"Maybe a school?"

"This far into the mountains?"

They stood there as the rest of the group drank fresh water from a running stream they found nearby.

"Whatever it is, we should stop. The Germans haven't been here yet. We should see if they have any food. It's worth a shot, and it'll be quick."

They told the rest of the group to stay by the stream to wait.

And then Alexei and Costa went forward to investigate.

They started to climb and as they got closer and closer to the building they saw decorated stained glass windows, quiet gardens surrounding the low walls, and a crucifix above the entrance.

"It's a monastery," Alexei said, realizing.

"I guess if there's anywhere we might find some charity," Costa smiled, "then this would be the place."

They went to the door and before they could raise their fists to knock it opened and there was a middle-aged woman in a simple and plain white gown standing on the other side, who had clearly seen them coming.

"Who are you?" she asked them.

"My name is Alexandros," Alexei said, "and this is my friend Constantinos."

"I'm Sister Adelpha," the woman told them. "What are you doing here?"

"We're just passing through. We wanted to see if you had any food that you might be able to spare. We've gone awhile now without enough. We have money to pay, of course."

She looked at the rifles slung across their shoulders. "You'd bring guns to a house of God?" she asked them.

"We're soldiers."

"Are you with the Resistance?"

"Yes."

"Where are you going?"

"We're going to Athens."

"For what? To leave Greece?"

"Yes."

She waited a moment longer, then opened the door a bit wider, and invited them inside.

"Please, come in ..." she said.

"Thank you."

Alexei and Costa walked inside and looked around at the crucifixes and nativity scenes on the walls, the high-vaulted ceilings, and the other sparse and humble decorations.

"Do you have news of the Germans?" she asked them.

"They're in Attica now. Not very far behind us."

"So it won't be long, then ..." she said quietly.

"No. I'm afraid that it won't be."

"We'll give you all the food that you can carry. But there's something that I need to show you first."

"We don't really have time."

"It's important."

They looked at her and saw the look that was on her face, and how important this seemed to her, and then behind them the door opened again and sunlight flooded in as they turned to see Koukidis standing in the doorway, urgency in his eyes, a pair of binoculars in his hands.

"What is it?" Alexei asked him.

"We have to go."

"What?"

"Now. They're behind us."

"How far?"

"Ten kilometers, maybe less."

Alexei walked back outside and Koukidis handed him the binoculars. He pointed them back towards the northwest and saw the cloud of dust gathering in the distance, rising above the mountains.

He knew what it meant.

He handed the binoculars back to Koukidis, then turned to Sister Adelpha, who had followed them outside.

"If you want to leave Greece, then you have to go now," he told her.

"We can't leave the monastery."

"They'll take everything that you have."

"We don't have very much."

Alexei looked at her and knew that the sisters would most likely be spared. They weren't desirable to young men, and even the Germans wouldn't want to risk offending God in the worst way that he could be offended.

"Any food you could spare would be greatly appreciated," Alexei said again. "But we need it now."

"We'll give you all that we have, all that you can carry . . . anything that we keep will just end up with the Germans."

"Thank you."

"But you need to come with me first."

"We can't. That cloud right there is the Germans. We don't have time."

"You have to."

"Why?"

"Because I know now what brought you here. It was God's will. It was his answer to our prayers."

"What prayers?"

"Come," she said. "I need to show you."

Alexei looked from Costa to Koukidis—

"Quickly ..." Koukidis said impatiently.

Alexei and Costa followed Sister Adelpha as she walked further into the monastery, through the dining hall and cloisters, across a small courtyard, and then finally to a shrine, where she took out a key.

"Follow me," she said as she unlocked the door and walked inside.

The shrine was dark and damp, and smelled like wet stone and mildew, and she led them past it all and behind the altar to where she used another key to open a second door, which revealed a staircase spiraling downwards into the darkness towards the crypt.

She lit a torch, and they followed her down, until they came to one last door.

She looked back at them, so much in her eyes, and then she opened the door and used the torch to illuminate what was on the other side.

Children.

All huddled together.

They were of all ages, though most looked like they were between four and thirteen, and they were scared.

"What is this?" Alexei asked.

"You have to take them with you."

"We can't," he said. "They'll slow us down."

"You can't leave them here. They came to us from all over Greece so that we could protect them."

"Why? They're just kids. The Germans will leave them alone."

"No, they won't. The Germans . . . when they find them here . . . the Germans will kill them."

"I don't understand."

Sister Adelpha turned to Alexei again, and when she opened her mouth he knew what her words were going to be even before she spoke them, and also what it would now mean for them, and it made his legs weak—

"They're Jewish," Sister Adelpha said.

"We can't take them."

"You heard what she said," Alexei sighed. "The Germans will kill them."

"If we take them," Costa told him, "then they'll kill us, too."

"Not if we go as fast as we can."

"We can't. Not with fifty kids with us. Did you see how young some of them are? We'll never make it if we bring them."

"We have to try."

"Why?"

"Because if we don't, then there's no point to any of this."

"No point to what?"

"Could you start a new life knowing that this was the cost? They're kids, Costa. They're kids, and if we leave them here, then they'll die in the worst ways you could ever possibly imagine. You remember the men that they took at the Line ..."

They were standing outside the monastery with Koukidis, who was silent through all this, and then Costa and Alexei were silent, too, as they each thought about what had happened at the Metaxas Line. They thought of how the German soldiers had walked through their ranks and taken any Jews that they could find. Nobody wanted to think about what had happened to them, but everyone knew. They'd been put on trains and shipped north to the labor camps the Germans were making, the ones that would soon become death camps. It wasn't a secret in Greece.

"So what do we do, then?" Costa asked softly.

"Let's get them, and go as fast as we can."

"Are you sure?"

"No. But we have no other choice."

There was a very long moment, and then Costa finally sighed—

"Alright," he said. "Let's get them."

They brought the children up from the crypt, and their young eyes squinted into the bright light that they hadn't seen for too long. They came in a long line, and Alexei and Costa and Koukidis led them across the courtyard, and through the cloisters, and before they left Sister Adelpha gave them the food that she had promised, and some water, too, and she knelt and bowed her head and said a prayer to bless the rest of their journey.

They left the monastery.

They went back down the mountain, to where the rest of the group waited, and when Worthington and the British soldiers saw them, he walked over to talk to Alexei.

"What is this?" he asked.

"They're coming with us," Alexei said.

"They can't come with us. They'll slow us down. You've seen the Germans and how close they are."

"That's why we have to hurry," Alexei said.

"Alexei …"

"They come with us."

Worthington could hear the steel in Alexei's voice, even if he could also see the pain and the doubt in his eyes.

He too knew what it would mean if they left the children behind, and so he nodded.

"Alright," he said. "We'll go as fast as we can."

The British went in front of the group as an advance guard.

The rest followed closely behind.

They continued east through the valley, the mountains high on either side, guiding their way towards Athens. The children struggled to keep up, and the others struggled to help them, carrying them, offering words of encouragement, anything they could think of to make a difference. Alexei couldn't keep his eyes off of Philia, how she was with the children, and he thought of their own, and how she'd be with them, and his heart broke for a reason that he didn't quite understand yet as he watched her.

Behind them, the Germans were getting closer.

They tried to go faster.

Alexei helped his mother when his father got too tired to help her. Costa was behind them, carrying a small girl on his back, encouraging the other children to go as fast as they could, and that's when Koukidis came running back to the group from the high peak where he'd been standing, looking back along the valley behind them.

"What is it?" Alexei asked him.

Koukidis' eyes flicked to Eleni, and Alexei let Iannis help his mother as he fell back to speak with Koukidis.

"They're gaining on us," he said softly.

"How far back?"

"Three kilometers now. Maybe four?"

"They didn't stop at the monastery?"

"No," Koukidis said. "They passed it by. We're going to have to do something."

"Not yet," Alexei said.

"What are you waiting for?"

"I'm not sure. But not yet."

"Alright," Koukidis nodded, after a moment, and they continued on. Alexei picked up a young boy to carry on his back, too, and he saw the look in Philia's eyes, and in his mother's, and he knew that they understood what was happening, and that they weren't going to make it.

Still, they pressed on.

Alexei was hoping for a miracle, some form of divine intervention that would cause the Germans to slow down, stop and make camp somewhere, somehow change their direction for some reason that they'd never know but would always be grateful for and could chalk up to God and faith and the answering of their prayers.

But a miracle didn't come.

They were to the end of the valley, and there was just one more pass that they had to cross, the last jagged and craggy peak before they would then come to the plains on the other side that stretched on all the way to Athens and the sea. The children were having more trouble now, climbing the incline with their short legs, and when they reached the peak, Alexei raised his hand, signaling to everyone.

"Let's stop a minute for some water," he said, after he'd caught Worthington's eye, and saw that he wanted to talk. Philia nodded, and along with Eleni and Iannis she started passing out the last of the water that they had to the children.

Alexei raised a canteen to his mouth as he stood with Worthington.

It was clear why he'd stopped.

Behind them, through the valley, where they'd just come, they could clearly see the Germans now. They were closer, and Alexei could make out the swastikas on their Panzers without having to use the binoculars. Costa came to stand next to them, and Koukidis, too.

"We aren't going to make it," Worthington said, once they were all there.

"No. Not all the way across the plains," Costa agreed.

"They'd be on us before we even went a hundred yards."

"And there's no cover out there, after we leave the mountains."

"So what do we do? We can't hide."

"We're going to have to try to stop them," Alexei said, looking back at the army behind them.

"What?" Costa asked.

"Just for a short time. Send the rest on ahead. Fight long enough that they make it to Athens, and then we follow after."

"That's a whole division down there," Koukidis said, looking at Alexei. "You realize that, right?"

"We'll have the high ground. We can't beat them, but we can hold them. That's what this whole war's been, anyways."

"And then what?"

"They'll stop, to take care of their dead, and regroup, and that's when we run, just like we did after the Line."

They all looked at each other.

There wasn't any doubt that it was the only plan that would at least give them a chance. Alexei nodded, and went to stand next to Philia. She'd been watching, from a distance, and she couldn't hear their words, but she knew what they'd been discussing, and when she saw Alexei's eyes, she knew what they were going to do.

"Why?" was all that she asked him.

"Because it's the only way."

"Let somebody else fight, Alexei. Please. For once. We've already given so much. Let somebody else give now, so that we can live."

"There's no one else left."

She was silent for a moment, looking at the ground, and then she looked back up at him—

"We're not going to make it, are we?" she said softly.

"Yes, we are."

"There's too much out there, Alexei. There's too much darkness."

"I read once that there's no such thing as darkness. You see, all darkness is, really, is the absence of light. And even if it goes away for a time, the light . . . the light always returns."

She closed her eyes, and when her tears leaked out, and down her cheek, Alexei gently brushed them away.

"We'll be right behind you, alright?" he said. "You're going to keep going, and we're going to be coming right behind you."

She opened her eyes, and met his, and he knew that her look was something that he'd never forget.

He took her hand in his.

He held it in front of them, and brushed his thumb across the soft underside of her wrist, where his initial was tattooed and set deep into her skin in dark ink, in the exact same place that hers was set into his.

"I'll always be right behind you, alright? Always. When

you turn around, before you even know that I've been gone, I'll be there, whenever you look for me . . . I'll always be there. Know that."

"I've always known that."

"Come here."

She tilted her head up, and Alexei kissed her again, one of his hands on her cheek, the other across her belly, where their child was waiting, unaware of the trials and great moments of his parents as he quietly slept. Alexei let his fingers linger on Philia's cheek, and on her belly, and then he turned to his parents.

They were waiting for him, standing behind and watching as their son said goodbye to his wife.

Alexei didn't say anything to them.

He embraced them, his mother first, and then his father, and before he left, his mother reached up and touched his cheek.

"When did you get taller than me, Alexei?"

"You already asked me that."

"Tell me again."

"It was a long time ago, Mana. When I was ten."

"That's right. The first summer you went out on the boat alone. What a beautiful summer that was."

He looked back at her.

He didn't know what to say.

"Come on, Eleni," Iannis said, meeting his son's eyes. "We need to keep going. We need to hurry."

Eleni stood on her toes and she kissed her son one more time, on the top of his head, the way that she used to do when he was a boy, and then Alexei turned away because goodbyes had always been too hard for him and he'd said too many of them already.

Alexei and Costa stood and watched as they left.

Philia was out in front, with Eleni and Iannis, and Nico was behind them, with the children, encouraging them along, a boy who didn't realize that he should have been one of them, and that he wasn't, because it was something that had been taken from him. When they were a ways into the distance, Worthington turned to Alexei and Costa, and the rest of the Greek and British soldiers that had stayed to defend the pass—

"It's about time that we got this place wired, don't you think?"

"Wired?" Alexei asked.

"Explosives. Bombs. Dynamite."

"You have explosives?"

"Of course we do. The British always come to war prepared. And we love explosives."

"I told you," Koukidis said. "Didn't I tell you that?"

"You did."

They all looked at each other—

"I guess it's time to get started then."

They all knew the odds.

Even with the British soldiers, they were still only going to be thirty men against five hundred. But they'd have the high ground, and they'd have the emotional advantage. That was one thing that they'd learned never to discount. They'd be fighting for everything on this earth that they loved. The Germans were fighting to not die.

They laid explosives under rock and dirt.

They hid them as carefully as they could, and then ran lines back up towards the position where they'd wait at the top of the pass. It was the same thing that they'd done at the bridge outside Larissa. They laughed as they worked, which Alexei found strange, the way that men handle the thought of imminent death. It's always laughter that comes, and if these were to be their last moments, then at least they'd be happy ones, and they'd smile.

They looked and saw that the Germans were closer now, less than a kilometer away. So Alexei and Costa and Koukidis checked their explosives one last time, and then they climbed back up the pass to where they'd hide. The British took positions on the southern side of the pass, while Alexei and Costa and the rest of the Greeks took their position to the north. They'd form a gauntlet, and fire down on the Germans for as long as they could hold them.

Alexei sat next to Costa.

They shared the protection of a large boulder, and they took their rifles out, checking their ammo, making sure that they were prepared for everything that was about to come, or as prepared as they possibly could be. Alexei peered around the side of the rock and he could see the German divisions very clearly now—the men in their uniforms, marching next to their Panzers, and the large and heavy artillery guns mounted on wheels that they were pulling behind their jeeps.

Alexei and Costa tried to steady their breathing.

"There really is a lot of them, aren't there?" Alexei said.

"It doesn't matter," Costa answered.

"It doesn't matter?"

"No."

"Why's that?"

"*Because only we, contrary to the barbarians, never count the enemy in battle.*"

Alexei smiled to hear Costa quote Aeschylus back to

him, the same thing that Alexei had said to Costa high in the mountains at the Metaxas Line, the first time that they'd faced the Germans together, and then Costa smiled, too. Alexei looked back at him and they both knew that there was more between them than could ever be spoken, or explained, and then it all passed because the moment was now on them once again, and they were alone, high in the mountains, one last time.

And everything was going to be decided.

Alexei reached out and grabbed the back of Costa's neck, and he pulled their heads closer together until their foreheads were touching, and they were as close as they'd ever been.

"One last fight, alright?" Alexei said to him.

"One last fight."

"And then we leave."

"Yes."

"We've been brothers, haven't we?"

Costa looked back at his friend, and smiled in the way that only Costa could, with the beauty of perfect truth in his eyes—

"We've been more than that."

"*Palikari*," Alexei said.

"*Palikari*," he smiled.

And then there was a soft whistle next to them.

They turned to see Worthington gesturing towards the valley and the distance.

"Get ready," he whispered. "They're here."

Alexei and Costa turned back to where their enemies approached. The Germans were starting to climb the pass, and they were almost to the area where explosives had been laid under the rocks.

They waited as the Germans came closer.

Worthington had the detonator.

It would begin on his move.

Alexei held his breath as he made the sign of the cross over his body the same way that he always did—his right shoulder first, then his left—the orthodox way, the way of the land that they'd now fight for, the land that they'd never stop fighting for.

Washington's finger hovered over the trigger.

Germans stepped on the rocks where the explosives were hidden. One of them saw a wire beneath him, and he looked at it curiously, tilting his head to the side, then realized what it was, but it was already too late—

Kabooooooooooom!!!!

The hills shook beneath them.

The ground tore apart in a giant fountain of earth.

Germans were thrown from their feet, and limbs were torn from bodies, and lives ended before any final moments were had. The British lobbed more grenades down at the Germans.

Kaboom kaboom kaboom kaboom kaboom!!!

Then Alexei and Costa and the rest of the Greeks fired their rifles into the confusion and mass of bodies.

Bang bang bang!!! Bang bang!!! Bang bang bang!!!

Germans fell by the dozen.

Death echoed through the hills.

The Germans ran to take cover behind their armored jeeps and Panzers, and the dust from the initial explosions started to settle, and that's when the Germans swung their own weapons around to return fire above them—

Rat-a-tat-tat-tat-tat-tat-tat!!!

They were devastating automatic rounds from MP40s.

The Greeks and the British dove for cover as bullets peppered into rocks all around them.

"How many do you think we got?" Costa asked, out of breath.

"Looked to be about fifty," Alexei said.

"Jesus. That's a lot."

"It is. But it's not enough. It's not nearly enough."

More bullets exploded around them, and more chips of stone rained down, but they were safe behind their boulder. Alexei looked across the pass and saw Worthington open his mouth and scream something but it was too loud for them to hear what he said. He pointed into the distance, and Alexei peered from behind their cover to see two German soldiers with *panzerschreck* rocket launchers pointed at them.

"Shit," Alexei said.

The Greek and British soldiers came from behind their rocks and opened fire on the soldiers with the rocket launchers as quickly as they could and they cut one of the soldiers down—which cost too many Greek and British lives, as they were riddled with enemy fire—but the second soldier got his shot off, aimed at the southern pass, where the British were, a rocket flying through the once quiet hills towards them, and—

Kabooooooom!!!!!

Alexei and Costa shielded their eyes from the shrapnel and debris as one single rocket killed half the British soldiers fighting with them. Alexei tried not to think about who they were, and what they were certainly leaving behind, and that just a short time before they'd been friends.

They had to keep going.

They kept firing at the Germans.

Bang bang!!! Bang bang bang!!! Bang bang!!!

Alexei and Costa ducked back behind their boulder again to reload: they were quickly running out of ammunition, and when they spoke they had to scream to hear each other over the noise of the battle because the mountains on either side of them were keeping all of the chaos so close.

"Holy shit, there's still a lot of them!"

"They got too many of us!"

"Worthington made it!"

"Half his men didn't!"

Alexei and Costa finished reloading and peeked around their boulder again to fire down on the Germans and when they did they saw that their enemies were making slow progress up the pass, steadily getting closer.

It wouldn't be long.

Alexei and Costa knew what was left.

They'd continue firing with everything that they had until they'd run out of bullets, and then the Germans would finally break them and in one giant unstoppable wave come flooding over the top of the pass, and that would be the end of their resistance.

Then Alexei saw their end coming quicker than he thought.

"Hey!" Alexei shouted.

He yelled as loud as he could across the pass and Worthington saw him and then turned to see where he was pointing, and then he too saw what Alexei saw: that the Germans were moving their tanks into position and angling their large gun barrels up towards where the Greeks and British had taken cover in the pass.

It was the same as the Panzers had done at Larissa.

"*Shit*," Worthington yelled. "*Fall back! Higher up the pass, as far as you can go!!*"

All the Greeks and British picked up the cry for retreat and fired another volley of bullets, to make the German soldiers dive for cover, and then they ran towards the top of the mountains, trying to make their escape up and over to the other side, and they ducked as they ran, going as fast as they could, knowing their lives depended on it, until the tanks fired—

Kaaaabooooom!!!!!!!

The hills were shaken again, and Alexei and Costa weren't hit, but the sheer force of the blow knocked them from their feet and threw them roughly to the ground.

More automatic German gunfire followed—

Rat-a-tat-tat-tat-tat-tat-tat-tat!!!

They got up and tried to run the rest of the distance, to the other side of the pass, but they were pinned down by the German fire and had to slide to cover again behind another boulder, and when they looked around them they saw that the battle was turning into a massacre now.

"How close to Athens do you think they are?" Alexei asked Costa, both of them drained, breathing heavily, thinking about those of their group that had gone on ahead of them.

"Not close enough," Costa answered.

Alexei looked around them.

There were only six British soldiers left, and five Greeks, including Costa, Koukidis, and Alexei.

"*One more volley down below on my move!*" Worthington shouted.

They waited until everyone had reloaded, and when Worthington made his signal they turned together to shoot back down onto the Germans for one final time—

Bang bang!!! Bang bang bang!!! Bang bang!!!

But as soon as they stood from their cover, Alexei saw a bullet tear through Worthington's skull, and his body fell onto the rocks, and his blood spilled across the dirt.

"No!" Alexei shouted.

Alexei tried to run to him, but Costa grabbed him by the waist, and held him back—

"*He's dead, Alexei!*" Costa shouted. "*They shot him in the head!*"

Alexei knew he was right.

"*We have to get out of here!*"

There were eight soldiers left now.

"*We have to fire one more time!*" Alexei yelled to all of the surviving soldiers. "*We fire one more time, then we make the last run and we don't stop until we're to Athens! Do you understand?*"

The soldiers that were left on the mountain nodded.

One more volley would give them the time they needed to make their final sprint over the top of the pass, and to safety on the other side, before they had to keep running and running and running across the plains all the way to Athens and their future. And so the Greeks and the British rose together, one more time, and one more time they turned and fired a volley of bullets down onto their enemies, the hills around them echoing with the brave sounds of their final defiance—

Bang bang!!! Bang bang bang!!! Bang bang!!!

Then they turned and ran.

The Germans returned fire.

Rat-a-tat-tat-tat-tat-tat-tat-tat!!!

The Greeks and the British pushed themselves towards the peak of the mountain, and they made it, starting to head down the other side, and then Alexei tripped and fell.

He felt a searing hot pain in his thigh. Costa stopped to help him, but Alexei pushed him away—

"*I'm alright!*"

Alexei tried to get up but he stumbled and fell again.

His body wasn't responding to the commands he'd given it, like it had all his life, until this moment.

Rise, he told himself.

Stand.

But he couldn't.

Costa ran back to him.

"*Don't move!*" Costa shouted.

And since Costa and Alexei had been boys together, Alexei could read his friend's voice, and then feel Costa's fear—it wasn't the fear of battle, but something else, and something much worse.

And then Alexei was scared, too.

He looked down and saw the blood as it started to spread across his thigh, turning his clothes dark red, and then he saw more blood beginning to pool, this time coming from his stomach.

He lifted his shirt.

There was a small hole just above his belly button, and for a moment longer it was just that, a curiosity on his body, something that had never been there before, and had come now in innocence, but then the bleeding began. He watched as blood started to pour from the hole and Costa quickly ripped a strip of cloth from his shirt and pressed it down on the wound, pushing as hard as he could to try to stop the bleeding.

"We have to go," Alexei said, and his voice was faint. "We don't have much time now."

"Don't move," Costa said again.

Then he turned to Koukidis, who was standing above them—

"Put pressure here," Costa said to him, and he let Koukidis take over and put his hands where Costa's hands had been as Costa took a needle and thread from their supplies and came back to Alexei's stomach.

"This might hurt."

"I can't feel it."

"What?"

"I can't feel it."

"Where."

"Anywhere," Alexei said, realizing. "I can't feel anything."

"Shhh," Costa said. "Don't talk."

Every time Alexei spoke or moved, more blood poured out and made everything more difficult as Costa tried to use his needle and thread to sew the hole in Alexei's stomach shut.

"Is it bad?" Alexei asked as Costa worked.

"It's just a flesh wound."

"How deep is it?"

"You're going to be fine."

"You're lying, Costa."

Alexei didn't know much about anatomy, and neither did Costa, but they both knew enough to know that there were too many vital organs in Alexei's stomach on the trajectory that the bullet had passed for Alexei to ever be able to leave these hills again. Costa kept working, but his sutures wouldn't hold, and the wound kept breaking open and more blood poured across Alexei's stomach, making it slick as he tried to work, but he was unwilling to give up. Behind them, Koukidis ran back to the top of the hill with another soldier to fire more shots back down at the Germans, to keep their enemies at bay for just a little bit longer and give them a little bit more time.

"Peace, Costa," Alexei breathed heavily.

"I've almost got the bleeding to stop."

"It's not the bleeding."

"What?"

Costa looked up, and his eyes met Alexei's. He wouldn't let his friend give up. Not now . . . not after how far they'd come.

"No," Costa said, shaking his head.

"I can feel it inside of me."

"You're going to be fine."

They both knew that it was over. Alexei looked into the distance—

"It's strange."

"What?"

"I always thought I would have had more time."

"You will, Alexei. You will."

Alexei started to feel cold all over, even though it was April in Greece, and almost summer, and he shouldn't have felt cold. He reached up to his collar and took the orthodox cross from around his neck, the cross that he'd worn every day since his father had given it to him when he was thirteen years old and told his son to never take off until he gave it to his own son, when he was thirteen. Alexei's hand was slick with blood as he handed it to Costa, and he was struggling to breathe now, and struggling to speak.

"Give it to him, alright?"

"You give it to him."

"Take care of her," Alexei said. "Promise me that you'll take care of her. She won't have anyone else. She only has you now."

"Alexei ..."

"Promise me, Constantinos. Promise me as my brother."

Costa was silent for a moment, and then the tears finally came as he took Alexei's hand, and he nodded—

"I promise."

"Do everything that you can to make her happy. That's all that I'd ask of you."

"I'll do everything in my power."

Alexei lay back now, his head on the rocks, resigned to what was going to happen, and so he tried to make himself as comfortable as he could for the end that was coming.

The sound of the Germans was getting closer, almost to them now.

The last of the British soldiers fell, cut down by foreign bullets.

Alexei looked up at the sun above them, the perfect sun over this beautiful land that was theirs, and his eyes were beginning to fail him now, too, but in that moment he could finally see, and what he saw made him smile in a way that he'd never smiled before.

When he spoke, Costa knew that he spoke truth—

"You're going to make it, Costa," he said. "They'll all be there waiting for you, when you get to the city, and then there will be a boat."

"It's not supposed to happen this way," Costa choked through his tears.

"There will be a boat that takes you away from here, and to a new life. You'll think of these mountains and these hills often, where we were born, and you'll think of me, too, and sometimes you'll be sad. But it's going to be a good life. It's going to be such a good life."

"It's your life, too. It's *our* life."

"Don't tell him about me, Costa. Raise him as your own."

"I'll raise him to honor his grandfather."

"He'll be an American. Raise him to honor his country. Promise me this one last thing, Constantinos, because it's very important. Raise him to love above all else the land where he'll be born, the same as we did."

Alexei knew that Costa couldn't refuse him—

"Alright, Alexandros, my brother. I'll do as you say."

Alexei opened his mouth to speak again, and he was shocked to hear that his voice that had used to be so strong was little more than a whisper now—

"I never realized it before."

"Realized what?"

"It's beautiful, isn't it?"

"What's beautiful?"

Alexei tried to answer him, to tell him what he was seeing now, and how he wasn't scared anymore, but he could taste more blood in his throat and he started to choke. It took a moment for reality to hit him, but when it did, he knew that there would be no more words, and that he'd spoken the last that he'd ever speak on this earth.

Costa knelt over him.

He held Alexei's head in his lap, and looked down at his friend as the light finally left Alexei's eyes, and he lay dead in the mountains, in the land of his father, with the smell of the sea breeze in the air, sweeping across them from over the peaks in the west. Alexei's last thoughts had been contentment, because in his final moments he knew that his death would be a good death, and that he'd been given what he'd asked for—he'd died fighting for what he believed in, more than his own life, with the taste of the sea on his lips, and the love of the girl that had made him hers in his heart.

It was a death worthy of Odysseus or Achilles or Alexander.

It was a death worthy of a Greek hero.

27

April 24th, 1941

A LL STORIES END, AND THERE ARE final things to be said, even when heroes die.

Philia had made it to Athens with Iannis, Eleni, Nico, and all the Jewish children that they'd saved from the monastery, and they were fortunate to find a boat at Piraeus that would take them away from Greece, just the way that Alexei had planned.

Costa and Koukidis were the only survivors from the battle in the mountains, and Costa, the born runner, along with Koukidis, who didn't know how to quit, or to let himself feel pain, ran all the way to Athens and they reached the city not very far behind the others. The battered German division that they'd fought against in the hills would come slowly after, because with each step they took now, they'd be wondering if there were more men like the ones they'd just fought waiting to ambush them along the way.

When Philia saw Koukidis and Costa alone, she knew what had happened, and she fell to her knees in the streets before Costa could catch her, and she wept. Eleni would live for another fifteen years, but she died that day at Piraeus, when she learned that her only son was gone, and wouldn't be coming back to her, and she fell next to Philia, and they wept together.

There was a panic at the docks because the Greeks knew that the Germans weren't far now. Koukidis saw everything and it was familiar because he'd seen panic on Greek docks before, and he thought of his childhood, and the way that it was taken from him, and the anger inside of him built until it was stronger than it had ever been before.

With Alexei gone, Costa took charge, and he led Philia and Eleni and Iannis and Nico to the boat that they'd already found, along with the Greek children, and he helped load them into it.

There wasn't much time now.

But they were going to make it.

Costa had everyone in the places where they were supposed to be, and they were set to leave, and then he turned to see that Koukidis was still standing at a distance from them, alone on the dock.

"C'mon, Koukidis," Costa said. "We have to go."

"I'm not leaving."

"What?"

"I'm staying here."

"The Germans are almost to the city."

"Yes," Koukidis said quietly, more quietly than Costa had ever heard him speak before. "The enemy is at the gate."

Costa looked into Koukidis' eyes, and in that moment, with the way that he spoke the words that he spoke, Costa knew that Koukidis had already made his peace with death, that perhaps he'd even made it long ago, and that he would never leave this land.

This land where he was born.

This land where he would die.

Costa also knew that no one can ever really leave where they began, and as Greeks that's always been their blessing, and it's also been their curse.

"*Koukidis* ..." Costa would try one last time.

"There's still Germans left to kill."

"There's always going to be Germans left to kill."

"One day there won't be."

"How many more have to die?"

"As many as it takes until Greece is ours again," Koukidis said. "What else is there?"

Costa knew that he wouldn't be able to say anything to change Koukidis' mind. And perhaps he shouldn't. Greece would need men like Koukidis now, and so would the world. So Costa smiled a sad smile and took a cigarette from his pocket and handed it to him.

"I think you were looking for one of these once," Costa said.

Koukidis took the cigarette, and looked down at it for a moment.

Then he finally smiled, thinking about the past, and the journey that had brought them there, and how everything began.

Then he looked back up at Costa.

He spoke with truth.

"He'll be smiling, you know," Koukidis said softly, perhaps seeing something that was still yet to come. "He'll see you, and he'll be smiling, at both of you."

"I'm glad that we were friends."

"I'm glad, too."

And with that, Costa embraced Koukidis one last time, and then he turned back to the boat that would take them to America. Koukidis stayed on the dock. He lit the cigarette that Costa had given him and smoked it as he watched the boat drift further and further out into the wine-dark sea, a smile on his face as he waited, because Koukidis was sure that it was the best cigarette he'd ever had.

Costa thought he would never hear from Koukidis again, but he was wrong. The entire world would hear the story of what would happen to Constantinos Koukidis after he left the docks at Piraeus that day.

Koukidis joined with the remnants of the Greek Army in the city, and with them he would make one last stand against the Germans, and they fought bravely in the hills outside Athens, causing the Germans even more harm, delaying their occupation by even longer than they'd already been delayed, killing more of them than they'd ever thought would be killed in Greece.

But the fighting didn't last forever.

The Germans broke the Greeks, once again, and the city finally surrendered. The people of Athens watched with tears in their eyes as the Nazis drove through their streets, and past their agora, and straight to the heart of the city—the massive Acropolis, and the Parthenon perched on top of it. In an act of humiliation, this is where the Germans had decided that they'd force the formal Greek surrender to take place.

This is where they wanted to raise their Nazi flag.

Every German officer had come for the ceremony, along with the Greek commanders who were still left, and all the surviving Greek soldiers that had been captured or surrendered. General Papagos had seen first-hand how bravely Koukidis fought outside the city, and how he killed Germans with reckless abandon, and little thought for his own safety, and when the General had asked Koukidis about his story, about how a young man could have become so good at killing, the General cried as Koukidis told him of his childhood in Smyrna, and everything that had happened since, and it was Koukidis that Papagos chose to be the soldier that would represent Greece in their surrender to the Nazis.

The ceremony took place at midday.

There's a large Greek flag that always flies above the Parthenon. Its colors are blue and white, and they're the same colors that were on the shield of Achilles, and the colors that were later carried across the sands of Egypt and Asia, and all the way to India and the ends of the earth by the great conqueror Alexander. They were colors that meant a great deal to the Greeks, and to their history, and to their pride.

The German plan was standard for a ceremony of surrender.

The flag was to be gradually lowered, and then when it had completed its descent, Koukidis would come forward and receive it. He would fold it three times, into a square with the cross facing upwards, the stripes neatly underneath, and then he would walk between the two armies and hand the flag to the German commanding officer in the formal act of laying down of arms.

Koukidis did as he was told.

He took the flag from where it flew proudly above the city, and he folded it as he had been instructed how to fold it. He began his walk between the armies, but when he was halfway to the Germans, in the middle, between the two armies, he paused.

The German officers looked at him curiously.

They wondered what he was doing.

Koukidis gently unfolded the flag, as they watched, and then when the flag was whole again, he put it over his shoulders and wrapped it tightly around his body. A German soldier raised his rifle and took aim at Koukidis, ready to fire the shot that would end his life, but the German officer in charge shouted at him— "*Nein!*"—and used his arm to shove the soldier's rifle to the ground. Koukidis and the officer looked at each other, across the top of the hill, and the German recognized in this Greek across from him a great spirit, the same way that Hitler had recognized the great spirit of the Greeks, and the German officer nodded to Koukidis.

It was a solitary act.

It was an act of respect.

Koukidis nodded back, and then he turned away from the Germans, his body wrapped in the flag of his country, protecting him from anything that could touch him. He was invincible now. He turned back to the Greek Army and with tears in his eyes and streaming down his cheeks he offered them a final salute, and when the army returned his salute as one, tears in the eyes of the soldiers now, too, his countrymen, Koukidis turned and began to run.

The Germans and Greeks alike watched as he ran between them.

He kept running, aware of nothing now except what he was meant to do. He ran towards the edge of the great Acropolis, the symbol of the strength of his people, and of their history, and when he reached the edge he leapt off the cliff, and for a moment his body was suspended in the air, above everything, and for a moment there was nothing else.

And then gravity came.

It was a force that even Koukidis could not defeat, and when it came he began his final plunge down towards the rocks and the city below, and he disappeared from their view. But the Germans and Greeks were both taken with this final act of bravery and sacrifice, that rather than handing the flag of his people over to their enemy, a single man would give his life to inspire a nation with one final display of courage and defiance.

The men and women of Athens who had gathered below the Acropolis to watch the ceremony saw Koukidis make his leap, and they watched as his body came flying down from the sky to where it was finally broken by the stones below, the Greek flag covering his body now in death, and the people came to him. They raised him up and carried his body on their shoulders through the streets of Athens, and women and children came out of their houses to touch him as they passed by, to anoint his forehead with oils, to place coins on his eyes for his safe passage to the next world. They came to honor him in all the ways that they could think to honor him.

Once again, the Germans didn't stop them.

The Greek government had fled from Athens to the island of Crete before the city fell, and even though Athens had now fallen, and the Greek Army had been captured, the Greek Resistance was just beginning. The fighting would soon move to Crete and the other islands, and it would continue on for three more years, just as bravely as it had on the continent, until the Germans were finally defeated and left the world in peace.

All told, at the urging of the rest of the world, the Greeks resisted Axis occupation for 219 days, which was the longest resistance of any nation that would be occupied during the war. The next longest was Norway, who resisted the Nazis for 61 days, and then France, who resisted for 43 days. The Greeks had fought fiercely, as they'd been asked to, as they'd been called upon to do, and by the time the war was over, and more heroes were made, 10% of the entire population would be dead. By comparison, Russia lost 2.8% of its population, and the next closest nation was Holland at 2.2%.

The world had called upon the Greeks to help save them, and they had answered. They gave the Allies the time that they so desperately needed, and the Greek Resistance delayed the German invasion of Russia by more than six weeks, so that the Germans were defeated there by the harsh Russian winter, maybe the only thing that could have stopped them from completing their conquest, the same way that it had defeated Napoleon and his unbeatable army a hundred years before. It's a strange thing, history, but it's not a mystery, not when you take the time to think about it.

After the war, a memorial to the Greek sacrifice was erected, and on it was inscribed a quote from Thucydides, which Costa knew would have made Alexei smile, and the inscription read:

"By wrapping round themselves the dusky cloud of death these men clothed their dear country with an unquenchable

renown. They died, but they are not dead, for their own virtue leads them gloriously up again from the shades."

They had given all that they had to give, and it was enough. They had finally earned their place beside their mythic ancestors—they had earned the glory that had haunted them through years of occupation and genocide.

They had finally become heroes again.

July 27th, 2014

"YOU ASKED OF THE WAR, AND now you've heard of the war."

"I had no idea …"

"And I thank God for that every day, Andreas."

"I don't think I understand."

"Of course you will have many questions."

I looked across from me at the man that I'd known as my grandfather, a man that I couldn't believe had this incredible story in him, and that he'd kept it from me for so long. I'd had no idea what he'd done, what he'd overcome, and what he'd been a part of.

"The two characters in your story are Alexei and Costa."

"That's right."

"But your name is Gus."

"My name is Gus in America. It hasn't always been. Once, in our own land, I was called Constantinos."

"How does Constantinos become Gus?"

"I don't know, but it does. When we got here I was told

that my name was Gus in English. I didn't fight it. I didn't have very much fight left in me then."

I started to put the pieces of the story together, and felt the emotion rising in my throat, almost choking me.

"And . . . Philia . . . that's Yia Yia."

"It is."

"But Yia Yia's name is Maria."

"Philia was a name that Alexei made for her. It was the first thing that he thought of when he saw her, and so it's what he always called her, and soon after everyone else did, too. She stopped answering to it when he died."

"Philia ..." I said, shaking my head. "It's Greek. What does it mean?"

"What does it mean?" Papou smiled. "It means *love*."

"And the baby that she was pregnant with?"

"Your mother. Alexei's daughter."

I tried to gather myself as I took in all that I'd been told, and make sense of how it fit, and what it meant. Across from me, Papou took the picture that I'd found in my attic and reverently ran his thumb across it, looking at it one more time, and then handed it back to me—

"That's Alexei," he said, pointing at the man in the picture. "He was my best friend in the world, and he was your grandmother's husband before I was. That's your grandfather, Andreas. And even now, so many years later, he's still the greatest man I've ever known."

I took the picture from him, and studied it again, looking at the tall handsome soldier standing next to my grandmother. I looked at his face, the structure of his bones, the line of his jaw, the way that his eyes stared defiantly back across the years, the eyes that I knew now were my eyes, too, and I was filled with an immeasurable pride, but also a very terrible longing.

After a moment I looked back up—

"And so then, you and Yia Yia ..."

"We didn't for a long time. First it was both of us that resisted. Then it was just me. But we'd both gone through so much . . . so much that nobody else would ever be able to understand. We tried to fit in, but no matter what we did, no matter how hard we tried . . . the only thing that seemed to fit was each other. It seemed natural, and we were both so lonely. I'll understand if you hate me for what I did, or if you don't understand."

"Why would I hate you?"

"Because sometimes I hate myself."

He was silent, staring at his hands, and I was glad that he'd told me his story, but I was sorry that I'd asked him to, and that I'd made him relive what had happened.

"Your grandfather was the best of us, and he was everything that I wasn't. It should have been me that stayed behind. I should have died there with him, too."

"He was injured. He wasn't going to make it."

"I shouldn't have left."

"If you hadn't, then what would his sacrifice have been for?"

"The same thing."

"No. It would have been for one person less. One person that he loved very dearly."

"I often think that he's the only one of us that's achieved immortality," Papou said as he turned and stared out towards the great lake in the distance. "And I don't mean in the sense that he was able to escape death, but that he gave his life for something he believed in so much that he's lived on after he died."

"How has he lived on?"

"Look in the mirror, Andreas. You'll see his eyes. When you go to bed and you're in the place between sleep and wake you'll feel his spirit. He lives on in us, so that when our time comes, death will find us alive, like it did him, and what else can any of us really ask for?"

I thought about the others in his story—

"What happened to Iannis and Eleni?"

"Your great-grandparents. They came to America and died here, not soon after you were born. They're buried in the city at Graceland cemetery, next to where I'll be buried, and Yia Yia, too, when our times comes."

"I would have liked to have met them."

"You did. You were very young, so you wouldn't remember. But you met them, and they're with you, too. Iannis used to sit with you in his lap after he'd gotten sick. He would just sit and hold you for hours. You never cried when you were in his lap."

"I wish I could remember."

"He named you, you know."

"He did?"

"We were in the hospital when you were born, and he was holding you in his lap, looking down into your young eyes. Your mother asked what we should name you, and he didn't hesitate. 'This is Andreas,' he said. 'This is our great-grandson, Andreas.' And so it was."

"I never knew that."

"It's true. You smiled when you heard him say your name for the first time. I still smile when I think about it."

"And what happened to Nico?"

His smile faded, and a darker look came to his face—

"He was here for a time. I took care of Nico as best I could, as I knew his mother would have wanted. But he never fit in here. He never learned the language. He drank too much. He was a man by then, and I couldn't stop him from going back. He'd seen too much for a boy to see, felt more than a boy should have to feel. He was still young but he joined the Greek National Army and fought with them in the revolution after the war. He used to send letters to us, once a month, like clockwork, until one month they stopped coming. We never talked about it. We both knew what it meant."

"He died?"

"It was civil war, Andreas. So many people died."

"A civil war between who?"

"Men who wanted power in a broken country. The same as any other war."

"What side was he on?"

"It doesn't matter. They all died."

"Do you think about Agria anymore?"

"I think about Agria every day. I've heard that there's no more *lavraki* in the waters there now, that they've all been fished away, taken from the sea and never to return. It used to be so beautiful there, when it was ours. I imagine like all the rest of the beautiful places in the world it's probably mostly concrete and steel by now."

"And you've never wanted to go back?"

"There's been so much pain, Andreas. A place full of so many thoughts of what could have been. There was an earthquake in 1953. Your grandmother heard that the house she grew up in, the house where her father had been killed . . . it tore off from the land and fell into the sea. She wasn't sad . . . her childhood and her home had been taken from her long before the earth ever moved. You see, the land never really forgets. It's older than anything. And it will always remind us of what's happened, and that's what's too hard to bear." He moved in his chair, shifting his legs, making himself more comfortable as he lifted his hands, staring at the wrinkled lines pressed into them by time and age. "Or maybe I just never went back because I knew everything would be different, and I want to remember my home and the people I knew there the way that I remember them now only late at night when I stare into the fire for too long."

We sat in silence for awhile longer, and I knew Papou was quiet because he'd said so much already, and he'd never been a great one for words, not when a look or a touch would suffice, and I was silent because I was so over-whelmed by his story, this story that was a part of me. I felt the cross that I always wore around my neck, the cross that my mother had given to me when I'd turned thirteen, and told me to never take off until I gave it to my oldest son when he was thirteen. I hadn't taken it off, as she'd told me, but I took it out from underneath my shirt now and held it in the palm of my hand.

"So my cross . . ."

"It was his."

"It's the same one that he gave to you in the mountains."

"Yes. That was given to him by his father. And his father before that. And on down until it came to you."

"I had no idea . . ."

"We were happy there once, Andreas, when we were young, and we had our dreams. But then our world changed, and we came here to this land, and we were given new dreams to dream. They weren't the lost and ancient dreams of Greece, but the new and perfect dreams of America. That's what Alexei wanted. That's what he died for. Him and so many others."

He turned and looked at me—

"We have so much good in our lives, in our family, and I see him in all of it. I still hear his voice when I close my eyes. I didn't tell you before now because I'm a weak man, and I didn't want to return to Agria, even if it was only in my own thoughts, and I wanted to honor the last promise that I made to him. But soon there won't be anyone left to remember our story, to remember who we were, and what we did."

I finally understood.

"I'll remember," I said, slowly nodding. "And when they're old enough, I'll tell my sons, and they'll remember, too, and they'll be as proud of who they are as I am."

"I still think about him every day. I think about the way that he hoped. He thought that once we were perfect. Odysseus and Achilles and Alexander. But of course they weren't, and we aren't either. They were men then, too, the same as we're men now. But that's why we have their stories. That's what we learned, in the war. Men aren't perfect, but the stories are. That's what lasts through the hours, the days, the years. That's what lasts from then until now. That's the light at the end of everything."

I was silent, and still taking it all in, and then I looked out towards the lake in front of us, finally understanding at last all that it meant, where my grandparents had chosen to live.

"You found your new home by the sea."

"*Thalatta, Andreas-mou.* We Greeks can never be too far from the water," he said as he looked out at the lake that he loved, and he smiled when he saw something in the distance.

"Look," he said. "They're on their way back now."

I looked down to the beach where Yia Yia was walking back from the pier with my wife and our children, and then I smiled, too.

"You should go to them."

"Will you come with me?"

"No, I don't think so. I'm tired, Andreas. I think I'll take a nap now."

Papou stood, and he walked to me, and when he was in front of me he looked into my eyes, his hand on my cheek—

"We were here, Andreas. For a short time—your grandfather, your grandmother, and I—we were *here*. That's what I want you to remember." I looked back and saw emotion in his eyes, and the dampness coming to the edges of them, and I knew that he didn't mean that he was here with me sitting on a porch overlooking a great lake, but that he was thinking back to a time long past, and to everything that had happened between now and then, and that more than anything else he was proud that what he had done in his life had meant something.

And with that and nothing further he walked inside to take his afternoon nap, and left me to slip into my own thoughts and wonder how I could ever hope to do as much with the days that I had left. I sat there lost on the deck as his story grew all around me until I could feel it inside of me and that's when I knew for the first time what I'd do, what I'd do for my *papou*, for all that he'd done, and for all that he'd given. I'd tell his story. I'd tell his story and young children in faraway lands would read it, on beaches, on islands, next to the sea, in normal houses, on normal streets, and maybe even high in the mountains, too. They'd read it, the same as the stories that he'd always read, when he was a boy, and maybe it might mean something to them, the same way his stories had meant so much, and maybe they might even remember, too. Like I said, I'm haunted by my history, but I knew now how I'd make sense of my place in things. I'd tell the stories that I'd been given. I smiled as I thought about it, and all that it could be, and all that it could mean, and then I heard my name on the wind in the distance—"*Andrew, Andrew!*"—and I looked up to see my wife waving, and I finally stood to walk down to the beach.

I went down the long staircase until wood came to sand and I felt it warm under my feet and between my toes as I walked through the tall clusters of marram grass that mark the beaches of Michigan and lined the path to the water. And I saw them there on the beach in the distance, coming back from the pier with ice cream cones in their hands— my grandmother, and my wife, and my perfect sons next to them, the past, present, and future of the story I'd just been told. I saw my grandmother first, and in her look I could see that she knew that I'd been told her story, and I could also see that she was glad that I knew. As I looked at her across the distance, this woman that I'd thought I'd known, I thought about her past, and I thought about her and my grandfather, and the island that was theirs that she'd called happiness. I thought about the ring on her finger that had come to her from an oracle in a faraway land that I'd never known, and the small tattoo on her wrist, the ink that had surely faded but was still there, the promise that was set into her skin as a reminder of a great love that had been swept away by war and circumstance and forgotten by time.

But I would not forget.

I stood there waiting as they kept walking towards me, and when my boys saw me they began to run, kicking up sand, William out front, his younger brother behind him, almost catching up, his older brother almost letting him, and as they ran seagulls flew into the sky in every direction, and when I looked across the distance into their eyes I could see myself, and I could see Yia Yia, and Papou, too, and I could see Alexei, the grandfather that I'd never met, and I couldn't help it as I smiled in a way that I'd never smiled before that moment.

I lifted my words up, speaking to my grandfather for the first time.

"Thank you," I said very softly, my voice catching in my throat, a tear slipping down my cheek. "Thank you for everything."

In the distance, across the gentle waves of the great lake in front of us, the sun was low in the sky, casting everything in its soft orange glow, and I remembered his final words, and I knew as he knew.

"You were right," I whispered. "It's beautiful."

My boys kept running, almost to me now—

"It's all beautiful."

Author's Note

THIS BOOK WAS LARGELY WRITTEN ALONE. And while the story and characters are a work of fiction, except for the obvious historical references, the spirit of their struggle and sacrifice is very much true. There is, however, one exception to this. Growing up as a Greek-American, I'd heard first-hand accounts of "the War" for as long as I can remember, many of which are included in this text, and the one that I'd lay awake thinking about at night was the story of Constantinos Koukidis, the Greek soldier so full of pride for his country and his people that rather than turning the Greek flag over to the Nazis when Athens fell he wrapped himself in it and threw himself off the edge of the Acropolis to his death. I first heard the story when I was probably eight or nine years old, and while many have debated through the years since if such a man had ever existed, or whether it was just a story created as Greek propaganda, I decided when I was very young that I believed in this brave soldier, and in many ways it was during those nights as a boy that I lay awake thinking about what he did and what he gave and how history had forgotten him that I first started writing this story, long before the words came, and certainly before I ever thought of myself as a writer.

My sincerest hope in writing this book is that it might

be able to shed light on one of the great forgotten contributions in history. And while any errors in facts or details contained within these pages are mine alone, the statistics given in the last chapter are true: Greece resisted the Nazis, at the urging of the rest of the world, for 219 days, while the duration of Nazi resistance for the next closest nation that would eventually be occupied was Norway at 61 days. During the course of the occupation Greece lost an estimated 10% of its total population. In comparison, the Russians lost 2.8% and France lost 2%. The loss of a tenth of the population of an entire country is a staggering amount of people, and also something that you won't find taught in any history books, though its importance and contribution to the Allied war effort cannot be overstated.

As Leni Riefenstahl, the Nazi propagandist and close friend of Hitler, would say after the war:

"If the Italians hadn't attacked Greece and needed our help, the war would have taken a very different course. We could have anticipated the Russian cold by weeks and conquered Leningrad and Moscow. There would have been no Stalingrad."

This is a story for all those who fought and have been forgotten. I think about you every day.

ACKNOWLEDGMENTS

THE HISTORY AND JOURNEY OF A book is a very long one, and here are just a few of the many people that need to be thanked for their help in turning this into reality:

My deepest thanks to Russell Galen, who breathed life into this journey when before him there was none, and whose kind words I won't ever forget, not even when I'm gone.

A very big thank you also to Mark Gompertz, for his belief and faith in this story, and to Caroline Russomanno, Tony Lyons, and everyone at Arcade, Skyhorse, and Simon & Schuster, as well as Steven Pressfield, Victoria Aveyard, Caitlin Horrocks, and Paula McLain.

To the entire extended Cosmos family: Gus, Mary, Tom, Nancy, Karen, Bethany, and all those more distant, this is yours, too, and I love you, and my thanks and love to the entire Kelly and Ryan families, as well.

My deepest gratitude to the Holy Trinity Greek Orthodox Church of Grand Rapids and the entire Greek community of West Michigan, who helped raise me, and who shared so many of the stories that are contained within these pages.

And finally, for all those who have struggled against evil

and given everything to fight for freedom, both in this war and others, both in this way and in other ways . . .

Αίωνία ἡ μνήμη
May your memory be eternal.